SHADOWS AT MIDNIGHT

RICHARD TYLER JORDAN

OLIVERHEBERBOOKS

Shadows at Midnight Copyright 2024 © Richard Tyler Jordan

Cover art by Dar Albert at Wicked Smart Designs

Published by Oliver-Heber Books

0 9 8 7 6 5 4 3 2 1

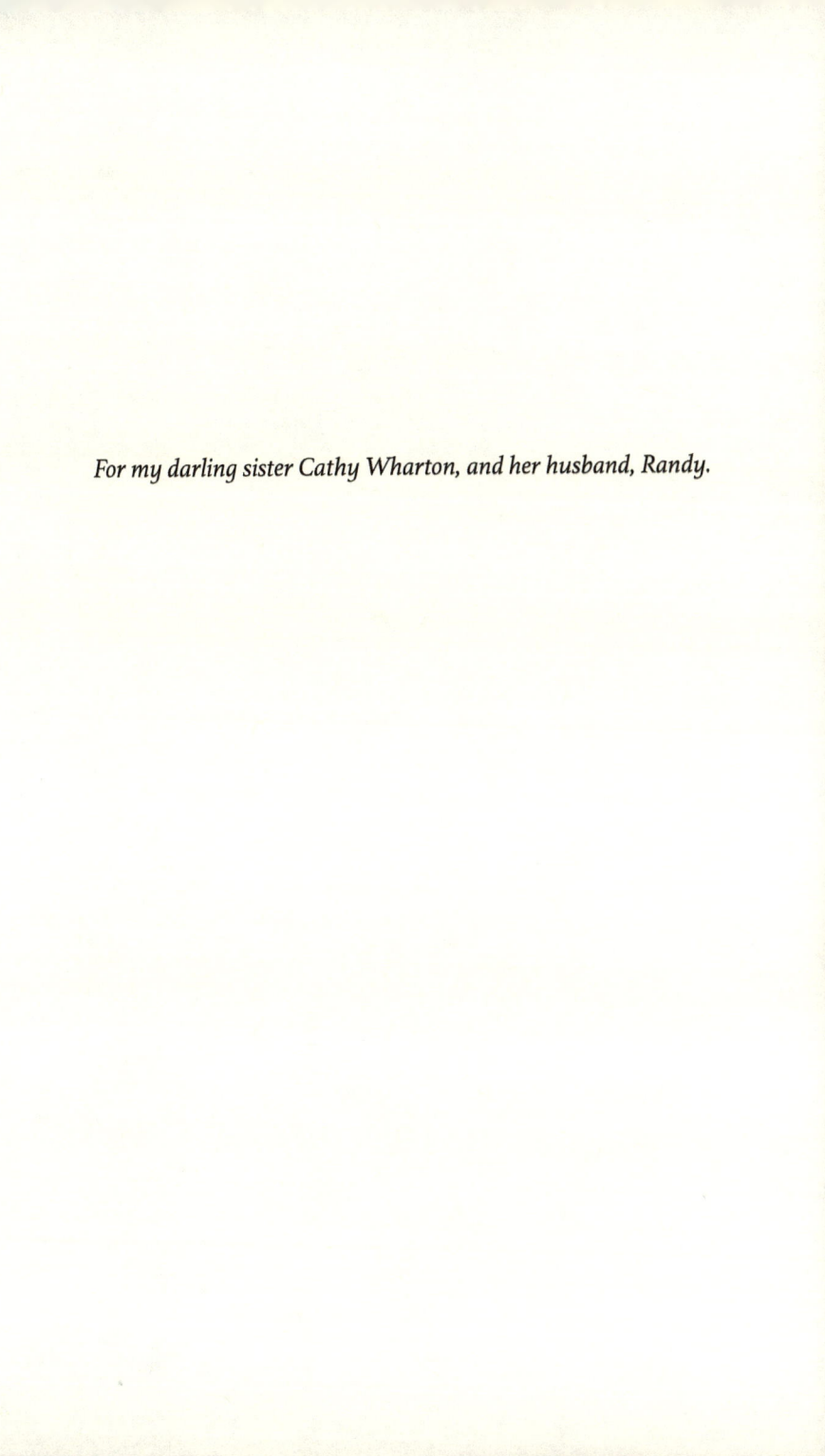

For my darling sister Cathy Wharton, and her husband, Randy.

"Fish *fingers*?" scoffed American TV legend Polly Pepper, sitting at the kitchen table in her inherited castle in England. "Dumbest thing I've ever heard. Fish don't have *fingers*!" She was studying the label on a box of frozen food that her maid and best friend, Tiara, was making for lunch. "They're fish *sticks*, for crying out loud. Unless Darwin was an idiot and English fish are more evolved than American fish. Or they've been swimming in nuclear waste—which, I guess, is entirely possible."

As Tiara prepared Polly's midday meal, she couldn't resist challenging her boss. "By your logic, get ready for a surprise because, last I checked, buffalo don't have *wings*, pigs don't have *blankets*, and there's no mud in a *mud* pie. So there's nothing weird about fish *fingers*." With a huff of satisfaction, she placed the tray of food in the oven, slammed the door, and relished the feeling of schooling Polly on culinary metaphors.

At that moment, Polly's adult but still living-at-home son, Tim, wandered into the kitchen, earbuds in place and head bobbing to music only he could hear. He glanced at the oven, then at the bickering duo. "What's for lunch?" he asked, pulling out one earbud. "Please don't say it's another toad in the hole."

"Fish *fingers*," Polly replied, rolling her eyes. "Or, as I call them, 'fish sticks with delusions of grandeur.'"

Once upon a long time ago, way before the Amy Schumers, Jenifer Lewises, and Tina Feys of the comedy world muscled in on her limelight, Polly Pepper reigned as America's queen of television. As a living legend, her weekly music/comedy variety show, *The Polly Pepper Playhouse*, dazzled audiences with its blend of funny sketches, clever songs, and celebrity guest stars. Millions of families faithfully tuned in on Sunday nights, and Polly's charm made them fall in love with her. The coastal elites adored her because she was funny and bright. The critics applauded because she was uniquely talented. Middle America treasured her because, as they unanimously agreed: "She's simple. Like us."

Along the way, Polly earned a dozen Emmy Awards and every other imaginable showbiz accolade, including a Macy's Thanksgiving Day Parade caricature balloon. Her iconic home in Bel Air—affectionately known as Pepper Plantation—boasted a whimsical rose garden adorned with life-size statues of Lucille Ball, Joan Rivers, and Rodney Dangerfield—her comedy gods.

Now, however, two decades after the stage lights on her show had been unplugged and sledgehammers had demolished the sets, Polly was grappling with professional inertia. As if that weren't bad enough, her checking account balance had plummeted below $500K—almost financial destitution in her world. And now, thanks to a well-meaning dead fan leaving her his English castle, she was saddled with the dual burden of maintaining her California mansion and Thistlethorne Lodge in the UK. Two expensive properties feeding on her dwindling bank account felt like voracious leeches racing to suck her dry.

Inheriting someone's estate is typically seen as a stroke of luck. One moment, you're clipping two-for-one coupons, and the next, you're catapulted into a 32% tax bracket and looking down your snout at everyone who isn't Jeff Bezos.

Life for this trio had instantly and dramatically changed. Only a few months earlier, Polly had been casually sipping her breakfast energy drink—a Bloody Mary—on the patio beside her pool, complaining about household budgets and the extortionate monthly cost of subscribing to Disney+. Then Mr. Mailman had delivered an envelope pasted with King Charles III's kisser. It was a letter from a lawyer in London informing her that she was now the owner of a real-life twelfth-century castle.

Ker-ching!

No one leaves a castle to a stranger. But Polly Pepper wasn't a stranger to loads of people. And once she confirmed the out-of-the-blue legitimacy of the inheritance, her thoughts exploded with dozens of ideas for capitalizing on the windfall. An English castle held undeniable romantic allure and potential revenue. Who wouldn't dream of visiting such a place? Polly envisioned a steady stream of tourists bowing and curtsying and tossing bucketloads of green moolah her way.

Alas, she'd discovered Thistlethorne Lodge was no Downton Abbey. It wasn't quite the Addams Family mansion either, but at a thousand years old, it had seen better millennia. After getting the keys to the kingdom, Polly, Tim, and Tiara were faced with the castle's ancient shortcomings: freezing cold drafts, ancient floorboards that creaked louder than Polly's joints, and even a resident flying rodent they affectionately named Bat Damon. Not to mention the murder of the castle's housekeeper.[1]

But what was there for a faded TV star to do with herself professionally in the sleepy rural village of Abbots Clover,

---

[1] Read all about it in *A Corpse in the Castle*. Available at all the fine places where you get your fun cozy mysteries.

England? Surprisingly, more than she'd bargained for. As a celebrity, Polly found herself hoodwinked into helping cast and direct an amateur stage musical production called *Cats on a Hot Tin Roof*—a corny fusion of Tennessee Williams' classic drama and Andrew Lloyd Webber's popular show tunes. In fact, this week, she was holding auditions for the show. A gaggle of wannabe Audra McDonalds were expected on Tuesday. She also had to interview for a new maid to assist Tiara. And of course, there was the small matter of finding time for canoodling with Terrence Marks, the dashing editor of the local freebie newspaper, the *Abbots Clover Overview*, who just might (knock on wood) become Tim's third stepdaddy. Yes, life in the English countryside was turning out to be far from dull!

Still, even amidst the chaos of village life, Polly couldn't help but grumble about the peculiarities of her new life abroad. As she lamented the name fish *fingers*, she also complained about other disparities between America and England. Now, dividing her attention between emails on her phone, she continued to beat the dead horse of what she perceived were the weird differences between the languages of two English-speaking countries. She was starting to get the hang of the British vocabulary with words like "torch" for flashlight, "plaster" for Band-Aid, and "sweets" for candy. Those made sense to her. But then there were words and phrases like "kip down" for a nap, "trolley" for a shopping cart, and "Bob's your uncle" for "there you go." Those made zero sense to her. "And don't get me started on some of the other names for foods here: 'bubble and squeak,' 'Eton mess,' 'faggots.' Oh, no offense, dear," she said, looking at Tim, who was nursing a Red Bull and scanning the BBC news on his phone.

"None taken." Tim yawned, paying more attention to his phone screen than his mother's mention of the traditional British meatball dish that happened to share its name with an unpleasant slur in America. Then, with a mischievous smirk, he added, "Just so we're clear, when I say I'm going out for 'bangers and mash,' I mean a meal at the pub. It's not a euphemism for my love life—although..."

"TMI, dear," Polly said dismissively as she perused her messages. Tim was the light of her life, and they were devoted to one another. But that didn't mean she wanted to know the nitty-gritty of his extracurricular activities. Tim was a son that most mothers would adore. He was handsome, kind, and artistic. Sure, he was a bit naïve and immature. But in his defense, life as the son of a celebrity and living in a twenty-room mansion hadn't exactly prepared him for life outside the cozy womb of privilege.

Polly sighed and considered the latest situation she'd found herself in: an American semi-expat living in England, in a much-too-costly-to-maintain castle. What had she been thinking? Oh, right: $/£ signs that had danced in her cranium like Vegas slot machines. They'd affected her ability to grasp reality. And this reality was turning into a money pit masquerading as a fairytale. The castle's deceased previous owner hadn't spent diddly-squat on preventative maintenance. Now the expenses for a new boiler, roof repairs, window and door restoration, insurance, and specialist craftsmen fell to her and would surely be astronomical in cost.

Yes, the idea of living in an ancient English castle had seemed like a fun idea at first. What started out as an exciting adventure now seemed foolish. And she missed her Rolls-Royce. Now every morning brought a variation on the same quandary: Do I stay in England and turn the castle into a fantasy retreat for Instagram influencers and their picture-perfect weddings? Or do I go back to the warm California sun and the cold-hearted way the public seems to have moved on from me?

It had been ages since her unctuous agent, J. J. Norton, had secured any sort of job for her—not even another Polly Pepper panini press endorsement on the Home Shopping Network. Her glory days in front of the television cameras were over, *so why*, she thought, *shouldn't I hang out in Abbots Clover?* And honestly, as long as the internet was working (it wasn't always), she had email, WhatsApp, and Zoom to keep in touch with her friends back home.

And now, on this wet and depressing afternoon, as she was about to log off from Gmail and prepare for the auditions for the village musical production, she heard the familiar ping of a new message. What was it this time? She'd already deleted one that said she'd won a national lottery prize in Albania. A couple that promised her good luck or dire circumstances if the message wasn't forwarded to others in her contacts list. And another Nigerian prince send-me-money scam. Polly's eyes narrowed as she looked at the sender's name: Lester Lynch.

"Lester Lynch? What the hell does he want?" she said with such sourness that Tim and Tiara looked up from their respective distractions and cringed at the idea of Polly interacting again with the costume designer from her old show.

Lester Lynch was an Emmy Award-winning wardrobe designer. He'd created beautiful clothes for Polly and dozens of other stars. Unfortunately, he was as well known for his vile temperament as he was for his dazzling dresses. His mean streak was so long it had pit stops. But Polly and many others put up with him because, honestly, he was the very best at his craft.

However, his professional relationship with Polly had come to a screeching halt after he'd intentionally flicked a lit match at one of the Polly Pepper Prancers (her in-house troupe of hoofers) and ignited her silk tutu. The dancer was fine. But Lester was fired. Other than occasionally bumping into each other at TV industry events, Polly and Lester hadn't seen much of each other since the conflagration. Now, he was sending her an email.

"Listen to this," Polly whined as she read the message aloud:

Polly, my all-time favorite funny lady! Guess who's in Europe and absolutely dying for long-overdue huggies and kissies? Yes, it's Moi, Lester the Dresser! I've had it up to here with horrid Hollywood. I can't work a moment longer with these too-young TV producers who don't know a sequin from a rhinestone. I'm turning my back on Tinseltown—for a few weeks at least—and accepting long-ago-offered invitations from chums in Italy, France, and Switzerland. You're next on my To-Visit list! I arrive on the 12th. Can't wait! Kissy-kissy. Love you! Mean it! Ciao, Bella! (I'm becoming almost fluent in Italiano!)

"Nope! No way! I'm not cooking and cleaning for Lester Lynch!" Tiara barked. "You know what he called me the last time we saw him at the Television Critics Association press tour! I've never been so insulted."

"Same here," Tim added. "Plus, he tells Helen Keller jokes. That's plain wrong in this day and age. And I hate myself for laughing so hard."

Polly looked at the email again. "He's not arriving until the twelfth. We can certainly think of an excuse to be away before then. I feel an invite from William and Kate coming."

Tim looked at his phone screen. "Um, today's the thirteenth. He must mean next month."

For a moment, everyone relaxed, thinking surely they could come up with an excuse to blow off Lester's visit by then. "Wait a minute," Tim said. "Lester's message said he's in Europe for 'a few weeks.' So he can't mean he'll be here next month."

Polly's phone pinged again. Another message from Lester:

Ha! My boo-boo.

Polly sighed with relief. "Oh, thank God. He says he's made a mistake. Gave me the willies for a moment." She chuckled before reading further.

Got my dates confused. I meant the 13th. See you in a tic! Smiley face.

Then the bell at the front gate clanged like a *come 'n' git it* chuck-wagon iron triangle. The color drained from their faces. "This is impossible," Polly said, horror registering in her voice. "Nobody appears unexpectedly at a friend's castle with plans to stay as an uninvited guest. We're not ready to host anyone. We're still recovering from last month's murder. I'm not dressed! My hair's a mess! Lester's always the first to issue a fashion police punishment. Plus, I'm holding auditions this week for that *Cats on a Hot Tin Roof* piece of doggie-doo. I'm too busy. Maybe he's just popping in for tea."

Tim frowned. "Nobody travels two hours by rail from London expecting to return on the same day. And he'll expect the full royal treatment."

"I'm happy to treat him like Anne Boleyn," Tiara deadpanned.

"How'd he even find us?" Polly asked.

"Some genius sent a round robin to all her email, WhatsApp, Facebook, and Instagram contacts, boasting that she'd inherited Balmoral, and wouldn't it be fun if everyone paid a visit some-time," Tiara sassed.

Polly rolled her eyes. "'Sometime' is code for 'I've got a castle, and you don't. Na-na na-na na!' It wasn't an offer for an all-inclusive holiday vacation. Hell, sixty percent of Americans don't even have passports, for crying out loud."

"Except in our social demographic," Tim said. "We're members of the 'been-there, done-that' world-weary class."

When the bell clanged impatiently a second time, Tim huffed and reluctantly set down his Red Bull. "We'll get you for this," he said in a mock threat to his mother.

2

A light mist was sifting through the afternoon air as Tim made his way from the house and over the graveled forecourt. Mr. Boots, the castle's resident cat and rodent ranger, tagged along in lockstep, eager to check out what all the commotion was about. When Tim reached the wooden double doors in the castle's stone curtain wall, he slid a small panel across its tracks to confirm who he feared—but knew—was on the other side.

"Your Lordship!" Lester sang out with an affected British accent. "'Tis I, a weary wayfarer, seeking to partake of your hospitality and gracious good cheer!"

Oh, brother, the histrionics begin. Tim smiled good-naturedly, and in a moment, he was welcoming Lester into the castle's courtyard.

"Kissy-kissy, hug-hug, my dear young chap," Lester trilled, adopting the most obnoxious impersonation of an overly enthusiastic nobleman. "It's been a lifetime since our last encounter. You're looking absolutely smashing!" He eyed Tim up and down with a mix of jealousy and admiration, clearly impressed by his handsome face and fit physique.

"Oh, how I envy you young people with your gyms and kale smoothies," Lester continued, feigning a dramatic swoon. "Enjoy your youth while you have it, dear boy. Before you know it, you'll be shaking your fist at the heavens, cursing the gods for their cruel sense of humor—making everything sag, shift, bloat, and fall out!" He let out an exaggerated sigh and gave a melodramatic shake of his head. "Now, be a good lad and lead me to my dearest dear Polly Pepper!"

Feigning delight at seeing Lester, Tim grabbed the smallest of two suitcases, expecting it to be a breeze. But as he tried to drag it over the graveled forecourt, the suitcase refused to budge, stubbornly embedding itself in the gravel. With a resigned sigh, Tim heaved the deceptively heavy luggage into his arms, his face turning crimson with effort. *What on earth did he pack in here? A collection of medieval anvils?*

At the entrance to the house, Lester was instantly in awe. The heavy oak door stood as a majestic sentinel, its surface adorned with an intricate tapestry of carvings. A faded heraldic crest was at the center, its once-vibrant colors now softened by time. Entwined with thistles and thorns, the crest told the storied legacy of the castle, a testament to its heritage and name.

Above the stone archway, bare vines clambered up the walls and hinted at climbing Lady Jane roses that would bloom in the spring. Stepping over the threshold and into the house, Lester was enveloped by an atmosphere of timeless elegance and old-world charm. With its soaring ceiling and wide staircase, the foyer was adorned with portraits of ancestors whose eyes seemed to follow with quiet curiosity. Polished mahogany and rich tapestries lent a feeling of warmth.

"How the hell did all of this happen? Your mother's just a comedy actress, and she never married particularly well," Lester said as he gaped with envy at the elegance and history around him. His voice was an irritating whine, like a nagging old aunt who always had a better way to do everything.

"Pretty cool, huh?" Tim agreed, leading Lester toward the main reception room, happy that their guest was obviously envious of Polly's good fortune. "Mom's putting herself together. We didn't get your message until a few minutes ago. Must be the lousy internet here," he chuckled.

"My bad. When I got on the train at Paddington this morning, I noticed I hadn't pressed Send on my last message—from weeks ago. I'm hopeless with modern technology. That blasted Siri or Sassy or Allegra—whoever she is—sometimes starts yapping at me when I haven't even asked her a question. One day, she recorded some unintentional vitriolic bluster I was spouting off and sent it to the very person I was ranting about! Now they won't speak to me. How did that even happen? What did I push? You young people are born with these devices clutched in your teensy-weensy mitts. You probably came out of the womb with a tablet and a sack full of bitcoin, for pity's sake! I always say, if you need tech support, call an eight-year-old!"

"Bitcoin isn't exactly a physical thing. But I get your point."

On one hand, it was amusing for Tim to see Lester in the role of obsequious, long-absent friend, shocked to discover that the black sheep had made good. On the other hand, Lester's sudden appearance probably meant Tim would be subjected to endless old Hollywood tales and have to play tour guide—when all he really wanted was to play cops and robbers with Constable Grayson Jenkins. Gray, the local police officer who'd collected the dead body they'd found in the castle, had also arrested Tim's heart. What on earth could Tim possibly find to keep Lester entertained? Heck, he didn't even like Lester. Tim was certain they'd all be bored out of their minds before the first day of Lester's visit was over. "By the way," he asked cautiously, "how long do we have the pleasure of your company?"

Lester stopped to admire the gown in a portrait of an aristo-cratic lady that hung in the reception room. "Hmm," he evasively stalled. "My plans are fluid. Lawrence and Bob—my billionaire chums in Italy, suddenly remembered they had a world cruise they'd booked eons ago, so I had to vacate their villa after only two days. Then Alissa and Grant, my two lovelies in France—they're billionaires too, you know, you'd adore them —she got her oodles from her dead grandfather who made a mint when he bought shares in Dynotech before their three-for-one split. They said they had a sudden family emergency and had to rush to the side of her sister's ailing mother-in-law in Bangkok, and would I mind awfully coming back the next time I was in Europe. I hardly ever get to Europe. But what could I say? They're a darling pair. Very posh."

Tim nodded, suspecting Lester's previous hosts had prob-ably quickly tired of him. *Who forgets they've booked a round-the-world cruise?* he thought, trying to devise a clever justification of his own to send Lester packing. "But we do get to have you at least for tonight, right?"

Lester was suddenly conveniently absorbed in another painting of someone in an eighteenth-century military uniform. As a costume designer, he was interested in historical fashion and fabric, and this particular painting offered an imposing figure of an officer in a scarlet coat, gold braiding, and epaulets. "Where's the bathroom?" he asked, further delaying a response to Tim's question.

After an inordinately long period refreshing himself in the powder room, Lester stepped back into the hallway just as Polly Pepper appeared at the top of the staircase.

"Lester the Dresser!" Polly cooed as she descended the stairs like Norma Desmond in *Sunset Blvd.* Wearing the only semi-elegant dress that she'd brought from the States, a floral, midnight-blue, knee-length concoction, and white high-heeled shoes, Polly Pepper looked every inch the Hollywood celebrity that she was. "Darling, it's been eons..." she smiled, leaning in for an air-kiss.

Lester beamed at seeing his old friend. Although it had been nearly twenty years since they'd worked together, Polly was still trim and elegant, contrasting with Lester's current state. *He's been at the Little Debbie snack cakes,* Polly thought to herself. Lester had never been lean, but now, with his round, pudgy face, he looked sort of like the Pillsbury Doughboy. Polly was almost certain that if she poked him in the belly, he'd let out a "hoo-hoo" giggle sound.

As for his attire, Lester sported a thrown-together ensemble that seemed more suitable for a rummage sale than for one in the fashion industry. But perhaps it was just right for a traveler with limited luggage space. His shirt strained against the buttons, while his trousers hung loosely behind his butt. A worn-out pair of scuffed and faded sneakers completed the sad look.

Tiara wandered into the entrance hallway and gave Lester the once-over, her eyes narrowing ever so slightly before she plastered on a forced smile. "I thought I heard a voice from the past," she said, her tone just a bit too cheerful to be genuine. "Lovely to see you again, Lester!" She lingered for a moment, her smile twitching with effort. "I'm serving tea in the reception room," she announced, seizing the opportunity to immediately excuse herself. She turned on her heel and walked away with a hint of urgency.

Soon, Tiara was wheeling a serving cart laden with a sterling silver tea service, Royal Dalton teacups and saucers, and small plates of lemon drizzle cake into the wood-paneled reception room. Polly pretended to want to hear all about Lester's travels through Europe. And as Lester reeled off a list of typical must-see tourist sites, Polly and Tim vied for the numbers of phony oohs and aahs they could muster. Tiara remained silent, listening distantly as Lester revealed that the queues at the Louvre in Paris were as long as the ones for the Jungle Cruise at Disneyland. And in Florence, Michelangelo's *David* was smaller than it was supposed to be. "Anyway, I've been too busy playing catch-up with my nearest and dearest," he claimed as Tim gave Tiara a knowing glance.

Polly's smile was beginning to hurt. She listened to Lester spin his tales with such grandiosity that she could hardly squeeze in any word other than *fantastic*! "First class? Fantastic!" she exclaimed, her enthusiasm feigned yet convincingly vibrant.

"Not just any first class," Lester elaborated, his eyes gleaming with the thrill of his narrative. "I was aboard the maiden flight of the prototype of the most technologically advanced airliner in history. Can't say which airline, of course. It's a secret. And the champagne they served? Vintage, from a boutique French vine-yard, so exclusive that the owner personally selects the buyers."

Polly's eyes widened, her "Fantastic!" echoing with disbelief and artificial interest.

"When you *think* first class, you *attract* first class!" Lester said.

"Fantastic!" Polly managed another hollow exclamation, her voice tinged with weariness.

Undeterred by Polly's fading energy, Lester barreled on. "Oh, and did I mention my visit to Rome? A Rolls-Royce whisked me from the airport to a secret dining experience underneath the Colosseum. We ate in a dining room dungeon where gladiators were once served up to hungry lions."

"Lester Lynch liver linguine?" Tiara deadpanned.

"The chef. None other than Alessandro Bellavita, the culi-nary genius himself. He prepared a feast fit for Caesar."

"Fantastic!" said Polly, the word now slipping out automatically. Lester's stories, brimming with extravagance and not-so-subtle self-promotion, were designed to dazzle, and Polly's responses, though repetitive, were the fuel to his ever-burning ego.

Finally, when Lester was feeding his face with lemon drizzle cake, Polly popped the question on the tip of everyone's tongue: "What time's your flight home in the morning?"

Tim looked at his mother with an ever-so-subtle grimace, a silent warning to prepare for an answer she wouldn't like. Mother and son were adept at reading each other's minds. Tiara, too, had developed that sixth sense between them.

And in the fraction of a moment that it took Lester to devour his slice of lemon drizzle, they girded themselves for his bombshell: "Hmm. Unsure."

"But you have a round-trip ticket. You had to prove that when you passed through passport control," Polly said, maintaining her taut smile. "Of course, you can always change the date…"

Tim's eyes grew wide. "More cake, Mom?" he said, trying to get Polly to fill her mouth with lemon drizzle rather than a suggestion as ghastly as the possibility that Lester could alter the return date on his airline ticket.

"So, Lester," Polly continued, her voice laced with a nonchalant charm, "we've been absolutely enthralled by your marvelous anecdotes, but what we're most eager to hear is when do you plan on taking your memories *back* to the States?"

Lester smiled broadly. "Ah, dear Polly," he sighed. "America will draw me home eventually. But apparently, the universe has laid out a mosaic of other plans for my immediate future."

"A *mosaic*, you say? Do tell," Polly said, raising an eyebrow, wary of Lester's pretentious wordplay.

Lester, not one to miss the opportunity for embellishment,

leaned back, his eyes twinkling. "I have a teensy-weensy situation. A couple of years ago, I signed a publishing contract for my
memoirs. You know I've dressed absolutely everyone who is
anyone in the biz for over a quarter of a century. I wrote what I
thought was a fun little outline for a book, and surprise, surprise
—they loved it! They gave me a thrilling advance without seeing
a single page of manuscript. Silly people. Who does that?
Apparently, some newbie editor who joneses for all things
Hollywood pop culture and celebrity gossip."

For the first time since Lester's arrival, Polly and Tim were
genuinely impressed by something he said. Polly knew all too
well the Herculean task of writing a memoir. Simon & Schuster
had published her own *PP Through Life* several years earlier, an
endeavor that, despite a major publicity campaign, had tanked
spectacularly. The book's dismal sales figures led to her editor's
abrupt firing, and the company had to lay off half their editorial
staff. The whole project had left a trail of wreckage behind it.
"This is marvelous!" Polly gushed, her eyes wide with admiration. "When's it coming out?"

"Well, that's sort of the situation..." Lester's whine was now a
drawl. He paused dramatically. "I sort of—well—I kicked the
can down the road, so to speak. They paid for a potboiler about
all the divas I've dressed." He sighed theatrically, rubbing his
temples. "I spent the advance money on a few too many
indulgences."

He threw a pitiful glance around the room, then added with
a hint of exasperation, "And now their legal department
bombards me with mean messages that make my lawyer cringe.
So, I need a quiet place to put pen to paper, somewhere serene
and inspirational. The English countryside worked wonders for
Jane Austen, so it should be perfect for *moi. N'est-ce pas?*"

He gestured expansively toward the sprawling estate. "You've got this fabulous castle with all this space and ambiance, so naturally, I'm staying here to write my memoir. Think of it as philanthropic. You're supporting the arts."

Polly gulped as she considered not only the horrifying possibility that Lester would be spending weeks or—heaven help her —months at Thistlethorne Lodge, but also the potential landmines he might reveal about her in his book if she didn't play along with his scheme.

"Don't forget your nondisclosure agreements," she said with a playful but pointed smile. "Not that you'd have anything but lovely things to say about me, right?" Her voice wavered slightly, masking the silent plea that Lester would stick to flattering anecdotes and not delve into the juicier, more scandalous bits of her past.

Lester's smile took on a mischievous curve, his eyes twinkling. "I never signed NDAs, darling. Those are for the little people. Assistants and apprentices," he said with a wink.

Polly's heart skipped a beat, her mind racing with the implications. "You wouldn't betray your friends," she said cautiously, her voice carrying a mix of hope and trepidation. "There's an unwritten agreement between costume designers and their stars: never utter a peep about what's under our clothes—or breaths." She attempted a light-hearted chuckle, but her eyes betrayed her anxiety, silently pleading for Lester to keep their glamorous secrets safe.

"Of course! I've been a clam all throughout my illustrious career," Lester declared, leaning forward as if to share a juicy secret. "Those Nosey Nancys at the *National Intruder* have been waving their checks at me for years. They tried every trick in the book to weasel out a tidbit about Cher or a morsel about Bette. They begged for a juicy snippet about Barbra, Sandra, and even Johnny. But did I ever spill the tea? Not a drop! I love my ladies.

We giggle and confide in each other about this wrinkle cream and that plant stem cell treatment."

He paused dramatically, his eyes twinkling with mischief. "I've endured the media's relentless badgering. And the stars' constant bitching. And all the while, my hidden tape recorder absorbed every groan, gripe, and naughty four-letter word. Who knew Julie had such a potty mouth?"

Lester sniggered, clearly enjoying the memory, as if he'd just shared the most scandalous secret imaginable. Polly's eyes widened in horror, realizing just how much leverage Lester held —both over his star-studded clientele and, quite possibly, over her. The room's atmosphere, already charged with anticipation and dread, seemed to grow heavier.

"And now," Lester said, with a dramatic flourish, "whether I like it or not, it's time for all those carefully guarded secrets to come to light. My book has to be a veritable treasure trove of the most delicious tales about the famous women, and some men, I've had the pleasure—and, too often, the misfortune—of designing wardrobes for. Their private moments, their unguarded whispers, the laughter, the tears, and the sex! Oh, not with me, of course! Too icky."

He winked conspiratorially, leaning in as if sharing a price-less gem of gossip. "Thankfully, a number of my divas are long gone, and I've been assured that legally, you can't libel the dead. And the others, well, if they dare fuss, I've got the audio proof!" Lester's eyes sparkled with glee, reveling in the scandalous potential of his revelations.

Polly's stomach twisted with a mix of dread and anticipation, realizing just how explosive Lester's memoir could be. She felt a cold shiver run down her spine. Her mind raced as she pondered the possible ramifications of Lester's planned exposé. She thought of her own shared confidences, which were now potential fodder for the public's insatiable appetite for celebrity gossip and scandal.

The stage was being set for a possible tragedy of Shake-spearean proportions. Polly struggled to maintain her composure, feeling the sense of betrayal tightening around her heart like a vise. How could Lester, a confidant and trusted friend to so many, even contemplate betraying their trust for a mere paycheck? How could he be so blind to the potential hurt and chaos his revelations might unleash? The specter of shattered friendships and ruined reputations loomed large, casting a shadow over her thoughts. Polly wondered if the glittering world they both inhabited was about to come crashing down around them.

"First thing in the morning, I must rush to the nearest stationery shop and buy a hundred notebooks and dozens of red pens—red is my good-luck color," Lester declared with a flourish, his voice ringing with a tone of self-importance that grated on Polly's already frayed nerves. "I detest those impractical little computer keyboards. They should make them bigger for my large hands and thick fingers. So, I'll be writing my story long-hand. I'll need to commandeer your library or study—you do have one or the other, don't you? I'll start my day at the crack of dawn, take my noon meals at my desk, and join you for well-deserved cock-il-tails in the evening. Doesn't that sound delight-fully *writerly*?"

His announcement, delivered as though it were the most natural demand in the world, left Polly and the rest of the Thistlethorne inhabitants exchanging wary glances. The audacity of his request, the presumption that they would accommodate his every whim for an extended period, was staggering.

"Perhaps Tiara will consent to type up my pages because, God knows, my editor won't be able to decipher my chicken scratches." Lester tittered, a self-satisfied smirk plastered on his face.

Tiara, barely able to contain her irritation, shot him a withering look. "Not even if you provided me with a lifetime supply of winning lottery tickets," she nearly spat, her voice dripping with disdain. "And good luck finding anyone in the village who won't repeat all your stories. We've been here long enough to know that your tales would hit the gossip circuit and become public domain so fast they'd be worthless by the time your book comes out."

Lester's smirk faltered, and Polly suppressed a chuckle. Tiara had a point, and the thought of Lester's precious secrets becoming tea-time chatter among the villagers was a deliciously ironic twist.

The silence that followed was thick with tension, each second stretching out as the room buzzed with unspoken objections and disbelief. Polly, mustering every ounce of diplomacy she possessed, tried to formulate a response that would convey their collective reluctance without igniting Lester's infamous temper.

"Lester," she began, her voice a carefully modulated blend of courtesy and firmness, "while we appreciate your... unique requirements, you must know that Thistlethorne Lodge isn't exactly equipped to serve as a personal office space for literary endeavors. And the village, charming as it is, may not provide the level of resources you're accustomed to."

She offered a tight smile, hoping to soften the blow. "Perhaps there's a lovely writers' retreat somewhere that's better suited to your needs? I hear the South of France is beautiful this time of year," she added, her eyes sparkling with a mixture of hope and humor. "Imagine yourself sipping wine, nibbling on croissants, and being inspired by fields of lavender instead of our moldy tapestries. Much more conducive to writing, wouldn't you agree?"

Lester's brow furrowed, a hint of irritation flickering across his features before he composed himself. "My dear Polly Pepper, I'm sure we can find a way to make do. After all, what's a minor inconvenience for me in the grand scheme of creating art? And my book will surely be a big success! Perhaps I'll dedicate it to you."

3

Morning barged in like a pushy stage mother, yanking Polly out of the cozy embrace of her bed and shoving her into the dreary reality of yet another rain-soaked UK day. She had a to-do list longer than a Shakespearean monologue: auditions for *Cats on a Hot Tin Roof*, interviewing a potential new maid, and—oh, phooey—hosting Lester Lynch while he scribbled away on his potentially explosive tell-all magnum opus. Drats! Was there no reprieve for a Hollywood expat diva? She sighed dramatically, wishing for a magic wand to poof her back to bed.

When Polly arrived in the breakfast room—still in her jammies and robe—she found Lester nattering away on his cell phone, his whiny voice carrying a tone of contempt as he told someone he "had proof," and if they didn't like it, they could "lump it." For added measure, he tossed in, "Oh, for the love of God! You're being melodramatic! She's dead! Why do you care?" He testily hung up and pretended to strangle the device. "I hate phones! Why did they have to go and make them so portable?" he spat. "And these touchscreens! I miss buttons! Real, clicky buttons! And don't get me started on autocorrect—it thinks I want to say 'ducking' when I definitely don't!" He cast a critical glance at Polly in her pink silk attire. "Why did you wear *that* to bed?" he asked, as if Polly had appeared on a red carpet wearing a muumuu from Walmart.

"You've obviously had your bowl of sunshine and lollipops," Polly said with a playful smirk as she reached for the Bloody Mary that Tiara had placed at her setting. "Any unexpected phantom visitors disturb your sleep?" she asked, referencing the night before when she'd shown Lester to his room and teased him about the castle's invisible resident. She'd quipped that she was thinking of naming the ghost Roz in honor of her favorite old-time dead movie star, Rosalind Russell.

Lester's reply had pierced the late-night air like the shrill cry of a banshee, his tone dripping with derision. "You can't name your ghost after *her*. She's my favorite! I hate that she's dead. You should name it after someone I didn't like. Lauren Bacall comes to mind. Now, there was a monster you'd hate to find under your bed," he said as he got down on his knees to investigate. "One week, when I was designing for *The Leslie Simpson Show*, Lauren came on as a guest star. I couldn't do anything right. 'What blind dope chose this color for my jacket?'" Lester mimicked the legend's distinctive patrician voice down to a T. "'It completely washes me out! I need fabrics that complement my skin tone and make me pop for the camera, for Christ's sake! This makes me look like I have vitiligo!' Yes, name your scary ghost Betty Bacall," Lester said again with a shiver of disdain.

Polly had endured her own run-in with the Oscar-nominated star and agreed that Mrs. Humphrey Bogart was more devil than angel and thus more apt to be locked out of the Pearly Gates. Maybe she was now a ghost wandering around Earth, or even Thistlethorne Lodge, looking for an escape hatch.

"Mind you, I'm not sure I believe in ghosts." Lester had scoffed while peeking into the wardrobe for zombies. "It surprises me that you do believe. Aren't we supposed to be smarter than that? Oh, I have a better idea. Name your specter after Paul Lynde. I'll never forget how he tore me a new one on my very first-ever TV job. I was young, nervous, and dazzled by celebrities. Then he came along and ruined everything. 'Whoever hired you for this show must have been tripping on acid! This outfit looks like it was fished out of a dumpster behind Goodwill! I need a costume designer with a sense of style, not a fashion nightmare who thinks polyester is couture! And those shoes—seriously, darling, even Liberace would scream in horror!'"

Polly had surreptitiously glanced at the bedroom ceiling in a "why me, Lord?" appeal as she realized Lester had a lot of pent-up anger from working with obnoxious stars. He seemed to remember, verbatim, all their personal insults and snubs. If this was a sample of what he'd reveal in his book, God help the TV industry.

Now, on this dreary morning in the breakfast room, forgetting about the castle ghost he'd discussed with Polly the night before, Lester took a sip of his Earl Gray and reached for a croissant from the muffin basket. "And then there's this perpetual rain!" He moaned a non sequitur as if they were continuing a conversation about the weather. "Honestly, what masochistic impulse drives anyone to choose to live in England? My mood was brighter when I used to visit my mother in her care home."

Feeling a surge of protective affection for her adopted homeland, Polly politely rebuffed Lester's negativity. "I almost don't miss the endless sun in California," she lied with a serene smile. "All those relentless blue skies creates this facade of unrealistic cheerfulness. People are forever saying, 'Have a good day!' when they really don't really give a flying fig."

Polly paused, giving Lester a playful yet pointed look. "And honestly, if the worst thing we have to complain about here is the rain, I'd say we're doing well. Besides," she added, her voice taking on a more whimsical tone, "it makes those rare sunny days feel like little rewards for our perseverance. It's a charm you only understand after you've danced through a few puddles like you were a little kid again."

"Well, I certainly don't get your attraction to misery," Lester sneered, shaking his head. "Compared to Southern California, there's nothing about England worth recommending. You should just go back to your mansion in Bel Air where you belong. By the way, you never invite me to your fabulous parties. All your old cast and crew get the golden tickets, and I'm left reading about them in the *Beverly Hills Courier*. Why is that? Afraid I might outshine you?"

Just then, coming in on the tail end of the conversation, Tim wandered into the breakfast room, his hair a wild bedhead tangle, the belt of his bathrobe dragging lazily at his sides. "Who's attracted to misery?" he asked with a yawn, giving his mother a peck on the cheek before plopping down at the table. He reached for a can of Red Bull with the air of someone grabbing their morning coffee, cracking it open with a flourish and taking a long sip. "Morning," he finally said, grinning through his grogginess. "What's today's drama?"

"Apparently, we are. Masochists, I mean," Tiara said, breezing into the room with a plate of scrambled eggs. She joined the family at the table, a glint of mischief in her eyes. "I could hear the complaints all the way in the kitchen. The ever-charming Lester Lynch thinks we're nuts for choosing to live in England." She rolled her eyes dramatically before fixing her gaze on Lester. "He conveniently forgets that a very generous Brit is the reason we're living here in the first place."

She looked at Lester, her tone dripping with sarcasm. "Tell me, Lester, which of your clients or adoring fans left you something fabulous in their will? Perhaps a chateau in the South of France? A penthouse in New York?"

"There's plenty of time," Lester replied, waving a dismissive hand. "I'll be around for ages. God willing." He reached for another croissant, then frowned. "Mind putting this in the oven for a quickie, honey?" he asked Tiara.

The room suddenly froze. Tiara set her teacup down with a precision that belied her irritation. Her voice was a saccharine blend of politeness and pointed sarcasm. "In this grand, old, former British Empire, they cherish a little thing called self-reliance. Especially when it comes to warming up one's croissants."

She flashed him a smile that was equal parts charm and challenge. "I'm sure a man of your many talents can navigate the complexities of an oven. By the way, if we're going to be sharing this house for God knows how long, you need to know *my* rules. I'll cook and serve the meals. I'll pour the champagne. But I won't make your bed, wash your tighty-whities, or play fetch when you want a warm croissant. Got it? *Honey.*"

Tiara's retort was more than a refusal to pander to Lester's whims; it was a clear reminder that one only tangled with her at their own peril.

Under the sudden heavy silence of the room, Polly and Tim involuntarily cast their eyes downward, seeking refuge from the brewing altercation. Their hearts raced as they silently acknowledged that Tiara's surface-level affability was like a frothy cappuccino—warm and inviting on top but scalding if you got too deep. Those who dared to underestimate her quickly learned that beneath the facade lay a drill sergeant in pearls.

"Well, I guess I done been told," Lester sassed, clutching the muffin basket with a dramatic flourish as he sauntered toward the kitchen.

With Lester out of the room, Polly pretended to pull out her hair as she rolled her eyes to the heavens, silently scolding, *It's a total crock that You never give us more than we can handle!*

"Make him disappear," Tim whispered urgently, as if plotting a magic trick.

"I can't."

"You could, but you won't," Tiara shot back.

"He'll settle down. He'll be so busy writing his darn book, we'll probably only see him at '*cock-il-tale*' time."

"Speaking of time," Tiara interjected, her gaze darting from the ornate clock on the wall to her watch, "we're interviewing the potential new maid at 10:30. She sounded lovely on the phone. I have a good feeling about this one."

"Fingers crossed she's not another diva in disguise," Polly quipped.

Chuckles rippled through the room; then Polly's expression grew more serious. She sighed, her shoulders sagging under the weight of her latest predicament. "I'm practically scraping the bottom of my bank account, and now I have to find money for a new maid. And a gardener, too. What's the going rate for a maid around here, anyway?"

Tiara's irritation with Polly was growing by the nanosecond. She was nearing the point where she'd again threaten to leave—a once-a-year state of exasperation where she'd declare her intent to work for Harrison and Calista, or Beyoncé and Jay-Z.

Taking a deep breath, Tiara finally let her frustration spill over. "Polly! I simply can't keep up with the dusting, let alone mop the floors and wash the windows in this big house. Don't start up again about the cost of a part-time maid! You're rolling in dough but won't admit it."

Polly raised an eyebrow. "Rolling in dough? If only I could find it! Maybe I accidentally stashed it in one of the rooms you never touch, or perhaps it's hidden in a secret safe behind a dusty portrait in the hallway. Care to join me on a treasure hunt?"

Tiara crossed her arms, tapping her foot impatiently. "Oh, please. Your 'woe is me' act is older than those curtains in the drawing room. Either hire some help or learn to love the cobwebs. I'm about two tantrums away from signing up with Team Taylor Swift."

"As for a gardener, Gray can help us find one," Tim said, absently draining his Red Bull as a dreamy look crossed his face. Constable Grayson Jenkins occupied pretty much every corner of Tim's mind these days.

Polly and Tiara exchanged a knowing glance, bracing themselves for yet another installment of *Gray's Greatest Hits*. Tim and Gray had become fast buddies ever since bonding over the discovery of a dead body in the castle larder. Grayson was in charge of that police investigation but had quickly made it clear that his most ardent investigation was going to be into Tim rather than into the boring old corpse.

Ever since, it had been "Gray said this; Gray did that." Gray's insights here, Gray's opinions there. To Polly and Tiara, it was like watching a dog with a meaty new bone—except Tim's bone was named Grayson Jenkins, and he gnawed on it incessantly.

"Gray thinks we should plant more roses," Tim said. "A good gardener can make all the difference. Don't worry. Gray knows someone. You'll see."

"Puppy love is irritating," Tiara whispered, half-annoyed, half-amused.

"Insufferable," Polly mocked, watching Tim, who was unaware that he'd become the topic of conversation. "He's practically writing sonnets with his eyes."

"Gray's got someone in mind who apparently knows a lot about plants."

"Sort of the requirement for the gardener job," Tiara said.

"Gray said the guy transformed Lady Barclay's gardens into a bloomin' paradise."

"I suppose he's cute, too," Polly quipped, her eyebrows lifting with intrigue.

"Could be a win-win." Tim nodded.

Just then, Lester returned, holding the muffin basket and what now resembled charcoal briquettes more than croissants. "Something's wrong with your oven," he griped, setting down the basket with a dismissive wave. "Clearly, it's not calibrated right. You need to look into that." He absolved himself of any blame for the reheating catastrophe before him.

Brushing off his hands as if he'd dusted away all responsibility, he continued, "I've lost my appetite. I'm simply too excited about diving into my book! Priorities, you know." He pushed the basket toward the center of the table, his enthusiasm barely contained. "This village of yours had better have a stationery shop! Perhaps one of those quaint little places where I can find all my office supplies."

Without waiting for an answer, he demanded, "Tim, you must take me there immediately! My muse has been overflowing with ideas. I was awake half the night with a million thoughts darting hither and yon. I need to capture every single one before they scatter away!" His eyes sparkled with a mix of zeal and self-importance. "Time is of the essence. I can't be concerned with mundane things like breakfast when there are memoirs to write and deadlines to meet!" He looked over at Tim. "Chop-chop!"

It wasn't a request for a lift into the village. It was a command.

4

The short drive from Thistlethorne Lodge to Bound to Read, the café and bookshop in Abbots Clover, quickly morphed into an infuriating journey for Tim. Lester's presence was an oppressive cloud, drenching the atmosphere with his relentless complaints, fears, and need for control. His anxieties filled the air. "You're on the wrong side of the road!" he wailed, forgetting they were on a British road, where Tim was driving correctly. "Why are the streets so narrow?" He denounced the millennia-old thoroughfares used for eons by travelers, cow herders, and maybe even Roman armies. He bemoaned every twist and turn, convinced they were careening toward disaster. "Mind the sheep! Don't hit the lambs! They're too cute to die at your reckless hands!" He pointed to a grazing flock in a distant field.

By the time they arrived in the retail center of the village and parked, Tim was silently seething. It had begun to rain again, and they dashed for the shop.

The tinkle of a bell on the door announced their arrival, and they were immediately absorbed in an enchanting setting. The air was scented with the aroma of freshly brewed coffee while music from the 1950s and '60s played softly in the background. Patrons, some accompanied by their canine companions, sat at small, mismatched tables, finding solace and respite from the cold and wet outside.

Lester's eyes widened in delight as he took in the surroundings. His usual demeanor of hypercriticism seemed to melt away, and he let out an unexpected exclamation of glee. "This place is positively *beguiling!*" he exclaimed, his voice carrying a rare note of genuine appreciation. His words seemed to reach every corner of the place, drawing the attention of patrons and staff alike.

Sarah Rogers, the owner-barista-bookseller of Bound to Read, was working behind the counter and looked their way with appreciation for what she'd heard. In her early thirties, Sarah was more than just the driving force behind this beloved establishment. Her passion for coffee, literature, and customer service was evident in every cup poured and every book recommendation made. She exuded a radiant charm that could brighten the dreariest of days—and Lord knew there were plenty of those in the Southwest of England. With a smile that even the grouchiest of guests couldn't resist, she welcomed customers with genuine friendliness. She was the best advertisement for the hospitality business, and loyal patrons responded, having already proved that they preferred her establishment to the short-lived Starbucks that had opened—and quickly closed —down the street.

Joining the short queue, Tim and Lester were impressed by Sarah's ability to multitask. She was a whirlwind of efficiency, her smile never faltering as she adeptly navigated the demands of her clientele. Today's immediate challenge: perpetually confused Mrs. Burnley and her changing coffee order. Cappuccino? No. Latte? No. Macchiato? Maybe. No. The poor old dear couldn't decide. With a grace that made it all seem like a dance, Sarah remade Mrs. Burnley's drink three times. Then she suggested a slice of Victoria sponge—on the house, of course— and her soothing voice quelled Mrs. Burnley's indecisive brain.

As the old biddy moved on with her tray to find a table, Tim seized the moment to introduce Lester. "Our visitor from America. Staying with us for... well, who really knows how long." Tim's voice wavered.

"Lester the Dresser," Lester said, shaking Sarah's hand.

Sarah flashed a radiant smile. "Nice to meet you, Lester. All Americans seem as lovely and charming as Tim Pepper." Her voice dripped with the kind of innate sweetness that usually disarmed even the sullenest of visitors.

"Charming?" Lester scoffed. "All an act, my dear. I assure you. Pure theatrics! Takes after his mother!"

Tim felt a prick of irritation. Lester was obviously trying to be clever, but at Tim's expense. Lester couldn't help making himself the center of attention when he had an audience. His words were sharp, and Sarah felt the equilibrium of their conversation begin to tilt. With a playful spark in her eyes, she deftly offered a counterbalance to the weight of Lester's critique. "Tim's nothing short of a sweetheart," she interjected. "And if I may add—a delightful bit of eye candy, too." Her smile was a mixture of cheek and charm, a bridge inviting Lester to cross back toward light-hearted chat.

For a fleeting moment, Lester found himself on the unexpected ground of agreement, his voice taking on a lighter note as he conceded, "I suppose some might consider him a visual treat." But the truce was short-lived as he swiftly veered onto another path laden with critique. "Speaking of treats, let's talk about your little *nibblies* there," he said, peering into the pastry display case. "They look yummy... but why are the chocolate chip cookies so *small*? American chocolate chip cookies dwarf these tiny English ones in size—and cost half as much."

Although one couldn't tell, Sarah was thrown off by Lester's disapproval of her sweets as she surreptitiously registered Lester's girth and decided he'd had far more than his fair share of "nibblies." However, instead of disagreeing with her guest, she cheerfully suggested that he have two cookies. "On the house. To make up for their diminished size."

Lester smiled in agreement, but then his gaze drifted to the display case glass. "Can't you afford to hire a decent *cleaner*?" He pointed to smudges and chuckled at what he thought was his adorable wit.

Tim felt a grimace of consternation cross his face. He was embarrassed. *This is precisely why Americans get a bad rap when visiting abroad. We're overprivileged and arrogant,* he thought. Yet he needed to maintain a semblance of light-heartedness, so he pressed on, his voice steady as he placed their order. "Two coffees, please, and... um, maybe a flapjack?"

"Flapjack?" Lester whined again, looking into the display case where Tim was pointing. "In America, flapjacks are pancakes, not brown bricks. Those are *brownies*, for crying out loud." Lester's lament caught the ear of everyone in line, eliciting a mixture of stifled laughs and sympathetic glances toward Sarah.

Feeling the weight of every gaze, Tim changed the subject. "Uh, Lester's here to work on a literary venture." He smiled at Sarah. "He needs loads of spiral notebooks. You've got those in the bookshop, right?"

"It's not a literary *venture*," Lester mewled. "You make my work sound *trivial*. This is not some vanity project. I have an important New York publisher. It'll surely turn out better than Prince Harry's boring rag. I'll need every notebook you've got and probably lots more. Is there another stationery store around in case you run out?"

With the grace of a saint and the smile of a diplomat, Sarah cocked her head to direct them down to the bookstore section of the shop. "Ben's your man," she said of her employee. "He'll sort you out with notebooks and anything else you need. Oh, and the coffee and—*dwarf* cookies—are on the house. A welcome to Abbots Clover present from me."

Tim guided Lester to a table by the front window and found himself caught in quiet turmoil as he absently stirred his coffee. Why, he asked himself, did Lester's presence create such a stifling air of intimidation? Yes, the man was also über-talented, had a whip-quick mind, and was draped in heaps of professional accolades. But Tim had been around equally illustrious and gifted people his entire life and never felt the urge to bop any of them in the nose the way he did with Lester.

He decided it was Lester's razor-sharp tongue that made him so uncomfortable. Lester could eviscerate anyone who might attack him first. That was what set Tim on edge—and high alert. People seemed to dance to Lester's tune not out of admiration but out of a primal fear of being the next spectacle under his scrutinizing gaze. To voice a dissenting opinion, to lay bare one's true feelings in Lester's court, was akin to painting a target on one's back. And so, like others, Tim found himself donning a mask of compliance, a betrayal of his own principles.

This acquiescence was a bitter potion for Tim. He was somewhat of a star in his own world—if only from the reflected glory of his mother—and was unaccustomed to shrinking or dimming his own light. Yet here he was, navigating the treacherous waters around Lester. Lester's quick wit and relentless need to be right cast a long shadow, making every word Tim uttered feel like a step on thin ice. His own authenticity was a luxury he couldn't afford. Cautiously, he said, "You know, Lester, I respect your opinion. Really, I do. But doesn't it get tiring, being so critical all the time?"

"Critical? *Moi?*" Lester's brows furrowed with irritation. "I'm no more critical than the next person. Observant, maybe."

"Well, you are. A bit. Sometimes." Tim pressed on, the momentum of his own courage propelling him forward. "Your insights are keen, for sure, but not everything needs to be about your opinions, you know? Sometimes things are just... they just are."

A brief silence ensued as Lester digested Tim's words. The notion that his straightforward comments could be impugned felt like a slap in the face. In his mind, he was simply stating obvious facts, pointing out truths that others were either too blind to see or too polite to acknowledge. "You just don't get my humor," Lester finally said, his voice laced with a mix of defensiveness and confusion.

Tim realized that Lester genuinely didn't understand the impact of his words on others and how his "observations" could cut deeper than he ever imagined. It wasn't only about Sarah's cookies being smaller than American cookies, the brownies in England being called flapjacks, or the display glass case being smudged; it was the relentless highlighting of flaws everywhere, the insinuation that nothing could meet his high standards. "Maybe it's about your tone of voice, then," Tim ventured.

"Well, forgive me for not graduating from the Miss Manners School of Comportment and Elocution!" Lester huffed. "I'm a direct person. I'm not one to sugarcoat things. That's what a lifetime in the tough world of show business has done to me!" he said, shaking his head. "At my age, the chances of changing are about as slim as one of those damn cookies becoming a full-sized cake. I'm set in my ways, for better or worse."

"Maybe you're right. Perhaps it's a matter of perspective," Tim said, tiring of the subject. "And maybe... maybe some things are just unchangeable. Let's enjoy our coffee, huh?" Tim offered, managing a half-smile. He sensed the shift in Lester's mood as the costume designer took an absent sip of his coffee, only to grimace.

"Now look what you've done. Thanks to your dissecting all my character flaws, my coffee's gone cold. If you hadn't been so intent on criticizing me, I might still be enjoying my cookies and a *hot* drink," Lester grumbled.

The irony of the situation wasn't lost on Tim. Lester was deflecting Tim's criticisms back onto him, blaming him for the coffee's loss of heat as if their exchange had somehow wielded the power to change the temperature of his beverage. It was almost laughable, yet deeply frustrating. "You're right, Lester," Tim finally said, his voice tinged with a weariness that felt too heavy for such a trivial matter. "Let's chalk it up to one of *those* days, shall we?"

With the remnants of their strained exchange still lingering in the air, Tim, aiming to shift the conversation to a less contentious topic, mentioned Lester's book project—a subject he knew was a point of excitement for the man. "So, Lester, what's the title? Of your book, I mean," he began, treading carefully but perhaps not carefully enough. "*Stitching on the Stars*? *A Threadbare Memoir*?" He laughed at his puns, but Lester didn't think they were at all funny.

"Threadbare?" Lester whined. "That would plant a negative connotation in readers' minds. I'm thinking of calling it *Behind the Seams*. Get it? Behind the *scenes*/behind the *seams*?" Now he was chuckling at his own double entendre.

"Have you ever done any writing before?" Tim asked innocently.

The question was merely meant to foster idle chitchat. Instead, it inadvertently struck a land mine. Lester's brow furrowed. "Are you implying that I need a ghostwriter?"

"No... I..."

"I'm not an uneducated illiterate, for crying out loud. I know what nouns are. And adverbs, too. I know the difference between interrogative sentences and imperative ones."

"I didn't mean..."

"What could be easier than writing one's own life story? You're born. Your mother's a shrew. Your father's a layabout who can't keep his fly zipped. Your siblings dislike you because you're different. You become wildly successful. You live happily ever after. The end. It's not like I have to make stuff up, like that Stephen King writer."

Tim rushed to clarify his question: "I didn't mean to imply you couldn't write it yourself. Just that writing a book is a huge undertaking. I have a friend who's been working on his novel for years. You said your publisher wants it by the end of summer."

Lester, however, wasn't quite ready to let Tim off the hook. "I understand the enormity of the task," he conceded, his posture relaxing as he considered his next words. "This book is my legacy—a candid exposition of my career's highs and lows and the backstage dramas and triumphs. It may affect a few people. Truth sometimes hurts. But that's not my fault, is it? What goes around comes around, right? They shouldn't have been so mean to me."

They shouldn't have been so mean to me. That sounded to Tim like a serial killer explaining the motive for stalking his old high school bully and chopping him into bite-size pieces for his dog. "I'm looking forward to reading it, Lester. Your perspective on the world of costume design. Your behind-the-scenes stories. They're bound to be as fascinating and vibrant as you are."

Lester, appeased by Tim's faux interest in his book, allowed a genuine smile to break through. "I assure you, readers will lap it up. They'll be unable to put it down! I'll be on the *New York Times* Bestseller List and appear on all the talk shows. A few people will be offended. Maybe even shocked. But that's the price they have to pay." Lester's internal anger hung between them, a promise of untold stories from a life painted across the grand canvases of television soundstages—and retribution. "Sorry if I can't forgive or forget."

Tim, intrigued and perhaps a bit emboldened by the turn in their conversation, couldn't resist pressing for a teaser. "So, it's going to be a potboiler! How 'bout a sneak peek? One or two salacious revelations?"

A brief flicker of irritation crossed Lester's features before he managed to mask it with a half-smirk. "You're quite the curious one, aren't you. You can't wait to read what I'll say about your mother and what it was like working on *The Polly Pepper Playhouse*, am I right? Will our beloved Polly make an appearance in my book? She has to. No question. So many years of my professional life were spent designing clothes for her and her guests each week. But my dear Tim, if I started spilling my secrets to you now, what would I leave for the pages of my book? I've already said too much to a couple of people I thought I could trust, and they're slightly, shall we say, displeased. I'll not make that mistake again. No, you'll have to buy the book like everyone else to discover the juicy details."

The deflection was playful yet firm, a clear boundary Lester drew to safeguard the treasures he intended to unveil in his own time and manner. Realizing he might have pushed a tad too far, Tim laughed and raised his hands in a gesture of surrender. "Fair enough," he conceded, a smile playing on his lips. "Consider one copy already sold—to me. I wouldn't miss it for the world. And I know you'll be kind to Mom. And to Betty White, for sure. And my all-time fave, Dolores Hayes, too. I know you designed for them. Don't tell me they weren't the best!"

"If you say so," Lester said ambiguously.

"And I don't think anyone would be interested in the time

Mom ended up falling in the Trevi Fountain in Rome and nearly being arrested for walking off with a handful of coins meant for charity."

Lester's eyes twinkled with amusement. "I'd almost forgotten that delightful incident," he said, seeming to make a mental note.

Tim, buoyed by the light-hearted truce and Lester's tales of impending literary fame, felt a spark of inspiration flicker within himself. "You know," he began, his voice infused with guarded enthusiasm, "hearing you talk about your book has got me thinking. I could write a book of my own."

"Why?" Lester said with a dismissive look on his face. "You've never done anything worth writing about. You're nobody except the son of a Hollywood legend. People don't buy books because the author is genetically linked to a celebrity. Well, maybe if it were Joan Crawford's DNA. I read her ungrateful brat's *Mommie Dearest*."

Wow! That was a stinging slap in the face. Mostly because it was true. Tim attempted a snigger, but it came out more like a pout. "I could write about the absurdity of being a celebrity and what it's like to be the son of a Hollywood icon. I have a few secrets of my own."

Just then, as if the gods were providing a cease-fire, the door to the café opened, admitting a blast of chilly air and—Constable Grayson Jenkins! Tim looked up, and all thoughts he had of writing a book—or punching Lester—were immediately wrenched away. He broke into a grin that could only be described as buoyantly cheerful.

Grayson Jenkins, Abbots Clover's one and only officer of the law, and Tim's reason for wanting to stay in England. "Tim! I saw your car in the car park and was hopin' I'd run into you," Grayson exclaimed, his enthusiasm genuinely sincere. "Sorry for interrupting," he added, smiling toward Lester, his eyes bright with curiosity.

Tim introduced them with a flourish. "Gray—I mean *Constable* Jenkins—meet Lester Lynch, a famous costume designer for TV stars in America."

"Not just *TV* stars," Lester whined, correcting Tim's omission of others in the firmament of the celebrity cosmos. "I've dressed movie stars, too. All sorts. A pleasure to meet you."

"You too, Mr. Lynch." Gray smiled, extending his hand. "We've never had so many celebrities in the village all at once," he said, insinuating Polly Pepper was attracting the upper crust of showbiz. "We're more used to the excitement of dealing with lost sheep. But it's an honor to have you visit."

Lester, taken aback by the unexpected, genuine warmth and addition of "famous" to his name, shook Grayson's hand, a wry smile forming. "The pleasure is all mine, Constable. And please call me Lester. I love your accent."

Gray smiled warmly. "Actually, if you don't mind me saying, since you're the visitor and I live here, you're the one with the accent."

Lester chuckled in agreement as Tim glanced at the antique clock that graced the café's far wall. The hands reminded him of tasks that lay ahead. "The morning's flying too quickly," he said, his voice mixed with an eager desire to complete their chores and get home. "We just stopped in to buy a bunch of notebooks for Lester. He's working on his memoirs while he's here."

"Memoirs?" Gray repeated, impressed that he was in the company of someone whose life was interesting enough to write about. "Then I won't keep you from that. Again, it was a pleasure, Mr. Lynch. I hope you find our little village as charming as we do. I'll do my best not to issue you any fines for vagrancy or noise offenses."

Lester rose, nodding once more to the constable. "I'm sure you're doing a fine job playing policeman. Speaking of noise, maybe you could do something about all that bell ringing from the church across the street! I suppose you're used to it, but it's rather annoying to visitors. Maybe consider fewer rings per hour?"

Tim exchanged a less-than-amused look with Gray. And Grayson, ever the embodiment of local diplomacy and accustomed to the quirks of village life, responded with a good-natured chuckle. "Well, Mr. Lynch, I'm afraid the church bells have their own schedule, one that's been around since before King Henry the Eighth. They're a bit like the weather here—something we all learn to live with. But I'll pass along your comments to the bell-ringing committee. Who knows? Perhaps your feedback might inspire a rule that it should be one o'clock all day." He looked into Tim's eyes for a fraction of a moment, registering his unspoken thoughts of *Good luck with that one!*

With farewells exchanged, Tim and Lester made their way to the other end of the café, where the scent of books mingled with the lingering aroma of freshly brewed coffee. The bookshop portion of the establishment was a cozy alcove. Shelves were filled with titles that ranged from well-loved classics to obscure local histories.

They found the stationery section, but Lester's dissatisfaction swelled with each notebook he inspected. His disappointment culminated in a pointed critique of the paper size. "Why are these different from American notebooks?" he lamented, his voice tinged with incredulity and exasperation as he held one up. "How am I supposed to get used to this awkward size?"

Witnessing Lester's growing frustration, Tim felt another involuntary eye roll claiming his composure. The difference in paper sizes—a triviality he'd scarcely pondered—suddenly took center stage, embodying a cultural chasm he hadn't anticipated navigating. In his mind, paper was merely a medium, its dimensions secondary to its purpose. Yet, for Lester, it appeared to be a matter of principle.

Spurred by a resolve that seemed to magnify with each passing second, Lester scanned the shop with the determination of a man on a quest. Spotting Ben, the shop employee wearing a forest-green Bound to Read apron and diligently arranging books, he made a beeline for the young man. "Where's the manager?" he asked, his tone teetering between demand and desperation.

Caught off guard by the sudden intrusion into his routine, Ben looked up to meet Lester's inquiry. "Sarah's at the coffee bar for another hour. Can I help you with something?"

Lester, already spiraling into a state of vexation, was quick to voice his grievance. "These notebooks. They're the wrong size. They're supposed to be eight and a half inches by eleven. I need American-size notebooks. Lots of them."

Ben, trained by Sarah to be patient with varied and sometimes peculiar customer requests, tried to navigate the conversation with a mix of diplomacy and practicality. "I'm really sorry, sir. I'm sorta new here. You'll have to talk with Sarah. To be honest, I think importing American-sized notebooks would probably be expensive. And really, what's the big difference anyway? Paper is paper, right?"

Visibly flustered by what he perceived as Ben's lack of cooperation, Lester struggled to articulate his frustration. "The difference, young man, is familiarity. It's about what I'm used to."

So go back to America! We don't really want you around here anyway—Ben and Tim simultaneously shared the same thought.

As Lester and Ben engaged in their standoff, Tim, as the bemused spectator, couldn't understand why anything as seemingly trivial as the size of a notebook was in any way a path to ending the special relationship between America and England.

It was simply utter nonsense. Soon it appeared that Lester decided that too, because he finally gave up. "Fine, you'd better have more stock. I'll surely need everything you have."

As they were leaving Bound to Read, Tim waved to Sarah and made a face that clearly expressed his torment at being in the company of Lester Lynch. She nodded in understanding and made the sign of the cross across her chest to let him know that she'd be praying for him to survive the visitor from America.

5

A t the very moment the grandfather clock in the hallway chimed for 10:30, the bell at Thistlethorne's entry gate clanged.

"Interview," Tiara surmised to Polly. "Always a good sign when the applicant's on time." Tiara had posted an ad for a maid on public boards at the Fox & Hare pub, Bound to Read, and the post office, but after more than a week, Elara Wells was the first and only one to respond. "Is it a reluctance to work in a castle where dead bodies turn up unexpectedly?" she asked. "Or is it the potential nightmare of working for a Hollywood diva?"

"She'd make a better first impression if she volunteered as an unpaid apprentice," Polly countered. "By the way, I'm leaving the interview and hiring duties up to you. This is all your idea, and when she turns out to be a dust-dogging layabout, I can say I told you so. And I'm keeping a respectful employer-employee distance this time. Look what happened when I got chummy with the help the last time I hired a maid twenty years ago," she said, making a gesture that reminded Tiara of their unprofessional joined-at-the-hip relationship.

Tiara made a face. "Yeah, hindsight being twenty-twenty, if

I'd known this would turn into a twenty-four-seven gig, I would have signed on with Naomi Campbell, her reputation for allegedly assaulting her staff notwithstanding."

"Let's hope this cleaner knows which end of the broom to use."

Tiara dashed from the kitchen, through the house, and out to the entry gate. She unlatched and opened the heavy oak door. Standing before her was a young woman wearing a simple, warm puffer jacket that spoke of practicality. Her hair was pulled back in a neat ponytail. There was a spark of eagerness in her eyes.

"Elara?" Tiara smiled and extended a hand. "Good morning. Lovely to meet you."

"Yes, ma'am. Thank you, ma'am. And thank you for seeing me," Elara replied, her voice a pleasant melody of respect, as Mr. Boots sniffed around and brushed up against her ankle.

"Darling kitty. I love cats. My Patches died a few months ago." Elara followed Tiara into the house, and as they passed through the reception hall, Tiara enjoyed watching Elara's wide-eyed wonder. Her gaze roamed the walls, drinking in the rich history of the place.

Upon reaching the library, Tiara ushered Elara to a wing chair opposite the antique partners desk and poured tea into delicate porcelain cups. Elara's eyes sparkled with nervous appreciation as she accepted the cup with a grateful smile, her fingers brushing lightly against the smooth surface. Tiara observed that she handled the fragile china with practiced ease, a silent testament to her proficiency in caring for delicate objects.

As they settled into their seats, Elara reached into her coat pocket and withdrew a neatly folded paper and offered it across the desk to Tiara. "A letter of recommendation," she said.

Tiara took a moment to read the typed page, her eyes

moving slowly across the lines, each sentence a flattering evaluation of Elara's diligence, trustworthiness, and attention to detail. Tiara nodded with satisfaction and took a small, delicate sip of her tea. With a serene smile, she said, "On the phone you said you saw our advert at Bound to Read. I love going there. It's charming. And we adore Sarah, the owner." Leaning forward slightly, she continued, her tone warm and friendly, "That little four-by-five card that I posted didn't give many details about the job. Or about us. Let me explain."

For the next few minutes, Tiara talked about the residents of Thistlethorne Lodge, Polly Pepper's Hollywood pedigree, and some of the family's idiosyncrasies. However, to her disquieting amusement, she found that Elara was already well-acquainted with the profiles of the castle's owners. Specifically, Polly Pepper.

"Google and gossip," Elara explained and began an eager run-on sentence. "Ms. Pepper is famous in America, and she's dating Terrence Marks from the *Abbots Clover Overview*, but nobody's supposed to know that. She's almost as well-known for finding murdered dead bodies; in fact, she found one right in this house. Her son, Tim, is dating Constable Jenkins—who I dated in high school... Where was I? Oh, the castle is haunted by two ghosts. One of which is a troublemaking doggie ghost named Loki, who was owned by the Duke of Droitwich, who lived here in the 1700s and had delusions of grandiosity and social behavioral problems as a result of family inbreeding. Loki's stinky flatulence—probably the result of a poor diet—still permeates the place..."

Tiara's mouth formed a perfect O shape as she tried not to look too unsettled. She wasn't sure if she was amused or disconcerted by Elara's wealth of information about Thistlethorne and its inhabitants. "I suppose you also know where my birthmark is and my thin versus thick crust pizza preference," she joked. "What's my astrological sign?"

"There aren't many secrets in Abbots Clover." Elara chuckled, explaining with a shrug. Her expression was tinged with a hint of apology for her encyclopedic knowledge.

"No secrets, indeed," Tiara said, not quite sure she wanted someone working in the house who would take more personal information back to the village tattlers. Finding her balance again, Tiara began to reveal the specifics of the job: washing, ironing, dusting, emptying the ashes from the fireplaces, etc. She emphasized the importance of punctuality and professionalism, her tone firm but fair. "I'm a stickler for being on time. Although Polly Pepper considers a clock merely a suggestion. And although Ms. Pepper—she'll soon tell you to call her Polly—Tim and I are all extremely easy-going and congenial, we expect reciprocity from anyone working here. It's only fair, don't you agree?"

Elara nodded. "Yes, of course. I wouldn't have it any other way."

"Now, tell me a little about yourself."

Over the next few minutes, Elara talked about growing up with her four brothers and three sisters. "We're a big family, but we pretty much all get along," she said proudly. "My parents—especially my dad—taught us the value of hard work. He subjected us to endless stories about how, as a kid, he had to get up before school at 5:00 in the morning to do chores on cold, rainy mornings. He persecuted us with tales about pulling carrots and milking cows with his frozen hands. We thought it was a big yawn at the time, but I guess he instilled a good work ethic in all of us. We always had jobs, even when we were at Uni."

"Sounds like we had the same father," Tiara joked. "He believed in the importance of perseverance." Leaning forward slightly, her curiosity piqued, she posed her next question. "Are you married? Children?"

Elara's gaze met Tiara's with a hint of hesitancy. "After A-levels, I attended university for a year. But life had other plans." A fleeting shadow of sadness crossed Elara's features as she continued, her words measured but honest. "I fell in love, as one does, and thought I was on the path to my personal happily ever after. I left Uni to focus on our relationship and took a job as a house cleaner. That letter of reference came from Mrs. McAllen, whom I worked for. Michael—my fiancé—had a few, shall we say, 'issues.' Love is blind, and I was attracted to him like everyone else because he looked amazing. But *he* thought he was amazing to look at, too. He liked to spread himself around. If you know what I mean. That wasn't the sort of future I wanted for myself. I'm too much of a romantic. And I was never very good about sharing my toys."

A flicker of sympathy crossed Tiara's features. "Life has a way of steering us onto unexpected roads," she offered gently. "But how we navigate those twists and turns defines us."

"I made the decision to take a different road. I still don't have a clear path, but I know that being here at Thistlethorne Lodge would be on the right track—if I'm fortunate enough to be hired." Elara cleared her throat. "But in the spirit of full disclosure, I'm not interested in a life-long career as a cleaner. I hope you won't hold that against me when you decide. I'd definitely commit to at least a year. But eventually, I want to return to Uni and study law."

Tiara assured Elara that she understood and that she originally hadn't thought she'd be working for Polly Pepper for more than a year herself. Still, two decades later, she was glad she'd decided to hitch her wagon to the star. Plus, she insisted she was more than just a maid. "Don't tell her I said this, but without me, she'd be wandering around in circles, searching for her phone while holding it."

Elara chuckled. "I'm ready to embrace whatever challenges come my way and make the most of opportunities," she said.

Tiara returned Elara's smile, her admiration for the young woman growing with each passing moment. "I have no doubt you'll succeed in whatever path you choose." Her voice filled with genuine confidence. "Now, what questions do you have for me? Any thoughts about working in the castle?"

Elara's eyes sparkled with a quiet intensity as she considered Tiara's question, her thoughts drifting to the weight of Thistlethorne's storied history. "I've always admired Thistlethorne Lodge. I passed by so many times when I was a kid. I never thought I'd have an opportunity to step inside, let alone maybe even work here."

A sense of understanding passed between them and a shared appreciation for Thistlethorne Lodge's sanctity and the duty of caring for the house. At that moment, Tiara knew Elara had the right attitude for working at Thistlethorne. She was almost tempted to share Polly's joke that if Elara had such a fondness for the place, perhaps it was payment enough for the opportunity to clean the house.

As the interview drew to a close, Tiara imagined Elara integrating into the rhythm of their lives. She was polite, attentive, and carried a warmth about her that Tiara sensed would endear her to Polly and Tim. *Or am I just an American sucker being charmed by a mellifluous British accent?* she asked herself. Tiara pushed her teacup and saucer aside on the desk. She took a deep breath and said, "The good news is, I'd like to offer you the position. That is if you're still interested after knowing all you do about Polly Pepper and her eccentricities."

Elara smiled. "I'd definitely like to accept. What's the bad news?"

"The bad news is... the salary is minimum wage. But there are a lot of perks."

Elara nodded. "When do I start? Oh, but should I meet Ms. Pepper and Mr. Tim first to see if they like me?"

"They do as they're told." Tiara chuckled. "Frankly, they're not very deep, so they pretty much go along to get along. If you know what I mean. Would tomorrow at 8:00 a.m. be too soon? There's a lot to do. Oh, by the way, we have a houseguest for an indefinite period, so there'll be four of us for a while."

As Tiara escorted Elara back through the front entryway, the echo of their footsteps on the parquet floor, blending with the quiet, faded grandeur of the Lodge, gave them both a flutter of excitement for the future.

6

Tiara sauntered into the breakfast room with a triumphant smile, singing, "Easy peasy lemon squeezy! I just hired us a maid!" Then she realized Polly was in the middle of a meeting with Mildred Banks, the Abbots Clover Am-Dram Society's piano diva. "My bad! Forgot about the vocal auditions today," Tiara backtracked, her smile melting into an apologetic grin. "Tea, anyone?"

Maestro Mildred, as Ms. Banks was affectionately known, barely acknowledged Tiara's entrance and continued to regale Polly with tales of her career triumphs in local village hall musical theater productions. *Hairspray, Annie, Little Shop of Horrors*. She boasted about being the pianist for all of them and many others. She wanted Polly to know that she was a village big shot. To hear her reel off her credits, you'd think she was a veteran of Broadway or West End orchestra pits. "Of course, I had to rewrite a lot of that Sondheim shit." She scowled as if recalling a repugnant task. "Why the hell was he sending in clowns? I know my musical theater, and there definitely weren't any clowns in that crummy show, for crying out loud."

Tiara glanced at Polly and could tell from her wide eyes that she was unsettled by Mildred's sacrilege of one of the greatest theater composers who ever lived and was bored with this woman's self-aggrandizement. Tiara's arrival was a welcome intervention.

"Mildred was just telling me how she came to create *Cats on a Hot Tin Roof*," Polly said, bemused. "Despite the suspicious title, she insists it's not at all a rip-off of Andrew Lloyd Webber and Tennessee Williams. And that little, inconvenient 'All rights reserved, unauthorized reproduction, copying, or performance is prohibited by law' on the sheet music and script is merely a recommendation and doesn't apply if nobody tells the copyright holder that the infringement is taking place in the first place. Pesky cease and desist letters are a dreary nuisance and hard to enforce when a show is only on for a weekend and doesn't earn enough dough at the box office to warrant legal action." Only Tiara could tell that Polly was making fun of the pianist.

As Tiara busied herself boiling water in the kettle and setting cookies—or "biscuits," as she'd learned to call them in England—onto a plate, she pointed out that it was nearly noon, and a horde of Patti LuPone wannabes was expected to descend on the castle at any moment. "How many karaoke casualties are you seeing today? Will I need earplugs?"

"Ah, the auditions!" Mildred trilled. Her voice was laced with an air of superiority. "It's like conducting a symphony, isn't it? Each voice must harmonize perfectly to create a synchronistic masterpiece..."

"Synchronistic masterpiece?" Polly whispered under her breath as she glanced cautiously at Tiara, who was trying not to snigger. *Who is she? Leonora Bernstein?*

"And, of course, my piano accompaniment is the *key* to everyone's success. Without my skillful fingers—I studied at Doncaster—guiding these amateur performers, they'd be lost in a cacophony of discordant sounds. I've whipped others into shape for village shows, and I'll do it again. Mark my words. There are some truly remarkable voices in our village. But it's my musicianship that elevates them to near-professional status. You'll be amazed."

I'm already amazed, Polly said to herself. *And terrified!*

And then, as if on cue, the resonant clang of the gate bell reverberated into the kitchen, heralding the arrival of the eager musical theater aspirants.

As Mildred left the kitchen to receive the auditioners, Tiara made a beeline for the liquor cabinet. "Fortification," she said, pouring a shot of whisky into a mug and handing it to Polly. Within minutes, they welcomed a gaggle of stagestruck villagers into the reception room.

Tiara had meticulously arranged chairs to accommodate the auditioning performers. The grand piano beside the mullioned multi-pane window transformed the space into an impromptu audition hall. Captivated by the artwork on the walls and the old-world charm of the room, the emerging thespians shifted their attention as Mildred loudly tapped middle C on the piano. As she began introducing Polly to the gathered crowd, Tim and Lester returned from their writing supply errands. Ignoring any sense of decorum, Lester swaggered in and unceremoniously plopped himself onto the Chesterfield settee.

Mildred's judgmental eyes scrutinized him. "Excuse me," she said, irritation dripping from her words. "If you're here to audition, please join the others and sit there." She pointed to an empty chair near the piano.

"Audition?" Lester snapped as if the very idea was offensive. "I live here, for criminy sake!"

Polly's eyes involuntarily rolled. "This is Lester Lynch, everybody. He'll be as quiet as a mouse." Her sarcasm was laced with thinly veiled annoyance. "Lester's our houseguest for... well, for the time being. He obviously ran out of touristy things to do today. Don't let his presence distract you. He's merely a fly on the wall. But no buzzing, please."

Moving on from the disruption, Mildred continued with her introduction. "Ladies and gentlemen, you've no doubt heard whispers and rumors about her, and maybe about the dead people who turn up on her doorstep, but it's my honor to formally introduce our honorary member of the Abbots Clover Am-Dram Society. She's the mistress of Thistlethorne Lodge and has graciously agreed to assist in bringing my magnum opus, *Cats on a Hot Tin Roof*... to life."

Lester burst into laughter at the sheer absurdity of the title. "You're joking! *Cats on a Hot Tin Roof*? You're serious?" Tim nudged him with a sharp jab in the ribs, prompting Lester to quickly stifle his laughter. He gasped for breath, wiping a tear from his eye. "Is there a sequel? *Fiddler on the Woof*? Or maybe *Camel-lot*?"

The room erupted in hesitant giggles, looking to Mildred for guidance. Mildred's face was reddening as she tried to regain control. "I assure you, Mr. Lynch, it's quite serious." Her tone suggested she wasn't entirely convinced it was such a great title after all.

"She's come all the way from that fabled land—Hollywood, California. Ms. Polly Pepper!"

Hollow smiles and polite applause ensued as Polly made an exaggerated curtsy.

"Ms. Pepper is a well-known American celebrity. She'll surely bring a lot of glamour to the proceedings of my—excuse me—*our* big springtime show," Mildred added.

Another aloof round of applause ensued as the audience of auditioners looked at Polly and tried to recall if they'd ever seen her in a television show or a movie. She looked familiar, but celebrities out of context and without their makeup or their signature hairstyles were often as hard to identify as a snowflake in a blizzard. Had she appeared in that thing with Judi Dench? Or was she on Graham Norton's show? Did she win an Oscar for playing that mother who freaks out in the hospital and screams bloody hell at the doctors because her daughter has a terminal disease, and they won't give her the right medication? It didn't matter. If village hotshot Mildred said Polly Pepper was famous, then she was famous. And apparently rich, too, if she lived in Thistlethorne Lodge.

Polly smiled and expressed her appreciation for those who had come to take part in the auditions. "I'm delighted to be here and to enjoy your wonderful talents. Let's get started!" she enthused, eager to get the whole thing over with.

First up was Frances Osmond. Tall and lean with weather-beaten skin and calloused hands, Frances exuded the rugged demeanor of someone accustomed to hard outdoor labor. She looked right for the role of Aunt Eller in *Oklahoma!* Her piercing brown eyes, framed by a tangle of unruly hair tucked beneath a weathered cap, held a steely no-nonsense demeanor. As she approached the piano, Polly couldn't help but feel a surge of dread. Frances handed Mildred a piece of sheet music, its edges worn from years of use. "I'm singing 'Memories,' from *Cats*," she announced.

"It's 'Memory' from *Cats*. Not 'Memories.' Sheesh!" Lester called out, ending his marathon run of twelve-point-three seconds of silence. Frances looked at the sheet music and then glared indignantly at Lester. "What's the diff? 'Memory'/ 'Memories.' Tomayto/tomahto. Everyone knows what I mean," she explained with a huff before starting her performance. And lo and behold, Frances Osmond was actually pretty darn good.

As she sang Grizabella's big song from the Andrew Lloyd Webber musical, her voice was soft and fragile where it needed to be and built to an acceptable climax. Tears actually glistened in her eyes, reflecting the pain and yearning in Grizabella's feline heart.

Must have watched Elaine Paige on YouTube and copied her performance, Polly said to herself.

Despite the lack of professional refinement, Frances' singing had a heartfelt quality. When she hit and held the final E-flat, Polly and the others in the room enthusiastically applauded. Frances smiled from relief, satisfaction, exhaustion, and gratitude.

Then she heard a muted, "Meow!" from the back of the room. It was Lester. Was he impressed with her performance or being (literally) catty? "Connect more with the audience, dear. Convey your emotions. Draw us into Grizabella's world. You want us to feel what the character is feeling," he said as Polly turned to give him a death stare. "Just a suggestion." Then he made the universal sign for locking his lips and throwing away the key.

"Thank you, Mr. Fly," Polly said with an edge to her voice.

Next up was Rose Wetherspoon, Abbots Clover's librarian, a petite woman in her sixties with spectacles perched precariously on the tip of her nose. With an air of determination that masked her nervousness, Mrs. Wetherspoon approached the piano, her hands trembling slightly as she clutched her worn sheet music. With a shaky breath, she began her rendition of "Time Heals Everything" from Jerry Herman's *Mack and Mable*, her voice quivering uncertainly with each note. Despite her best efforts, it quickly became apparent that she wasn't up to the task of expressing the lyrics' intent that time has the power to mend wounds and soothe pain. The lyrics, so familiar to her in the quiet confines of the library (or her shower), now seemed to slip through her mind like grains of sand, leaving her grasping at syllables and stumbling over verses.

As Mrs. Wetherspoon warbled through the song, Polly

couldn't help but feel a pang of sympathy for her. Being in the limelight was probably the woman's lifelong dream. Still, there was an obvious reason why she was a librarian instead of a singing star. Despite her valiant effort, it was clear that the stage was far from the familiar shelves of books where she felt most at home.

Tiara's heart, too, went out to the timid librarian as she struggled to find her footing. Though her rendition of the classic song might have been far from adequate, there was a sincerity to Mrs. Wetherspoon's singing. And the applause at the end was at least considerate.

Except for Lester. "When Bernadette Peters originally sang that song, I felt a range of emotions. Empathy. Nostalgia. A sense of resilience in the face of adversity. You certainly managed to capture the adversity." He tsked.

Polly shot a pointed look at Lester. Mrs. Wetherspoon, for her part, managed a weak smile, unsure whether to take Lester's comment as a compliment or an insult, but decided it was a put-down.

"Not another word," Lester promised and mimed, buttoning his lips again. At least until the end of the next song. And the next. And the one after that.

As the parade of other singers continued, Polly and Tiara exchanged resigned glances, their amusement growing with each passing audition. However, amidst the chaos, a few performers stood out.

There was Tommy Evans, a lanky teenager with a mop of unruly hair and a grin stretching from ear to ear. He launched into his rendition of "Good Morning, Baltimore," from *Hairspray*, and his voice rang out with so much enthusiasm it hardly mattered that he'd missed a few lyrics. An infectious energy to his performance had Polly tapping her foot in time to the music.

Tommy's liveliness was undeniable as he belted out the

lyrics with gusto. His passion for the music was evident in every note. While his performance might not have been flawless, a raw talent shining through left Polly nodding her approval, impressed by the young man's potential. And for once, Lester didn't have anything to say.

In that moment, amidst the chaos of the auditions, Tommy Evans emerged as another ray of hope for the show, a reminder that, sometimes, it's not only about hitting the right notes but about letting the music fill your soul and carry you away on a wave of joy and possibility. And for that, he earned a checkmark next to his name on Polly's list of performers to be seriously considered for primary roles.

Another check was placed beside Emily Bennett's name. Emily, a demure young woman with a quiet confidence that belied her nerves, had walked to the piano, taken a deep breath, and sang "The Man That Got Away." Though her tone lacked the polished perfection of a seasoned performer, a raw honesty to her singing tugged at Polly's heartstrings. She wasn't Judy Garland by any stretch of the imagination. But Emily poured her soul into the song, and her voice was filled with a poignant longing that resonated with each note. Polly was eager to see what the young performer could accomplish with a bit of guidance and encouragement.

One by one, after each person had performed, they bowed, thanked Mildred and Polly, and left the room, relieved that their ordeal was over. Several discreetly hung around outside the reception room doors to listen to their competition. But most had jobs to return to, or at least farm chores to do, and they had to get back to them. After the last performer had left, Polly and Mildred huddled to discuss who might be good for this or that role. Lester wormed his way into the consultation, and his contribution to the evaluations of each singer was as expected: critical and unhelpful.

"Good luck with that one!" he mocked as Polly and Mildred went down the list. "Rusty hinge!" "Nails on a chalkboard!" "Should consider a career as a mime!" One zinger after another erupted from Lester until Polly started to doubt her own intuition about each one's potential. But it hardly mattered because Mildred had already made up her mind about who would fill the important roles of Brick (Tommy Evans), Maggie (Frances Osmond), and Big Daddy (Jack Millfield) in this Southern Gothic musical mash-up.

"Well, that was fulfilling. Not!" Polly said to Tiara after they'd escorted Mildred out of the house and closed the front entry door. Lester had vanished into the library with his spiral notebooks, and Tim was texting Grayson. "Everyone wants to be a star."

7

When it came to his daily writing schedule, Lester was impressively disciplined. He was up at the crack, shaved, showered, caffeinated, and at his desk in the library even before Mr. Boots completed his final rodent run of the night. His career in television had instilled the importance of maintaining strict regimens. TV shows operate on tight production schedules. Delays disrupt the entire timeline, leading to cost overruns and logistical problems. Lester was a professional.

During the first few days of his residence at Thistlethorne Lodge, other than occasionally being spotted sprinting toward a potty mission, Polly & Co. rarely saw Lester. And as the next few days flew by, it was almost as if they didn't have a houseguest at all. *Heaven!* Polly could wear her jammies to the breakfast table without condescending remarks about wrinkles in the fabric matching the ones on her face. And she could concentrate on her *Cats on a Hot Tin Roof* duties. Tim could follow his favorite social media influencers or text Grayson without Lester's whining for attention. Tiara and Elara could focus on keeping the castle tidy. Even Mr. Boots could perform his exhibitionist grooming without sarcastic judgments.

Of course, Lush Hour began every evening precisely at 6:00, and work stopped for everyone. They all met in the main reception room and shared the events of their day by the fireplace. Well, Lester did most of the talking. But with the family sufficiently mellowed by their champagne, his self-aggrandizing reports were tolerable.

"It's almost like automatic writing!" Lester bragged about his creative process and how the words and anecdotes were gushing onto the page. "I'm simply the conduit through which the Nine Sisters—those delightful Greek Muses—pour themselves into me. It's so easy," he rambled as he massaged his stiff fingers, which were stained with red ink and cramped from squeezing his pen for hours. "I'll be finished in no time and on my way to winning a Pulitzer or whatever they give for outstanding achievement in memoir writing!"

On your way is the only prize we care about, the trio collectively thought.

Polly eyed Lester suspiciously. "No writer's block, sweetums?" Her tone was laced with skepticism. "When I wrote *PP Through Life*, it was a horror show. One day, I'd have a mountain of pages; the next, I'd be lucky if I hadn't set fire to the whole flipping manuscript in frustration. And Vlad, my editor? More like Vlad the Impaler with those ruthless notes of his! I still don't know what he meant by 'verb replacements' and 'sentence clutter.' I'm a legend. Not an English composition student. Writing is torture for most of us mere mortals. Honestly, you and J. K. Rowling must have magic quills or something!"

"It means you're not a real writer, Polly," Lester chided smugly. "Personally, I think if the work is hard, then you're not doing it right. Or you're not fully in touch with Saint Francis de Sales, the patron saint of writers. Shakespeare obviously tapped into the Divine. Jackie Collins and that *Fifty Shades* writer, too. I guess I have the gift as well."

"Easy writing makes for damn hard reading." Tiara surreptitiously whispered a quote from Hemingway to Tim.

"And la, the memories are welling up like a sparkling natural spring!" Lester continued. "I somehow don't need old photos or letters or diary entries to help recreate precise images of designing for Bette, Liza, Jen, Tom, Emma, and all the others! I think readers will feel they're practically hovering over my shoulder as I describe Diana 'Boss'—as I call her—flying into one of her famous tizzies and ripping off all the sequins and fringe that I'd spent weeks sewing onto her dress. That was before she shoved a peacock feather into my nose. She'll be sorry. Oh, the dish I have on all of them. That goody-goody Dolores Hayes, too."

At the mention of Dolores Hayes, Tim's all-time favorite Golden Age of Hollywood star, his interest was instantly piqued. He had fallen deeply in love with the legendary film icon from the first time he'd seen her in an old black-and-white movie musical on television when he was a kid. "This is the second time you've mentioned Dolores Hayes in the past week, Lester," Tim began. "There's no way you could write anything but love letters about her. Right?"

Tiara agreed. "I've never read a single negative thing about Dolores Hayes in my entire life. She devoted her post-career life to spaying dogs and neutering cats. Or is it the other way around?"

"Hmm," Lester groaned.

"She was Little Miss Sunshine and Shirley Temple all rolled into one beautiful, freshly scrubbed package," Tim continued and turned to his mother. "You guys did a couple of benefit shows together. She was the best, wasn't she?"

Polly nodded and smiled as warm memories of the beautiful

and talented Dolores Hayes came rushing back to her. Dolores had been a recording star with one of the popular bands of the 1960s. Then she got a studio screen test at Sterling Studios and was cast—almost by chance—in a comedy-romance musical. Then bam! Overnight, she became one of the industry's biggest and most enduring stars. She was #1 at the box office for a decade. A so-called "triple threat," Dolores excelled at singing, dancing, and acting. Comedy or drama, it didn't matter. She could do it all. She continued to have hit records and sold-out concerts for over fifty years. Her perpetually sunny disposition might have been mocked by spiteful wiseacres, but her wholesome charm, infectious optimism, and multifaceted talent made her a favorite of several generations of fans. She remained physically attractive and still sang into her seventies.

"Dolores was a genuinely loving and gracious lady," Polly agreed wistfully. "There will never be another like her—not even close. I wanted to model my own image after hers, but I couldn't pull it off. I'm not nearly as sweet." Polly stopped to remember the Dolores Hayes she'd gotten to know personally. "The general public thought she was all smiley and perky because she was a rich and famous movie star and therefore couldn't possibly have a care in the world. That was pure rubbish. Dolores had as many heartaches and challenges as the rest of us. She suffered quietly. She had abusive husbands who took advantage of her. 'I sure can pick 'em, can't I?' she once said to me."

"Dolores had a dark side—" Lester added.

"Not *dark* per se," Polly interjected, cutting Lester off and defending the legend from uncharitable accusations. "She learned to use her star power. Many people took advantage of her early on, and she finally woke up. I can smell a rat from a mile away, but she was too naïve sometimes."

As Tim continued to sip his champagne, he was desperate to

ask Lester for more information about his beloved movie-star crush and what he'd meant by Dolores having a "dark side." However, he knew better than to come right out and press for specific details. Anything Lester revealed would have to come organically. Lester could whisper hints about facing the testy spleens of the divas he worked with in television, but like a sadist (which he was) who controlled the level of pain inflicted on their victim, he was totally in charge of the scraps of information he dispered. Lester couldn't keep his mouth shut when it came to practically every other thought that sprinted through his noggin, but when it came to prematurely revealing advance gossip from his book, he was a miser.

The more Tim thought about Lester's interactions with Dolores Hayes, he realized perhaps it was precisely because seldom had anyone ever written a single negative thing about the star that might make Lester's own reminiscences, however harmless, grist for the gossip mill. Clever news editors or bloggers could contort facts and create clickable headlines even if there wasn't any real meat to a story. The *National Intruder* was brilliantly notorious for taking an innocuous morsel of truth and making it into something approximating sensational news. Emma Stone's Scandalous Scoop! equaled a revelation that the star was seen ordering an ice-cream cone with two balls of pralines and cream at Baskin-Robbins. Taylor Swift's Dramatic Confession! led to the not-so-earth-shaking revelation that the singer/songwriter/billionaire preferred jellybean-scented suds in her tub. Hannah's Hair-raising Encounter! divulged the incendiary yawn that Hannah Waddington had bumped (literally) into Miley Cyrus at the beauty salon. To heck with journalistic integrity.

But why, Tim wondered, since Dolores Hayes was now dead, would writing trash about her—if that was what Lester was doing—be of any value? Maybe disclosures of any kind were cathartic for Lester, like writing in a journal to get things off one's chest. More than likely, his publisher wanted insider showbiz dope, however unobjectionable, to generate public interest and sales of the book rather than offering a nuanced or deeply reflective portrayal of Lester's life. Whatever the reason, Tim was fairly certain that very few people would ever read *Behind the Seams* anyway.

By the second week of Lester's literary journey at Thistlethorne Lodge, the family's schedules became almost routine as they returned to their business-as-usual lives. Polly grappled with the increasingly controlling Mildred Banks over creative differences for *Cats on a Hot Tin Roof*—or *Claws*, as Polly was now referring to the show in general, and Mildred in particular. Tim snuck off for midday coffees (surely a euphemism) with Grayson. Tiara tutored Elara in the peculiar way that Polly liked her breakfast Bloody Mary (garnished with pickled okra). Polly even managed to squeeze in a couple of dates with her new beau, journalist Terrence Marks. But early evenings were, of course, devoted to the family's unalterable tradition of Lush Hour in the reception room.

Life was grand...

... And then it wasn't.

"Puppies and butterflies" was how the new maid, Elara, had described the atmosphere at Thistlethorne Lodge after her first week. But the honeymoon was a short one. Although she'd quickly assimilated into the family and was appreciated by Polly, Tim, Tiara, and even Mr. Boots—who hung around coaxing treats and taking advantage of her inexperience—Lester Lynch was a different story. Used to bossing around underlings and treating them as disposable things, he treated Elara like the lowly servant that she actually was. Monday morning had rolled around, and Elara made the near-fatal mistake of vacuuming the runner carpet outside the library door.

The whirring of the Dyson was intrusive enough, but she also bumped the machine against the base of the door several times. In an explosion of irritation and expletives, Lester flung open the door and cursed, "I'm writing, damn it all! Don't you know anything, you stupid girl? How do you expect me to concentrate when you're making all that rackety-rack racket!"

"Well, excuse me for working!" Elara blasted back at Lester in an unprofessional knee-jerk reaction. Elara cast her steely glare at him, and when he huffed and slammed the door in her face, she extended her middle finger and stuck out her tongue. In a loud whisper she hissed, "Watch your step, mister, or you'll be sorry."

At that very moment, Tim appeared and startled her.

"I didn't know you were... I didn't mean what I..." Elara stuttered, trying to cover for her outburst.

"Of course you meant it." Tim smiled and nodded in solidarity. "He deserved it. I totally get it."

"I don't usually let people get to me." Elara tried to find an excuse for her short temper. "But Mr. Lynch treats me like I'm not even human."

"He thinks you're beneath him. Lester only likes celebrities and rich people. But he hates most of them, too, so don't sweat it too much. Creative people are sometimes weird about distractions and interruptions while they're in the zone, so to speak," Tim said. "But there's still no excuse for his behavior. I'll have a word later."

The rest of the day passed with only the additional drama of Mildred Banks deciding that her name in the show's program needed to be surrounded by a red box to make it stand out. Then, at precisely 6:00, Tiara poured the evening's first bottle of

Verve and passed around a tray of her famous salmon tortilla appetizers. Everyone was in good spirits.

Except for Lester.

"What's up, Shakespeare?" Polly teased as Lester wandered into the reception room and plopped himself into a wingback chair by the fireplace. "To be, or not to be?" she chirped as she sipped her champers, and Dionne Warwick asked if they knew the way to San Jose, over the music system speakers.

"Not." Lester pouted before taking a long pull from his flute. "Thanks to your stupid maid, my patron deity has abandoned me! Elara ruined my train of thought this morning, and I haven't been able to turn the pump back on. She's got to go."

Polly and Tiara blanched in unison at Lester's absurd suggestion. "You can't sack someone for interrupting your muse, sweetums. Well, *you* probably can," Polly added, trying to make light of his sour disposition. "Is that why your design studio was a revolving door of assistants? Now, tell us the real reason for your abysmal mood."

Lester made a sound like a small outboard motor through his lips. His frustration was palpable as he considered how much information to reveal. "Too many interruptions!" he pleaded. "Constant pings from emails and text messages! And don't even get me started on those infernal social media notifications. It's a never-ending cacophony of distractions! I can't think straight with all this noise. That Jane Austen movie made the English countryside look like a place of peace and beauty where one can escape the pressures of society and find solace in nature. Wrong! How am I supposed to focus on my work when I'm bombarded from all sides by trivialities and nonsense?"

Polly arched an eyebrow, a mischievous grin dancing on her lips as she regarded Lester's melodramatics. "Darling, it's hardly rocket science! Simply press the power-off button on your phone. *Voilà!* Crisis averted!"

Lester made a face that suggested he thought Polly had made the most absurd statement in the history of absurd statements. "Press the power-off button..." he mimicked in a singsong, his voice trailing off into disbelief. "Yeah, I'll do that. Then life will be peachy. Brilliant."

Lester's nerves were already stretched taut when suddenly his phone erupted with his jarring, kazoo-like ringtone. He flinched so violently that the champagne in his flute threatened to slosh over the rim of his glass. His eyes locked onto the screen, and the color drained from his face as though he'd just seen Thistlethorne's own specter materialize before him. He jabbed at the Decline option with trembling fingers and sent the call to voicemail. "Probably my editor." He fumbled an explanation, his voice strained with barely contained panic. "He forgets we're five hours ahead of New York."

Lester gulped down the rest of his champagne, the bubbles doing little to ease the tight knot of anxiety in his chest. And then, like a relentless tormentor, the phone rang again with what Polly now recognized as the Beatles' "Paperback Writer." Lester recoiled, his hand shaking as he repeatedly stabbed at the Decline button again with growing desperation. "How do I make it stop!" he demanded, his voice cracking with frustration.

"Lester, darling, calm down," Polly interjected, her genuine concern evident as she patted his arm. "You can't let things like pesky book editors and their silly publishing schedules get under your skin. What's the worst that could happen if you miss your deadline? Beheadings are rare—outside of Saudi Arabia."

"You don't understand!" Lester cried, his voice laced with a raw edge of desperation. "Nobody understands!"

When Lester's phone rang for the third time, a surge of panic seemed to seize him like a vise, squeezing the breath from his lungs. With a jolt, he catapulted from his chair. He dashed from the room with the urgency of a hunted animal fleeing a predator. Despite the smooth strains of Ella Fitzgerald's lilting voice replacing Dionne's scratchy one through the speakers, Polly and her companions couldn't ignore the discordant notes of Lester's heated exchange reverberating down the hall. "No means no!" they heard him shout. "How many times do I have to repeat myself? And no, I'm *not* sorry!" The words carried a weight of desperation, and then he vanished behind the library door, leaving an uneasy silence in the air.

Polly exchanged glances with Tim, who grimaced at Tiara— their expressions a mix of confusion and concern. "Well, that was... weird," Polly said, her tone tinged with bemusement. "Someone needs their blankie. Or a Xanax."

"What happened to his grand impersonation of Truman Capote?" Tim mocked. "He used to flounce around the house, bragging about his literary genius and how his words flowed like champagne at a high-society gala!"

"Now he's pointing fingers at poor Elara and having a meltdown over a phone call," Tiara added. She paused, a memory dancing behind her eyes. "I haven't seen him this worked up since the Wardrobe Apocalypse at the Emmys that year. Remember?"

Polly grimaced, recalling the situation. "It was chaos backstage after someone replaced his designer suit with a janitor's uniform. He went ballistic. But this... this is a whole new level of drama," she said, shaking her head in disbelief.

"He was in a vile mood this morning," Tim explained. "Did Elara tell you? She accidentally bumped the library door with her vac. The way he reacted, you would have thought she'd dropped his phone in the toilet. Totally irrational. Elara was sort of scary too. She's got another side to her."

The family moved on to their evening meal, and Lester eventually wandered into the dining room, looking tired and defeated. "Apologies for that untoward scene," he said, not moving toward his chair. "Business stuff. I'm tired. I'll take my plate to my room if you don't mind. And I have an early appointment in the morning, so I won't be..." He mumbled something unintelligible and placed a modest portion of Tiara's roasted chicken, mashed potatoes, and steamed veg onto his plate. He refilled his flute. "Oh, I forgot to mention, I discovered a hidden panel in the library. I'll show it to you tomorrow."

8

"Mildred's driving me cuckoo!" Polly wailed to an audience of Tim, Tiara, and Mr. Boots when she wandered into the kitchen after rehearsals the next afternoon. "Get this! She wants me to use my Hollywood connections to get a fog machine, a confetti cannon, and a pyrotechnics expert for her dum-dum show! She wants fireballs and levitating performers, too! 'I dream of a boundary-pushing immersive experience for the audience.'" Polly mimicked Mildred's demands in an exaggerated theatrical voice. "I'll give her a boundary-pushing immersive experience she'll never forget," she said, then gestured strangling Mildred with her bare hands.

Polly sat down at the table, where Tiara and Tim were playing Scrabble against each other on their phones. She looked around for something else to grumble about. "Speaking of confetti cannons and pyrotechnics, is Lester in a better mood today?"

Tiara shrugged. "Haven't seen him. Hasn't returned from his meeting."

Tim, who was dividing his attention between Scrabble and

Mr. Boots, who insisted that scratches behind his ears were far more important than the lousy all-consonant S-L-X-P-W-M-T tiles on his rack, said, "Wherever he went, he walked. He knew better than to ask me to give up my pillow to drive him anywhere before nine o'clock."

"The kettle was empty, and his teacup unused," Tiara added. "So I guess it was a breakfast meeting."

For the rest of the afternoon, the trio busied themselves with their usual business of this 'n' that. Only when Lush Hour rolled around, and June Christy was singing "Something Cool" on Spotify did anyone remember that Lester still hadn't returned to Thistlethorne. "Should we be worried?" Polly said, nursing her drink and listening to the wind and rain lashing the house. "He should have called or texted to say he'd be away all day. Timmy, dear, call his cell and ask where he is and when he's coming home."

Over the next hour, several attempts were made to contact Lester, but the calls went to voicemail. "Did he say where he was going or who he was meeting?" Polly asked for the umpteenth time, her voice starting to express the anxiety she was feeling. "We should have asked."

"He'll be along any moment," Tiara added optimistically as an eerie stillness enveloped the room. Tim had turned off the music to better hear when Lester opened the door. The crackling logs in the fireplace, the tick-tock of the grandfather clock down the hall, and the wind and rain lashing the windows seemed amplified.

The dinner meal was subdued. On any other night, they'd be yapping over each other, debating how well the new maid was doing, or chuckling about something Polly had read in her online edition of the *Hollywood Reporter*. Or mimicking the bellyaching of Mildred and her overactive imagination and novelty ideas for staging the upcoming show. But tonight, with the candelabra throwing a creepy glow throughout the dining room, they ate in near silence, each thinking the same thing: *Lester's a pain in the butt, but I'm getting worried.*

As if they weren't feeling freaky enough, the music system suddenly interrupted the cast album of *Funny Girl* with Mozart's mournful *Requiem*—without anyone tapping their Spotify app. Even the apple crumble Tiara had made for dessert failed to summon anyone's interest. Something wasn't right. They all knew it.

On any other night, after the fire was reduced to embers, they'd drain the last of their champagne, slip into their jammies, place hot water bottles under the sheets on their beds, say their prayers, then hit the hay. Tonight, however, Polly paced the room, Tim pretended to read BBC news on his phone, and Tiara puttered around in the kitchen. They were doing all they could to stop thinking about Lester Lynch and why he wasn't home from his morning meeting.

Finally, the anxiety was too much, and Tim texted Grayson. A moment later, his phone rang. Of course, it was Gray, morphing from a lovey-dovey boyfriend into a serious police constable. "I'll be there in a tick," he said.

In a brisk fifteen minutes, Grayson was settled onto the Chesterfield settee in the reception room, accepting a cup of tea from Tiara. "Let's start from the beginning," he said, his tone firm yet composed as he opened his small memo book to jot down notes. "When was the last time you saw Mr. Lynch or heard from him? Can you walk me through the events leading up to his departure this morning? What was his demeanor like? Was there anything unusual or out of the ordinary about his behavior?" As Grayson spoke, his pen moved swiftly across the page, capturing key details of their conversation. "What about his appearance?" he continued. "What was he wearing? Does

Mr. Lynch have any medical conditions or special needs that
need to be considered?"

Polly fidgeted with the diamond and blue sapphire ring on
her right hand, considering Grayson's inquiries. "He was quite
agitated last night," she said, her tone heavy with concern. "He
got several calls that made him angry—or maybe fearful is a
better word. It was hard to tell if he was upset by the interruptions or something the caller said. He claimed it was his editor—
he's writing a book—but I don't believe that. He was definitely in
an unusual mood."

"Not completely uncharacteristic," Tiara interjected, her
voice taking on a subtle edge. "He's often sullen over perceived
slights or inconveniences. But this was different."

"He said he was meeting someone this morning, but didn't
say who," Tim added, his tone laced with concern. "He doesn't
have a car, so he would've had to walk. It couldn't be farther than
the village."

"Unless someone picked him up," Polly said, her eyes
widening slightly, her worry deepening. "If someone did, it
means he willingly went with them. But who would he meet so
early? He never mentioned knowing anyone around here."

"As for what he was wearing, we can't say for sure because
we didn't see him leave," Tiara said. "But he tends to wear the
same blue jeans and flannel shirt day in and day out."

"And no, I don't think he has any specific medical conditions.
At least he never said," Polly added.

As Grayson meticulously pieced together the puzzle of
Lester's disappearance, a sense of unease settled over him. "I've
never handled a missing persons case before," he admitted, his
brow furrowing with worry. "We've had our share of missing
Amazon packages, a kidnapped box turtle once, but nothing
quite like..."

His voice trailed off, a somber gravity weighing down his

words. "Lester's behavior sounds, well, troubling, to say the least," he continued, his expression growing more solemn. "If this were London or Bristol, they'd suggest waiting a full twenty-four hours before hitting the panic button. But given the circumstances, I think we need to jump on this sooner rather than later."

Grayson's gaze intensified as he leaned forward. "With Lester being sort of a lone wolf around here, he shouldn't be hard to locate. Everyone knows everyone else's business in Abbots Clover. Someone will have seen or talked to him. As a starting point, I'll check with the surgery over in Chaplainslade. We don't want to jump to conclusions, but we need to be proactive." He offered a reassuring smile, though it did little to dispel the tension. "We'll find him. That's a promise."

Although it seemed impossible that Polly and her troupe would be able to sleep, they eventually retired to their beds. In what seemed like very little time, the dull morning light gently seeped through the windows, casting soft shadows across their bedrooms.

In the breakfast room, an air of solemnity hung thick. Polly, Tim, and Tiara sat in uneasy silence, their usual lively banter replaced by a palpable worry and apprehension. Polly absently stirred her Bloody Mary. Tim tapped away idly at his phone, his usual enthusiasm for Wordle replaced by this new preoccupation. Tiara's usually sparkling eyes were clouded with concern, mirroring the heavy atmosphere that weighed upon them all. Even Elara, going about her cleaning duties with quiet efficiency, couldn't help but feel the tension.

When Grayson returned to the castle, a sense of anticipation filled the house. His report was brief but held a glimmer of hope amidst the uncertainty gripping everyone. "I've checked with all the hospitals down here in the Southwest," he began, his voice steady and measured. "There's no sign of Mr. Lynch."

Though the news was far from reassuring, there was a flicker of relief in knowing that Lester's absence hadn't led to a hospitalization.

"I've reached out to Constable Towers," Grayson continued, his tone taking on a note of determination. "She's agreed to assist in any way she can. We're not alone in this."

Constable Ella Towers, affectionately known as "Grandma Sherlock" to the locals, was long retired from the Bristol police force and had moved down to rural Abbots Clover for the tranquility and the sense of community she longed for after years in the bustling city. A plaque in her cottage recognized her years of "tireless effort, courage, and sacrifice"—though she'd spent most of her career behind a desk. And she proudly pinned her commemorative retiree's medal to her coat before Sunday church each week. But she was bored and loved it when Constable Jenkins called for assistance with police activities.

Even though crime was almost nonexistent in bucolic Abbots Clover, Grayson would summon her when overwhelmed with tasks like reuniting lost sheep, redirecting tourists who got lost following a treasure map they found in a local antique shop, or addressing calls about mysterious "monsters" at Duck Lake—inevitably inflatable toys from the village fête. Constable Towers was no longer spry, and her claim to local fame was investigating a "suspicious" package outside the bakery, which turned out to be a forgotten bag of scones and crumpets. Still, the pseudo-police work kept her engaged with life.

Grayson leaned forward, his expression grave as he addressed Polly and her family. "I've started asking around, but no one saw anything unusual in the area yesterday morning. Of course, if Mr. Lynch left before seven, it would still have been dark, and he might have been hard to spot."

Polly's concern was palpable as she fidgeted. "Well, I can't just sit around waiting," she declared, her voice tinged with worry. "I'll organize a search party. Maybe Lester wandered off and got lost. Oh, I feel dreadful. He was our guest, and it was our duty to protect him! I hope he was dressed warmly."

Grayson nodded in understanding but cautioned her against taking matters into her own hands. "I appreciate your concern," he began, his tone firm yet empathetic, "but leaving the search efforts to the professionals is the best thing. It could be hazardous. You haven't lived here long enough to know the area much better than Mr. Lynch. I don't want anyone getting hurt and making the situation worse."

"Gray'll do everything he can to find Lester," Tim said in support of his friend. "We need to trust him."

The day stretched on. The uncertainty of Lester's where-abouts weighed the family down with each passing hour. When the grandfather clock chimed 6:00, signaling the end of another anxious day, Polly & Co. gathered in the reception room. "I've never been so desperate for bubbles!" Polly said, her voice tinged with gloom as she took a long swallow from her glass. "If I weren't so worried, I'd be furious! He's making us all nuts!"

"I can't understand someone vanishing into thin air, especially when everybody in the village knows everyone else's business!" Tim said. "This place is one big microscope."

Seated on the Chesterfield facing the fireplace, Tiara agreed. "It's definitely weird. So how can it be that no one seems to have noticed Lester out walking yesterday morning?"

"Maybe 'cause there's nothing unusual about someone walking in Abbots Clover," Tim said. "We're not in car-crazy California, where the police in Beverly Hills give citations for being a pedestrian. But you're right. With all the gossip circulating around here, you'd think someone would have seen or heard something."

Rain pelted the windows of Thistlethorne Lodge, the relent-less downpour echoing the anxiety that permeated the interior atmosphere. "I hate to think of Lester out in this dreadful weather." Polly sighed. "We don't even know if he was wearing a scarf."

The lights flickered sporadically, casting eerie shadows that danced across the walls, hinting at the perpetual threat of a power outage.

"Everyone charged their phones?" Tiara's voice broke the uneasy silence, her words punctuated by the nervous glances exchanged between the group. Suddenly, Mr. Boots, who was curled up serenely on Polly's lap, jolted upright and cast a piercing gaze toward the door leading to the main hallway. His attention shifted to the window, where a lone branch scraped against the glass with a sinister whisper. When Mr. Boots eventually settled back down, his ears still twitched anxiously at every faint rustle and noise.

"Dinner'll be simple tonight," Tiara announced as she rose to start the meal preparation. Scooping Mr. Boots into her arms, she felt the cat purr contentedly against her chest. "Keep me company, you little devil," she cooed, pressing her cheek against his fur. "You'll get fish pie if you protect me from the spooks. If I see muddy shoeprints anywhere in this place, I'll fly back to California so fast on Elara's new broom!" Her joking added a lightness to the tension that hung in the air.

Then, suddenly, they heard the soft click of a door. Everyone froze with anticipation, and a chill swept through the room. In the tense silence that followed, Polly's voice rang out with a mix of hope and distress. "Lester? Dearest? It's about time. Where have you been? We were worried..."

But there was no Lester. An eerie quiet hung in the air, broken only by the sound of their hearts pounding. They exchanged anxious glances, uncertainty clouding their faces. "We all heard it, didn't we?" Polly's voice quivered as she voiced the question in their thoughts.

"It didn't sound like the entryway door," Tim said in barely a whisper, his eyes darting around the room as if searching for answers in the shadows.

"And I'm pretty sure it wasn't coming from the direction of the kitchen or the larder." Tiara's voice wavered, her hand trembling slightly as she clutched Mr. Boots closer to her chest.

"Check the bedrooms," Polly said, her voice laced with urgency. "I promise to be right behind you." Her false bravado suggested she'd throw her son under the bus if a zombie appeared. As they stepped cautiously into the hallway to investigate the sound, their eyes widened when they noticed the door to the library, which had been slightly open all day, was now firmly closed.

"Is it always that spooky down there?" Polly's voice quivered slightly as she peered down the hallway. Her gaze lingered on the shadows that seemed to dance and sway in the flickering light. "Maybe Lester came in and didn't want to bother us," she added, trying to inject optimism into the tense atmosphere, though her words sounded hollow even to her own ears. The lights flickered again.

"Okay! I'm a sissy! I admit it," Tim confessed, his voice trembling slightly. "I think it's best to call Gray for backup. He's a cop. That's his job. Your property taxes pay him for investigating stuff like spooky noises in thousand-year-old castles."

A short while later, they huddled together in the entry hallway, apologizing to cold and wet Grayson for dragging him out at such a late hour. "I'm always at your service," he assured them as he glanced at Tim. He was happy to be anywhere near Tim and show him how strong and brave he could be.

"We would have investigated the noise ourselves, but Timmy's a mouse when it comes to dark rooms and basements," Polly said. "Thank you, Jason Voorhees."

Grayson adopted a serious demeanor as he listened to their description of "the scary noise." He suggested Polly and Tiara remain in the reception room while he and Tim conducted the investigation.

"Implying that we mere women aren't brave enough?" Polly said, insisting they join the posse. "I was once stuck in an elevator with Debbie Harry. I know what scary is."

As they ventured down the dimly lit hallway with Grayson holding a flashlight and leading the way, the suit of armor standing against the wall cast an ominous shadow, its metallic form appearing almost lifelike. Each creak of the floorboards echoed through the corridor, heightening their sense of unease. When they finally reached the library door, they halted, the tension in the air palpable.

Grayson exchanged a glance with Tim, and they all strained their ears to catch any sound from beyond the door. Suddenly, the silence was shattered by the solemn chime of the grandfather clock marking the stroke of midnight. Grayson switched on a flashlight and placed his hand on the door knob. After a moment's hesitation, he slowly turned the handle. The door protested with a creak as it opened.

The room was freezing cold, and as the flashlight's beam penetrated the dark, Gray found the light switch and flipped it on. With the fullness of illumination from the overhead chandelier, they all breathed a sigh of relief. Other than one of the French doors leading to the back garden being open, a few wet leaves and twigs scattered on the carpet, and Lester's notebooks strewn across the desk, the room was not the safe house for a demon or creatures with glowing red eyes they'd feared. It was just the library. Decorated with its odd collection of celebrity-autographed photos and posters from Hollywood movies and Broadway and West End shows. Alastair Drake, the enigmatic former owner of Thistlethorne Lodge, had left a legacy of passion and obsession, his collection a shrine to the luminaries he revered.

Grayson reached out to close the French doors, and then his eyes focused on the large partners desk that dominated one side of the room. Lester's notebooks were scattered like discarded magazines in a doctor's office. Red pens were strewn on the desktop and the floor.

As the tension dissipated with the realization that the sound from the library door closing was likely just a casualty of the blustery weather, a collective sigh of relief swept through the group. The explanation seemed straightforward enough, and a welcome sense of reassurance came with it. Their fears of an intruder lurking within the shadows seemed unfounded.

Yet, amidst the calming atmosphere, Polly couldn't shake a nagging sense of unease. The open French doors and the gust of wind seemed a plausible explanation for the library door closing, but something didn't seem right. Lester hated the cold. It was unlikely he'd have opened the doors and willingly exposed himself to the elements.

However, with the group seemingly content to dismiss the matter, Polly opted to set aside her concerns. After all, there were more pressing matters at hand, and dwelling on the peculiarities of the situation would only serve to distract them. With a reluctant nod, she resigned herself to letting the matter rest— at least for now.

Grayson basked in the glow of his self-appointed role as the gallant protector, relishing the admiration he sensed radiating from Tim's appreciative gaze. With a confident demeanor, he declared, "I believe we've unraveled the mystery," a smirk of satisfaction playing across his features. Yet, as if to mock his sense of triumph, the lights above began to flicker erratically. Outside, the wind howled menacingly, causing the French doors to tremble in their frames. At the same time, the ominous brush of tree branches against the windowpanes echoed through the room.

And just as they were preparing to retreat, Mr. Boots wriggled from Tiara's arms and walked tentatively toward the fireplace. Emitting a cautious meow and sniffing at the hearth and built-in bookcase next to it, he meowed again. He placed his front paws against the bottom shelf containing famous actors' biographies.

"Probably a mouse," Tim suggested as he moved toward the fireplace. "A tasty mousey in the wall?" he asked as he began to examine the shelves of books. "He's definitely interested in... Lester said he'd found... What if..." Tim started to feel around the shelves and used his phone's flashlight to scan behind the old collection of books. He pressed and tapped and examined the intricate molding framing the shelves. Then his fingers traced an intricately carved rose applique. As if guided by an unseen hand, he gave it an almost imperceptible push.

Suddenly, with a barely audible click, the entire bookcase slightly shuddered; ancient hinges groaned in protest as it moved on a hidden mechanism. The whole unit protruded from the wall. All eyes focused on this strange revelation, and the lights flickered again. Then, with a combination of intrigue and apprehension, Tim gave the built-in bookcase a small tug.

The weight of something behind the shelves forced it completely open.

At that very moment, the lights went completely out!

But the very last illuminated image was forever seared into their eyes: Lester Lynch.

Looking exactly like a dead body.

Because he was... a dead body.

9

L ester Lynch was zipped into a cadaver bag. Gurneyed to an emergency response van. And whisked away from Thistlethorne Lodge before dawn had fully embraced the English countryside. As Polly & Co. silently watched the vehicle's red taillights recede in the distance, they were morose. As sad as they'd ever been about anything. Sure, dead bodies weren't exactly a novelty to Polly Pepper. She'd been an unintentional amateur sleuth in Hollywood and Beverly Hills and had stumbled upon a few stiffs there. And she'd briefly known the last corpse—Gwellyn Clogg, the castle's housekeeper. But this was different. Lester Lynch was an old friend. Not exactly a bosom buddy. They hadn't swapped favorite recipes or beauty secrets or anything like that. But they were palsy-walsy enough for Lester to have been Polly's house-guest at the time of his death. Now, she and her troupe were each thinking variations of the same theme: *Another day. Another death.*

As dreadful as Tim felt for dead Lester, he also felt a pang of misery for his chum, Grayson, who didn't seem to know what the heck he was supposed to do in this crisis. Gray was still somewhat green as a cop. Crime school had probably been entirely theoretical. It was one thing to pass Body Finding 101 class or watch an instruction video during police academy training. But he still wasn't all that comfortable with face-to-face interactions with something the Grim Reaper left behind. Tim wanted to provide emotional support but didn't know how.

As Tiara was offering the umpteenth cup of tea, Grayson announced that he was returning to the station. "A report to file. The American embassy to call. Do you have Mr. Lynch's passport?"

Elara arrived for work, but what could she do? Yes, the place needed a mop-up after the EMT guys had tracked mud onto the floors and carpets. But there was a depressing cloud hanging over the whole place, and at least for a few more days, the house would be a hotbed of evidence-collection activity. She'd only be in the way. Furthermore, Grayson had made it clear that no one was to disturb the library until a forensics team from Bristol could comb through the scene. But who knew when that would be, considering budget cuts to His Majesty's police operations. Abbots Clover wasn't exactly a high-priority village.

As Polly sat at the kitchen table, sipping tea instead of her usual Bloody Mary (somehow, even the concept of blood, however artificial or idiomatic, seemed plain wrong this morning), she was in a near-catatonic state. All she or the others could see in their mind was Lester's lifeless face when he tumbled out from the hidden niche and crumpled to the floor just as the lights went out. Poor Lester. He'd looked as miserable as anyone unexpectedly dispatched to the afterlife would.

As the trio sat staring into space, unconsciously picking blueberries out of muffins and mechanically eating them morsel by morsel, they were silently going over the events of the past two days:

Lester's excitement about writing his book...

Lester being a pill about Elara and her noisy vac...

A phone call driving him into a rage...

Something about a morning meeting...

Lester hiding in a secret space...

Never coming home—because he'd apparently never left home.

They recalled the previous evening when he'd mentioned discovering a hidden panel in the library. How had that happened? And had he decided to check it out while everyone else slept? When Tim had shown off the secret passageway in his bedroom, Lester was sure there must be another and was eager to find it. Now, it seemed he had managed to locate one. While exploring, he must have become trapped inside. Had the castle ghost closed the panel on him? Could he have been saved if Polly had come down to breakfast earlier and heard him pounding on the wall?

The image of Lester being entombed in the castle was hard for Tim to block out of his head. *It's only about the size of a phone booth,* Tim thought of the claustrophobic space. *Without ventilation, I guess he'd only last about a day or so. And what if he'd had to go to the bathroom?* He shuddered as he recalled reading Edgar Allan Poe's *The Cask of Amontillado* in school. One of the characters was lured into the catacombs of a palazzo under the pretense of sampling a rare wine. Then he was chained to a wall and bricked up—while still alive! Tim had been traumatized by the story. "If Lester was in the house all along, why didn't he make a noise or call us? Why didn't we hear anything?"

Polly shook her head as she silently considered all the possible scenarios, even the possibility, remote as it might be, that an intruder—a murderer, in fact—had been in their house too. But she kept those thoughts to herself.

Polly and her cohorts were drained from the awful turmoil of the previous night and the adrenaline they'd spent. They agreed they should put their weary heads down for an hour—which turned into five.

Awakened from her black, dreamless sleep by the impatient clanging of the gate bell, Tiara was the first to stir. Groggy and disoriented, she made her way down the stairs and through the entryway hall, emerging into the courtyard and lurching toward the main gate.

It was Mildred Banks. "The curse of Polly Pepper strikes again!" Mildred exclaimed when Tiara opened the peep plate in the door. Mildred seemed excited to be at the forefront of breaking news and gossip. "I've heard all about it. I didn't know Mr. Lynch very well—we only met the day he destroyed the collective self-confidences of Nancy Mann, Rose Wetherspoon, and Emily Bennett with his sarcastic critiques of their audition performances. I'm told they're still destroyed. But I'm sure he didn't deserve to die so young."

"He wasn't young, and there's no Polly Pepper curse," Tiara insisted, still drowsy and trying not to yawn.

"Two deaths at Thistlethorne Lodge in two months? I beg to differ," Mildred said as she scooted through the gate past Tiara and into the courtyard. "Three, if you count old Mr. Drake!"

"We weren't here when Mr. Drake died!" Tiara countered. "And obviously, Polly isn't in any emotional shape to attend rehearsals today."

"The hell she isn't!" Mildred declared as she barreled toward the open front door. "Wakey-wakey. Time to partake in the day's sweet cakey!" she yelled into the entry hallway. Her past days as an annoying preschool teacher were evident by her juvenile incentivizing rhymes. "It'll take her mind off the drama. The show must go on, and we open in a tick. Polly's professional contribution is essential. Now, bring Madam Starshine to me."

Tiara was too tired to argue and followed Mildred into the house. "A cuppa?" she automatically asked and instantly regretted the encouragement.

"Milk, two sugars, and I saw a lemon drizzle cake the other day. I'll have a slice of that."

Having been warned that Mildred Banks was in the kitchen, insisting Polly would feel better if she immersed herself in creative activities, the Lady of the Castle eventually wandered down to confront her antagonist.

"Nancy Mann's out." Mildred announced the change in the show's casting. "It's lambing season, and she can't take the time away from her flock long enough to learn the songs. That's the last time I put her mutton-loving bum in one of my shows!"

Polly maintained a calm exterior, nodding sympathetically as Mildred rambled on about Nancy's abrupt departure and the urgent need to find a suitable replacement. Inside, however, her mind was in turmoil. She couldn't care less about Nancy Mann, her sheep-birthing chores, or this latest show drama. All that consumed her thoughts was the discovery of yet another dead body in her castle. The macabre find overshadowed everything else, rendering Mildred's trivial show utterly inconsequential.

Despite the chaos within, Polly knew she had to uphold her reputation as the epitome of sweetness. She couldn't afford to let her disdain slip through the cracks of her carefully constructed persona. Taking a deep breath, she forced a smile and agreed to help with the auditions. It was the easiest way to keep up appearances, and for now, keeping up appearances was all that mattered.

It was going to be a very long day.

Just as she resigned herself to the exhausting task ahead, Polly's phone rang. It was Terrence, who had heard the news of

Lester's death and called to offer support. "I know how to take your mind off this horrible event," he said. "I'll pick you up at eight." Polly couldn't say no, feeling a small sense of relief at his offer of distraction.

Meanwhile, Grayson Jenkins returned to the castle in his official police capacity. He gathered Polly, Tim, and Tiara into the reception room, the air thick with tension. "It's early in the investigation, but I think it's probably a slam dunk," he began, his tone attempting to be reassuring. "You all saw Mr. Lynch's body. There weren't any lacerations or blunt force trauma, so I'm guessing his death was accidental. It'll take a few days for the autopsy report to confirm, but I'd say he probably suffocated. The space just ran out of oxygen. He somehow got stuck in there, and that was that. I'm sorry."

Polly felt a chill run down her spine. The idea of suffocating in the dark space was horrifying. Tim looked pale, and Tiara clutched her hands together, eyes wide with shock and confusion. The room fell silent as they absorbed the news, each of them wrestling with their own thoughts about the circumstances of Lester's death.

"This is like one of those awful news stories," Tiara said, her voice trembling slightly. "You know, where people get stuck in chimneys or fall between walls and can't get out, and no one finds them until someone starts a remodeling job years later. It's terrifying to think that something so dreadful could happen right here."

Tim's imagination ran wild as he pictured the grim scenario. He envisioned Lester, desperate and claustrophobic, trapped in the dark, narrow space. The walls closing in. Every breath becoming more labored as the oxygen dwindled. He thought of the frantic pounding that might have gone unheard through the castle, and the helplessness Lester must have felt as the desperate hours turned into the last defeated minutes. It was a chilling thought, and Tim shuddered.

But Polly wasn't ready to accept Grayson's cause-of-death conclusion just yet. Doubt gnawed at her, and she had pressing questions. "You don't think Lester's head seemed a bit too loosely connected and wobbly?" she asked, her voice laced with skepticism and her brow furrowing in confusion. "And what on earth was he doing in there in the first place? It doesn't make any sense," she added, her eyes narrowing as she tried to piece together the puzzling circumstances.

"He said he'd found another hidden place. Maybe he wanted to see what it was like then couldn't get out," Tim suggested. "You know how he was intrigued by those things."

Tiara's mind spiraled into more horrifying possibilities. She imagined Lester peering into the narrow, hidden space, initially thrilled by his discovery. But then the panel suddenly closed behind him, plunging him into impenetrable darkness. She pictured his panic, frantically feeling around for an escape, fingers scraping against unyielding stone. She envisioned him yelling for help, his desperate cries absorbed by the thick, uncaring walls. A shudder ran down her spine as she thought of him trying to call them on his phone, only to realize there was no signal in the suffocating depths of the castle. She imagined the battery dying, the screen flickering before going black, leaving him in utter isolation. Every breath would have grown more frantic, the air becoming oppressively thin and stale, his heart pounding in his chest. She could almost hear his gasps, each one more desperate than the last until, finally, he succumbed to the horrifying, suffocating silence.

"He could have yelled or called us on his phone!" Tiara demanded, trying to come up with ways his death could have been avoided, even as the chilling images filled her mind.

"He didn't have his phone. He hated that thing," Polly said.

"Complain, complain. That's all he did. He was frustrated by his lack of twenty-first-century skills. How many times did he threaten to take a hammer to it? Maybe he finally got fed up with the calls from his editor—or whomever—and ditched it somewhere."

Over the next hour, Polly, Tim, and Tiara continued giving Grayson information and details about Lester's life, career, and state of mind during the past few days. Yes, he'd been upset the last time they'd seen him. But he was also excited about writing his book. Yes, he probably had a few enemies because of his often-vicious tongue, and he let his impatience for anything slightly inconvenient turn ordinary situations into uncomfortable ones. But...

"And who knew that we had another secret room!" Polly said, returning to the curiosities of this constantly self-revealing house. "We've got a secret passageway in Tim's bedroom. Our very own dungeon. And now a concealed hideaway! What could someone want to hide from? Royalists? Parliamentarians? Witch-hunters?"

"I think it's called a priest hole," Grayson said of the hidden niche. "They're not entirely uncommon in really old places like yours." He explained what he knew about priest holes and religious persecution centuries ago. "In those days, Catholics couldn't worship openly. The Protestant Church was the only religion the king allowed. Some Catholics built secret hiding places in their homes to shelter priests, who risked death for practicing their ministry. These spaces were ingeniously concealed. Like behind panels, under floorboards, or in chimneys. Some were accessed through hidden doors or trapdoors, while others, like yours, required intricate mechanisms to reveal their existence."

"This house seems to want to swallow people up!" Polly said. "Mr. Boots got stuck in the secret passageway in Tim's room.

Then we were locked in the dungeon, where no one might ever have found us for a million years. We even have a ghost that can't seem to get out."

By the time Grayson finished his inquisition, it was late afternoon, and the sun was going down. Although it was technically too early for Lush Hour, Tiara popped a cork and served Polly and Tim. "Ach! I don't feel like going down to the pub tonight, even if it is with dreamy Terrence," Polly whined. "I won't be in a chatty mood. And kisses are just a temporary Band-Aid. My thoughts will be filled with Lester and why he died in a priest hole. A priest hole, for crying out loud! I'm already imagining the obscene headlines this bit of information will generate in Hollywood! The late-night comics will have a field day!"

Tiara snorted. "They'll say things like, 'Lester's last confession was so scandalous, he had to bury himself to keep it secret!'"

Tim laughed. "Or 'Lester Lynch took skeletons in the closet to a whole new level—he became one!'"

Polly slipped into a reflective mood as she sat petting Mr. Boots and felt the tingle of champagne bubbles on her tongue. "Secret hideaways," she muttered, then turned to Tim. "Lester was excited when you showed off the passageway to the dungeon. He said a house this size probably had other secret spaces and was actively looking for one. He had such an imagination. I think he actually wanted to meet our ghost, even though he said he didn't necessarily believe in ghosts. Maybe he went inside the space to check it out and then got locked in. Oh, it's too dreadful to think about!"

Polly couldn't stop thinking about the upsetting calls Lester received and the possibility of a link between them and his death. "Where is his phone, anyway?" she asked, standing up and looking around for the iPhone she'd last seen clutched in Lester's hands, his finger jabbing at the screen. For the next hour, she searched the house to no avail, growing increasingly frustrated and anxious.

As she approached the library door, Tim spoke up, breaking her train of thought. "Gray told us not to go into the library," he reminded her, his voice tinged with caution.

"He said not to 'disturb' the library," Polly countered, "totally different." She peeled away the blue and white police caution tape obstructing the doorway. "Just a quick peekaboo."

The library was silent and cold, and remnants of what the wind had previously blown in were evident on the carpet by the glass French doors. The overhead chandelier gave the room an icky, sallow glow as Polly wandered around and inspected the autographed celebrity photos and classic posters that Alistair Drake had collected over the years.

There was a black-and-white picture of Judy Garland dressed as a hobo during her 1951 engagement at the Palace Theatre in New York City. "Come Rain or Come Shine," Polly said to herself, knowing the song her favorite singer had performed while wearing that costume during her legendary concert series. There was a color photo of dancer Juliet Prowse looking elegant in a beaded, form-fitting dress during her triumphant engagement at the Stardust Resort and Casino in Las Vegas. Polly stopped for a moment and made a face. Was there a picture missing from the wall? There were so many stars represented in the room, she couldn't remember. Still, she noticed a gap between frames and an empty nail protruding between pictures of Debbie Reynolds and Ella Raines.

"Do you see me touching anything?" Polly said to the room as if to convince all the eyes on the walls that she was following orders to not disturb potential evidence. "But I do need answers. Help me out here. Please?"

With Tim, Tiara, and Mr. Boots in lockstep, Polly wandered to the partners desk. Spiral notebooks and red pens were scattered about, an unusual state of disarray that would have sent Lester's obsessive-compulsive tendencies into a tailspin. She also noticed a fine dust and tiny fragments of white paper littering the desk. "Better get Elara in here the minute we have the all clear," she said, frowning at the mess.

Her thoughts shifted to Lester's meticulous nature. "How many notebooks did Lester buy?" Polly asked, looking at Tim.

"Twenty."

Polly counted eighteen, her brow furrowing as she swept the room with her eyes one final time. She scrunched up her face, making a sound that suggested she was disappointed but had seen all she needed to see. With a resigned sigh, she headed for the door. "Time to paint my face," she said. "Terrence expects glamour."

10

The Fox & Hare was the only place in Abbots Clover to go for a pint and a meal. With all the charm of a quintessential British pub, the main room was dominated by a large inglenook fireplace, which spanned a significant portion of the wall. The wood-beam ceiling was low, and the flagstone floor was uneven. A dozen wooden tables and mismatched chairs were haphazardly scattered throughout the room. The walls were a collage of dartboards, framed pictures of famous footballers lifting championship trophies above their heads, and royals doing royal things—waving, cutting ribbons, and fake smiling.

Behind the bar was a large painting of formally attired fox hunters galloping on horseback and blowing bugles, accompanied by a pack of eager hounds in full pursuit. The scene was set against a backdrop of rolling green hills and a clear blue sky, capturing the essence of a classic English countryside hunt. The Fox & Hare was everything an anglophile like Polly Pepper could want in an English country pub, and when she and Terrence closed the door behind them, they felt embraced by the warmth of the roaring fire.

Just being away from Thistlethorne was more of a tonic than Polly had anticipated. And the brief kiss she'd exchanged with Terrence in the car temporarily dislodged all thoughts of dead Lester Lynch. They walked past a group of locals parked at the bar, and one of them nudged another. "That's her," he whispered as though Polly had been the topic of recent conversation. And undoubtedly, she had been.

Polly was used to causing a slight stir when she entered a restaurant. It didn't happen all that often anymore in California, where celebrities were as common as luxury cars on Sunset Boulevard. And she usually enjoyed being recognized. But here in Abbots Clover, she knew she was being judged. She was an outsider. An entitled American. A foreigner who'd inherited the local castle.

As Polly and Terrence took their seats at a table for two at the far end of the pub, Terrence reached for Polly's hand, silently broadcasting that he didn't really know what to say but wanted to be supportive in any way he could.

Polly nodded. *Rotten things happen sometimes*, she seemed to say and offered a slight grimace. "Change of subject," she announced with a big fake smile, searching for any topic to discuss other than the elephant in the room. "Tell me about the annual cheese-rolling contest. I saw a poster for it. And the Duck Parade. I've heard it's darling. And what's the headline for the next issue of the *Abbots Clover Overview*? Maybe avoid printing 'Lester Lynch' and 'priest hole' in the same sentence." Polly chuckled quietly.

A server arrived to take their drink and meal orders, and when they were alone again, Polly became pensive. "It's curious. Lester's death, I mean. Naturally, I'm crushed, but I guess I didn't realize how utterly gutted I really am," she said, looking into Terrence's eyes. "I'll be honest, Lester Lynch was sometimes a pain in the neck. He was negative. He had a short fuse, which kept everyone around him on their toes. I don't know why we remained friends all these years. Shared history, I guess. But my goodness, he was talented. He designed costumes for me and so many others. He won all sorts of awards and commendations. The industry has lost one of their finest creatives."

Terrence carefully navigated the delicate terrain of Polly's grief, cognizant of the weight of her loss. While he longed to offer solace drawn from his own experiences with sorrow, he hesitated, wary of overshadowing Polly's mourning. When their drinks arrived, he raised his pint of beer to Polly's effervescent Prosecco in tribute. "To Lester," he said solemnly, the words tinged with reverence. "Although I never had the privilege of meeting him, I've seen some of your shows on YouTube, so I've also seen his work."

"To Lester," Polly repeated, letting the bubbles cascade over her tongue. Her eyes sparkled as she leaned back, a genuine smile spreading across her face. She raised her glass higher. "To life!" she declared, her voice ringing with unrestrained cheer. She paused for a moment, her fingers drumming a quick, happy rhythm on the table.

"Here's some good news." Polly's grin widened. "We might have to cancel the annual village musical!" She clinked her glass against Terrence's with a satisfied nod, her shoulders relaxing as if a burden had been lifted. "I'll drink to that," she added, taking a joyful sip, her eyes twinkling with delight.

"That's *not* good news." Terrence winced, his voice rising louder than intended. "It'd rob us of our annual chance to laugh at Mildred Banks! The woman is blissfully unaware of our sniggering behind her back. That's more fun than the annual Sheep Beauty Pageant!"

A sheep beauty pageant? Polly laughed as images tumbled into her head of a showcase for the most photogenic ewes in the village. "Poor Mildred being the object of ridicule," she said with approval. "The thing is, we've lost our star," she explained and described the awfulness of the concept for *Cats on a Hot Tin Roof* and how the cast was falling apart. "Nancy Mann, who was to play one of the leads, was actually pretty darn good when she auditioned. I think she could have done well. But now, unless Peggy Sawyer's hiding in the village, we're screwed. Or maybe saved, depending on how you look at it."

"Peggy Sawyer?" Terrence asked. He knew everyone in the village, and the only Peggys were Peggy Merchant and Peggy Newman.

"Fictional," Polly explained. "Peggy Sawyer's that wide-eyed kid in the chorus of a big musical who steps in and takes over the lead in the show when the star breaks her leg being mean to someone. Peggy tap dances her way to saving the show and making it a great big hit. But I rather hope we don't find Peggy. This project is total doggie-doo, and I want out."

Most evenings Polly and Terrence spent together flew by; this one was no exception. When they found themselves among the last to leave the pub, they were still fully engaged in lively conversation. They'd covered every subject from Thistlethorne's new maid, Elara, whom Terrence said he'd met at the fishmonger's and thought she was a bit aggressive... sugar on the outside, vinegar on the inside, to Polly's concern for Tiara's love life. "She's adorable. But men don't appreciate vintage. They want shiny, new toys. If you know anyone who might be suitable..."

By the time Terrence paid the bill, it was nearly 11:00, and the pub was empty.

"It's cold outside, but I know a fun way to warm you back up," Terrence teased with a lascivious grin as they bundled up against the night air.

"Rain check, handsome." Polly smiled back, reading Terrence's mischievous thoughts. Although she was eager to touch Terrence's bare skin again, she wanted that moment without distractions. And right now, she had another man on her mind: Lester Lynch.

Arriving at Thistlethorne, Terrence escorted Polly through the main gate. Mr. Boots was waiting outside under the front portico, sheltering from the cold and wet. He greeted them with a quiet meow that seemed to say, "Listen up, buddy. I'm the top cat around here. Scram before I cough up a furball on your shoes!" Terrence gave Polly one more long kiss, watched to ensure she was safely inside the house (with Mr. Boots), and departed.

Polly locked the door behind her and dropped the keys onto the antique console table in the foyer. As quietly as possible, she followed the light into the reception room. The fire was reduced to embers, and the cold had begun to reclaim the room's temperature. She shivered and looked up at the portrait of the duke over the mantel. "What's up, old man? I think you need a haircut," she said to the pasty-faced nobleman who, centuries ago, built this house inside the fortified castle walls.

The house seemed particularly quiet tonight. Tim and Tiara had obviously gone to bed, and Polly was alone and feeling gloomy. Sure, she'd had a lovely evening with Terrence. She was growing fonder of him with each passing day. But she was unsettled. Not only because she was still getting used to living in England but because of the gnawing feeling that Lester's death wasn't the accidental suffocation that Grayson had suggested. *Trust your instincts, girl*, she said to herself.

Polly wandered around the room, touching the frames of paintings, admiring pieces of porcelain on the side tables, and imagining who the weavers of the tapestries were. Her entire life had been one extraordinary surprise after another, and now she had all of this, too! Looking up at the intricately molded ceiling, she wondered about the unseen spirit rumored to occupy the house. The one she wanted to name after her favorite old-time movie star. The one she still suspected of coming to their rescue when she and Tim and Tiara had been thrown into the castle dungeon by a killer. Now she stood motionless, listening to the sounds of the house, and wondered if she dared give in to temptation and call on the spirit world to ask what had really happened to Lester.

Polly sat on the piano bench, rested her arm on the keyboard lid, and closed her eyes. After a quiet moment, she whispered tentatively, "Is there someone here from the other side?"

Silence, except for the tick-tock of the grandfather clock.

"Give me a sign. But please don't scare me." She stopped to listen again.

Silence.

"Spirit world..." she continued with more authority. "I don't believe this earthly life is the only one. There has to be more. Maybe not a Heaven or Hell, or a big ol' VIP rapture party for Jehovah's Witnesses' top picks, but there must be a Great Beyond where creative energy and talent go. There has to be a place where I'll sing, dance, and tell jokes when this life is over. Judy will be there. And Elvis. And dear Karen Carpenter, too." She recalled those she admired or knew. "If you can hear me, please give me a sign."

Again, Polly stopped to listen. But the only sounds in the room came from the soft crackling of the dying embers in the fireplace, and Mr. Boots purring contentedly on the Chesterfield settee. "I'll give you one last chance," Polly said, her patience with the dead wearing thin. "If there's anybody here... even that damn dog Loki from that painting in the hallway Old Granny Grumbles put a curse on way back in the day... please reveal yourself... now."

Again, Polly waited, her eyes closed, trying to tune her ears to whatever the sound frequency was that ghosts used to communicate with the living. She was just about to say, "Nobody listens to me anymore," when she heard an unexpected sound. She opened her eyes and looked around the room. She was sure she'd heard... something. A sound like a deep sigh of resignation. Like someone giving in to a lost cause and accepting things as they are. Or was it the wind from outside blowing against the window? Or Mr. Boots having a dream?

Despite her eyes telling her one thing, Polly started to feel another presence in the room. Like in the movies, there was a sudden drop in temperature. She thought if she were wearing "specter specs" she'd surely see someone next to her.

Then she detected a subtle scent wafting through the air. She sniffed, trying to identify the odor. Was it the damp smell of hay or freshly mowed grass? Was it the pages of a newly printed book? That was her favorite smell, a nostalgic reminder of her school days. Back then, being good meant she was given the special privilege of opening the box of new extracurricular reading books when they arrived. This was a similar scent. Polly sniffed again. This time, she was almost certain she smelled one of the scented dryer sheets that Tiara threw into the machine on wash day.

And then it hit her. Lester had tracked hay on his shoes after visiting grazing cows in the field behind the castle a few days ago. The scent of paper and ink could be from his notebooks. The smell of something like a Downy dryer sheet was from him having to do his own laundry. Lester Lynch was in the room! Polly was sure of it!

"Lester?" Polly whispered almost frantically, "Are you here? Give me a sign. I know you just gave me a sign. I mean a different sign. Just to be sure. Say something. Play the piano. Prove that you're here in this room." In that moment, an ember in the fireplace unexpectedly popped and startled her. It glowed like the taillights on the EMT van that had carried Lester away. "That's the best you can do?" Polly grumbled. "I was thinking something a little more dramatic. Making something levitate. Like maybe a card table. Or a kid's head spins around. Not that I want my head to spin, for crying out loud. Definitely not!"

Polly stood frozen in anticipation, her heart pounding in her chest as she strained to make sense of an eerie noise that began emanating through the stereo speakers. It sounded like the crackling of an old, scratched vinyl record. Then distorted musical notes clashed and twisted like a violent car crash, jagged and jarring. The music seemed to splinter into shards. A shiver traveled down her spine as an ominous male voice whispered the bone-chilling words: "Polly's dead."

Polly bolted from the room, the echoes of the haunting message reverberating in her ears. They seemed to follow her like something nipping at her heels and trying to catch up to her. Her footsteps echoed loudly against the staircase as she ascended, her breaths coming in ragged gasps.

Reaching Tim's bedroom door, Polly pounded frantically. Each desperate knock was a plea for help, a prayer for refuge from the terror that engulfed her. Her hands trembled with fear as she turned the knob. Tim stumbled out of his sleep, eyes wide with alarm. At the same time, Tiara emerged from her own room, drawn by the commotion. Polly collapsed into their arms, her body racked with sobs of terror and confusion. "I've done something so stupid," she cried, her voice choked with fear. "I've summoned the dead. I contacted Lester! I heard his voice! He was in the reception room!"

As the trio huddled on Tim's bed, tension hung heavy in the air, palpable in their exchanged nervous glances. Polly's usually vibrant demeanor was eclipsed by a storm of anxiety, her features contorted with distress.

With trembling hands and a quivering voice, Polly recounted the events, her words tumbling out in a torrent of desperation. Each syllable dripped with urgency as she confessed her ill-fated commune with the other side, her voice laced with guilt and remorse.

"I didn't mean for this to happen," she confessed, her eyes brimming with tears. "I thought maybe, just maybe, the spirits in this house could provide some answers about what happened to Lester. I didn't perform any rituals. I didn't light candles or burn incense, I swear! I just... I started talking, reaching out to the... wherever."

Her voice faltered. "I never imagined it would lead to... to this. I've meddled with supernatural forces."

Tiara's reaction was immediate and visceral. She threw up her hands as she bemoaned their predicament. "You've gone and stirred up the spirits!" she exclaimed, her voice filled with equal parts fear and frustration. "Now we're doomed!"

"You're supposed to tell me everything's okay and there's no such thing as devils, demons, and poltergeists!" Polly pleaded. "Help me out here. I'm a distraught old woman, for crying out loud!"

With a pained expression, Tiara invoked stories from her grandmother, her words laden with superstition and foreboding. "Ghosts are often heralded by mysterious scents," she explained, her tone laced with dread. "The smell of flowers, perfume, or tobacco smoke... they're all signs that the deceased are trying to communicate with the living. And now, thanks to your poking around, you've invited them in."

Polly was mortified. "Maybe it wasn't Lester. Maybe it was my fan Alistair Drake. Or Gwellyn Clogg. She died here just a month ago. Or the duke and his stinky dog. I think I smelled that little monster."

Tim's expression twisted into a grimace, his mind still reeling from his mother's phantasmagorical ordeal. "Well, brava to you," he declared sarcastically. "You've managed to thoroughly freak me out. I'll never be able to sleep in this house again. Ever! And

I'm steering clear of the reception room, the library... heck, I might even avoid the bathroom if a ghostly presence decides to join me for a soak!"

Tiara paced the room, her mind racing to understand what Polly had experienced. "Let's backtrack," she began, her voice laced with curiosity. "You said you heard someone say, 'Polly's dead.' It came through the stereo speakers." Pausing momentarily, her brow furrowed in thought. A glimmer of an idea flickered in her eyes. "Remember that Beatles documentary we watched recently? There was that story, from back in the '60s, about Paul McCartney supposedly dying and the group keeping the information from fans?" Her tone grew increasingly animated. "Conspiracy theories are nothing new, and back then, according to the documentary, Beatles fans were dissecting every lyric and utterance for signs of Paul's demise. The song 'Strawberry Fields Forever' was at the center of it all."

Turning her attention to Tim, she fixed him with an inquisitive gaze. "You used Spotify tonight, didn't you? I heard you playing stuff from the Fab Four."

Tim thought back to his earlier evening entertainment. "I played a bunch of stuff with Gray..." He turned and looked assertively at his mother. "Yeah, you're not the only one who gets to have a date! And yeah, we played the Beatles' *Magical Mystery Tour* album. I wanted to hear 'Penny Lane' again."

"Where's your phone?" Tiara's gaze fell on Tim's nightstand; her curiosity piqued as she reached for the device. "Let me have a look. Don't worry, I won't read any of your DMs with Gray." With practiced ease, she navigated through the apps until she landed on Spotify, her expression morphing into amusement and disbelief.

"The Cowsills? Really?" Tiara deadpanned and looked at Tim with a mocking chuckle as she saw his Recently Played artists list. "How on earth do you even know that group?"

"Sometimes I need a little sunshine pop to brighten my day," Tim smirked.

Tiara's chuckle bubbled as she continued scrolling through Tim's recently played song selections. Her finger finally landed on the title she was searching for. "Aha! 'Strawberry Fields Forever,'" she exclaimed triumphantly. As she tapped on the song, she watched Polly's face.

When the music reached its end, Polly declared, "That's it! That's the voice!"

"I suspected as much," Tiara declared. "That's John Lennon's voice, you silly twit. He said, '*Paul* is dead.' Not '*Polly's* dead'! As a matter of fact, according to the documentary, he actually said, 'Cranberry sauce.' Go figure."

"But how...?" Polly sat on the side of the bed, shaking her head in confusion.

Tiara explained, "Siri sometimes starts babbling on her own without any prompts, thanks to Steve Jobs eavesdropping on our every word. Background noise or a random trigger phrase can unintentionally set off your so-called 'virtual assistant.'"

They all breathed a sigh of relief. But only for a moment. "But I wasn't anywhere near Tim's phone," Polly said skeptically. "Siri, or Alexa, or whoever couldn't have heard what I was saying way downstairs in the reception room! Plus, I never used words like strawberry... or fields... for crying out loud. I haven't even thought about that song since Ringo came on my show, and we did a parody of their old tunes."

"I wanna believe Tiara's right," Tim said, "because I can't spend the rest of my life hiding my head under my pillow. Or being afraid of ghostly eyes watching what I do online. Do you think the undead know what Chaturbate is?"

Polly surrendered. "Fine," she relented, her voice tinged with resignation. "I'm not entirely convinced I didn't dial into Casper's hotline, but to preserve what's left of my sanity and ensure we all get some shut-eye, I'll play ball. However," she added, pointing a finger for emphasis, "someone's going to have to brave the depths of the haunted downstairs and switch off the lights. And let me tell you, it ain't gonna be me. Not unless it's high noon or the room's lit up like Times Square!"

With that, Polly walked purposefully to her bedroom, eyes scanning the hallway for spooks. She slipped under the covers, her heart still racing from the night's events. Although she couldn't shake a feeling of unease—despite Tiara's confident bravado—exhaustion soon consumed her, and she drifted off into a deep and much-needed sleep.

While Polly found refuge in sleep, Tiara steeled herself and descended the staircase alone, each step amplifying the eerie silence of the house. Shadows danced on the walls, and her footsteps echoed like a heartbeat. As she reached the bottom step, a strange noise rippled through the hallway, a soft rustling followed by a faint thud. Tiara froze, her pulse quickening. Was it her imagination, or was something lurking in the darkness?

Summoning her courage, Tiara inched forward, her senses on high alert. The hallway stretched before her like a tunnel of suspense, every creak and groan of the old house magnified in her ears. As she reached the source of the noise, she tensed, ready for anything. Then, out of the gloom, Mr. Boots emerged, his eyes glowing mischievously as he brushed against her ankle.

Relief washed over Tiara, and she let out a shaky laugh. "You little troublemaker," she whispered, scooping up the feline, who purred contentedly. With Mr. Boots in her arms, she made her way to the reception room. After turning off the lights, she hurried back up the stairs, her steps quickening with every shadow that seemed to flicker at the edge of her vision. The feeling of being watched clung to her, and she couldn't shake the sensation that something unseen followed her ascent.

11

That night, even Mr. Sandman was too chicken to visit Tim and Tiara in their beds. And when they shuffled down to breakfast the next morning, they were amazed to find a smiling Polly Pepper sitting like a queen on her throne, phone in hand, looking as fresh as a daisy, and scrolling through posts on her Facebook page. "Sleep well, my cherubs?"

The answer was in their bloodshot eyes.

"I zonked out the moment my head dented the pillow," Polly bragged. "Woke up at the crack and couldn't bear to squander a perfectly moist morning. I put the kettle on. Whipped up my tomato-flavored energy drink. And... *voila!*"

Tiara's jaw practically hit the floor as she marveled at her ladyship mixing her own hand-crafted Bloody Mary (pickled okra garnish, too).

"You're welcome," Polly added with a mischievous grin.

"You recovered from your supernatural encounter," Tim said, popping the tab of the Red Bull Polly had thoughtfully set out. "I'm still traumatized by what happened. I'll never get over last night. Never, ever in a million years. Like when I discovered

Darren Criss, who played Blaine Anderson on *Glee*, was straight." He made a sound that resembled a wounded animal.

"I'm starting to think your mama's been possessed," Tiara quipped, eyeing the basket of warm muffins Polly had also placed on the table. "Please, dear Lord, whoever's taken over Polly Pepper's body is welcome to camp out there for as long as they like. We promise not to summon an exorcist!"

Polly grinned as she buttered a piece of muffin and shrugged as if to say, *What? I'm just being my ever-helpful, independent me.*

The clock was ticking toward nine, and as the sun tried to squeeze through the clouds, Polly & Co. silently thanked the heavens that it was at least semi-dry outside. Yet, living in soggy England meant expecting the unexpected—weather-wise. The climate was as reliable as predicting the next winning lotto jackpot number. And then another surprising thing happened. Polly's cell phone erupted with the whimsical theme music from the classic television comedy show *Rowan & Martin's Laugh-In*. The Caller ID displayed a string of digits. Clearly, the call wasn't from someone in her Contacts. Furrowing her brow, Polly asked, "Who do we know with a number ending in 1244?"

"When you find out, let us know," Tiara quipped as Polly hesitantly tapped the Accept option on her screen.

For the next several minutes, Polly mainly listened. She contributed a few "uh-huhs," an "I see," and a couple of "maybes" before saying, "I hardly think so, dear." Then she thanked whomever and said goodbye.

Tim and Tiara's eyes asked, *Who?*

"Eliza Doolittle, for all I know. Her accent was so thick I couldn't understand half of what she said."

Tim groaned. "The other day, Gray said, 'Mah-tin pahk'd'is cah by the pah'ey house doah.' Took me hours to translate: 'Martin parked his car by the party house door.' Thankfully, his actions are more of an international-body-language type thing. If you get my drift." He chuckled seductively.

"We do, dear. Drift, I mean," Polly said dismissively, ignoring her son's attempt at lascivious levity. "This Audrey... Someone... I think she mainly called to say she'd heard about Lester's death and wanted to convey her condolences. At least that was part of it."

"Who was she to Lester?" Tim asked as he took another swig of Red Bull and glanced at breaking BBC news on his phone screen (something about Prince Harry being miserable because Meghan canceled their Netflix subscription). "A friend? A fan? He never mentioned knowing anyone in England—except that guy he called 'posh.' Ever notice that Lester only knew 'posh' people? And how'd this Audrey person get your number?"

"Beats me," Polly said, "but she definitely wasn't posh. I can't imagine she was ever within spitting distance of the Judi Dench School of Cultural Linguistics." As she sipped her Bloody Mary, Polly continued to think about the call and decided it was weird that Lester's acquaintance knew how to contact her.

"Maybe Lester boasted that he knew Polly Pepper and broadcast your number to prove it?" Tiara said, reading Polly's mind.

"Maybe he listed you as his emergency contact in England," Tim suggested.

"She did say something sort of curious. She was glad Lester wouldn't be finishing his book because there was too much negativity in it."

"He's only been dead a couple of days. How'd she—or anyone—know Lester was writing a book, or who or what he was writing about?" Tim asked.

"Maybe there was something in a gossip column? Or a blog?" Tiara said.

"I click on *Reel Rubbish* every day. They publish all the latest showbiz dish," Tim said. "I'm addicted to that sleazy rag. But I don't remember seeing anything about Lester or his book mentioned on there."

As Polly sat thinking about the call, something else dawned on her. "She also said, and I quote, 'It's your responsibility to clean up his filthy manuscript, or you'll be personally contributing to the decline of Hollywood.'"

Tim laughed. "As if all the superhero franchises, sequels, and streaming services haven't done that already. Hollywood's responsible for its own tarnish! Not you or Lester Lynch."

Tiara scrunched her face. "Sounds vaguely like a threat if you ask me." She was starting to feel uneasy about a stranger having access to Polly's cell phone number and somehow knowing details about Lester's unpublished manuscript. "Maybe she's one of those word wardens from the page patrol who want to censor and control what everybody else reads. Lester had a right to his own thoughts and opinions and to write about what-ever he wanted. Even if someone didn't agree with what he had to say about their golden calves or celebrity crush."

"Good grief, it makes me furious when *Reel Rubbish* publishes insane things about Axel Stuart," Tim exclaimed in agreement, defending his flavor-of-the-month celebrity. "I mean, who needs to know that he only eats white foods? A diet of rice, spuds, and oatmeal can't be all that interesting or even good for him—even if it's to achieve what he calls 'purity and spirituality.' He needs a rainbow on his menu. I'd volunteer to be on his plate."

"Anything else of a dubious nature from this Audrey?" Tiara asked.

"Just that she hopes I like my castle."

"So this person knows where you live," Tiara scoffed with apprehension.

At that moment, Mr. Boots sauntered into the breakfast room and proudly dropped a half-dead mouse on the floor beside Polly's chair. "Meow," he said as if to offer the rodent equivalent of a bauble from Cartier. Polly looked down and grimaced in revulsion. "Such a good kitty! Yes, you are! Yes, you are!" she cooed ambivalently. She looked away and cringed from the crunching sound of the cat chowing down on his raw, still warm, breakfast wrap. She took another sip from her breakfast drink to tamp down a rising urge to barf.

And then Polly's ringtone blared again. This time, her face lit up with happy anticipation. "It's Sarah. From Bound to Read." She grinned happily and eagerly tapped Accept. Sarah Rogers had quickly become Polly's favorite resident of Abbots Clover—well, other than her sexy beau, Terrence Marks, of course. Clever and bright, Sarah seemed to have the gift of everyone liking her. Even those few who were initially suspicious of her sunny disposition were soon won over by her authentic charms.

Polly's mood lifted instantly as she engaged in the conversation. Engrossed in what Sarah was saying, Polly enthusiastically nodded and punctuated the conversation with an occasional "I see!" a couple of "Reallies?" and a "very interesting!" After a flurry of animated exchanges and saying, "Eight is perfect," she hung up.

"Something's up," Polly reported. "She wouldn't say what. Potential prying ears around her. But it might be important. Maybe not. She's not sure. She can't leave the shop, so I've invited her to dinner tonight."

"Another mystery?" Tim asked, eyebrows raised. "We're already up to our ears in drama, and now Sarah's bringing more."

"Shush," Polly pleaded, a glint of excitement in her eyes. "You know I love a good mystery. Besides, I'm already bored with the dead people. They just lie there, doing nothing interesting. I need something to liven up the day!"

Tim rolled his eyes, but Polly's enthusiasm was contagious. The anticipation of a new puzzle hung in the air as they moved on with their day.

12

T im busied himself shaving, showering, and assembling an outfit of jeans and flannel, aiming to channel the rugged charm of an American lumberjack to impress Grayson. Meanwhile, Tiara orchestrated Elara's efforts in polishing the silver and cutlery, her keen eye ensuring every piece gleamed. Polly, on the other hand, was deep in her own plans, scheming to get her hands on Lester's notebooks for a covert look-see. The peculiar call from Audrey Someone gnawed at her curiosity. Despite Grayson's orders to avoid the library, Polly's natural inquisitiveness had morphed into full-blown suspicion. She simply couldn't resist the lure of the unknown.

While the others in the house were preoccupied with their this 'n' thats, Polly quietly and stealthily sneaked down the hallway and into the library.

The room was freezing cold. The glass French doors leading to the garden were closed, and thick brocade curtains were drawn over them, yet it still felt like the penguin enclosure at the zoo. Polly scanned the room. Lester had forbidden Elara to enter his inner sanctum once he'd begun writing, and dusty cobwebs clung to the molded ceiling corners. A worn-out Persian rug, threadbare in places, lay beneath a leather Chesterfield settee and two wingback armchairs. The settee's once sumptuous leather was now cracked and weathered, the deep buttoned tufting hinted at its former elegance. The side tables, marred with scratches and water rings, held tarnished brass lamps. Polly hadn't noticed before, but a musty scent with the faint aroma of mildew permeated the air. A sense of gloom lurked everywhere.

But Polly was only interested in one thing and made a beeline for the antique partners desk. She noticed that one of the side drawers was slightly open. It hadn't previously occurred to her to examine the desk's contents. With the imminent arrival of the police forensics team from Bristol any day now, she realized this might be her only opportunity to investigate. As she settled into the executive chair, an odd sensation enveloped her. She realized she was seated in the very chair that Lester had occupied, seeing the room from his perspective. She imagined her own eyes looking out through Lester's.

Polly looked around at the memorabilia on the walls, the furniture, the fireplace, and where she knew the hidden priest's hole was located. Then, with a tug of a brass handle, she opened the desk's center drawer. No big deal. Paperclips. Stapler. A book of stamps. An expired London Underground train ticket. These odds and ends were left over from when Alastair Drake was alive. She didn't see anything that could be considered unusual. No revolver or switchblade knife. No bottle of poison or rope ligature. She checked the side drawers. She rifled through them one by one, but nothing caught her eye as particularly interesting.

Her eyes came to rest on the desktop and its collection of notebooks. She picked one up and held it reverentially for a long moment, her fingers tracing the surface of the cover. As she opened to the first page and peered at Lester's words, written in a small, red-ink scrawl, she felt the weight of their significance. The hand that had written these pages belonged to a man who was now dead. These were some of Lester Lynch's very last thoughts and words. The realization hit her with a profound sense of loss and intimacy. Each word seemed to whisper his presence, a bittersweet reminder of the man who had poured his heart onto these pages, now left behind for her to discover. And she was the first person on the planet to read them.

Polly leaned forward and began scrutinizing the page. It quickly became clear that it was a continuation from a previous notebook. Wanting to read Lester's work chronologically, she examined the others, arranging them in the order she thought they'd been written.

"Insert into Chapter One," she read at the top of the page of the first notebook. With that, she began a journey through Lester's rise to success as a costume designer in television, uncovering the passion and creativity that had driven him. Each page revealed a piece of his life's puzzle, drawing her deeper into his world and legacy.

It was sometimes challenging to follow Lester's narrative. Almost entirely lacking in punctuation, Polly quickly pitied the editor who would have to decipher and make sense of it all. *Lester Lynch! Use a dictionary!* she wanted to scream. Despite this, she was drawn to his life story, captivated by tales about the people who worked in her showbiz world.

As she delved deeper into the pages, Polly couldn't help smiling at the way Lester immediately managed to savage his family. He decried having been born into a family that, although middle class, lacked the slightest elevated level of wit or sophistication he craved. His dad was a low-level loan officer in a bank who was horrified to discover the gods had punked him into having four kids before he was twenty-five years old. Moreover, he found it impossible to keep his manhood sequestered behind his trousers' zipper when it came to the women he'd met at work.

His mother, a nurse who loved her kids but didn't necessarily like them all that much, obsessed over why Lester spent all his time sketching women's clothes. Lester's peculiarities disappointed his parents and confounded his siblings, who condescendingly nicknamed him "Lester the Dresser." However, he embraced the moniker and accepted it with a determined "I'll show them someday" vow.

His brothers hung out with thugs and called in bomb threats to get out of school. His sister smoked marijuana and drank Boone's Farm apple-flavored rotgut. While Lester immersed himself in classic black-and-white films on television, his siblings only went to movies starring spiders or ants with silly superpowers. Lester, meanwhile, reveled in the golden age of Hollywood, with *The Philadelphia Story, His Girl Friday*, and *The Thin Man* mysteries. He longed to belong to the refined on-screen worlds of Katharine Hepburn, Cary Grant, and Grace Kelly. Instead, he was stuck with what he called "knuckle-draggers"—those who'd be baffled by more than one fork at a dinner table. Determined to escape his stifling small hometown, Lester dreamed of living in New York, or at least a world like the ones inhabited by Nick and Nora Charles or Auntie Mame. Drinking martinis and mingling with the New York glitterati was surely his destiny.

However, fate had other plans. In a last-minute twist, he moved to Los Angeles instead. Enrolling at the Fashion Institute of Design & Merchandising, it wasn't long before he hopped, skipped, and jumped under the bedsheets with several Warner Bros. studio marketing execs, catapulting himself into the entertainment industry. Almost immediately, he snagged an apprenticeship at Style Atelier, the famed costume design shop in the San Fernando Valley owned by the legendary, Academy Award-winning designer André Marsh.

Lester knew it would happen. He willed it to happen. He made it happen. It was as if he had personally arranged all the stars in the universe to align perfectly with his grand scheme through sheer force of will. Then, one day, in a serendipitous turn of events (though Lester insisted he didn't believe in serendipity), André Marsh found himself overwhelmed with other projects and unable to design the wardrobe for Nathalie Sullivan's television special. Seizing the opportunity, André persuaded the diva to consider Lester's design portfolio. Sullivan, a notorious harridan, was instantly enthralled by Lester's unique, cutting-edge work.

"Clear the tracks 'cause there's a new kid on the costume-design block, baby!" Lester boasted in bold, underscored letters in his notebook.

After subsequently creating costumes and wardrobes for TV shows starring Eartha Kitt, Dolly Parton, and Olivia Newton-John, he was hired to work on *The Polly Pepper Playhouse*. For the next twelve years, he was so much in demand that he not only designed for Polly and her in-house troupe of sketch comedy players and guest stars, but he also created clothes for nearly every television musical variety program and network special and Las Vegas nightclub act of the era.

Ah! Now we're getting somewhere! Polly thought to herself when she got halfway through the fourth notebook and started to see names of celebrities and friends she recognized. In block letters and overused exclamation points (Lester's rare concession to punctuation), she discovered that Danny Kaye—whom Lester had dressed when the star was a guest on a Gloria Silvers comedy special—had refused to wear a colorful tuxedo designed expressly for him.

"It had taken weeks to find the right fabric," Lester wrote.

"I embellished it with metallic sequins, and it turned out to be a masterpiece on par with Picasso's finest work! I remember my excitement about the opportunity to design for one of my movie idols. Danny arrived for the tech rehearsal—and he destroyed me. A part of me literally died that day. Nobody warned me about him. His image was that of a laid-back entertainer with a flair for physical comedy and witty word-play. He had a charming and charismatic presence on-screen. But he sneered at the jacket and told me that Larry wouldn't approve (I didn't get his reference to Sir Laurence Olivier, his boyfriend at the time), and I should shove it somewhere impractical. He despised my work. And I came to feel the same about him."

A few pages on, Lester was ranting about the level of anxiety that legends Bette Davis, Marlon Brando, and Lucille Ball had perpetrated on him. "I'm glad they're all gone," he wrote and described horrific encounters he'd had with each of them.

"But I never let on. Not to anyone. I was 'Lester the Dresser,' the meek and smiling underling they thought didn't quite get the mean jokes or hear the whispered aspersions and so-called 'playful' ribbing at my expense. They never knew how much they hurt my feelings. They thought they could get away with treating me like something to wipe off their shoes. I get it. Stars are demanding because they're spoiled-rotten perfectionists who think they have the only vision for how they are to be seen on camera. But I know what's best for them! I'm the one who studied and trained to make them shine brighter than they otherwise would have. I alone have the perfect eye for what works for each of them! Would they listen? Hardly ever! They were mostly all hopelessly stupid!"

By now, Polly was intrigued and horrified by what Lester had written. "I loved Danny Kaye!" she whispered. She could tell Lester believed he was superior to these legends. Lester was also resentful toward them for not appreciating his brilliance and expertise in the clothes he designed or selected for them.

Lester's colorful language was filled with grandiosity and contempt. He lacked empathy and respect for others. Polly knew he'd always tended towards manipulation and a desire for control. However, the words she was reading were still revelations. She'd had no idea Lester had experienced so much frustration with not being seen and listened to. His belief that he alone knew what was best for others seemed consistent with what she knew about narcissistic personality disorder. "An inflated sense of self-importance," she said quietly as she read the pages. "This industry is a breeding ground for psychos."

Polly now thought she understood why the caller, Audrey, had been eager to have her edit or sanitize what Lester had revealed in his notebooks. But again, how could Audrey—or anyone—know what Lester was writing? Maybe Tim was right that Lester's reputation was such that someone would naturally come to the obvious advanced conclusion that a mean-spirited Lester Lynch would write mean-spirited things in his book.

As Polly continued reading Lester's gossip and vitriol, a growing dread gnawed at her. She wanted to skip ahead to his recollections of the years he worked on her own TV show, but the fear of what she might find held her back. She braced herself for the sting of his machete-like acrimony. If he could be so cruel in his revelations about the famously humble Lillian Hart—who, at the time of their collaboration, was the last known surviving star from the silent-screen era—what might he say about her? The thought made her stomach churn, but she was desperate to know. Simultaneously, she didn't want to miss anything he might have written about her beloved Goldie Hawn, Doris Day, or Rosemary DeCamp. Torn between fear and curiosity, she forced herself to read on.

But midway through notebook number seven, as Lester

continued tearing into some of America's favorite entertainment legends and flash-in-the-pan celebrities, Polly became aware that the text seemed to jump mid-rant from one big kahuna to another without any noticeable transition. She understood that Lester's writing was almost a stream of consciousness, but she suddenly had to flip back and forth to figure out if Lester was lambasting Olympic gold medalist Peggy Fleming during one of her TV specials or legendary comedian Bob Hope during one of his. It needed to be clarified.

She reasoned that Lester probably wouldn't have begged Bob Hope not to wear an inordinately long scarf—à la Isadora Duncan—lest he accidentally skate over the fabric and land on his tush. Polly knew for a fact the comedian didn't figure skate. So, his words must have been about beautiful Peggy. "Lester's vitriol is melding into one big steaming pile and burying everyone under it! It's hard to tell who's who," Polly said, trying to keep track of whom Lester aimed his arrows at.

Then it suddenly dawned on her! What appeared to be a lack of continuity, or transitions was actually a result of missing pages in the notebook. Of course! That was why there was an abrupt vault from Peggy Fleming to Bob Hope. Pages had been torn out. Perhaps they were pages on which he determined he'd gone too far about a particular celebrity. But which celeb? And why a change of nasty heart? Lester hadn't considered any of his previous offensive thoughts to be over the top. He seemed to write whatever he wanted—like it or lump it.

Polly looked down at the wastebasket and made a face. It was empty. Then she looked at the surface of the desktop with its accumulation of dust and tiny fragments of paper, a result, she'd previously thought, of the room being off-limits to Elara's feather duster. Now, she supposed the debris was bits of paper being torn from a spiral notebook. An idea started to form in her head, and she gingerly closed the notebook and placed it on top of the pile she'd made of the others.

Leaving the library, Polly made a feeble attempt to readjust the police caution tape at the doorway to make it look like it hadn't been touched. She tiptoed to the reception room, then quickly re-emerged as if to suggest to anyone paying attention that she'd been there all along.

"I'm on to you, missy," Tiara smirked. "FYI, I've sent Elara shopping. Tim is playing strip search the perp with Grayson—although that's not the game he admitted to. And your new girlfriend, Mildred Banks, called to say she'll be here at two o'clock. Something about a potential replacement for the rat—err, cat—that dropped out of her cockamamie show."

"That's nice," Polly said, completely disinterested in anyone else's activities. She was too busy hatching the far-fetched theory in which Lester Lynch uncharacteristically decided he'd gone too far in writing about one of his former divas and had ripped the offensive pages from his notebook. That idea didn't actually make any sense because he'd trashed almost everyone he'd ever worked with and hadn't seemed to show remorse by crossing out a name or any of his scathing reflections.

But where, Polly wondered, if Lester had taken pages out, *had he put them?* They weren't in the library wastebasket. Maybe he had ditched them in the fireplace, where they had burned to ashes. It was a mystery.

Tiara could tell Polly's thoughts were far from the mundane world of maids' shopping duties, Tim's extracurricular distractions, or village musical stage extravaganzas. She knew that Star Lady was wafting off to another psychic realm where kittens and fireflies ruled, and it was best to let her float off to the Great Wherever. She'd eventually run out of gas and drift back to reality. "I'll make you a cuppa. But I suggest you come to your senses before Mildred gets here," Tiara said and wandered to the kettle.

"If she starts gossiping about the lady in the castle flying off to Neverland, Arlene down at the post office will slap a *Lost in Space* stamp on you, fast..."

But that was exactly where Polly was: outer space. Or at least a parallel universe. She'd been distressed to read Lester's showbiz revelations and insider knowledge about her chums Bill Murray, Sissy Spacek, and Faye Dunaway. It was one thing for him to talk about Virginia Supplee's halitosis, Trey Lester's potty mouth, or even the closely guarded secret that William Nash wears toupees. But to talk about Linda Hamilton and Miranda Richardson as freely as he did was just plain mean. And she was terrified of reading whatever Lester had written about herself!

They say, "look before you leap," but Polly couldn't resist sticking her surgically sculpted nose back into Lester's spiteful world. However, she was distracted by the nagging question of what had happened to the missing pages in his notebook. Were there other pages torn from the other notebooks? She had to find out.

But phooey! As Polly was about to reach for the doorknob and sneak back into the library, the bell at the front gate clanged. She looked at her watch. Mildred wasn't due for another hour. As Polly was pretending to be merely passing by the library door, Tiara arrived with three uniformed police officers. "Forensics. From Bristol," she said to introduce them. Polly had had enough experience with police investigations in Los Angeles to last a lifetime. However, when she looked at their official identification patches, something within her glowed. She had always loved watching forensics teams at work, and the thought of seeing them in action again excited her.

Polite—but all business—the officers explained that they'd be accessing every room of the house before settling in the library, which, according to their instructions, was where they were to concentrate their investigation and search for clues about how the American, Lester Lynch, died.

Donning protective latex gloves, shoe coverings, and goggles, the officers finally entered the room where Lester's body had been found. Polly watched with fascination from the doorway. The forensics team had brought portable lights to enhance the room's illumination, casting stark shadows against the walls and showbiz pictures. The men proceeded to carefully comb through everything. They photographed, measured, and collected samples of trace evidence such as fibers, hairs, and microscopic particles of anything that might prove important.

Polly marveled at their equipment: chemical test kits and handheld ultraviolet and infrared lights that revealed hidden or subtle evidence that might not be visible to the naked eye. Their assortment of tools and methods for carefully examining evidence and gathering potentially crucial investigation information seemed staggering to her.

The atmosphere was somber, too. Polly eavesdropped as discreetly as possible from the doorway and strained to catch the officers' comments and conversations. With her nerves on edge, she wondered what she might have disturbed or left behind that they'd uncover and then accuse her of tampering with evidence. Weren't all those police chief inspectors and detective chief superintendents on TV always finding teensy-weensy bits of proof that sank a seemingly innocent's alibi?

"I found a hidden compartment under the desk," said one of the officers scouring the partners desk.

Polly's stomach dropped. "I hadn't noticed that!" she blurted out, immediately realizing her slip. She was supposed to have left the room untouched, per protocol.

The officers exchanged a brief, knowing glance. Polly felt a flush creep up her neck as she tried to gauge their thoughts. Were they judging her, or was it something worse?

"No one's been in here since Constable Jenkins—he's the entirety of the Abbots Clover Police Department, you know," Polly told the officers, trying to exonerate herself from ignoring official instructions.

"Ma'am," said one of the officers, who gave her a withering look that anyone would interpret as "please stay out of this!"

Polly's nerves were on edge as the trio went about their tasks. She knew her fingerprints would be discovered on all the surfaces and objects she'd touched. With each passing moment, her anxiety intensified. Her mind raced as she replayed her movements in the room. She winced at the realization that her prints would undoubtedly be on the desk, its drawers, and Lester's notebooks. She unconsciously wiped her hands on her trousers.

It's my house, for crying out loud, so of course my prints are everywhere, she said to herself. For a moment, she wondered whether modern technology could tell the exact age of fingerprints. *If fingerprints are time-stamped, I'm in trouble.*

As she continued watching the investigators, she noticed that one of them was paying particular attention to the top of the desk. He seemed fixated on a specific characteristic—a rough, uneven edge near the bottom right-hand corner—which Polly had also seen but dismissed as insignificant. A subtle menace lurked—a small, jagged patch of exposed wood that threatened to snag the unwary with splinters if they brushed against it carelessly.

With practiced precision, the officer retrieved his magnifying glass, his gaze sharpening as he scrutinized this area of the desk. His gloved fingers traced the contours of the rough surface with cautious deliberation, and he tweezed out a bit of something that Polly couldn't see. And then, amidst the grainy texture of the wood, he observed a faint red stain, barely discernible to the naked eye.

Although the presence of red pens scattered across the desk suggested a mundane explanation for the red stain, the officer's professional instincts urged him on. Ignoring the temptation to dismiss it as inconsequential, he recognized the importance of gathering all potential evidence, no matter how seemingly trivial.

"According to the report, there's a hidden door next to the fireplace," one officer said to another.

Polly's eyes lit up, and she couldn't contain her excitement. "It's over there!" she called out, her voice bubbling with enthusiasm like a little girl who knew a big secret and was eager to earn brownie points. "You just have to push something, and it magically swings open!"

"Ma'am," barked another officer, clearly perturbed by Polly's presence.

"Well, excuse me for being a big fat carbuncle on the face of humanity," Polly whispered to herself. She made a face, just shy of including her tongue. From the doorway, she watched the officers' methodical precision as they examined the area and traced the wall as if feeling for a pulse.

The officers, whose professionalism demanded dispassionate detachment, were suddenly animated when they unlatched and opened the priest hole.

"This is amazing," one of the officers exclaimed, his eyes widening with excitement as he shone his flashlight into the narrow space.

They peered into the cramped chamber with a mix of curiosity and awe, their initial caution giving way to fascination. The stark, inhospitable interior of the hidden room captivated them. The stone walls pressed in on all sides, barely large enough to accommodate one person. The low ceiling added to the sense of confinement, creating a stifling atmosphere that felt suffocating even to those standing outside.

"This must have been a last resort for someone," one officer mused, his voice echoing softly in the confined space. "Imagine hiding here for days on end."

With bated breath, Polly observed their every move, her curiosity piqued by the aura of intrigue surrounding the hidden chamber. With each passing moment, her fascination grew, and her imagination began to run wild with speculation about what clues they might find in the secret chamber. What tip-offs might it hold that would unravel the enigma surrounding Lester's last hours of life?

"That's interesting," said one policeman to another as they scrutinized something Polly couldn't see from her distance away.

And at that very moment, when perhaps incriminating evidence was about to be revealed, a voice identical to Mildred Banks' punctured the air behind Polly and spoiled all the fun. "You don't want to watch all this boring police work!" Mildred snapped, rolling her eyes dramatically. "If you're a mystery maniac, tune in to reruns of *Murder, She Wrote*. Angela Lansbury is far more interesting than these stuffed-shirt monkeys," she added with a condescending sneer, as if Polly's interest in the investigation could only be due to the presence of attractive men.

"We have a real show to put on!" Mildred declared loudly, her voice grating on Polly's nerves. Without waiting for a response, she grabbed Polly's arm in a viselike grip and yanked her down the hallway.

"Come on, let's leave that work to the professionals," she said with a dismissive wave towards the officers, dragging Polly into the reception room, where three women sat nervously waiting to audition to replace Nancy Mann in *Cats on a Hot Tin Roof*.

Mildred's grip tightened as she pulled Polly forward. "Let's get this show on the road! We don't have all day to waste on nonsense."

13

By the time Lush Hour rolled around, the forensics guys had wrapped up their gumshoe tasks, Mildred had cast a fifth-rate Betty Buckley, and Polly had fielded phone calls from *Daily Variety,* the *Hollywood Reporter*, and the *National Intruder*. Thanks to a leak at the media desk of the American embassy, Lester Lynch was finally about to be a story on *Eyewitness News at Eleven*.

Lounging on the Chesterfield by the fireplace, with Mr. Boots purring on her lap and a flute of Veuve in her hand, Polly lamented that she suspected poor Lester might not be getting the most flattering of obituaries in any of the showbiz industry papers and rags. "The *Times* wanted me to confirm that I'd fired him from *The Polly Pepper Playhouse* for intentionally building that embarrassing wardrobe malfunction into Pamela Anderson's gown. You know the one."

"I can't unsee all her bits and pieces!" Tim grimaced.

"I'm still traumatized. They also wanted to know why he was recently sacked from designing for a Bow Wow Wow tribute band. I had no comment on the first question and no idea who or what a Bow Wow Wow is or was. And the *National Intruder* said they're running with the headline 'Sew Long: Lester the Dresser Hangs it Up.'"

As the trio sat before the crackling fire, sipping their fizzy golden cure-all, the stereo speakers channeled Linda Ronstadt, asking the age-old question, "When will I be loved?" Otherwise, the house was quiet.

Elara had set the dining table before she'd left for the day.

Tiara had chopped and diced her meal-prep ingredients.

And Tim was concentrating on cheeky DMs from Grayson suggesting he'd violated some obscure municipal ordinance and would soon be cited and properly punished at the hands of the law. That sounded good to Tim. After tapping a response in which he assured the constable that he'd offer appropriate resistance before being eagerly subdued, he thought to ask his mother about her day with the forensics investigators.

"Not very cuddle-worthy, if that's what you're after," Polly said. "A bit up their own bums—to use that lovely new descriptive phrase I learned."

"In other words, they know your mother's reputation for obstructing inquisitions," Tiara translated.

"And they refused to speculate about what Lester was doing in the priest hole in the first place," Polly continued. "I offered the hide-and-seek-gone-wrong theory, but they stared at me for the longest time then said something about 'protecting the integrity of the investigation.'"

"Not to worry. Grayson's got his detective hat on," Tim said, relaying the latest scoop from Constable Jenkins' investigative initiatives. "He's been working the phones and drumming up intel from a friend in Bristol's medical examiner's office. The guy thinks Lester's cause of death is probably cut and dried. I guess that means Gray was probably right. Lester accidentally got trapped in the secret room and eventually ran out of air. That was that. Sad."

"Hmm," Polly said dismissively as she stroked Mr. Boots and contemplated the life and death of her friend.

"Grayson's brilliant," Tim continued, pushing his early-stages-of-puppy-love character reference. "The forensics guys can turn over every stone and pore over minute details, but they'll eventually circle back to Gray's initial conclusion that there's nothing to see here, so move along and have a nice day. But until they can slap an official cause of death on the table, Lester's body can't go anywhere. The embassy contacted his sister in Florida. She wants him shipped to her, but she's too broke to pay the repatriation fees. Apparently, Lester and Louise weren't very lovey-dovey."

Not very, Polly said to herself as she reflected on Lester's condescension for his uncultured and boring family. She knew the costume designer would rather be buried in an unmarked grave with random John Does than to have the dusty particles of his once physical form packed into a cheapo urn from Walmart and taking up space on a sibling's fireplace mantel—especially a mantel in Florida, where fireplaces were fake and/or merely decorative.

Polly sat quietly for a long moment as she once again saw Lester's dead body in her mind's eye. She felt weepy as she imagined Lester excitedly discovering the concealed space behind the library bookcase, stepping inside to investigate, then pulling the panel closed on himself, only to be trapped. But why would he have done such a foolish thing? Was it for the novelty of the experience? Had he even considered that there might not be a release mechanism inside?

"The buddy system," Polly murmured. It was a simple rule meant to prevent such tragedies: never explore alone. If one person runs into trouble, their buddy can render aid. Yet Lester had ignored this safeguard, stepping into the darkness solo, leaving no one behind to hear his cries for help.

A sinister chill clawed its way down Polly's spine as she absorbed the harrowing truth of Lester's ordeal. As an actress, she was trained to dive deep into the psyche of her characters—to live out their brilliant triumphs or darkest fears in her own flesh. She had mastered character-switch exercises and improvisations designed to merge her identity with those she portrayed. And now she found herself empathizing deeply with Lester, mentally and emotionally reliving his final ordeal.

She could almost smell the dank, stale air of the ancient secret place and feel its claustrophobic grip tightening around her. Her heart beat in her ears. She imagined herself groping blindly through a suffocating blackness, her fingers scraping against the rough, unyielding walls. Lester's desperate search for a latch, a way out, spiraled her into terror.

Polly experienced the all-consuming void that had swallowed Lester whole, and the stark realization that he was utterly alone. He'd had no cell phone, no lifeline, and had been stranded alive in a silent tomb. She almost called out—as Lester surely would have—imagining his voice echoing through the silent halls of the house, but falling on deaf ears, swallowed by the stillness of the empty library. Help for Lester had been this close—just on the other side of the wall—yet impossibly far away. Lester could only have hoped that someone would rescue him before it was too late.

But it *was* too late. And as Polly grappled with unanswered questions, a determined resolve ignited within her. Suddenly, returning to the moment, she bolted upright and beckoned to Tim and Tiara, her voice resolute despite the lingering unease that gripped her heart. Setting aside her champagne flute and an irritated Mr. Boots, she rose and strode purposefully out of the room. Her troupe trailed behind.

14

They arrived at the library door, which was now adorned with a new placard that issued a sterner warning from the authorities: Do Not Enter Under Penalty of Prosecution! But Polly paid no heed to the sign—it was her house, after all. She opened the door and stepped inside. She went immediately to the priest's secure hiding place. "Try it out," she said, looking at Tim.

"Try what out? You'd better mean a meditation and wellness app," he said warily, suspecting his mother had something unsettling up her sleeve.

"The secret panel. Open it. Take a seat inside."

"No way! We read the tale of *Bluebeard* in school! Plus, I'm claustrophobic! I have nightmares about being buried alive or locked in a cage! You go in! It's your house!"

"How did you end up such a delicate little snowflake?" Polly tsked, rolling her eyes at Tim's distinctly unadventurous attitude. "It's a quick experiment. In and out. Mommy's here. I need to understand why we didn't hear a peep from Lester if he was hollering for help? Pretend you're him."

"Dead?"

"Imagine you've just discovered this incredible secret chamber. It's the coolest thing ever. You're totally jazzed. And then, because apparently you left your brain in your other pants, you step inside and close the panel. Bam! You're part of the castle wall. Now, I need you to bang, kick, and holler. Really sell it. Pretend you're trapped in a cheesy Roger Corman horror flick, begging for help!"

"I am trapped! My mother's a Stephen King crazy: Annie Wilkes. Carrie. Cujo!"

"We're not Oliver Cromwell's priest hunters," Tiara said, siding with Polly that Tim was the logical guinea pig for this experiment to better understand why they hadn't heard Lester's calls for help.

Tim looked to the heavens in a "why me, Lord" pique. However, with the dramatic resignation of a martyr walking to his crucifixion, his hand reluctantly reached out for the carved rosette beside the fireplace. With a push that was more of an angry jab, he triggered the latch with a melodramatic sigh. After a soft click—the panel creaked open. "*Voila*," he muttered, "the portal to my doom."

"It won't take more than a nanosecond," Polly promised. "Pretend you're hiding behind the clothes in Gray's closet. We'll know right away if we can hear you or not."

With more dread than that fateful day he'd boldly asked Neil Patrick Harris out on a date—only to be met with polite laughter —Tim touched the flashlight icon on his phone. He shot a look at his mother that could only be described as feeling deeply betrayed yet not entirely surprised. Then, with the air of a gladiator about to face the lions, he ducked his head and ventured into the void.

"Easy peasy." Polly smiled and blew him a kiss. She closed the panel, giving it an extra push to ensure it was tightly shut into its undetectable place. Then she stood back to admire her accomplishment.

"Can you hear me?" Tim yelled, panic taking over his voice. "Out! I want out! Now!"

"Yes, dear. We hear you," Polly said. "Keep complaining. Louder. We're stepping out for a wee moment-o. Back in a tick. Entertain yourself. Recite the Gettysburg Address. You know, 'Four score and seven years ago...' Or maybe 'The Lord is my shepherd; I shall not want...'"

"That's the one about the shadow of death!" Tim shot back, his muted voice dripping with disbelief.

In the hallway, Polly and Tiara strained their auditory nerves. They could barely make out Tim's muffled protests— which sounded like historical facts mixed with existential dread. They exchanged puzzled looks. If they could hear Tim's impromptu history lesson—even faintly—why hadn't they heard Lester? As they retreated incrementally down the hallway toward the reception room, they could still detect a dull thumping sound from within the library. Then, suddenly—

Their thoughts were interrupted by the sound of the house phone ringing in the reception room. Polly rushed to pick it up. "You can be late, but you may not cancel," she said, smiling brightly, expecting Sarah's voice on the other end of the line to say she was slightly delayed. Instead, another woman said, "Polly Pepper, we spoke this morning. I tried your mobile, but it went straight to voice-mail. I want to confirm that you handled the Lester Lynch situation. If you haven't, we will. There isn't much time." Then she hung up.

Polly stared at the phone, a faraway look in her eyes.

"Who?" Tiara asked, curious about the sudden change in Polly's demeanor. At that very moment, the bell at the front gate clanged. "Sarah," Tiara guessed, still eager to discover who had called and why Polly looked distracted. But not wanting to keep their guest waiting outside in the cold, she quickly set Polly on the Chesterfield, handed her a refilled glass of bubbly, and positioned Mr. Boots on her lap—like a tableau. "Pretend you're posing for an episode of *My Lottery Dream Home*," Tiara said, then hustled down the hallway to the front entrance.

"Smooch, smooch," Polly purred theatrically as Sarah entered the reception room and leaned down to place an air-kiss next to Polly's cheek. She presented Polly with a bottle of Pinot Noir. "I wasn't sure what culinary masterpiece Tiara is conjuring tonight," she said, her eyes twinkling, "but one simply doesn't arrive at a movie star's castle empty-handed. Even in Abbots Clover, we uphold the sacred tradition of hostess gifts."

Polly smiled enthusiastically. "Screw tops are such a convenience!"

But in the next second, Tiara looked around as if smelling cookies burning in the oven. "You're forgetting something!" She began humming "You Are My Sunshine, My Only Sunshine." In a sudden burst of understanding and alarm, Polly threw Mr. Boots aside and leaped from her seat.

"I'm coming to rescue the stranded little Thai boys in the cave!" Polly called out to Tim as she raced down the hallway to the library. She hadn't paid close attention to the precise location of the lever that opened the secret room, so she pushed and pulled and pounded her fist at disparate places on the wall. "How the hell do I open this damn thing?" she called through the wall to Tim. "Where's the little doohickey?"

"You'd better find it! I've been in here so long I could have solved Sunday's *New York Times* crossword puzzle! In front of you! Look to the left! That carved rosette! Next to the fireplace!"

With Tim nearly hysterical on one side of the wall and Polly panicking on the other, she finally pushed the rosette applique, and the door burped open. Tim tumbled out as Lester had and fell to his knees, theatrically gasping for breath. "How could a mother do that to her own adorable child! I hope you have nightmares about how this could have tragically played out! You should be in a cell with Susan Smith!" he wailed, trying to catch his breath. "There could have been rats..."

"Yeah, and the boogeyman could have grabbed your butt and dragged you down to his love lair. But he didn't. You should be happy! I just set you free!"

"Boogeyman? Love lair? You've never understood how fragile my psyche is! I'm calling Child Protective Services! And I think I smelled that stinky ghost dog, Loki."

"Shifting the blame to a dog is usually a cover-up for one's own behavior, sweetums," Polly said, pinching her nose. "Talk about histrionics! Marlon Brando's Method acting wasn't nearly as convincing as your little scene. Splash some water on your face and pull yourself together. Sarah's here, and she won't want to spend her night seeing you whine about something as insignificant as being entombed in a castle wall, for crying out loud."

When Polly and Tim returned to the reception room, Sarah was seated and accepting a glass of champagne from Tiara. The glow from the fire danced across the room, casting a warm and flickering light that, combined with the rich voice of Jane Olivor singing "Stay the Night" wafting through the speakers, gave the impression that Thistlethorne Lodge was the most peaceful place on earth. But it obviously wasn't.

As Tiara returned to her kitchen domain, she begged Sarah and Polly to withhold gossip until they were all seated for dinner. "I always miss out on juicy dish!" she declared. "You can hold your tongues for at least twenty minutes. They won't atrophy from lack of use."

The castle never failed to impress Sarah, but she pretended to be nonchalant. Thistlethorne Lodge had seen far better days, but it was still the grandest house she'd ever been in. When they were eventually summoned to the table, she once again felt that she was dining at a palace. "It's still Downton Abbey to me..."

"Or Downton *Shabby* as a friend who thinks he's clever—but isn't—calls it," Polly said.

Regardless of Thistlethorne's far-less-than-flawless condition, Sarah was happily absorbed in the ambiance of the candlelit dining room. The polished mahogany table, with seating for twelve, was set for four at one end. The Royal Doulton rose-pattern dinner plates sat on sheer lace embroidered placemats accompanied by Waterford cut-crystal glasses and antique silverware. Two five-arm silver candelabras buffed to a high sheen with tall, tapered candles dominated the center of the table.

As they settled into their seats, the quartet was soon treated to a culinary masterpiece. Tiara, a masterful chef, had prepared pan-seared salmon fillets with a lemon-dill butter sauce, roasted asparagus spears with garlic and parmesan, and creamy mashed potatoes with chives. The meal was a perfect balance of simplicity and sophistication. By the time Tiara served chocolate lava cakes with raspberry coulis and whipped cream, they were ready to be regaled by Sarah with whatever she had come to discuss.

"I'm singing for my supper." Sarah chuckled. "Here's what I wanted you to know. Yesterday, a couple of tourists came into Bound to Read. It's a little early in the year for tourists—it's not quite spring. But a couple of Americans—at least they sounded like Americans—a man and a woman—ordered coffee and cakes. One of them, the man, asked me if I'd ever seen Polly Pepper around the village. He said they'd heard that you lived here."

"Were they impressed?" Polly asked, curious.

"I didn't really know what to say. It's not a secret that you own Thistlethorne, is it? But I sometimes get vibes from people, a feeling—I meet so many—and I decided to be vague. I said I'd heard that a celebrity from the States had been visiting Abbots Clover, but I wasn't sure which one or exactly where she was. That's sort of dumb because everyone here knows everything about everyone else. And I think he knew I was being evasive."

Polly nodded, appreciating Sarah's discretion. Although she loved her fans and was fairly accessible to anyone when they approached her for an autograph or a selfie, she appreciated Sarah's judgment. "I'm not hiding out, but I never broadcast my good fortune. Well, except to Barbra and Bette. And, of course, Meryl and Glenn. Maybe George and Amal."

"I get it," Sarah agreed. "But that's not all. They seemed somewhat—I don't know—I haven't spent much time with Americans, so I might not be the best judge. There are probably a lot of cultural differences that I don't understand, which might explain... When I was wiping off a nearby table, I overheard them talking about your friend who died. I know they were talking about him because Lester called himself 'Lester the Dresser' when we were introduced, and that's the name they used. Then the man said, 'He's history,' and, 'Gotta get our hands on them,' and, 'The boss calls the shots.' Then I saw a customer waiting at the counter and had to get back. The next time I looked over again, they were gone."

American tourists visiting Abbots Clover early in the year? What was the big deal? Some people crave a Caribbean beach. Others may want to avoid the summer vacation crowds. However, Sarah's revelation that Lester had been the subject of conversation in her shop sparked everyone's curiosity. "Who's 'the boss'?" Tim asked. "Springsteen? And what shots was the boss calling?"

"And what did they mean by 'he's history' and 'get their hands on' something?" Polly said, making a face. "I suppose his costume sketches will be of some value now that he's gone. Maybe they wanted to get their hands on some of those."

As Tim began helping Tiara clear the dinner plates from the table, Polly took another pull from her champagne flute. She stared for a long moment at the glowing candles in the candelabra, contemplating all that Sarah had revealed. "I wonder if there's a tie-in with the call from this morning," she said. "Just before you rang, someone named Audrey called. She made what might be interpreted as a vague threat. Nothing overt. Just suggestive. She phoned again this evening, before you arrived. She asked if I'd taken care of the 'Lester Lynch situation,' and if I hadn't or wouldn't, she said 'they' would. I don't know who 'they' are."

Polly retold the story about Audrey's original call, repeating what she wanted Polly to do with Lester's notebooks and emphasizing that it was Polly's responsibility to clean up the language in them.

"I still think it's strange that this Audrey person knows that Polly lives here at Thistlethorne and even that we have a ghost in the castle," Tiara said, setting down a bottle of Grand Marnier with a plate of chocolate truffles. "That's too much information even in this know-it-all, Google age."

Being the subject of tourists' conversations or envy was nothing new to Polly Pepper. She was accustomed to the buzz of gossip and opinions. Even her home in Bel Air was a regular stop on the Glamor Galore Sightseeing Tours bus route, with tourists eagerly snapping photos and soaking up the guides' tales of celebrity lore. The sight of open-topped vans with their blaring bullhorns was a familiar backdrop to Polly's daily life, as enthusiastic but often woefully ill-informed guides regaled tourists with stories about the homes of Katy Perry, Kristin Wiig, or Jason Bateman, and other Hollywood stars who lived nearby. Polly sometimes chuckled at the exaggerated tales she heard being offered as truth. Often enough, she'd wanted to yell out, "No, Steven Spielberg does not live under the Hollywood sign!" and, "Ellen and Portia fled to Montecito decades ago, along with Oprah!"

"More disconcerting is that the caller not only had Polly's cell phone number but somehow got the landline, too," Tim said. "I don't think you can call an operator anymore—do they still have operators?—and ask to be put through to Polly Pepper at Thistlethorne Lodge."

Sarah sat contemplating the revelations and sipping the liqueur that Tim had poured into snifters. "You've told Grayson about this, right? I think you have to. Strangers asking about where you live and unexpected, potentially threatening phone calls are concerning. I know he's busy with a new play toy" — Sarah glanced at Tim with a salacious grin— "but he's got a job to do. And now has a vested interest in keeping you all safe."

Polly's mind raced. The report of American tourists poking around Abbots Clover and trying to uncover the location of her private castle, combined with phone calls from a stranger urging her to do something unethical, like fictionalizing Lester's memoir, was unsettling. Polly & Co. wanted to dismiss Sarah's information as unimportant and continue with their daily routines, but they couldn't shake the sense that the strange call Polly received, and the nosy tourists were possibly connected.

Fortunately, Polly had other things to think about. Like how the heck did she get roped into working with amateurs on a less-than-mediocre stage production that was no more than a vanity project for Mildred Banks?

15

FINAL SEAM. LESTER LYNCH. DEAD! The obituaries began appearing in the Hollywood trade publications. By morning, Polly's phone was flooded with messages. Mutual friends were eager for the lurid details. The *Los Angeles Times* ran a short piece in the Calendar section of the paper and listed titles of a few of the television shows Lester had worked on and the stars he had dressed. Out of respect for an accomplished member of the entertainment community, *Daily Variety*, the *Hollywood Reporter*, and the *Times* all focused on Lester's professional achievements and awards, emphasizing his creative legacy rather than his notoriously poisonous tongue. But scandalmongers feed on a steady diet of malicious gossip, and Polly's social circle was starving for salacious info. They all seemed to harbor unresolved cynical feelings or ill will for Lester.

As Polly scrolled through her messages, she shook her head in despair. "They all start off saying they're sorry that Lester is dead. But then they tell me they can't get over something that he said or did to them that left lasting impressions. And not very good impressions," Polly said to her audience of Tim and Tiara at the breakfast table.

"Diana Cartwright says that Lester was a narcissist and loved emotional manipulation. Anita Bregman says Lester sabotaged her work to deliberately undermine her advancement in the fashion industry. Rich Trent brought up the subject of being humiliated by Lester at a dinner party.

"I was at that dinner," Polly vividly recalled. "Lester was holding court and nattering about a newly unearthed recording by some obscure singer he liked who'd never achieved mainstream success. The chanteuse had a small—very small—but loyal following among the New York cognoscenti. Rich should have just sat quietly and listened, but he had to try to top Lester by bringing up his pop music idol and a new biography someone had written about her."

"I know where this is going," Tim interjected. "Lester loved putting others down—especially in public."

Polly nodded and continued, "I overheard that witch from Disney marketing, Stephanie What's-her-face, say something to Rich along the lines of, 'Don't let him get away with insulting you! Here's what I would do...!' I didn't hear her plans—she's known to be pretty damn mean—but Rich was too weak to do anything. Instead, he turned red and drank more."

"Maya Angelou was right," Tiara said. "'People might forget what you said about them, but they never forget how you made them feel.' I know from personal experience how Lester made people feel inferior or stupid."

"He made Rich feel like caca, that's for sure," Polly said. "When I ran into him at the Hollywood Bowl last summer, he was still yacking about that evening—from five years ago!"

Polly continued scrolling through messages and came upon one from Cherise Roberts. "Listen to this one," Polly said.

"Blah, blah, blah... So sad (☺). I'll never forget when Lester designed the dress for the grand finale of my last Vegas act. The sketches he showed me weren't what I had in mind. I merely suggested it might not dazzle audiences enough. Where were the shimmering fabrics, intricate beadwork, and other eye-catching embellishments to capture the essence of my performance? I had a gorgeous body back then. Of course I wanted to show it off!

"I said I thought the sketches weren't his best work, and he got angry. And then I discovered that Lester had been recording what was supposed to be our private conversation. You know as well as I do that chats between a star and her designer are sacred and confidential! I said a few unflattering things about—well, several of our mutual nearest and dearest. I demanded he erase all the voice memos from his phone, but he said I deserved payback for another time when he thought I was being difficult. I'm never difficult! Assertive, maybe. So what if I have design ideas of my own? I guess I'm not really sorry that he's gone, bless his soul. I wonder if he kept the recordings. I'd die if they ever got out!

"Cherise is the third person to tell me that Lester recorded private conversations," Polly said. "He wouldn't have dared to record our conversations, would he?"

The trio thought for a long moment about Lester's clandestine practices. "If we could find his phone, we might find out," Tiara said. "Where the heck is that thing?"

As they pondered the mystery of Lester's missing phone, Polly's mind wandered back to the unsettling calls she'd received the day before. She was plagued by the fact that someone would go to the trouble of finding her cell and the castle's landline numbers to inquire about Lester Lynch's memoir. Who was this Audrey No-Last-Name person anyway? And why was she so concerned with what Lester might reveal in his book?

As the day progressed, Polly couldn't shake the sense that she was being watched. Was it the castle ghost? Or simply that a stranger knew where she lived and how to contact her. Then she had an idea. She looked at her phone and scrolled through the list of recent calls. She found the number from yesterday morning and sequestered herself in the reception room for privacy. Polly tapped on the number from which Audrey had called. Someone answered on the second ring. Surprisingly, it was a man's voice—and he sounded American. *This had better not be to a US number. I don't have an international plan. It'll cost me a fortune!* she said to herself.

Polly hadn't thought about what she would say if someone answered, and now she was flustered. She waited a beat until the man demanded, "What?" a second time. "Dreadfully sorry," Polly said, using her idea of a posh English accent, "I had a missed call from this number. Someone named Audrey, I believe?"

There was a long pause before the voice said, "No one here by that name. You dialed wrong." And then he hung up.

"I didn't dial wrong," Polly said, annoyed. "I merely *redialed* the number that called me first." And then she tapped the number again. This time, after several rings, a woman answered. Her greeting was cautious, and she spoke with a heavy, unattractive British accent. Polly knew it was the same voice she'd heard twice yesterday. "Ms. Audrey?" Polly asked, knowing full well whom she was speaking to.

"Who wants to know?" The voice was sharp and sent a chill down Polly's spine.

Summoning all her acting prowess, Polly maintained her composure and morphed into one of her most popular sketch comedy characters: an English nanny. "This is Miss Ursaline Reid, in service to Ms. Polly Pepper," Polly said, her voice professional and earnest. "Ms. Pepper asked me to relay a message to you. She said she would preserve Lester Lynch's work in progress just as he left it. And she plans to hand over Mr. Lynch's notebooks and recordings to his publisher in New York for publication at Christmastime. She feels it is unethical to do otherwise and is certain you will understand. She also said that she would appreciate it if you would please try to respect her position and Mr. Lynch's legacy."

The silence that followed was heavy with unspoken thoughts. Finally, after what felt like a minute but was probably several seconds, Audrey's dull voice pierced the stillness. "We're sorry to hear that. Polly Pepper will be sorry, too. Guaranteed."

With that ominous statement, Audrey abruptly hung up, leaving Polly staring at her phone in disbelief. The encounter had left her shaken, a sense of foreboding settling over her like a dark cloud.

However, Polly had only a moment to think about Audrey and the call when suddenly Mildred Banks flung open the doorway to the reception room with the force of a gale.

"Emergency!" Mildred hollered, her voice quivering with agitation. "The theatrical grapevine is a short one, and word's gotten around to Andrew Lloyd Webber that Polly Pepper is putting on a show and using his songs!"

Polly's heart skipped a beat. *Sir Andrew Lloyd Webber knows who I am?* That thought was enough to send a thrill through her. She imagined the legendary composer sitting at his grand piano, perhaps even discussing the possibility of a starring role for her in his next show. *Polly Pepper—a name on the lips of a musical genius!*

But her excitement was short-lived. Mildred's next words brought her back to reality. "They've sent a cease-and-desist letter!"

Drats! The reality of the situation snapped Polly back into focus. Her eyes widened in shock. "It's not *my* show! All yours!"

she exclaimed, hastily dissociating herself from anything potentially illegal or unethical.

"He can suck an egg!" Mildred spat, pacing back and forth
with fury, her hands clutching the letter from the Really Useful
Group's legal reps. "I've worked my buns off putting this
together!"

Anyone else who received such a threatening letter would be
intimidated by potential legal action. But Mildred was on the
warpath. "All those years spent crafting the perfect script! The
meticulous planning of each scene!"

Her despair suddenly transformed into steely determination. "Who does he think he is? A lazy-ass songwriter! What's he
even done lately?" Mildred snarled. "I will not have my brilliant
show snatched away by some egomaniac big shot with fancy-
pants lawyers!"

Mildred's eyes sparkled with defiance as she crumpled the
cease-and-desist letter into a tight ball. "I refuse to let anyone
intimidate me or dictate what I can and cannot do creatively.
This production is my passion, my vision, and I won't let anyone
take that away from me."

With a dramatic flourish, she tossed the crumpled letter into
the fireplace and crossed her arms in defiance. "Sir Andrew
Lloyd Webber be damned! This show will go on, even if I have to
stage it in my own barn!"

With newfound resolve, Mildred straightened her shoulders
and posture. "I'll show them," she vowed, her voice tinged with
determination. "We're proceeding with the show as planned. Try
to stop me! Licensing rights, my ass!"

16

Over the decades, Polly had grown accustomed to the efficiency and resources of the Los Angeles and Beverly Hills police departments. They had big budgets for state-of-the-art equipment and technology. But in Abbots Clover, England, things were decidedly different. Constable Grayson Jenkins, the lone ranger of law, was adorable in his hi-vis jacket and dark blue trousers, but his professional tool kit needed his California counterparts' shiny gadgets and high-tech wizardry. When Gray popped over to the castle to deliver a book he'd promised to loan to Tim (an obvious ruse), Polly cornered him. She spilled the beans about the calls she'd received and implored Gray to use whatever means were at his disposal to identify who Audrey was.

While Grayson agreed that it was possible, in theory, to track someone down based solely on their phone number, he admitted that it was extremely difficult and unlikely to happen in wee Abbots Clover.

"At police college, we learned about working with telecommunication companies to trace calls, retrieve data storage, and use monitoring devices and such to locate people," Grayson explained. "They mentioned things like *triangulation* and *GPS tracking*, but I don't know anything about those. And those methods typically require a court order or a warrant. Even that isn't always straightforward, especially if a caller hides their identity by using burner phones."

Shoot! Polly knew this was true; her own phone was set up so that her number was not displayed when received by others. She had to use many precautionary measures to protect her privacy, security, and professional relationships in this age when personal information was so highly sought after. But, creeped out by whoever Audrey was, she felt it was imperative to find her —with or without help from the police.

As Grayson's attention drifted to the real reason for his visit, Polly found herself alone in the reception room, her mind buzzing with thoughts of the mysterious Audrey. Frustration gnawed at her as she scrolled through her emails and tried to take her mind off the enigma.

With frustration absorbing her, the phone rang and pierced the silence with its familiar *Laugh-In* ringtone. It was Sarah from Bound to Read, her voice tinged with urgency. "Can you drop over? It might be important. I can't leave the shop."

With Tim and Grayson engaged in—whatever, Polly summoned Tiara and asked to enlist Elara for a lift into the village. Within minutes, Polly was speeding toward the town, anticipation building with each passing cow pasture.

"The midday rush is through," Sarah said in greeting, her characteristic warmth slightly diminished. Polly returned the smile, though she knew Sarah well enough to sense that something unusual had prompted the urgent summons.

"Tea? Coffee? Take a seat by the window."

"Tea, please. And a slice of something yummy."

A few minutes later, Sarah set a teapot and mug in front of Polly, along with a slice of Victoria sponge. She sat opposite with a worried look on her face. She glanced around the coffee shop, ensuring they were alone, before leaning in closer, her expression uncertain. "Those two tourists came in again a little while ago. Although I now think only one of them is American. The man. The woman had an English accent. They were talking about you, Polly. I heard one of them—the American—say, 'Polly Pepper may be famous, but she won't get away with it. She's maybe got to go.'"

Polly's heart skipped a beat at Sarah's words, a knot of unease forming in her stomach. Her mind raced as she processed Sarah's words. Who was the so-called American tourist and his English sidekick? And what did they think she was getting away with? And why or where did she "maybe got to go?" What did that even mean? The air in the café shop seemed to grow heavy with tension as they exchanged concerned glances, sensing that something sinister was afoot.

"And that's not all," Sarah continued. "When they left, I watched through the window. They met another man across the street in front of the church. They seemed to be having an argument. There were a lot of body gestures. The other man pointed a finger in the American's face and shook his fist. Even from a distance, I could see the two scowling. I was distracted for a second when a customer came in, and when I turned back, they were gone."

Polly took a deep breath. "They were definitely talking about me? One was an American man, the other a British woman? This might make sense," Polly said, explaining to Sarah about her call to the unknown phone number that was first answered by an American-sounding voice and the next time by a woman with a British accent. "What did they look like?"

Sarah didn't have to think long. "The American was rather good-looking. Maybe five feet eleven inches tall. A sort of rugged masculinity. Chiseled jawline, high cheekbones, and piercing blue eyes. Sandy brown hair."

Polly painted a picture in her mind's eye and liked what she saw. *In other words, attractive,* she said to herself.

"The woman was shortish with a slight build. Skinny. I liked her eyes. They were brown and expressive, although she never smiled. Her hairstyle was—it wasn't a style. It was—basic. And brown. The other guy—he looked like another American. I only say that because—and I don't mean to bash my countrymen—but he was far better looking than the average Brit. At least the ones in this village. They were all about the same age, which I'd say was maybe nearing fifty. Oh, and the guy across the street had a very interesting umbrella. It had the RCA Records logo on it. You know, the one with a dog sitting in front of an antique gramophone? Hard to forget."

Just then, the bell on the door rang, and Sarah looked up. A group of five came in laughing as if one of them had just told a funny story. They wandered to the counter and stood reading the coffee menu board. "Gotta get this," Sarah said, making a beeline for her station behind the counter.

Meanwhile, Polly retrieved her phone from her coat pocket and tapped Tiara's number. "Lots to tell you when I get back," she said cryptically. "Can Elara pick me up?"

Tiara explained that she was in the middle of teaching Elara the delicate task of making a souffle and couldn't leave for at least thirty minutes. Slightly annoyed, Polly said she'd wait at the Fox & Hare by the fireplace. "If Grayson's still there, keep him around until I return. Distract him with something. He's already distracted? Hmm." She chuckled knowingly.

As Bound to Read started to get busy again, Polly caught Sarah's attention from a distance and waved goodbye. She stepped out into the chilly late afternoon and pulled the coat collar around her neck. She quickly crossed the narrow, cobbled street and walked the short distance to the Fox & Hare. She loved entering this establishment because it was always warm and cozy inside. It was nearly dusk and a bit too early for the after-work crowd to be knocking back a pint or two, but several patrons were seated at the bar. Polly looked at her watch. She had time for a tea.

Two men bookended the short bar, and Polly took a stool between them. In the relatively brief period that she'd been coming to the pub with Terrence, she was becoming friendly with the bartender and waitstaff. Nigel was on duty. "The usual, Polly?" he asked in the jovial way he had.

"A tad too early for my 'usual.'" Polly laughed. "How about an Earl Gray? With lemon."

"Righto!"

A short while later, Nigel set a teapot, a cup, and a mismatched saucer in front of Polly. She thought the disparity in the patterns was actually quaint and took a tentative sip, testing the temperature. As she savored the taste and the warmth, a man from several seats over cleared his throat and, in a soft, almost embarrassed voice, said, "Excuse me, ma'am."

Polly smiled and looked to her right. She saw a good-looking face smiling at her sheepishly. She knew this salutation well—it was the prelude to a fan asking for an autograph or a selfie. Polly cherished these moments of recognition, especially now that they were so rare. Too often, she felt invisible, even in the Los Angeles restaurants that once tripped over themselves to show their appreciation for her patronage. There had been a time when she was instantly recognized on sight. Now it pained her when a young hostess looked right through her and asked if she had a reservation. Polly's name meant nothing to them—just another person to escort to a table. The sting of anonymity was a bitter pill to swallow. So, she was genuinely delighted and touched when she heard the voice asking, "Is it possible that you're Polly Pepper?"

The beam in Polly's smile was known for lighting up entire theaters, and at this moment, the Fox & Hare pub was engulfed in her star shine. She nodded humbly as she looked into the blue eyes of her obvious admirer. "Not if you're a bill collector." She laughed at the old joke as the man shook his head in disbelief.

"This is awesome!" He was clearly American and excited to meet Polly Pepper. "I'm a huge fan. We've actually met before. At my mother's funeral. Her name was Dolores Hayes."

"Dolores Hayes!" Polly shouted involuntarily, her voice piercing the air with the urgency and volume of someone yelling, "Fire in the theater!"

"Dolores Hayes!" she screeched once again, nearly at the top of her voice range, as if never in a million years could this be possible. "I worked with your mother! I loved your mother! I was devastated when she died... granted, she was old, but I loved her. I still play her records! I watch her old movies! Oh my gosh. Then you must be..." Polly thought for a short moment until the name finally came to her... "Jerry! Jerry Corley. And your father was... he produced some of your mother's movies." Polly couldn't recall the first name of Dolores' second or third husband. Still, she remembered that Dolores had wed him later in life, and it hadn't gone well—like the others before—except it produced the light of her life—Jerry.

"Howard. Howard Corley was my father." Jerry held out his hand for Polly to shake. "You can't possibly remember me."

Polly might not have really remembered meeting Jerry Corley, but she absolutely remembered attending Dolores Hayes' funeral. "It was only for a moment," she said, imagining that she probably had at least said hello and "I'm sorry for your loss." "What are you doing in Abbots Clover? This tiny dot in tiny England?" she asked, now fully invested in the conversation, completely forgetting her tea and still disbelieving that someone from her own Hollywood world was visiting her village. "It isn't even spring yet! I'm told tourists don't start wandering here until mid-May!"

Jerry had scooted a couple of seats over and was directly next to Polly. They were talking as though they were old friends and reminding each other of this mutual acquaintance and that old friend. "I remember when your mother lived on Tower Grove Road. Extraordinary view! Do you still have the house? She was a major star but always so down to earth. Everybody loved her. What are you doing here? Are you married? Do you have kids..." Polly was flooding Jerry with questions and was so excited that she hardly let him get a word in edgewise.

Not married. No kids. Failed miserably as an actor despite having a mother who, like Polly herself, was a major star. "Now I run the Dolores Hayes Foundation, her animal charity. And I oversee all of Mom's copyrights and try to keep her memory alive. That sort of thing. It's not the creative career I wanted, but it keeps me off the streets."

Being a Hollywood brat, Jerry knew that celebrities—especially the larger-than-life ones like Polly—were not interested in the lives and careers of ordinary people. Therefore, he deftly steered the conversation back to her. "And you?" he asked, genuinely interested but knowing better than to ask a long out-of-work celebrity what they were doing professionally. And he definitely didn't want to bring up the end-of-career jobs that he knew Polly had had on the Home Shopping Network. "I think I heard you retired from Hollywood and bought a big ol' castle in England. Which is a huge shame. The retirement, I mean. I think it's great that you can afford a castle!"

"Retire!" Polly rolled her eyes. "I'll never retire, dear!" She filled Jerry in on the truth that she hadn't willingly left Hollywood. And the castle was an inheritance from a fan. "The place needs a ton of work, and I'm not sure I can afford to maintain it," she said with a frown. "It's almost a pile of stones. Where's the big Netflix deal when you need it?" she joked. "I'm still deciding if I want to stay in England. It's lovely here despite the constant rain. I'm told it gets a little better in summer. I'll see if I can hold out that long."

Just then, Polly's phone rang. Tiara told her that Elara was on her way and would meet her outside the Fox & Hare in a few minutes. When she disconnected the call, she turned again to Jerry. "What are you doing for dinner this evening? Please come to Thistlethorne Lodge—that's the name of my castle."

"I love the way you say, '*my* castle.'"

"Tim, my son—you may have met him at the funeral—will be thrilled. He absolutely worships your mother—as we all do. Forget about Taylor Swift, Billie Eilish, or Ed Sheeran. Tim is *devoted* to Delores Hayes. She's still his all-time-favorite Hollywood icon. I'm not even on his list. The ungrateful little sod. He's not too annoying, I promise. Oh, please say yes! And I need gossip from La La Land! You'll have to tell me what's been going on in Hollywood lately. Please?"

Jerry was thrilled. "What time? What can I bring?"

"Eight o'clock. Just bring yourself. And don't bother to dress up. We're a very casual castle. I'm not sure what Tiara—our darling factotum and BFF—will serve, but she's divine in the kitchen. Oh, this will be so much fun! I need this! Still can't believe that you're here!"

17

The energy Polly brought into Thistlethorne Lodge was like the wind before a hurricane. As she burst into the kitchen, Tim and Tiara immediately sensed that something momentous was up. Polly's eyes were wide with excitement, and she could barely contain herself. "You simply will not believe who I ran into!" she gushed, her voice ringing out as if she were trying to be heard in the back row of a theater. Before anyone could take a guess, she practically shouted, "Jerry Corley!"

"A new baker at the Tasty Tart?" Tiara asked.

"The plumber who fixed the leaking toilet in the Henry the Eighth suite?" Tim suggested.

"Oh, for heaven's sake," Polly said impatiently. Looking directly at Tim, she said, "'Silent Shadows at Midnight.' Who sang that song? Your one and only girlfriend. The mother you wish you'd had."

"Wait a minute! I know that name! Jerry Corley is Dolores Hayes' son!"

"Ding! Ding! Ding!" Polly tapped her nose as she exclaimed,

"Dolores Hayes' son is right here in Abbots Clover. On vacation! And... drum roll... He's coming to dinner. Tonight!"

"Dolores Hayes' son!" Tim shouted with as much enthusiasm as Polly had shown in the pub. "What the heck is he doing here? OMG! You know I'm not usually starstruck. But when it comes to anything Dolores Hayes-related, I can't help myself!"

Polly plopped herself down at the table and explained the serendipity of it all. "Jerry's staying at the Fox & Hare. He was in the pub having a brew. He overheard that adorable bartender, Nigel, I think it is, say my name and then recognized me. I'm not even wearing my signature Polly Pepper lollypop-red hair color! We started chatting and hit it off! It seemed right to invite him to dinner."

Tiara made a face and said she hadn't planned anything fancy but would throw something together. "Elara failed miserably with her souffle this afternoon, so I'll have to think of something else for dessert. Heck, I don't think I'd be more excited—or nervous—if Charles and Camilla were dropping in."

"I should have invited him for Lush Hour," Polly lamented. "I wasn't thinking because I was so excited!"

Polly deigned to help set the table and arrange the throw pillows on the Chesterfield in the reception room. Tim lit the fire and selected what he thought was appropriate music from Alastair Drake's CD collection. Tiara sliced and diced mushrooms, shallots, garlic, and fresh parsley for a chicken marsala. To an outsider, you'd think the frantic atmosphere resulted from expecting royalty. In a manner of speaking, Jerry Corley was royalty. At least the offspring of showbiz royalty. They couldn't have been more nervous if Barbra and Jim Brolin were coming to tea!

The family had completely forgotten about Lush Hour. When the grandfather clock in the hallway gonged eight times, they were all in need of something to calm their nerves. And just as the clock's chime ended, they heard the dull thud of the front door knocker. Polly looked at Tiara, who looked at Tim. "I've got to give him my patented Polly Pepper hostess-with-the-mostest entrance."

"In other words, hide until you hear the champagne cork pop," Tiara said.

In only a few minutes, Tim was playing docent. He explained what he knew about the paintings and tapestries hanging along the entryway walls. Jerry oohed and aahed in the reception room at the portrait over the fireplace mantel. "The duke," Tim said as if introducing an old relative. "From all accounts, an insufferable so-and-so with bad breath."

Tiara entered the reception room, wearing an apron and wiping her hands on a dish towel. "Just want to introduce myself and make sure Tim offers you something to drink," she said, reaching out to shake Jerry's hand. "Her Highness will be along any minute. She's putting on her face. As if another layer of Max Factor Facefinity All Day Flawless three-in-one Foundation will wipe away even a minute of her... fill-in-the-blank years."

Immediately after Tim opened a chilled bottle of Veuve Clic-quot, and as Etta James sang "At Last" over the stereo speakers, Polly Pepper slid open the double pocket door dividing the reception from the dining room. "Jerry," she purred, offering an exuberant greeting. "We're delighted that you're able to join us in our humble little castle."

"Humble?" Jerry smiled, leaning in to plant a whisper of a kiss on Polly's cheek. "I'm the more delighted one. If I'd had anything else planned for this evening, I would have canceled to be here. Such an amazing coincidence running into you this afternoon. Obviously, it was meant to be."

For the next half hour, Jerry talked about the touristy things he'd done in England. He'd rented a car in London and set out for the countryside. "My mother talked a lot about wanting to come back to England ever since she made *The Desperate Life* for Clark Walters way back in the 1970s. I still think she was robbed of the Oscar that year." He said he was enjoying boutique hotels that were once manor houses and a few centuries-old pubs that offered accommodation. "The Fox & Hare is every Anglophile's fantasy of a charming English inn." He still had a long list of places he wanted to see: Stonehenge, Gloucester Cathedral, and the ruins of Tintagel Castle. He'd booked tickets for a couple of National Trust houses over the next few days and was open to suggestions for anything he shouldn't miss.

When Tiara announced that dinner was served (and apologized for the simplicity of the meal), Jerry was as in awe of the formal dining room as Sarah Rogers and others had been. He made the very same reference to Downton Abbey. Since the joke was new to Jerry, Tiara repeated her line about Mr. Carson having the night off. Of course, Jerry laughed, and the others pretended it was a funny off-the-cuff remark.

As the quartet enjoyed Tiara's chicken marsala, Jerry engaged them with reminiscences of his legendary mother. They'd all read the bestselling *Dolores Hayes: Her Story*, written with Simon Randolph, so they knew the basic story of her life and career. But he also offered anecdotes that very few others knew about. They'd heard that Dolores' last husband—a so-called "restauranteur" in Beverly Hills—had invested a lot of her money in get-rich-quick schemes only to see them fall apart and lose their investments. And then there was the horrifying story of her stunt double in the musical western *Prairie Serenade*, who placed herself between Dolores and a thief who was robbing the star at gunpoint and ended up shot and killed. Dolores had been devastated by that tragedy and unable to work for a year. But overall, Jerry stayed true to all the stories and fables about his legendary mother that fans always wanted to hear. He was a master at doling out tidbits that further burnished Dolores Hayes' legend.

As the evening wore down and they were lingering over Tiara's sticky toffee pudding dessert and snifters of Grand Marnier, Jerry began to ask about Thistlethorne Lodge and its history. He was astonished that a fan had bequeathed the property to Polly. He revealed that no one had ever left anything in their wills to his mother because they figured she was rich. Which, he said, definitely was not true. And then, as politely as possible, he asked if they would give him a tour of the house. "I never ask that," Jerry said. "Not even when Barry Manilow and his husband, Garry, invited me to their place in Palm Springs. I hope I'm not being rude or impolite. But this castle is so amazing. Do you mind?"

House proud and eager to gloat, Polly couldn't wait to guide him around the ancient rooms. Along the way, she pointed out this painting, that marble bust, and what she knew about their history. "The fox hunt painting," she said, pointing to a large canvas in an ornate gilt frame. "What's wrong with this picture?" she asked. After a brief moment of silence, she continued, "See the lazy dog lying down on the right?

"For one thing, it's a German pointer, which is totally different from all the foxhounds on the chase. You'd think he would be excitedly joining in, but he's a total lump. According to legend, the real-life dog, Loki, was annoying and had gassy intestinal explosions. So Old Granny Grumbles, the castle witch, put a spell on him and absorbed him into the painting. We can smell him when there's a full moon. In the myth, he supposedly guards the house."

As they all laughed at the folktale, Polly moved her charges farther down the hallway. Jerry pointed to the police tape across the library door. "I was sorry to hear about your friend Lester Lynch. I should have said something earlier."

"We're devastated, of course," Polly said, stopping before the door. "Such a dear. Well, not necessarily dear. But a friend nonetheless, and certainly a brilliant costume designer. You must have known him. He designed for your mother when she did her last television special."

Jerry was quiet for an introspective moment. "Lester Lynch. The prodigal son," he said. "Yeah, I knew him. Or at least I knew *of* him. Mom mentioned him a couple of times. She actually wasn't much of a fan, I have to say. They had some sort of falling-out. Still, what a terrible way to die." He seemed to suddenly remember that Polly had been through the trauma of a death in her house, and reined himself in, not wanting to stir up more pain for his hostess. "I'm sorry I've come around when you're probably still grieving. I don't know what to say."

"Lester was using the library to write his memoir," Tiara said. "He needed a quiet place to work, so he came here to stay with us while he wrote."

"Right," Jerry said distantly.

Tim added, "It's not really a library anymore. More like a museum. Mr. Drake, who left the castle to Mom, collected celebrity memorabilia. It's a pretty cool shrine to his favorite stars. Want to take a look?"

"Off-limits," Tiara interjected. "The forensics guys haven't given the all clear to go in again."

"Nonsense!" Polly said as she pulled away the police caution tape. "One short peek won't make a difference. Jerry's not a thief. He won't touch anything." She opened the door and turned on the lights. "I think Mr. Drake has autographed photos of every major star of the twentieth century. And posters from classic films. When we get around to appraising everything, I'll bet the value will be phenomenal. My picture is right over there," she said, pointing to the framed eight-by-ten-inch black-and-white glossy. "I was so young then. And cute," she joked. "A publicity shot taken when I was appearing in my very first off-Broadway musical, *Bacteria: The Typhoid Mary Story*. God, that was a dreadful show. Although my personal notices were brilliant! Ashford Longacre in the *Times* said, 'Although this show should be quarantined, Polly Pepper's "Sanitizer Tango" is a star turn.'"

"I remember the hit song, 'Germs in My Soup, and Everywhere Else,'" Jerry said, scoring huge brownie points with Polly. "I saw Lacy Canningford's revival at the Pasadena Playhouse about fifteen years ago. She was okay, but surely not as good as you were. I wish I'd seen your production."

As Jerry wandered around and examined the pictures, he seemed pleased to see the faces of many people he'd met through his mother. He had an anecdote to tell about each of them, and when he'd finished oohing and aahing, he wandered to the desk. "I guess this is where Lester worked. That's quite a brave thing—writing your autobiography. Although I'm not sure there's much of a market for a book about a costume designer bashing the stars he dressed. I know he was well-known in our circle, but who in Caldwell, Iowa, will care?"

Jerry reached out and was about to pick up one of Lester's notebooks when Tiara politely suggested that it would be best not to touch anything. "The police have already dusted for prints, but they seem to be fussy about anyone interfering with their work. They'll probably never come back, but just in case."

"As soon as the police give the okay, I'm sending the notebooks to Lester's publisher," Polly said. "Funny story, Lester told us that he signed a contract for this book a couple of years ago and then didn't bother to write it! He spent the advance and said they threatened to sue if he didn't hand in a manuscript by August. That's why he was with us. I must say, he's got some dreadful stories in there!"

"Mother!" Tim declared. "You read them? We were told not to touch anything!"

Polly shrugged. "And let me tell you, Lester held nothing back! He had a lot of anger issues. I sort of—and sort of not—feel sorry for Sally Dresden. They'll have to put her on suicide watch after reading what he said about her! Bye-bye Pollyanna image. Fred Astaire's horse-loving widow has a lot to be worried about, too, but she's old, so maybe she'll be joining Lester before publication."

As Jerry took one last long look around the room, Polly followed his gaze. He seemed to be absorbing all the elegant details and fine craftsmanship. "I love the intricate plasterwork," he said, looking to the ceiling. "And the fireplace is amazing. It just needs a bit of TLC." He ran his hands over the mantel and appeared to be studying the architecture and furnishing of the room. His gaze surreptitiously landed on a lone nail in the stone wall surrounded by picture frames.

Polly made a face. "I think that's where your mother's picture was. I'm almost sure of it. There's Joan Blondell. And Anne Miller. And Olivia de Havilland. Maybe the police absconded with it."

"Mom started charging fans for autographs in the 1990s. A hundred percent of the proceeds went to her animal foundation. Maybe Mr. Drake didn't want to pay for a photo, and the cost of mailing from the States might have been too steep for him."

"He was eccentric," Tiara agreed. "He was left a fortune by his parents but apparently squandered it. By the time he died, he was property-rich but cash-poor. Which is why this place needs so much work. He couldn't afford to maintain it."

As Jerry's eyes lingered on the walls and desk, Polly steered the looky-loos out of the library. Returning to the reception room, Jerry made it clear that he'd had one of his life's most unexpected and delightful evenings. "Almost better than when

Mom received her Kennedy Center Honors. Sometimes the best things that happen are unplanned," he said. "I have two more days booked into the Fox & Hare. It's my base until I return to London for my flight back to LA. Please let me reciprocate and play host for dinner in the pub. Nothing fancy, obviously. Unless you know of a fine dining restaurant in the area."

"Forget about Michelin stars anywhere for miles." Tim snorted.

"The pub is perfect." Tiara spoke for the group. "It'll give me a night out of the kitchen."

Jerry was still beaming as they walked down the hallway to where his coat was hanging. "Darn. I think I left my umbrella in the bar at the Fox & Hare," he said. "Mind if I borrow one of yours? I'll bring it back when we meet up. How 'bout day after tomorrow?"

When the family had agreed on the night for a pub meal with Jerry, they all exchanged goodbye hugs and wished their guest safe travels. "Don't drive on the wrong side of the road." Tim chuckled. "I almost hit a pheasant the other day!"

Even before Jerry's car was out of the car park, Tim nearly whooped excitedly! "OMG, he's Dolores Hayes' son! I was, like, one degree of separation from *the* Dolores Hayes! Did I behave myself? Did I act like the sycophantic fan that I am? Was it okay that I said we had a lot in common, like we're both handsome and the only sons of national treasures?"

"You were adorable, as always," Polly assured Tim as the trio returned to the house and closed the door. "I'm sure he thought you were charming. But he's a tad exhausting. Has anyone ever worshipped their mother the way he does?" She looked directly at Tim.

Tim offered a guarded laugh. "I thought it was sorta weird that he's still so devoted to her that he rewatches all her old TV interviews and subscribes to a service that searches the internet for any mention of her. Reminds me of that crazed Judy Garland fan we met."

"He's the head of the Dolores Hayes Foundation, so he needs to be aware of how her image and music are being used," Tiara said. "But yeah, I thought he was a bit weird about it sometimes. Still..."

When "good night and sweet dreams" were exchanged, Tiara started to peel away and head down the hall to the reception room to clean up and turn off the lights. Polly stopped her. "Did you think it was odd that Jerry seemed to know Lester was dead? He's on vacation, and the American newspapers just reported that news this morning."

"We live in a twenty-four-hour news cycle," Tiara reminded her, disregarding Polly's question. "No doubt he keeps up with showbiz news. Probably has a digital subscription to *Reel Rubbish* like Tim."

Polly nodded, agreeing that show business was in his veins, so he'd be up to date with what was happening in the industry. Then they all went to bed.

W ith only a week left before *Cats on a Hot Tin Roof* had its first of only two performances, Polly was frantic. It didn't help that Mildred was impatient and bossy and could only get a few members of the cast together at the same time. What did she expect? The Abbots Clover Am-dram Society was a troupe of dilettantes. They all had jobs and other obligations and responsibilities. They could never be counted on to all be available at the same time. Mildred had bragged about having been involved with many previous shows, so surely, she knew the complications with small theater productions. Apparently not. Polly ended up filling in for all the roles during rehearsals and sing-throughs.

Needing a break from the chaos, Polly met with Terrence for lunch and filled him in on the behind-the-scenes disasters. As they sat together at the Fox & Hare, Polly monopolized the conversation with complaints about Mildred Banks, the maybe/maybe not threatening calls from a mysterious Audrey, the happy happenstance of meeting Dolores Hayes' son and, of course, Lester's death. The bar portion of the pub was empty, and Polly glanced over and noticed an umbrella set against the wall next to the seat where Jerry had been sitting the other day. She remembered that he'd said he'd left his umbrella at the pub and made a mental note to retrieve it before Sticky Fingers got there first.

Just as they were settling into their conversation and enjoying their ploughman's lunch of cheese, crusty bread, Branston pickles, and chutney, a small woman with an ancient face approached their table. "Sorry for interrupting," she said to Terrence in a tone that didn't sound like any sort of apology. "When are you going to correct my advert in the *Overview*? It's 'psychic,' not 'psychotic,'" she said, obviously perturbed about a typo in her newspaper ad.Terrence swallowed a bit of his food and smiled at the woman. "You know I'm really sorry about the ad, Emma. The paper comes out on Thursday, and I've checked and rechecked the copy. It now says, 'Don't let uncertainty cloud your path! Visit *psychic* Emma Tunsing today and unveil the secrets of your destiny. Satisfaction guaranteed or your money back!'"

"I'm the one who should get my money back!" Emma said. "Your mistake makes me sound like a nutter."

Terrence grimaced and apologized again, promising to run Emma's next ad for free. "Do you know Polly Pepper?" he asked, trying to change the subject. "She's from America."

"Of course. I know all about Polly Pepper," Emma said, not smiling and sounding as if Terrence had asked a stupid question. "You're the one who keeps finding dead people up at Thistlethorne Lodge. You almost ended up a corpse yourself."

Polly smiled. "Can you check your crystal ball to see if there'll be any more dead-people surprises in my future?" She was joking, but Emma didn't laugh.

Instead, Emma stared silently into Polly's eyes for a long moment. "I don't usually give impressions for free, but in your case... I sense a negative energy surrounding you and Thistlethorne Lodge. I'm picking up on an unsettling presence lingering within its walls. Darkness and a shadowy figure are lurking in the corridors. Unseen eyes are always watching you. There's also a ringing phone. Someone is trying to reach you. But they wish you ill." She stopped and emerged from her sudden trancelike state. "If you want more info, it'll cost you. Here's my card."

Then, turning her attention back to Terrence, she added, "Don't forget. A free advert!" With that, she walked away.

Polly was dumbfounded and unsettled. "What was that? She was sort of specific. A presence lingers in the walls? A shadowy figure lurking in the corridors?' The last time I went to a psychic, all she could tell me was that I knew someone with psoriasis."

Terrence shrugged and made the sound of a soft chuckle. "Emma's sort of a joke in the village. She's offered her psychic services to Constable Jenkins, but as far as I know, she's never even found a missing garden gnome. I wouldn't pay much attention to her if I were you."

Still, Polly felt a sense of unease. "I don't know how much information about Lester Lynch's death has gotten around the village, but..." She summoned Terrence's ear closer and whispered, "He died in a secret wall space in the library."

Whoa! That was news to Terrence. "I've usually got my pulse on all the scandals and malicious gossip, but that's insane."

"Emma said there was a presence lingering within the walls. That's a little too on the nose."

By now, Polly had lost her appetite and pushed aside the wooden board on which her lunch had been served. She looked at her watch. "No! Don't send me back to Satan," she pleaded and rolled her eyes. "I suspect Emma's reference to the negative energy following me is Mildred Banks. She definitely lurks and lingers. And sends a chill down my spine."

They exchanged a hug, and Terrence initiated a quick kiss to Polly's lips. Then they agreed to have dinner in the indefinite "soon." Terrence left the pub and walked to his small office at the *Abbots Clover Overview*. Polly collected Jerry's umbrella from the bar and walked to the village hall.

P olly arrived at the village hall just as Mildred was pounding the piano keys and upbraiding Stacy Steinlaw for flubbing a lyric—a lyric that Mildred had changed in the Andrew Lloyd Webber–Tim Rice song "I Don't Know How to Love Him." Polly knew this was a theatrical no-no due to copyright rules, which required asking the author's permission first. For the next two hours, Polly focused on encouraging Stacy and propping up her ego.

After rehearsal, as she waited for a ride home from Tim, Polly's thoughts drifted back to what psychic Emma Tunsing had said to her in the pub. The ominous warning lingered in her mind, but her musings were interrupted by the ringing of her phone. The caller ID said *Trouble*. Actually, it displayed a sequence of numbers—the same numbers that had preceded the calls from the otherwise anonymous Audrey.

Their conversation was brief, but Audrey was clearly upset about receiving a call from Polly's made-up assistant, Ursaline Reid. "You're a funny lady, Ms. Polly Pepper. But you won't be laughing much longer." Then she hung up.

Tim arrived a few minutes later as it began to rain again.

Polly opened Jerry's RCA Records umbrella and dashed from the village hall to the car, muttering all the way about her hair and a pothole next to where Tim had set the car. "I'm melting!" she exclaimed as she closed the umbrella and slipped into the passenger seat.

"Cute doggie. On the umbrella, I mean," Tim said as Polly tossed Jerry's brolly into the back and released a loud huff.

"What a day!" she said. "Remind me to hang myself by my thumbs before I ever agree to work with amateurs again!"

"You think you've had a bad day. Mine was worse! Gray and I had a fight. It's all your fault!"

"They always blame the mother," Polly said with a roll of her eyes. "I do my best to provide love, support, and guidance to my child, and this is the thanks I get. What have I done this time, and why can't you take responsibility for your own love life?"

"Gray stopped by earlier and noticed that the police tape was no longer across the library door, and the door was open. He knew someone had been in there."

"I didn't think his eyes ever strayed from you," Polly said, chuckling. "I hope you lied for your dear old mother and blamed the new maid."

"I did. But Tiara gave you away. And that's what got me in trouble. He says he can't trust me if I lie. And it's all because you're so nosey!"

"You could have said our ghost opened the door! He'd never be able to prove otherwise."

"He said that he was disappointed in me. *Disappointed!* That's the worst thing anyone has ever said! He also said that in light of my lying, he has to rethink our friendship. He's angry. At you and me. Not only because you disobeyed police orders but because I covered for you. What should I do?"

"Breakdown of trust is never a good thing," Polly said. "Did you apologize? Did you explain your motives?"

"Yes, and yes. He said I'd have to regain his trust. I don't know how to do that!"

Polly stared straight ahead as rain pelted the windshield, and she tried to make sense of Tim's plight—and her own. It was bad enough that she had the specter of Lester Lynch's corpse hanging over her house and was inadvertently supporting Mildred Banks' infringement of a famous composer's intellectual property. But she also had someone threatening to cause her some sort of harm if she didn't revise dead Lester's memoir. Not to mention that her maid and best friend Tiara was about to be renamed *Judas Iscariot*. "You picked a lousy time to break up with the law," she said. "I'm about to be crucified by whoever the local theater critic is. Plus, I've got a psychic telling me there's a dark shadow hanging over Thistlethorne. And that Audrey woman's back making trouble. I could use a bit of police protection right now."

Tim glanced at his mother. He was suddenly contrite for allowing his personal problems to eclipse his mother's potentially dire ones. "What's this about Audrey?" he asked. "This might be a good excuse to work things out with Gray. If I can get him up to the castle."

"Maybe if I call him?"

"He'll think I can't fight my own battles. Tiara holds sway. She'll have a plan."

Gray couldn't resist Tiara baiting him with her spaghetti and meatballs. And when the meal was over, the quartet sat in the reception room, apologizing for things they'd said and done and promising to do better in their relationships. Tim said he'd never again be untruthful with Gray. Polly vowed that she would henceforth be a good girl and follow instructions from the law (although she'd surreptitiously crossed her fingers behind her back). Tiara insisted that combining beef, pork, and veal was the secret to making great meatballs. Everyone was happy. Until Polly brought up the subject of the threatening calls from Audrey, and Gray wanted to know why she waited so long to tell him.

"I did tell you," Polly insisted. "You said you couldn't trace the calls, so I figured you weren't interested."

Gray looked annoyed. "You say you've had four calls, one of which you placed yourself, to the same number, and each call has become progressively more hostile. May I?" he said, pointing to Polly's phone. She tapped Recent Calls and handed the device to him.

Grayson studied the number for a moment before saying, "Right off the bat, I can say it's a cell phone and not a landline. Landline numbers are ten digits long. This is eleven. I wish it were a landline because it would have an area code, and we'd have a general idea of where they were calling from. This could be anywhere. What does this person say when she calls?"

Polly repeated the messages and added what Emma Tunsing had said about hearing a ringing phone and the caller wishing her ill will.

Grayson rolled his eyes. "Emma Tunsing? Really? I hang my Out to Lunch sign in the window when she wanders toward the station. She insists that her dreams are prophetic. She gets telepathic messages from her neighbor's cows, too. When the *Overview* ran her last ad and mistakenly said she was 'psychotic,' everyone laughed because it was pretty much spot on. Frankly, we think Terrence did that on purpose."

Shifting his focus, Grayson dragged his fingers through his hair and tried to offer comfort to an increasingly distraught Polly. He knew she was concerned not only for her own safety but for the safety of the family. However, without knowing who

Audrey was or where she lived, there wasn't much he could do. He could alert the police in the next village, but otherwise...

"What if we could get a physical description of her?" Polly said, accepting a top-up to her glass of champagne and leaning forward. "Sarah, down at Bound to Read, told me about a couple of tourists who'd come in for coffee. She thinks they're tourists because she didn't recognize them as being from around here. One's American; the other is British. She thought they were suspicious because she's twice overheard them talking about me... and Lester Lynch. It might be worth talking to Sarah. Maybe get a police sketch artist."

Grayson looked at Polly. "You said earlier that a male American-sounding voice answered the phone when you called Audrey's number back. Then, when you redialed, Audrey herself answered. That's curious. Okay. First thing in the morning, I'll take a statement from Sarah and get a description of the suspects. As for a police forensics sketch artist, don't count on it. Bristol might send someone if they thought the crime was serious enough. I can check the protocols, but I wouldn't be too optimistic."

Grayson thought for a long moment, then nodded as an idea flickered through his mind. "I think I've got an idea. There's a guy, David Durham, who does those drawings of St. Clematis Church and country cottages that Sarah has in the window at Bound to Read. He's a good artist. Maybe he'd be willing to draw a composite from Sarah's description. In the meantime, remain vigilant. Call me if you notice any suspicious activity around the house or castle grounds. I'll check in again in the morning."

Before going to bed, Tim and Tiara moved in tandem through the house, checking that all the doors and windows were locked. After all the talk of threatening phone calls and a psychic who claimed to see "a shadowy figure lurking in the hallways," they were plenty spooked and on high alert. The front entryway door was bolted, and the kitchen door leading to the larder was locked too.

"What about the door in the larder that leads to the courtyard?" Tiara asked.

Tim had thought about that, but he didn't want to open the kitchen door and venture into the dark room to investigate. "I think it's closed," he stammered, his voice barely above a whisper. "It probably doesn't matter as long as the kitchen door is locked," he added, his words hollow and weak—a feeble attempt to convince himself and Tiara, hoping she would agree.

She didn't.

Tim cautiously pulled open the door to the larder, and a bone-chilling gust of wind rushed in, sending shivers down their spines. Darkness engulfed the room, and Tim felt around the void for the pull-string light switch. He gave it a tug. The feeble glow of the bulb overhead barely pierced the inky blackness, casting long, sinister shadows that seemed to dance on the walls. To his surprise—and horror—the door to the outside was indeed open!

He stepped cautiously into the larder, his heart pounding in his chest, and practically dove to the old wooden door, slamming it shut with a loud bang.

However, when he reached for the sliding barrel bolt lock, his stomach dropped. The catch plate mounted on the door frame had come off and was dangling by two of its four puny screws. As he turned around, he noticed the other two rusted screws that had held the plate to the doorframe lying on the floor like tiny, lifeless insects. He looked at Tiara, who was standing in the doorway between the kitchen and the larder, her arms folded across her chest against the cold, her eyes wide with fear.

Tiara saw the look on Tim's face. "What?" she asked as the outside door blew open again.

Tim looked at the door. "The lock is broken." Then he pointed to wet leaves and a bit of mud accumulated on the larder floor. "I think someone's been in here." Terror caught in his voice as he looked around for further evidence of an intruder.

"Can't be!" Tiara insisted, trying to convince him, and herself, that there was nothing unusual in the larder. "The force of the wind pushing against the door made the lock fall off. That's all. And the wet leaves? The wind brought them in."

Tim looked around suspiciously, then dragged a sack of potatoes resting against a shelf of homemade preserves and pickled veg and propped it against the door. "I don't like this," he said. "I don't like this one little bit!"

The wind rattled the outside door again, sending Tim tearing back into the kitchen and bolting the door. "I want my mommy," he whined as he and Tiara skedaddled to the safety of their bedrooms.

"They'll obviously hang my portrait in the National Gallery in London," Polly declared as she sauntered into the breakfast room the next morning. Dressed to impress in a tailored suit that screamed confidence and professionalism, she'd accessorized with a dazzling diamond brooch on her lapel and a silk scarf artfully draped around her neck. Taking a seat, she theatrically retrieved her Bloody Mary energy drink.

Tim and Tiara were staring at her, wide-eyed.

"What?" she asked, knowing they were intrigued by her outfit. "I'm trying to encapsulate my essence for the artist."

"You're not having your portrait painted," Tim reminded her. "Gray's getting a sketch artist to do a composite from Sarah's description of those two tourist dudes. This has nothing to do with you."

"Scout's motto: Be prepared!" Polly retorted. "Mr. Crayons might look at me and decide I'm his muse. When I met Jean-Michel Basquiat at a gallery opening, he said I exhibited 'layered symbolism.' He wanted to draw my 'raw energy.'"

Tiara looked askance at Polly. "Basquiat painted graffiti. This village artist draws churches and thatched cottages. Ancient things."

"Well, she is a timeless classic," Tim quipped with a grin.

Elara wandered into the room and whispered into Tiara's ear.

"Back in a tick," Tiara said, following Elara to the larder. Elara pointed to the center island workstation, where a box of Meow Munchies cat treats lay on its side. "It's been gnawed clean through," Elara said, indicating the chewed edges, holes, and scattered debris. "Mice!"

But the box of Meow Munchies wasn't what caught Tiara's attention. "What's the candlestick doing out here?" she asked. "It belongs on the sideboard in the breakfast room."

Elara gave Tiara a quizzical look. "This is weird. I didn't want to say anything because I thought you'd think I was nuts. But the other day, after I'd polished it and set it back down on the sideboard, I went on to polish the napkin rings, and... it toppled over. You know how heavy the base is. It couldn't have fallen over by itself. But it did. And now it's out here."

Tiara nodded in fascination. This very candlestick was the object that had probably saved her, Polly's, and Tim's lives when they were abducted and thrown into the castle's dungeon by the deranged killer who'd visited them the previous month. They had joked that the castle ghost had clobbered the villain, but they only half believed that. It was too weird to be true. Nevertheless, Tiara picked up the candlestick and returned it to the sideboard.

"Mice," she said as she sat down to her now-tepid tea. "The rodents found Mr. Boots' treats."

"He's supposed to catch the mice!" Tim grumped. "I think he's gone soft. We feed him too much. There's no incentive to do his job."

Mr. Boots, resting on Polly's lap, looked up. He knew they were talking about him.

"That's not all," Tiara said. "That candlestick... it was on the island workstation. It's supposed to be there on the sideboard. I don't suppose either of you moved it."

"Why would we?" Tim asked. "The power hasn't gone out for a few weeks, so we haven't needed it."

"Don't look at me. I don't polish silver," Polly said. "My nails, maybe, but not the silver."

"Like everything else wacky around here, we can blame it on the ghost." Tim sniggered. "By the way," he said, looking at his mother, "you were going to give it a name. Prudence? Algernon? Euphemia? Do we need to establish that it's a girl ghost or a boy ghost? Is gender identity even valid in the afterlife?"

"If they're disembodied, how would you even tell?" Tiara shrugged.

"Maybe they rattle different chains." Tim laughed at his own joke.

"I'd like to try being a different sex in my next life," Polly mused. "Imagine the simplicity: getting ready in fifteen minutes flat. Cheaper haircuts. Never enduring the torture of high heels."

"A wardrobe of only jeans and T-shirts," Tiara agreed. "Plus, men never face long lines for the bathroom. They can age gracefully into distinguished silver foxes without the pressure to stay eternally youthful."

"On the flip side, if you come back as a man, you've got the societal expectation to be stoic and tough all the time," Tim said. "No crying watching *Somewhere in Time*. Then there's the handyman stereotype. You're supposed to know how to fix things even when you have no idea what you're doing. And don't get me started on shaving. The daily ritual of scraping a razor across your face gets old really fast. Then there's the constant challenge to avoid anything deemed too sissy—like enjoying a spa day or a fruity cocktail. So, while being a man has its perks, it's not without drawbacks! But I definitely recommend being a man the next time 'round. For the novelty."

At that moment, they heard the bell at the main gate clang. "Mildred's not due until noon," Polly whined.

A short while later, Tiara returned to the breakfast room with an orange plastic shopping bag with the Tesco supermarket logo printed on the side. "Don't freak out," she warned, dropping the bag on the table in front of Polly. "I didn't see who left it, but I have a hunch."

Tim joined his mother and Tiara as they peered into the sack. "It's... Lester's phone," Polly said as she reached into the bag. "It's got that dumb sticker of Ariel from *The Little Mermaid* on it."

"Fingerprints!" Tim interrupted his mother. "I don't think we should touch it."

"Call Gray," Tiara said. "The forensics guys in Bristol can dust it and maybe even figure out who Lester was talking to the night he died."

"What's this under the phone?" Polly said as she gently tugged on a slip of lined paper: *A generous trade in exchange for the notebooks.*

The Abbots Clover village police station could only be described as "quaint." Tucked away on a narrow cobblestone street, the station was a relic from a bygone era. The building was a modest structure with weathered stone walls and a sloping slate roof that gave it a period charm. A small sign above the entrance, its faded letters barely legible against the backdrop of peeling paint, proclaimed Abbots Clover Constabulary.

Inside, the station was a labyrinth of clutter, with old-fashioned filing cabinets bursting at the seams and stacks of old case files teetering precariously on every available surface. A single desk dominated the center of the room, its surface an organized chaos of paperwork, half-empty coffee cups, and the odd crumpled snack wrapper. Despite its lackluster appearance, the station buzzed with the quiet intensity of village law enforcement at work.

Grayson looked up as Polly and her troupe entered the station, brandishing Lester Lynch's smartphone. "You didn't see who dropped it off?" he asked, eyebrows knitting together in concern.

"It's got to be that Audrey person," Polly said, her tone laced with frustration. "She obviously wants to trade his phone for his notebooks. From what I read—okay, so I peeked—Lester was revealing a lot of salacious gossip. Can't imagine why anyone would care. Nobody reads showbiz bios much anymore. My own *PP Through Life* was a disaster, so who would care what *he* had to say?" Polly rolled her eyes, a mix of annoyance and curiosity flickering across her face as she handed over the phone.

"Fans," Tim said. "You love them. They lift you up. But some become dangerously obsessed."

"A fan tried to assassinate President Reagan to impress Jodi Foster," Tiara added. "Annie Wilkes severed one of Paul Sheldon's feet with an axe to force him to write another *Misery* book. Oh, I wouldn't want to be famous. No thank you!"

"A fan wants Lester's notebooks, but they can't have them," Polly said. "I dislike being bullied or given ultimatums. That's not how I roll. Sacha Barron Cohen learned that lesson the hard way when he tried to force me to remove the bamboo from between our two properties. Cybill Shepherd was just as unlucky. Nope! Lester's publisher is getting his notebooks. They probably own them anyway."

Tiara was suddenly agitated. "Wait a minute. Whoever left

Lester's phone at the gate obviously knows where we live. What's to stop them from... I don't want to be an alarmist, but we need to put the notebooks somewhere safe."

Grayson agreed and felt a little sheepish about not thinking of that himself. "I'll collect them and put them in the safe here if you want." But at that moment he was interrupted when David Durham, the artist, walked into the station.

"Sounds like a fun assignment," Durham said, eager to put his sketching skills to work. "It's been ages since I did a sketch of a person. I mostly do souvenir art like iconic buildings or street scenes. But I'll give it a try."

Grayson looked at Tim. "I'll be up at Thistlethorne to collect the notebooks right after we see Sarah."

Sarah was too busy to take a break, even for a police matter. "You can see for yourself," she said, suggesting Grayson and David return after the morning rush. When Grayson suggested enlisting help from her other employee, she pushed back firmly. "He's not trained. Cappuccinos, macchiatos, and espressos don't just drip out of the machine," she explained, her voice tinged with impatience as she simultaneously frothed milk and took orders.

Grayson's frustration was evident, and his usually calm demeanor started to crack. Sensing the mounting tension, Sarah's unflappable composure also began to fray. She wiped her brow with her hand, managing a tight smile. "I'm pretty good at multitasking," she said, her tone a mix of determination and exasperation. "David can sit here behind the counter with his sketch pad, and I can try to give a description while I'm making coffees. Otherwise, you'll have to wait at least an hour."

The coffee shop buzzed with activity, the hum of conversations blending with the hissing of the espresso machine. Customers shuffled impatiently, their eyes darting between their watches and the barista. Sarah's hands moved with practiced efficiency, yet the strain of the rush was beginning to show. Grayson nodded, recognizing the take-it-or-leave-it edge in her voice.

"Alright, let's try it your way," he agreed, motioning for David to sit on several boxes stacked behind the counter. "Not ideal, but if you're willing..."

As Sarah made drink orders, she described the two tourists she'd seen, her words punctuated by the rhythmic clinking of coffee equipment. David Durham's charcoal pencil flew across the paper, translating her hurried descriptions into images. The scene in the shop was a chaotic dance of multitasking, but Sarah's resilience and Grayson's determination kept them moving forward.

Grayson watched the scene unfold, admiring Sarah's ability to juggle ten things at once. "You're doing great, Sarah," he said, hoping to offer some encouragement.

She shot him a grateful smile before returning to the next customer. "Large latte with almond milk? Got it."

Durham's sketch began to take shape, and the two tourists started to emerge on the paper. "This is really helpful, Sarah," he said, pausing to adjust his lines. "You've got a sharp eye."

Sarah handed a cappuccino to a customer and took a fleeting moment to look at the sketches. "That's them," she said with certainty. "I'd recognize those faces anywhere. Maybe change the woman's nose and make it a wee bit smaller. And the man's hair was a little shorter. Otherwise, that's them!"

With a wide smile of satisfaction, the two men again apologized for interrupting Sarah's day. "Now I have a better idea of who to keep my eyes open for," Grayson said. "If they come in again, give me a call. Can I get an Americano to go, please?"

"Sure... but no jumping the queue. You'll have to go to the back of the line," Sarah said with a chuckle but was totally serious. She wasn't about to make the other customers wait while she served him ahead of them. No way!

It was raining again when the two men left Bound to Read, and Grayson struggled to protect the sketches. He stashed them inside his coat and zippered it up against the elements. "You've been a big help, David," he said, giving the artist a firm handshake before they parted ways. Grayson planned to copy the sketches and study them and keep a lookout for anyone resembling the two figures.

As he entered the station and headed to the copy machine in the back, his phone rang. He smiled when he saw the caller ID: **YANK**. Aka Tim. "Hey, you," Grayson said seductively, tucking the phone between his ear and shoulder as he turned on the copier.

Tim's voice crackled with urgency. "Gray! We need you. Please get over here! Quick!"

Grayson dropped the sketches on his desk and raced out the door. He rarely had an opportunity to use the blue lights and siren on his police car, but now, as he switched on the ignition, he instantly engaged the emergency warning devices. The siren's wail cut through the pounding rain, and the flashing lights painted the wet streets in a kaleidoscope of bursting blues. He tore along the slick roads, the tires barely gripping the pavement as he navigated sharp turns along the narrow lanes. His pulse raced, and within minutes, he came to a gravel-spewing stop in front of Thistlethorne Lodge.

Grayson scrambled out of the car and dashed through the main gate door. Tim was waiting at the front entrance.

"We've been burgled!" Tim led Grayson into the house and down the hallway to the reception room. There, Elara was seated on the Chesterfield between Polly and Tiara, who were cooing words of comfort and support, their hands gently patting her back and shoulders, trying to console the young woman, who was visibly shaken.

Elara's hands trembled as she clutched a teacup, the liquid inside quivering. Her usually composed demeanor was shattered, replaced by a fragile vulnerability. She looked up as Grayson entered, her eyes searching his for reassurance.

"First of all, are you okay?" Grayson asked in his most compassionate yet professional voice, kneeling down to her level to meet her gaze. "Did they hurt you?"

Elara swallowed hard, her voice barely above a whisper. "No, they didn't hurt me, but they were right there. In the library. I... I didn't know what to do." Her voice cracked, and she took a deep, shuddering breath.

Grayson nodded, his expression softening. "Elara, you're safe now. Can you tell me exactly what happened?"

Elara nodded and explained that shortly after Polly and her troupe had left the house, she'd heard a loud thud coming from the vicinity of the library. She went to investigate, and when she opened the door, two people wearing balaclavas were coming through the French doors. "They looked surprised as if they thought no one was home," Elara explained. "I was so shocked I just froze. We looked at each other for a split second. Then, like an idiot, I said something stupid like, 'What do you want?' They grabbed several of Mr. Lynch's notebooks on the desk and bolted away. They were gone in a flash."

"This is exactly what I was afraid would happen," Tiara snapped, her voice edged with frustration and a hint of accusation, implying that this could have been prevented if Grayson had been more vigilant. "The important thing is that Elara's okay. But I'm sure they were watching the castle and waiting for us to leave."

Grayson's jaw tightened at Tiara's words, but he focused on

the task at hand. He took detailed notes from Elara, gently prompting her for all the specifics she could recall. Grayson then walked through the library, his eyes methodically scanning every detail. He inspected the French doors, noticing immediately where they had been forced open. The splintered wood and bent lock spoke volumes about the burglars' determination. "I'm calling the guys back from Bristol," Grayson announced, pulling out his phone. His tone was authoritative. "Don't touch anything in this room," he added, his gaze locking onto Polly, who had been absently righting a picture frame that was askew on the wall.

Polly quickly retracted her hand, nodding in understanding.

Grayson stepped into the hallway to make the call, his mind racing with the implications of the break-in. As he spoke with someone in Bristol, arranging for a forensic unit to be dispatched, he couldn't shake the feeling that this was more than just a random burglary. The timing was too perfect, and the execution was too precise.

Returning to the reception room, he found Tiara pacing, her frustration simmering just below the surface. "This wasn't a coincidence, Grayson," she said. "They knew exactly what they were doing." She stopped and looked him in the eye, her expression softening slightly. "It's your duty to make sure Polly and Tim are safe."

Grayson nodded, understanding the gravity of the situation. And unlike last time, when it took three days for the forensics team to arrive in Abbots Clover, they were there in a matter of hours. The same three police officers appeared, their faces a mix of professional detachment and thinly veiled irritation, as if they blamed Polly for pulling them away from more pressing matters in the big city.

The forensic team moved through the room with practiced precision, photographing, dusting, and tweezing microscopic fibers with the meticulousness of surgeons. Polly made a concerted effort to stay out of their way, but she hovered near the door, observing their every move. Despite her efforts to remain inconspicuous, her curiosity got the better of her.

When she heard one of the men say, "I've got something," her ears perked up, and she couldn't help but step closer. She watched intently as one of the team members leaned in to photograph a minuscule smudge on the handle of one of the French doors.

Polly stole a glance at Grayson, who met her gaze with a steady, reassuring look. His eyes held a quiet determination, and he gave her a small nod.

"We're on the right track," he murmured, his voice a steady anchor in the storm of her thoughts. The confidence in his tone made her feel slightly lighter, her spirits buoyed by his certainty. "We'll get to the bottom of this, I promise."

Three hours later, as the sun dipped lower in the sky, the team began to pack up their tools and equipment. The lead officer, looking weary yet resolute, turned to the group gathered near the library door.

"No one is permitted inside the library until we say so," he instructed firmly, his tone brooking no argument. He affixed the "Caution Police Investigation" tape across the entrance, the bright blue stark against the dimming light. Then, with a tip of his cap, he led the others out of the house, leaving the room to settle back into an uneasy silence.

21

"Well, this was a truly rotten day," Polly said as she collapsed in exhaustion onto the Chesterfield in the reception room. As the trio sipped their Veuve Clicquot and tried to put the enervating day behind them, Polly wondered aloud if anyone thought Elara's traumatic experience was enough to send her fleeing her employment. "I don't want to lose her," Polly said. "She's a lovely girl. A little high-strung, but I'd probably be bouncing off the walls too if a gang of desperados invaded the castle and threatened to kidnap me and do... whatever it is that kidnappers do to maids who catch them in the act of burglarizing a TV star."

Listening to his mother's dramatic tirade, Tim reluctantly tore his eyes away from his phone screen. With a heavy dose of sarcasm, he said, "Right, Mom. Clearly, we're living in the Wild West with gangs, desperados, and kidnappers lurking around every corner. The reality? Two intruders scared Elara. Not exactly a Liam Neeson movie plot."

"She won't quit," Tiara predicted of Elara. "I doubt there's another steady house-cleaning job for miles around. She needs the work. But we should give her a bonus."

"Changing the subject," Tim said, "there's a piece in *Reel Rubbish* about Lester's death." He scanned his phone screen and suddenly looked up. "How'd they find that out? It says, 'Award-winning television costume designer Lester Lynch, affectionately known as "Lester the Dresser," was found dead Sunday while on a working holiday in England. Eyewitnesses said he was staying with comedienne Polly Pepper at her castle. He completed a memoir, which is to be published by Elysian Press in December. A spokesman for Elysian said they were heartbroken by the news of Lynch's death, but that Lynch had written an informative book, and they would hold to their publishing calendar. The release day is December 2.'"

Polly cocked her head and tried to make sense of what Tim had read. "Lester said he hadn't written the book. He said he'd spent the advance long ago, and the publisher threatened to sue for not turning in a manuscript."

Tiara poked at the logs in the fireplace as she considered what *Reel Rubbish* had revealed. "There's something that hasn't made much sense to me ever since Lester came here," she said. "Here's a guy—talented and successful. He worked in an industry that required hard work on tight schedules. Deadlines are a harsh fact of life, but they're essential. Miss one, and you're history because TV is expensive, and they can't wait. No excuses. Lester was a pro. He might have been a terrible person in many ways, but he was disciplined. I've thought it odd that he'd been given a deadline to produce a manuscript—even if he'd never written anything before and didn't know what he was doing—and then just blow it off. That's not Lester. That's not anyone who's achieved any level of success in any business. You meet deadlines, no matter what."

Polly sat up and set Mr. Boots aside. "But why would he lie about needing a quiet place in the countryside to write?"

As the trio pondered the question, Tim reminded his mother

of when she was writing her own memoir. She'd worked for several years on a manuscript and had been over the moon when she'd finally turned it in. It was a major accomplishment, and an albatross off her neck. But then, surprisingly, that was when an equally challenging amount of work began. "Remember your editor, Vlad, and how excited he was when you turned it in? He said he loved it. He wouldn't consider changing a word. He might have a few notes with relatively tiny suggestions for tweaks or improvements. And then he pulverized it. He threw it into the editorial meat grinder, and we spent another full year making his changes. Confirming dates. Providing corroborating documentation for the accuracy of quotes. It was a year of hell."

"Maybe Lester was doing a *rewrite* of his book," Polly said. "If his editor was anything like Vlad, he wanted more showbiz gossip."

"Publishing an autobiography of someone famous behind the scenes in Hollywood—like Lester—is risky," Tiara said. "It's expensive to print books. Even e-books need marketing. You're an honest-to-goodness star, and sales were still stinky."

Polly nodded in agreement and suggested that perhaps Lester hadn't been booted out of the homes of his other European friends simply because they had other plans and unexpected emergencies. "You know, Lester didn't have much of a filter when speaking whatever was on his mind. What if he told so-and-so in Italy about changes or embellishments he was asked to make to his book? What if they were as aghast as I was when I read his notebooks. Maybe they didn't want to have anything to do with supporting that kind of behavior. So, they made excuses to send him away. Then he got to us and decided to keep his trap shut."

Tim jumped on that idea. "He talked freely about everything else in his life, but when it came to his book, he was pretty quiet," Tim said. "He made a few blunders and hinted at what he was doing, but not enough that we would have a clue and send him packing as the others had."

Knocking back her champagne, Polly said, "Along those lines, what if his two hosts, both of whom had lots of Hollywood friends, told their chums in the industry about what Lester was writing. I got several emails suggesting they knew Lester was working on a book that might not be flattering to them or our mutual friends. You know what happened to Truman Capote when he ratted on his Swans. I'm beginning to think—"

"I'm beginning to think we've all lost our minds," Tiara suddenly said and bounced off her seat. "We've forgotten that Jerry Corley's taking us to dinner tonight!"

"Ach! I'm not in the mood!" Polly wailed. "I loved his mother dearly. Tim worships her for the legend she is. But I'm exhausted after having invaders and pillagers plunder our castle. Not sure I can stand another evening of Jerry's obsequious memories. 'Mother said this. Mother preferred that. All of my mother's roles are my favorites. I can't choose my best-loved of all her songs. What's up with him vowing never to get rid of her clothes? She's been dead for five years! Someone shoot me before opening my big mouth and agreeing to dinner with a movie star's offspring in the future."

22

It was a lively Saturday night, and the Fox & Hare was buzzing with energy. The massive inglenook fireplace, dominating the room, glowed warmly with embers, casting a cozy light across the space.

Nigel, the bartender, was busy and harried, juggling drink orders. Leslie, the hostess and server, greeted Polly and her troupe with a warm smile.

"Jerry, sweetums! We've kept you waiting," Polly trilled as she expertly leaned in for a kiss on her cheek. "Why does anyone put up with an old woman who was absent the day they taught time management skills?" She laughed. "I don't know the big hand from the little hand, but thankfully, when you're a star, people make allowances," Polly looked hastily around and caught Leslie's eye. "A bottle of whatever is cold, fizzy, and contains forty percent water," she said, eagerly anticipating a potion to get her through the evening.

Now, focusing on Jerry, she returned his umbrella. "I nicked it before someone came along and admired it too much. Yes, there are petty thieves in Abbots Clover, believe it or not. Now, tell us all about your fascinating visit to Ludgershall Castle! I hear it has lots of old stones!"

As the evening began, Jerry described all of the fun tourist activities he'd been enjoying. He regaled them with anecdotes about visiting Clevedon Court, Dyrham Park ("I recognized it right away as the location of one of Mom's favorite movies, *The Remains of the Day*"), Corfe Castle, and Kingston Lacy. "After a while, all the manor houses start to look the same." He chuckled as if he'd become world-weary and could no longer be impressed. "But enough about me. I've heard you all had a horrifying day! Is your maid okay?"

Polly and Tim exchanged glances. *The village grapevine is working overtime.* "Having one's castle invaded by bandits is too unsettling to think about," she said, giving Jerry the play-by-play and shaking her head at the previously inconceivable idea of intruders entering her home. "It's an old fortress, for crying out loud. Robert the Bruce couldn't get in. Somehow, an infantry of two made it!"

"They could have taken the silver! How about that hand-painted mantel clock? Or Polly's favorite diamond ring sitting out in the open on her dressing table," Tiara added. "They were obviously after one specific thing: Lester Lynch's notebooks."

Jerry looked skeptical. "You can't know exactly what burglars have on their must-steal lists."

"They got in through the French doors in the library," Polly continued. "And someone returned Lester's missing cell phone this morning with a note attached saying it was a trade for the notebooks," Polly said. "They obviously came to make the exchange."

"At least we have a composite sketch of the perpetrators," Tiara said.

Jerry squinted, envisioning the scene. "I didn't think your maid got a look at their faces."

Polly shook her head. "They wore masks, but she got a general physical description of heights, body proportions, and eye colors. That sort of thing."

"But Sarah at the coffee shop gave the police a good description," Tim said. "Well, a description of a couple of tourists who came into her shop who she said were displaying unusual behavior. They're persons of interest to the police."

Jerry snort laughed. "Tourists displaying 'unusual behavior'? That describes every sightseer. I probably stand out like a sore thumb taking pictures of cottages and castle ruins. My accent alone gives me away. Would that be considered unusual behavior around here?"

"They were also overheard talking about Lester Lynch before we even discovered his body. He was just a missing person then," Tiara added. "And a couple of days ago, they asked Sarah if she knew where Polly Pepper lived."

Jerry made a face. "I was shopping in Argyle on Rodeo Drive in Beverly Hills recently and overheard two Japanese women wondering where Justin Bieber's house was," he said, dismissing Tiara's suggestion that asking for the location of a celebrity's house was unusual. "I was tempted to impress them with directions, but I decided to mind my own business."

"Maybe just coincidences," Tim agreed, "but the police can't disregard the possibility of a connection between the tourists and our burglars."

"Any other leads?" Jerry asked. "Do you think there's a chance the burglars will come back and try to steal the rest of the notebooks?"

"Good luck with that." Polly chuckled. "Thistlethorne is one big warren of clever places to hide things. The notebooks are safe and sound where no one will find them—unless they torture our ghost for details. We've got secret passageways, a dovecote, a ruined chapel. Only the castle ghost knows where we've put them."

Leslie, the server, returned to take their meal orders and patiently waited as the quartet decided on the minimal pub grub offerings: fish and chips, cottage pie, scotch egg, and toad in the hole. In the end, they all ordered fish and chips.

23

Of course, it was raining outside. As Polly prepared to leave the Fox & Hare, she realized that she'd returned Jerry's umbrella but hadn't brought one for herself. Tiara caught up with him as he climbed the stairs to his room above the pub and asked to borrow the brolly again. It would be returned before he left for London the next day. Polly pointed the umbrella into the night and ran the fastening mechanism up the shaft to open the canopy against the rain. She dashed to the car. "I'm melting!" she wailed—her go-to exclamation when it rained.

At Thistlethorne Lodge, Mr. Boots was in a state when Polly and her posse returned. Meowing and pacing the reception room, he seemed agitated and unable to calm down. "I know how you feel," Polly cooed to the cat as she settled onto the Chesterfield and accepted a champagne flute from Tiara. "This entire day has been one big episode of *Stranger Things*!

"Even Jerry was a bit weird. He wasn't nearly as much fun as the other night," Polly said. "And he got his castles confused. He said the artwork at Corfe was awe-inspiring. Corfe is a ruin! No walls. No artwork. There's something fishy going on here."

Tim added, "I guess the village grapevine is working on overdrive. He knew there were two intruders here too, and that Elara saw them."

"I feel sort of sorry for him," Tiara said. "He seems lost without his mother. Of course, he's reminded of her every moment of every day because he runs her animal foundation. He doesn't have a life of his own. Divorced. No kids. Not even one of the dogs his mother was so keen on. He probably doesn't have time for fun and games. It's probably an all-consuming job negotiating licensing agreements for his mother's likeness and recordings and documenting copyright infringements."

"I won't be spending my days monitoring streaming platforms and social media for potential infringements of *your* copyrights," Tim said to Polly, putting her on notice. "Writing cease-and-desist letters is no way to spend my post-PP retirement. I'll be living it up on a tropical beach with Gray."

Just then, a plaintive meow broke the silence. Mr. Boots cautiously ambled over to the floor-to-ceiling window in the room. It was pitch black outside, but he placed his paws against the glass, seemingly interested in something in the front forecourt.

"When was the last time Mr. Boots caught a meal?" Polly asked, trying to inject some levity. "Maybe he wants a midnight snack."

"I hope that's all he's interested in," Tiara replied, her voice tinged with unease. She tentatively approached the window, unhooking the curtains from their tiebacks. "Just in case anyone's looking in," she explained, pulling the curtains closed before quickly retreating to the safety of her seat beside Polly. "This place is too spooky at night."

"Please, no scary noises tonight," Polly pleaded. Then, as if on cue, an unfamiliar sound reached into the room. It wasn't loud but enough to set their nerves on edge. A dull bump came from the direction of the breakfast room, a sound foreign to the usual creaks and groans of the old house.

They exchanged uneasy glances, each of them acutely aware of the noise. The silence that followed was thick with tension, every creak of the floorboards and rustle of the wind outside amplifying their anxiety. Polly's heart raced as she strained to hear other sounds, her mind conjuring images of unseen watchers and creeping shadows. The cozy warmth of the room was suddenly filled with unseen terrors lurking just beyond the drawn curtains.

"That's all I needed to hear," Tim announced, making a show of stretching and yawning. "I should be off to dreamland, not investigating strange sounds at this time of night."

Polly and Tiara stared him down, their eyes demanding action.

"Fine." Tim conceded defeat, holding his hands in mock surrender. "I'll investigate the mysterious bump in the night. But if I get eaten by a zombie, I'm haunting you for the rest of your days—and beyond!" He shuffled towards the door. Polly and Tiara exchanged a relieved, albeit slightly guilty, glance. The tension eased somewhat as Tim's exaggerated grumbling faded into the next room. However, the eerie ambiance of the house still lingered, keeping them on edge.

Tim cautiously ventured down the hallway and into the breakfast room, with Polly and Tiara right behind him. He reached for the light switch. To everyone's relief, the room was empty—no monsters, no serial killers.

"What about the kitchen?" Polly suggested, cocking her head toward the door at the end of the room. The kitchen, too, was deserted. However, as they retraced their steps through the breakfast room, Polly stopped. The others followed her gaze. Their eyes came to rest on the silver candlestick—lying on its side.

A chill ran down Tim's spine. "We need to keep an eye on that," he murmured, his voice barely audible. They all exchanged uneasy glances before heading to bed, each lost in their own thoughts about the mysterious candlestick.

The next morning, Polly's voice was hushed and serious as she sipped her Bloody Mary. "I think Lester's spirit is still in the house."

Tim nodded, his expression grim. "He's trying to send us a message."

"'Boo! Go back to California!'" Tiara deadpanned, sipping her tea.

Polly ignored Tiara's sarcasm. "I'm serious. I was awake half the night thinking about it. Why else are we hearing strange noises and finding that damn candlestick on its side again? He's trying to tell us something!"

The room fell silent, the air heavy with curiosity and unease. Tim glanced around nervously. Polly's eyes gleamed with conviction, her words hanging like an unsolved riddle. The house seemed to hold its breath, as if the mysterious presence of Lester lingered just beyond the edge of their understanding.

Just then, Elara walked in from the kitchen. "We're nearly out of milk. The sink's starting to clog up again. And I think I saw someone in the old chapel. Maybe it was a magpie. But I thought I should mention it."

Polly & Co. immediately went to the breakfast room window, which had a view of the castle's inner ward and the chapel beyond at the far end. Like the rest of the castle, the chapel was basically a ruin. Despite centuries of erosion, its thick stone walls, now partially crumbled, still had distinguishable remnants of rounded

Romanesque arches. The stained glass in the windows was long gone, leaving only stone tracery through which to view the space's interior. As they peered into the distance, they were slightly relieved when a magpie did indeed fly out from the interior.

"Guess I'm still jumpy after yesterday." Elara chuckled guardedly. "Thought there might be another intruder."

Tiara was still unsettled. She'd worked with Elara for a week now and had found her to be conscientious and pragmatic—like herself. Elara had even taken the episode of the burglars in stride. Other people might have been too upset to return to work after such an encounter, determining that all the drama was well above their pay grade. But not Elara.

When Polly and Tim abandoned the table to dress and start their daily activities, Tiara decided to investigate for herself. She walked across the ward to the chapel.

As Tiara pushed open the heavy wooden door, the creak of the ancient, rusted hinges echoed through the misty morning air. The drizzle outside seemed to seep into the ancient stone walls, lending the chapel a damp, musty smell.

Inside, the chapel lay in ruins, its once grand architecture now crumbling and overgrown with ivy and moss. Tiara's footsteps echoed softly as she cautiously made her way into the small interior space, which was no larger than the reception room in the house. Her senses were on high alert for signs that she wasn't alone.

It was freezing cold, and the dim light from the outside cast eerie shadows on the stone walls. Tiara's heart raced with a mixture of fear and curiosity. She paused at what was once the altar. An ancient stone crucifix stood there, weathered and worn. The air felt heavy with the weight of centuries of prayers, and Tiara couldn't shake the feeling of being watched. With a deep breath, she steeled herself and continued her investigation.

Like the main house, she suspected the chapel held many secrets from the past.

Tiara stopped for a long moment to listen to the silence. The air was still, and the quiet felt almost heavy, pressing down on her like a physical weight. The peace was so profound that it amplified every faint sound from the outside: distant bird calls, the whisper of wind passing through the chapel's open arches and windows, and the occasional rustle of leaves. Standing amidst the weathered stone walls and crumbling archways, Tiara could almost hear the echoes of the chapel's history. The walls seemed to whisper old hymns, prayers, and confessions, adding an eerie layer to the oppressive silence.

Suddenly, something brushed against Tiara's ankle, the touch as soft as a feather yet startling in the stillness. The unexpected contact felt like a jolt of electricity, and she jumped, her heart leaping into her throat. She looked down, her mind racing with wild possibilities—had some creature emerged from the shadows, drawn to her presence?

She nearly screamed as her eyes locked onto the source. "Mr. Boots!" she shrieked, her voice sharp with fear and relief. The black cat nuzzled against her, his tail upright and waving nonchalantly. Her pulse still pounding, she scolded him, her voice trembling. "I'm not the superstitious type, but sometimes I think those medieval folks were onto something when they believed witches shape-shifted into black cats."

She gently shook her head, trying to calm her racing heart, but the oppressive atmosphere of the chapel lingered, making every rustle and whisper feel like a hidden threat lurking just beyond her sight.

Trying to steady her nerves, Tiara turned to leave the dilapidated structure, but something caught her eye. The old baptismal font—a large stone basin that once held holy water for the sacrament—stood eerily in the dim light. She noticed that its round wooden cover, usually securely in place, was now set aside against the font's pedestal. A small chill crept up her spine as she registered this odd detail. Had she misremembered, or was it a sign that someone else had recently been in the chapel? She had only explored the ruins a few times before, but an unsettling feeling washed over her.

By the time she returned to the house, Polly was ready for Tim to drive her to the village hall for yet another dreaded rehearsal with Mildred and, hopefully, several cast members. The days toward opening night were ticking away too quickly, and Polly could feel the anxiety gnawing at her. The show was teetering on the edge of complete chaos, and every rehearsal seemed to highlight new issues rather than solve existing ones. Polly sighed, bracing herself for the inevitable confrontations that awaited her.

Meanwhile, Tiara anticipated a relatively peaceful day, a rare respite from the usual whirlwind of activity. She looked forward to the simple, meditative tasks of washing clothes and over-seeing Elara's ironing techniques. There was something oddly satisfying about the rhythmic hum of the washing machine and the hiss of the iron, a welcome contrast to the frantic energy Polly was about to plunge into. Tiara hoped the tranquility would hold, allowing her to breathe and perhaps even enjoy a quiet afternoon tea, a fleeting indulgence before the household's inevitable return to its usual bustling state.

When Polly arrived at the village hall, the scene was already charged with tension. Mildred Banks sat at the piano, her fingers poised but not playing, as she sternly addressed Frances, the dairy farmer-turned-West End hopeful who was cast as Maggie. "Your emotion when you sing 'Memory' is uninspired," Mildred snapped. "And you're off pitch! How many times must we go through this, Frances?" Her voice echoed through the hall. "We're not here to serenade the floorboards with your flat notes!"

"I'm sorry, I thought—" Frances began, her voice trembling, but Mildred cut her off sharply.

"You *thought*? If you spent as much time tuning your voice as you do thinking, we'd have a show worth paying money to see! I'm counting on you, and you're disappointing me."

Frances nodded meekly. "I'll try harder, I promise."

"*Try* harder? No, you will *do* harder! I won't have you making a mess of this production—my most ambitious work to date. Get your act together. Now, from the top! And let's see if you can keep it on pitch this time. And for heaven's sake, emote!"

Polly watched from the doorway, feeling the oppressive weight of the hall's high expectations settle over her. She couldn't help but sympathize with the beleaguered performer; Mildred's relentless drive for perfection wore everyone down. Polly was aghast at Mildred's harsh treatment of Frances, an amateur who had only sung in the St. Clematis Church choir or serenaded her cows. From Polly's experience in professional theater, she knew berating performers was unnecessary. Instead, combining technical guidance with psychological support brought out their best. As Frances prepared to sing again, the room seemed to hold its breath, thick with fear and determination. Then Mildred slammed the piano keyboard and started to shout again.

"Good morning, Frances!" Polly intervened as she walked through the small auditorium. "I'm delighted that you're in the show! I've listened to your song, and I think you're almost there!" As she wandered toward the stage, she said, "'Memory' is a really hard number to sing—Betty Buckley, the original Grizabella in the Broadway production of *Cats*, told me so herself.

She should know; she did eight shows a week for over a year! But I can tell you're getting the hang of it."

Much to Mildred's annoyance, Polly made her way to the stage and took over the rehearsal.

"Let's start with thinking about Maggie's journey in the Tennessee Williams play and Grizabella's journey in Andrew Lloyd Webber's musical," Polly said to Frances as an introduction to this master class in stage performance. "Both characters have something in common. They're nostalgic and heartbroken —yet hopeful. Your goal is to bring their emotions to life through this song."

"I rented the Elisabeth Taylor and Paul Newman movie from Amazon and thought she was sad. How do I bring out her hope?" Frances asked.

"Good question." Polly thought for a long moment. Then she reached out and took Frances by her hands. "Perhaps if you think of it this way, you'll understand the two characters. Both are outsiders in their respective worlds—and you're an outsider to the theater. Maggie is estranged from her husband Brick's family due to her different social background and their strained marriage. Grizabella has been rejected by the other cats because of the way she looks. Maggie seeks Brick's love, and Grizabella wants to relive the days when she was admired and loved. Maggie looks back longingly on the early years of her marriage. When Grizabella sings 'Memory,' she's reflecting on her past beauty and the days when she was celebrated, which contrasts with her current state. Both have inner strength and determination. Both characters are driven by a longing to overcome their present circumstances, which makes them tragic yet inspiring."

Mildred interrupted. "That's exactly what I've been saying!" She harrumphed as if she had any psychological insight into those two fictional characters. "Now, let's start from the beginning," Mildred huffed. "And get it right this time!"

Polly held Frances' eyes and cocked her head toward Mildred in a not-so-subtle knock at Mildred's pedantic control. Frances smiled gratefully at Polly for her support and encouragement. "Start softly with the opening lines of the lyrics," Polly suggested. "Let your voice carry the weight of loneliness. As the song progresses, you'll transition from reflecting on past memories to a stronger, more hopeful tone."

"And watch that bloody B-flat!" Mildred demanded. "Breathe! Belt it out!"

Frances still didn't live up to Mildred's expectations, but there was no way she ever would. It was a simple fact that, yes, she could sing the notes (most of them) with mechanical accuracy. But she didn't possess genuine talent, so they lacked any emotional depth and resonance that might make the song meaningful to her or the listener.

Looking at her watch, Mildred finally lifted her hands from the piano's keyboard. "That's enough," she said, excusing Frances to return to her cows. "Keep practicing, and we'll get together one more time before the dress rehearsal. God help us."

Polly felt a knot tighten in her stomach. She knew that Mildred was right about the show being in trouble. But admitting that would mean conceding power to Mildred, and Polly wasn't about to give her that satisfaction. She squared her shoulders and offered Mildred a faint smile, projecting an air of unwavering confidence that she didn't actually feel. Her ringing cell phone rescued her from what she knew was an oncoming tirade from Mildred.

It was Terrence calling. Could Polly get away for lunch? You bet she could! Polly was thrilled to have an excuse to escape from the oncoming cavalcade of semi-talented villagers who were expected to rehearse in the afternoon. They were all sure that if a talent scout from *Britain's Got Talent* showed up, they'd be "discovered." Susan Boyle wasn't the only amateur who could become rich and famous. "Meet you at the Fox & Hare in ten," Polly said before making the sound of a kiss. She turned to Mildred. "I'll be back in time to catch Big Daddy's number." She gave a wiggly finger wave. "Tah!"

When Polly entered the pub, shaking off the drizzle that clung to her coat, the Fox & Hare was nearly deserted. The cozy warmth, dim lighting, and the faint crackle of the fire provided a welcome reprieve from the dreary weather outside. Terrence was already seated at what had unofficially become "their" table in a secluded corner. The familiar setting offered comfort and intimacy.

After studying the worn paper menus and placing their lunch orders with Leslie, Polly settled into her chair, feeling the weight of the day's worries start to lift. Terrence reached across the table, taking her hand in his. Usually filled with a playful glint, his eyes now held a serious, contemplative look.

"There's actually something I wanted to tell you," he began, his tone heavy with significance. The words seemed to hang between them, filled with unspoken emotion and the promise of a revelation. Polly's heart quickened as she looked into his earnest face, bracing herself for whatever was about to unfold.

Polly fought to control a smile, her mind racing with possibilities. She was pretty sure it was too early in their relationship for a marriage proposal. Maybe Terrence was planning a romantic holiday getaway. Somewhere warm, far from the dreary UK winter. *Yes! The Caribbean!* she thought excitedly, almost feeling the soft, powdery white sand beneath her feet and seeing the gentle turquoise waves caressing the shore. In her reverie, palm trees swayed gently in the warm, salt-kissed breeze, and the air was filled with the scent of tropical flowers. The call of seabirds punctuated the soundscape as she and Terrence walked hand in hand, feeling the cool water lap at their ankles while sharing whispered conversations and laughter.

Then another thought rudely interrupted her tropical daydream. *God, I hope he's not going to ask for a loan!* Her excitement was suddenly tinged with apprehension. She prepared herself for either scenario, hoping for the best but bracing for the worst.

Terrence cleared his throat and began hesitantly. "This is about... I need you... I ran into Constable Jenkins this morning."

For a fraction of a moment, Polly's mind raced. Was Terrence about to reveal some shocking secret? Maybe he was actually Tim's rival for Grayson's attentions! She stifled a laugh at the absurd image of Terrence and Tim in a dramatic showdown, both vying for Grayson's affection with over-the-top declarations of love and maybe even a duel in the village square. The mental picture of Terrence brandishing a bouquet of roses while Tim wielded a poetry book was almost too much. She quickly composed herself, ready for whatever unexpected twist was coming.

"He showed me the composite sketches that David Durham made."

Oh, fudge! she thought. *This doesn't sound like the prelude to my tropical erotic fantasy... On the other hand, this has nothing to do with Tim, so that's a positive sign.*

"Well, I didn't tell you or anyone else about this before because I didn't think it was important. I mean, you're famous, and people are bound to be interested. When Grayson showed me the sketch, I immediately realized that it matched two people who came by the station the day before yesterday. They said they'd read the interview I did with you last month in the paper and were massive fans from America—one of them sounded American. They said they wanted to take selfies outside your house but weren't exactly sure where you lived.

They promised not to disturb you, so I told them where Thistlethorne Lodge was."

Drats! Polly's spirits plummeted. All those delightful images of strolling hand in hand on a beach with a shirtless Terrence bronzing in the sun and tiki torches flickering romantically at night instantly vanished. *The Girl from Ipanema* playing in her head came to a screeching, needle-across-a-vinyl-record halt. Despite her disappointment, she managed to keep a smile plastered on her face.

"What's the biggie?" she asked, trying to sound nonchalant. "Unless—"

"That's what I'm thinking." Terrence shrugged. "I feel dreadful that I told them *exactly* where to find you. Then they broke into Thistlethorne."

The corners of Polly's mouth turned downward, and her eyebrows knitted together. "We don't know for sure that they were the intruders," she said, dismissing Terrence's need to apologize. "It's common knowledge that I'm here in Abbots Clover. It said so in your article in the *Overview*. They could have asked anyone for my location. Glyn, the postman, knows it by heart. The Amazon delivery guy, too. There aren't many castles around here. Even if they were my burglars, it's far from your fault that they got in. Now, take my hand again and tell me you've booked a secluded seaside villa with an infinity pool in Antigua."

Terrence smiled sheepishly and bobbed his head in understanding. Polly was right, of course. A couple of fans asking where she lived was hardly any indication that he was an accessory to the crime of breaking and entering.

Polly was only annoyed that her *Fantasy Island* adventure was nothing more than that: a fantasy. But she still felt something thrilling around the vicinity of her navel. It was that fantasy of a shirtless Terrence on the beach. She absorbed his smile, which revealed a glimpse of bright, straight teeth. And those dimples! She could forgive almost anyone almost anything if they had Terrence's deep dimples. And the scent of his cologne...

Her reverie was abruptly interrupted. "Oh drats," Polly muttered from the corner of her mouth. "Madam Mysteria is here again. And she's heading our way."

Terrence looked up just as Emma Tunsing, the self-proclaimed village soothsayer, shuffled to their table. He forced a smile while bracing himself for another round of eccentric predictions and unsolicited advice. He started to say, "The *Overview* is out next Thursday. I'm sure you'll be pleased..."

But Emma took control. "I have a message for Polly Pepper, from the realm of the spirits!" she declared, cutting Terrence off and fixing Polly with an intense gaze. "Someone who has passed from this physical world has chosen me to convey a message from beyond," she continued, her eyes locking onto Polly's with an unsettling intensity.

Polly felt a shiver run down her spine as Emma's piercing stare seemed to delve into her very soul. "They said you alone will understand this," Emma intoned, taking a deep breath and squaring her shoulders. After a long, pregnant pause, she whispered in a barely audible voice, "I know things now..."

The words hung in the air, laden with a sense of foreboding. The room seemed to darken, and Polly's mind raced. She tried to grasp the meaning behind Emma's cryptic message. What could she possibly know? What secrets from the past were about to resurface? Emma's eyes never wavered, their depths suggesting knowledge of things better left forgotten.

After a beat, confused by Emma's words, Polly asked, "What do you know now?"

"Nothing. I mean, it's not me, for pity's sake. The spirit gave me that message to give to you: 'I know things now.' I'm sure it's a warning."

Terrence grimaced. "Maybe the spirit is saying they learned something important before their death."

"Like pants are optional on Zoom?" Polly deadpanned.

"I wouldn't be so flippant about the spirit world if I were you," Emma said almost belligerently. "People without bodies aren't easily amused."

"A sense of humor helps manage stress and boosts physical and mental well-being," Polly said. Then she corrected herself. "But then again, they're no longer physical, are they."

"That's all I came to say," Emma said as she turned away and left the pub.

Polly and Terrence were quiet for a long moment. Then, from the corner of her eye, Polly noticed another woman approaching the table. The woman looked vaguely familiar. "So sorry to bother you," the smiling woman said. "I'm Jane Lassen. Do you remember me? I auditioned for you a couple of weeks ago."

Must be why she looks familiar, Polly said to herself, bracing for some sort of personal criticism. "And you were amazing, my dear!" She offered an ambiguous compliment. "It's a crime that I don't make the casting decisions," she added, in case Jane was about to bop her on the nose for destroying her musical-theater-career dream.

Jane sniggered. "Mildred said the same thing. About not making the casting decisions, that is. Anyway, I wanted to say that I was sorry to hear about your friend's death. He was particularly vile about my audition: 'Your voice could make onions cry,' he told me."

Polly now fully remembered the woman and Lester's clever but mean barb.

"He deserved some sort of punishment for making fun of me in public," Jane said, "but I wouldn't wish being entombed in your castle on anyone—except maybe my ex-husband. That's all

I wanted to say. Please accept my condolences. And I hope Lester Lynch didn't suffer more than necessary."

"Didn't suffer more than necessary?" Polly quietly repeated Jane's comment and scowled.

As Jane wandered back to her table, Polly looked at Terrence. She asked the question to which she already knew the answer—did everybody in the village know the specific facts about how Lester had died? "Constable Gray wouldn't have revealed that plot point. He's too professional," she said.

The police had not yet revealed the cause of his death, nor had any of the news outlets—even in America—described the specific circumstances of his demise. This English village had its own way of broadcasting local events—almost telepathically.

24

"Nice to see you again, too, Mrs. Banks. That's a lovely beanie you're wearing," Tim lied to the miserable Mildred with his best Eddie Haskell two-faced charm as he collected his mother from the village hall. The afternoon's sing-through had been a disaster. Polly again had to mediate between merciless Mildred and another wannabe singer's sensitive ego. She was exhausted. By the time they returned to Thistlethorne, it was half past Lush Hour—way off the family's preferred schedule—and Polly wanted to put the dreary day behind her. By the time the trio was comfortably settled in for the night, their dispositions had melted away at a rate equal to the draining of their champagne flutes.

After a few long minutes of staring at the fire, listening to "Something Stupid" by Frank and Nancy Sinatra, and trying to forget Mildred Banks and her crummy show, Polly hesitantly said, "I got a message today."

"Email? WhatsApp?" Tiara said.

"Ghoul-o-Gram, I think." Polly made up a name for an end-to-end encrypted spirit world connection. "Madam Woo-Woo—Emma Tunsing. She said she was relaying a dispatch from the dispatched. She quoted someone dead saying, 'I know things now...'"

Tim made a face. "I know things now, too. Babies aren't delivered by storks, and gum doesn't stay in your stomach for seven years if you swallow it."

"Maybe it was dead Stephen Sondheim recalling his song 'I Know Things Now' from *Into the Woods*," Tiara remarked with a touch of sarcasm.

After a moment of introspection, Polly decided to bring up a topic she'd been mulling over since running into psychic Emma Tunsing. However, she knew the idea would be met with skepticism. She took a deep breath, steeling herself. "I've been thinking—for a little while. Why don't we host a—séance!"

Six eyes, including Mr. Boots', pinned Polly like butterflies in a collector's case, their mouths agape in astonishment.

"Maybe we can get some insider information on what it's really like over there. Beyond the veil," she continued. "We might reconnect with Lester and hear his awful Helen Keller jokes again. Maybe Dolores Hayes will sing," she added, appealing to Tim's fandom to support her idea.

When Tim and Tiara finally found their lost voices, they erupted in unison. "No way! Don't mess with the unknown!" Their objections tumbled over each other, a cascade of sheer panic. It was obvious that Polly was cooking up another of her Lucy Ricardo harebrained schemes, and they were desperate to distance themselves from the impending cuckooness of it all.

"What?" Polly exclaimed, not exactly surprised by the fervor of their pessimism. "We're living in England, for crying out loud! In an ancient castle!" She paused for dramatic effect, her eyes sparkling with excitement. "Think of all the history—the battles, the severed heads," she continued, waving off their concerns with a dramatic flick of her wrist.

Tim and Tiara exchanged uneasy glances, their skepticism

palpable. Polly pressed on, her enthusiasm undeterred. "This country is probably one of the best places on the planet—outside of a morgue—for a tête-à-tête with spirits from the other side. Why would we deprive ourselves of a potentially enlightening experience?"

Tim opened his mouth to protest, but Polly cut him off. "Besides, we need to get to know our castle ghost better. Who else will tell us if there are more hidden treasures around here?"

"Mother, I know how séances generally work out. I've seen *Drag Me to Hell*."

"You'll end up possessed by the spirit of Bathsheba like that poor woman in *The Conjuring*!" Tiara added.

"What's next on your to-do list, animal sacrifices? I'm out!" Tim said, giving his mother a stern look of disapproval.

"Polly, you dive under the pillow if the wind so much as whispers against your bedroom window," Tiara reminded her.

"You don't know the first thing about holding a séance," Tim said. "You could Google it, but you'll probably end up spooking the spooks! No, you're a bigger snowflake than me. And you have the emotional spine of a cotton ball!"

"The spine of a cotton ball? Surely that's a slur in this age of diversity, equity, and inclusion," Polly pushed back. "I'll ring Emma first thing in the morning and see what she thinks."

"She'll think it's great 'cause she'll make money off you," Tiara said.

"She's a pro! She's been doing this for years. We'll relax and let her bring back the dead," Polly said.

"How'd that work out for Dr. Frankenstein?" Tim said as he crossed his arms in defiance. "I don't like messing with things we don't understand or have no control over."

The flicker of the living room lamp cast shadows that seemed to echo Tim's unease. But Polly was undeterred. Her eyes sparkled with a mix of mischief and excitement. "Where's your sense of adventure?" she teased, playfully nudging Tim in the ribs. "Emma can guide us step by step. What could go wrong?"

"Apart from demon possession and opening a portal directly to Hell?" Tim looked at his mother, his gaze softened slightly, but his stance remained firm. "It's not about adventure. It's about stirring up things that are better left unstirred. We don't know anything about the spirit world—except what Neil Gaiman and Stephen King tell us."

Polly scoffed. "Emma's probably done this a million times. She knows what she's doing. It's a way to preview the Great Beyond and see if there's anything interesting over there. Maybe we'll get some ghostly gossip or find out where the lost silverware went!" She paused, her gaze intense and probing. "Don't you ever wonder if there's more after this life? Aren't you the least bit curious about the mysteries of the universe?" She took Tim's hand. "It's for an hour. If it gets too weird, we can always say we've got another appointment and scram."

Tim sighed, knowing that arguing with Polly when she had her mind set on something was like trying to hold back a hurricane with an umbrella. "At the first sign of anything strange, we're out of there," he conceded, still uneasy but swayed by Polly's enthusiasm—and her calling him a "snowflake."

Polly beamed. "Deal. And just think, if we run into a demon, we'll have a great story for the next dinner party!"

Tiara bit her lip, torn between curiosity and caution. "I don't know, Polly. It seems... weird," she admitted, her voice uncertain.

Polly grinned, undeterred by their hesitation. "Trust me, Tiara. It'll be a night to remember!"

"So was the night my neighbor was hit by a train."

Demon possession. Portals to hell. Tim's flippant reply to Polly's rhetorical question about séances gone wrong echoed in her ear. She braced herself and eventually summoned the nerve to call Emma Tunsing.

Polly probably shouldn't have been surprised that psychic Emma was expecting her call. "What did you expect?" Emma said, her tone dripping with imperious pride. "My spirit guide told me you'd be in touch." Emma seemed almost giddy at the thought that Polly might attract glamorous Hollywood spirits like Grace Kelly, Ingrid Bergman, or Greta Garbo.

However, Emma insisted Polly come to *her* domain: Daisy Dell Cottage. "We must protect your castle from disruptive energies," she explained dramatically. "Spiritual sessions can attract entities that may not leave willingly. Holding the séance here prevents these entities from invading your personal space."

"A sort of spirit quarantine zone?"

"You must come tonight. Midnight. When the veil between the physical and the spirit world is thinnest, making communication with the other side more accessible."

Polly asked if there was anything she should bring—objects associated with Lester Lynch, like his red pens or an item of clothing containing his scent, to help establish a connection.

"Bring an open mind. The spirits will take care of the rest."

A short while later, Polly sat at the kitchen table, explaining to Tiara that she'd scheduled the séance. "She insisted we go to her place. 'To protect Thistlethorne from disruptive energies,' she said."

Tiara rolled her eyes so hard it was a wonder they didn't get stuck. "Of course she did. Polly, don't you see? Emma's playing the part perfectly. She's a fake medium and a charlatan."

Polly frowned.

Tiara leaned forward, her tone firm. "Emma knew you would call because she planted the idea at the pub. She set the stage with all that talk about her spirit guide. And now she's got you going to her place. At midnight, no less! It's all part of her act."

"What if there really are entities that could invade our personal space?" Polly argued.

"Entities? Please," Tiara snorted. "The only entities Emma's worried about are her unpaid bills and your gullibility. She's probably setting up her spooky sound effects as we speak."

Polly chuckled despite herself. "Maybe she's a bit theatrical. But what if she's the real deal?"

Tiara shook her head, smirking. "Sure, Polly, spirits have nothing better to do in the afterlife than chat with Emma Tunsing. Out of all the billions of people on the planet. Face it, she's just another performer, and you're about to be her starstruck audience. By insisting on holding the séance at her place, she's controlling the environment. She can do all sorts of things in advance to make it seem like she's communicating with spirits. It'll all be smoke and mirrors."

Polly looked down at her hands, uncertainty clouding her eyes. "But she said the veil between the physical and spirit worlds is thinnest at midnight. That it makes communication easier."

Tiara couldn't help but chuckle. "Oh, come on. Midnight? The witching-hour cliché? It's designed to add drama and mystery. Emma's using every trick in the book to make you believe she's authentic."

Polly looked up, a hint of defiance in her eyes. "What if she really can communicate with the other side? Shirley MacLaine talked to the dead! Or was it aliens?"

Tiara reached out, taking Polly's hands in hers. "Polly, I know you want to believe. But you have to protect yourself from being taken advantage of. These so-called mediums prey on people's grief and hope. They use theatrics and psychological manipulation to make you think they have some special connection to the afterlife."

Polly took a deep breath, her resolve wavering. "I just... I want answers, Tiara. I need to know why Lester died. And I need to know why dead bodies keep popping up on our doorstep."

"I get that. But be cautious. If Emma's real, she won't need all these elaborate setups to prove it. Don't let her exploit your vulnerability."

25

As the clock struck 11:30—long past the family's usual bedtime—the wind outside Thistlethorne was like an eerie harbinger. And the journey to Daisy Dell Cottage was filled with trepidation. As Tim drove Polly and Tiara through the narrow, twisting lanes of the village to the outskirts where Emma's secluded cottage awaited, they were nearly silent the entire way.

The cottage itself was an enchanting sight by day—a quaint, three-bedroom thatch-roofed charmer nestled gently in the verdant embrace of the countryside near the tranquil waters of Duck Lake. During her previous daytime excursions around Abbots Clover, Polly had admired the cottage for its picturesque pastoral beauty. She'd described it as "darling," a hidden jewel amongst the rolling landscape.

However, under the cloak of night, the cottage's charm transformed into something more mysterious—even foreboding. As they parked their car and stepped out, the only light came from the full moon, casting long shadows from the tree branches. The shadows danced across the ground like dark wraiths in a silent ballet. The air was thick with the scent of earlier rain, mingling with the wild, earthy aroma of the surrounding woods and sheep pastures.

Approaching the front door, the group could not shake off the chilly breeze that seemed to whisper warnings. When Polly knocked, she discovered the old wooden door was ajar. She pushed against the portal while simultaneously calling Emma's name. The door groaned on rusted hinges, its creak a slow, drawn-out screech that seemed to echo into the depths of the house. Inside, the atmosphere shifted palpably; the quaintness of the outside gave way to a jumbled mess.

The trio grimaced at each other, transmitting the same thought, *Emma's a hoarder!*

The nooks and crannies shadowed ominously under the dim candlelight that flickered sporadically, casting peculiar patterns on the walls. The faint smell of incense hung in the air, its smoky tendrils intertwining, suggesting the many evenings Emma had spent here in communion with the dead. As they moved deeper into the main room, the floorboards creaked under their feet, and the windows rattled sporadically, as if the cottage was reacting to their presence.

This was a different Daisy Dell than expected. Every surface was cluttered with a curious assortment of objects: skulls of small animals, ancient books piled in corners, and countless jars filled with herbs, each labeled with fading script: **Mugwort. Yarrow. Lavender. Sage.** The walls were decorated with celestial maps and arcane symbols. A small altar was set up in a corner with an array of talismans, pentacles, and bowls of dried calendula flowers and incense ashes. There were also framed photographs showing blurred figures that were perhaps meant to be proof of spirit manifestations captured during past séances.

Amidst this disarray, a large, round table with a velvet cloth and six mismatched chairs dominated the room. A large quartz crystal ball on a wooden stand carved with mystical symbols was placed where Emma would probably sit. At the table's center was a Ouija board displaying the alphabet in two arcs above a line of the numbers 0 through 9. The words "Yes" and "No" were in large letters on the upper corners of the board, and the word "Goodbye" was found along the bottom of the board. A heart-shaped planchette, the tool through which spirits communicate by pointing to specific characters or areas of the board, sat in the center.

Emma Tunsing came from behind a beaded curtain, smiled enigmatically at her guests, and welcomed them to her home. She was a small, wiry woman with piercing black eyes. She hadn't intimidated Polly when they'd met in the fullness of daylight at the Fox & Hare. But now, on her home turf, Emma exuded an unnerving magnetism. "The others will be here shortly," she said, explaining that she had invited two "believers" to join them. "They know not to be frightened."

Polly, Tim, and Tiara exchanged looks of apprehension.

Soon, Emma welcomed Reginald Hawthorn—who looked almost ready to join the spirits on the other side himself—and Charlotte Blackwell, a woman Polly recognized from the first *Cats on a Hot Tin Roof* auditions. She also remembered that Charlotte's voice was not unlike the rusted hinges on Daisy Dell's front door.

"Please be seated and join hands," Emma instructed, her voice steady and steely. "I will soon enter a deep trance. This will allow me to be open to receiving visions or messages," she explained. "As I gaze into my crystal, I look for symbols or images. I will communicate with the spirits and gain their insights about the past, present, or future. It is important to remember that these spirits were once people and should be treated with respect. Let no fear cloud your heart."

As the assembled sat and linked hands, Emma began to chant in a rhythmic, hypnotic tone. The air seemed to grow thicker, and the atmosphere was heavy with anticipation. Polly felt a chill run down her spine as the temperature in the room dropped. The candles flickered aggressively as if in protest.

"Is there anybody here who wishes to communicate with Polly Pepper?" Emma asked, her voice cutting through the silence.

Tiara squeezed Polly's hand. Tim's eyes darted around the room, their skepticism battling the eerie reality unfolding before them. Charlotte Blackwell whispered something that sounded like a prayer, while Reginald Hawthorn's eyes were fixed on the medium.

"Who is with us tonight?" Emma's voice was a whisper, almost drowned out by the wind outside, which had begun to howl.

Then the table moved slightly as if someone had bumped into it. A cold gust of wind swept through the room, extinguishing the candles. A faint whisper could be heard in the sudden darkness: "I should not have died…"

The table began to tremble, its center pedestal rising slightly. The room grew colder, making everyone's breath visible even in the darkness. Then, without warning, a flash of lightning—on an otherwise clear night—momentarily illuminated the room. Again, a faint whisper snaked through the darkness, a hollow and familiar voice to Polly. "I should not have died…" it moaned, the words repeating and overlapping as if spoken by someone trapped between worlds. The air felt thick with the presence of something unseen, anguished, and desperate.

Emma's quivering voice again asked, "Who is with us tonight? Reveal your identity." The table tilted again as if it had a life of its own. It moved jerkily as if resisting the force that compelled it.

A low laugh, almost inaudible, emanated from a corner of the room, sending a shiver down everyone's spine. "Retribution..." The whisper returned, colder and more urgent. "Retribution..." it breathed again, the word left hanging in the air.

"Who requires retribution?" Emma asked, her voice strong but tinged with fear. "Tell us what you wish us to know."

The darkness seemed to press in closer, the chilling presence in the room growing more intense. The voice said, "Polly Pepper must know. She is next..."

Polly swallowed hard. *Next for what? An Oscar? A Tony? Gum disease?* she wondered. The eerie atmosphere overwhelmed her senses. She glanced around, trying to make out the faces of Tim and Tiara in the dark, seeking reassurance but finding none.

Suddenly, the faint glow of the candles reignited by themselves, casting long, sinister shadows against the walls. The light revealed Emma Tunsing, her face frozen and her eyes unseeing.

"Who are you?" Emma asked again, her voice barely audible. The wind outside rose, this time howling with such force that it rattled the windows and shook the cottage to its core. From the shadows near the fireplace, a figure started to materialize. At first, it was nothing more than a misty silver outline. But slowly, it became more defined like Captain Kirk and Spock in the starship *Enterprise*'s transporter beam. When all the particles coalesced, it revealed an image that somewhat resembled Lester Lynch—but his features were twisted in anger. His eyes, hollow and dark, locked onto Polly.

"I am the spirit of Lester the Dresser... They were mean... Polly Pepper is next..." Like a radio signal breaking up, his next words were unintelligible. But everyone clearly heard, "Polly Pepper is next."

Emma, her usual commanding presence somewhat shaky, asked, "Tell us what Polly Pepper needs to do."

The apparition began to groan. "Silent shadows at

midnight," it said weakly and cryptically. "Silent shadows at midnight... is her answer—and her fate." As the form faded back into nothingness, Polly and the others heard the final faint and perplexing words: "Remember... silent shadows at midnight..." The wind outside died down, and the image evaporated. A heavy silence settled back over the room.

The group exchanged nervous glances as they released their collectively held breaths and disengaged their hands. Slowly emerging from her trance, Emma looked dazed. She glanced around, confused, as if trying to remember a quickly fading dream. "Were we successful?" she asked.

The drive home to Thistlethorne was made in complete silence. Polly sat in the front passenger seat, staring blankly ahead as the car's headlight beams sliced through the night, revealing the narrow lanes and the hedgerows on either side. Beside her, Tim gripped the steering wheel, glancing occasionally at Polly with concern and curiosity but respecting the unspoken need for silence. In the backseat, Tiara sat with her arms crossed, her cynical expression not hard to read.

When they finally arrived home and settled into the reception room, Tiara broke the silence. "What a crock!" she said, setting Mr. Boots aside on the Chesterfield, her voice tinged with indignation.

Polly turned to her friend, her eyes reflecting a blend of confusion and vulnerability. "I don't know," she admitted, her voice barely above a whisper. "I've spent my whole life saying that I don't know anything about anything but that anything was still possible. And now..."

"And now what?" Tiara sighed, shaking her head slightly. "You don't seriously believe we actually spoke to Lester's spirit, do you? It was all clever tricks and emotional manipulation. And it cost you five hundred pounds. Cash!"

Tim reached out, placing a comforting hand on Polly's arm. "It's okay to be confused. What happened tonight was—pretty extraordinary."

Polly stared into space. "I know we saw Lester. We heard his voice. It was real."

"Maybe Emma somehow recorded Lester's voice and used a hologram," Tiara countered, her tone dismissive. "We heard words and a voice that sounded like Lester's. But we didn't have a conversation with him. There are plenty of ways to manipulate voices and images these days, especially with AI technology."

Polly clenched her hands in her lap, trying to reconcile this night's experience. "It wasn't just the image and voice, Tiara. It was—the feeling. I felt his presence. It was like he really was there with us. He said things like, 'They were mean to me.' That has Lester written all over it! He was always complaining that he'd been unfairly treated by others. And what about identifying himself as Lester the Dresser? That's a nickname! Emma couldn't have known that!"

Tiara leaned forward, her expression softening slightly but still skeptical. "I'm stumped about that. But feelings can be powerful, Polly. They can cloud your judgment. You're a rational person. Think about how easy it is to be convinced when you're emotional and vulnerable."

Polly's gaze remained fixed, her mind replaying the séance over and over. "I've considered that, believe me. But each theory I come up with doesn't hold. The way he spoke, the things he said. It was beyond what I can rationalize away."

Tim nodded in agreement. "I felt it too, Tiara. I don't know how to explain it, but it felt genuine."

Tiara sighed, leaning back in her seat. "I don't want you to get swept up in something that isn't real. Grief can make us see and hear things we desperately want."

They sat there a moment longer, the silence filled with unspoken understanding and lingering doubt. Eventually, Polly took a deep breath and stood up. "I need time to process all of this. We'll talk about it in the morning."

26

Jerry Corley called. His vacation was ending. He wanted to collect his umbrella and say goodbye. An hour later, in the car park outside Thistlethorne's curtain wall, Polly and her brood were fussing over him like a flock of worried hens.

Polly fluttered around Jerry, adjusting his scarf and ensuring he had everything he needed for the journey. "Got your passport? What about snacks for the road?"

Tiara double-checked the backseat, ensuring he had his luggage. "Make sure to take breaks along the way and stay hydrated."

Even Elara was there, offering a thermos of hot tea for the road.

Looking slightly overwhelmed by the attention, Jerry laughed and reassured them all. "I've got everything, really. You've all been so wonderful. I'll miss this place—and all of you. Mom would have loved it here. But one last thing. You were kind enough to give me a tour of the house the other night. I wonder if you'd think I was being too nosey if I asked to see the ruins. I'll probably never know anyone else with their very own castle."

For the next hour, Tim reveled in his impromptu role as a museum docent, showcasing the Thistlethorne grounds with the pride and passion of a seasoned historian. Jerry eagerly oohed and aahed, his smartphone snapping pictures at every turn. Tim had learned the proper names for the different parts of a Norman castle: curtain wall, bailey, keep, tower, dovecote, arrow slits. With unrestrained enthusiasm, he guided Jerry through each area, his explanations animated and thorough.

"And here's the old stable," Tim announced grandly, sweeping his arm towards the dilapidated structure. "Beyond that is the chapel." He pointed to the ivy-covered stone walls. "Both are obviously in ruins now, but if you use your imagination, you can almost see how amazing they must have been a thousand years ago."

Jerry leaned in, his eyes wide with fascination. "A thousand years," he repeated, unable to comprehend that long a period. "Who can fathom that amount of time gone by?"

"Aside from the history of the Native Americans in the US, all you've got there is four hundred years of post-colonialism wretchedness," Tim added. "You know, stealing lands and eradicating indigenous cultures. Like that."

"The craftsmanship is incredible," Jerry said, admiring the ancient remains. "You can almost hear the sound of horses' hooves and the solemn chants from the chapel," he mused, snapping a close-up picture of a particularly ornate stone carving.

Tim grinned, pleased with Jerry's enthusiasm. "Exactly! This dovecote housed hundreds of pigeons, a vital food source in medieval times. And these arrow slits in the tower walls—they were ingeniously designed to defend against invaders while giving the archers a perfect vantage point to shoot from."

Tim's voice became more dramatic as they moved along the bailey. "And here, you can see the remains of the great hall, the heart of the castle. Imagine feasts, knights in shining armor, the manor lord presiding over it all."

Jerry's excitement was palpable. "This is like stepping back in time!" he exclaimed, capturing a panoramic shot of the majestic ruins.

"What's the most amazing thing you've discovered here since moving in?" Jerry asked, an excited glint in his eyes. "Other than the priest hole in the library."

Tim hesitated, a mischievous smile playing on his lips. "Well," he began, lowering his voice conspiratorially, "there's a passageway that leads to the dungeon."

"You have your very own dungeon?" Jerry's eyes sparkled with intrigue. "Can we see it? Please?" His enthusiasm was like that of a young boy discovering the entrance to a mysterious cave.

Tim paused, glancing around to ensure no one else was listening. He cocked his head and leaned closer to Jerry. "Follow me," he whispered.

With a shared sense of adventure, Tim led Jerry back to the larder. He pushed aside the tall Welsh dresser concealing an ancient door, revealing a narrow, winding staircase descending into darkness. "Watch your step," Tim warned, his voice echoing slightly in the confined space as they both turned on the flashlight feature on their phones.

As they descended, the air grew cooler and damp, and the stone walls seemed to close around them. They stopped at another heavy, ancient-looking door. Tim pulled it open, the metal creaking on ancient hinges. The air grew even colder and mustier as they ventured deeper. Finally, they reached the bottom. "Welcome to the dungeon," Tim said.

The room was vast, with cold, rough stone walls enclosing the space. Two flat-iron cells loomed ominously in the corners, and rusty iron manacles hung menacingly from the walls, a reminder of the cell's purpose. Old wooden beams, weathered and splintering, supported the low ceiling, and the uneven floor was strewn with straw that crunched softly underfoot. The dim light from their phone flashlights cast long, flickering shadows, making the space feel both mysterious and forbidding. A faint, stale odor of decay lingered in the air, mingling with the earthy scent of damp stone.

Jerry's eyes widened in awe. "This is incredible!" he exclaimed, his voice echoing in the cavernous space.

Tim grinned. "We haven't explored all of it yet. There are still nooks and crannies we've yet to uncover. We found an old chest over there"—he pointed to a dark corner— "but it was empty."

"Who knows what else might be hidden down here," Jerry said as he wandered around, examining this isolated place of punishment. "We had a wine cellar in one of Mom's houses, but this takes the cake," he added, his voice filled with wonder.

Tim chuckled. "It's one of Thistlethorne's many secrets. And who knows, maybe one day we'll find something extraordinary down here."

After exploring the dungeon, they made their way back to the house. Jerry seemed genuinely sorry to be saying goodbye and leaving Abbots Clover. "I've had my fun. Now I have to return to an eternity of Dolores Hayes." He sighed, a sad, wistful tone coloring his words. The name "Dolores Hayes" seemed to carry the weight of unfulfilled dreams and mundane routines.

Under a light drizzle they all exchanged hugs and promised to keep in touch. As Jerry was about to climb into his car, he realized he'd almost forgotten the very reason for his return: his umbrella.

"Hold on!" Tim said and sprinted back into the house, returning moments later with the umbrella canopy open to shield himself from the rain. He handed it to Jerry with a flourish, the fabric rippling in the breeze.

"We've all admired this umbrella," Polly said, examining the RCA Records logo on what was probably once a promotional giveaway item. The umbrella had an air of bygone elegance, its brass handle worn smooth from years of use. "Antique?"

Jerry smiled, twirling the umbrella with a practiced hand. "More sentimental value than anything else," he said as he placed the umbrella on the passenger seat of his rented car. A few moments later, his vehicle disappeared down the narrow lane, and the trio dashed back into the house.

"I feel sort of sorry for the guy," Polly said wistfully as the trio gathered in the kitchen and Tiara poured mugs of tea. "He's pretty much forced to live in the past, what with all the work he does for the foundation. His mother's voice and image are a constant presence. I suspect most regular non-showbiz people can move through their grief faster because they don't see and hear their loved ones singing and dancing or whatever they did in life. But a celebrity is different. They're on-screen or on records forever."

"It's probably a double-edged sword," Tim agreed. "Jerry's proud of his mother's legacy but seeing her all the time has to bring back the reality of her absence."

"If you ask me, I think the guy needs a shrink," Tiara added. "He's going cuckoo! Jerry's intense adoration of his mother doesn't seem healthy. I know he wants to protect her legacy, but his entire identity seems wrapped up in Dolores the Legend Hayes, like a bonkers fan. He even said he didn't want any other relationship. Not even one of his mother's dogs. That's weird, if you ask me."

Polly's phone vibrated, and she looked down at her phone screen. "I've missed a call," she said, shaking her head and changing the topic. She looked at the time stamp and the clock on the wall. "Must have come in while we were saying goodbye outside." Then, looking closely at the number, a chill went down her spine. "Oh, fudge. It's Audrey's number." The trio exchanged nervous glances. She tapped the Voicemail tab, then touched the speaker option on her screen.

"Polly Pepper, you're a big disappointment. You've made our job more difficult than it was supposed to be. We sent Lester Lynch's phone to you in exchange for his notebooks. A fair trade. But you didn't play along. Fun and games are over. I hope you know what you've done and can accept the consequences."

Polly, Tim, and Tiara exchanged uneasy glances, the weight of Audrey's threat enveloping them. Polly's heart pounded in her chest. The air seemed to thicken with a mix of fear and tension. "You know how much I hate bullies and people who think they can push me around. I've said it before: they're not getting Lester's notebooks! No way! I don't care how offended they are by what he's written."

Tim's jaw clenched, his eyes darting towards the shadowy corners of the room as if expecting danger to emerge from the darkness. "What do you think they'll do?" he muttered, his voice barely above a whisper.

Tiara, usually composed and unflappable, looked shaken. Her hands trembled as she pointed to Tim's phone. "Call Grayson. We're in deep doo-doo."

Polly, Tim, and Tiara perched uneasily on the edge of the worn Chesterfield sofa; their eyes fixed on Constable Grayson Jenkins. His usually calm demeanor was marred by a deep frown as he replayed the message for what felt like the hundredth time. Each repetition seemed to darken his expression further, the gravity of the situation sinking in with every chilling word.

The voice on the other end of the line was dripping with

malice: "You've disappointed us...Fun and games are over... It didn't have to turn out this way."

The message ended, leaving a heavy, oppressive silence in the air. The room seemed to grow colder. Polly felt her heart pounding in her chest, each beat echoing in the silence.

Grayson cleared his throat. "I need to get as much information as possible. First of all, are you sure this is the same voice that called before?"

Polly nodded, her voice barely above a whisper. "She said her name was Audrey. It's the same phone number, too."

Grayson scribbled in his worn notebook, the pen scratching against the paper relentlessly. "We're a small village, Polly. We don't have a tech team that can analyze recordings. The guys in Bristol might be able to trace it, but they'd need a court order. That could take time. And I'll have to take your phone."

Tim's face grew pale. "What can we do in the meantime? We can't sit here waiting for someone to knock on the door and say, 'Bang-bang, you're dead.'"

Grayson looked thoughtful, tapping his pen against his notebook. "First, I'll speak with the local magistrate to see if we can expedite that court order. In the meantime, we need to make sure you're safe."

He scanned the cozy but ancient reception room, taking in the antique furniture and the old family portraits lining the walls. "Do you have any place you can stay, somewhere out of the way?"

Polly shook her head in defiance. "Nope! And I'm not leaving my home. This castle was built to ward off armies. Our castle may not be under siege like in a scene from *Braveheart*, but surely, we'll be safe from a couple of lunatic marauders masquerading as tourists."

Grayson gave a nod, his voice steady and reassuring. "Alright, we'll make do here. We might be a small village, but we look out for one another. I'll ask that everyone keep an eye out for anything suspicious."

Her normally composed demeanor faltered, and Tiara asked, "What about us? What should we do?"

Grayson met her gaze with a firm look. "Stay vigilant. Keep all the doors and windows locked. Don't go anywhere alone; if you see or hear anything out of the ordinary, call me immediately." He offered what he hoped was a reassuring smile. "We'll get through this. And we'll catch whoever's behind these threats. I promise. In the meantime, you're not alone. The whole village will be looking out for you."

Polly watched him leave the house and felt hopeful. "I remember one night when I was a little girl, and a big storm raged outside," she said wistfully. "There was nothing my daddy could do about it, but for some reason, I felt completely protected because he was in the house with us." She looked at Tim with a sly smile. "Now's the time you and Gray should have a sleepover. But honestly, you'd probably be too busy making your own spooky noises to hear any others."

Tim put a comforting arm around her. "We'll figure this out, Mom. We'll be alright."

Polly nodded, trying to draw strength from his words. They were all in this together, and somehow, they would find a way to weather the storm closing in on them.

And then another storm arrived. With the bell clang at the front gate, Polly knew it was Hurricane Mildred.

27

Rehearsal was over, and Polly stood in the doorway of the village hall, the rain pouring down in relentless sheets, drumming on the pavement with a steady rhythm. She glanced at her watch for the umpteenth time, her impatience growing with each passing second. *Where is Tim? It's well past "save me from Mildred" time. Has he forgotten?*

Without her phone, which Grayson had taken as part of the investigation, she felt stranded in pre-digital-era limbo. She couldn't call or text to confirm Tim's five-thirty rendezvous or distract herself with emails, Facebook, or even a quick game of Wordle. All she could do was wait and watch the world go by, a once-favorite pastime she hadn't indulged in since childhood.

This is like the days before screens and internet distractions, she mused, a wry smile tugging at her lips. Back then, people-watching had been her best-loved game. She would invent elaborate stories about the strangers who passed by, imagining their lives, secrets, and adventures. She grinned now as she recalled the lady in the big purple hat with a peacock plume sticking up like an antenna. The woman always sat on the same park bench at the same time each day. She was a secret agent on a mission to infiltrate the government and wreak international havoc. The feather—which wasn't really a feather, of course—sent and received electronic communication signals.

Then there was the man with the rainbow socks who walked his three-legged dog around the block every day at the same time. Polly had decided the dog's name was Pincus—she'd heard the name somewhere and thought it was hilarious. They were retired from the circus. The man used to train the animals, and Pincus had been the star attraction because, despite his infirmity, he could do all sorts of flips and amazing tricks. But they'd had to run away from the circus because one of the clowns planned to kidnap Pincus and sell him to a rival circus.

Polly smiled at another memory: an older couple always wearing matching sweaters. They weren't just any couple. They used to be pop music stars—like Sonny and Cher. In the 1960s, they toured the world with their folk music band, the Sweater Swingers, and recorded #1 hit songs. They'd vowed to always match their sweaters as a symbol of their love and their wild, rock 'n' roll past.

It was now nearly dark as Polly waited under the protective awning of the village hall. Only a few people were out on this cold and wet late afternoon. The shops had closed, and the streetlamps were on. Polly noticed a lady walking briskly through the downpour wearing a red raincoat. *She's a time traveler from the future, here to observe how people dealt with weather before global warming turned the planet into a desert. Her red raincoat is a high-tech instrument that keeps her dry and invisible to other travelers who want to stop her research.* Polly grinned at her imagined scenario.

Polly watched her disappear into the misty distance, and a shiver ran through her as a slight wind picked up. *I'm freezing! Where the hell is Tim? The little bugger.* But as she was about to turn away, she was caught off guard by a flash of something in the distance. Something familiar. A distinctive umbrella—with the RCA Records logo of a gramophone and a dog. *Is that Jerry?* she said to herself. But as quickly as the umbrella appeared, the figure holding it vanished between the Fox & Hare and the Tasty Tart bakery. Polly squinted through the drizzle.

No. Of course it couldn't have been Jerry or his umbrella. He was a hundred miles away in London—probably boarding his plane at Heathrow this very minute. But Jerry's umbrella was unique. Or was it? Polly had earlier decided it was probably an old promotional item from Dolores Hayes' record label. Maybe there were still a few around. But in Abbots Clover, England? Sure, there were charity shops in the village and even the Dusty Attic antique shop, where anyone could have picked up an old umbrella. But what were the odds?

Polly tried to convince herself of various logical explanations. She glanced back at the now-empty corner, but the honk of Tim's car horn snapped her back to reality. Shaking off her unease, she focused on staying as dry as possible as she dashed to the car.

Upon their arrival at Thistlethorne, Tim immediately set about his new security duties. He closed the heavy iron latch on the main gate, the clang of metal against metal echoing in the damp evening air. He tugged on the gate to ensure it was firmly closed, nodding in satisfaction when it didn't budge.

Next, at the house's entryway door, he checked the sturdy oak door, examining its thick bolts. Satisfied with the initial inspection, he slid the heavy iron bolt into place with a resounding thud. He repeated the action with the bolt at the base of the door, ensuring that it, too, was securely fastened.

Turning to Polly, who watched with appreciation, Tim gave a

small, reassuring smile. "Unlike some people, I follow Grayson's orders," he said, his tone light but resolute. "I even got Elara to fix the larder door."

Polly nodded, feeling a sense of relief wash over her. The day's unsettling events had left them all on edge, and Tim's careful attention to security provided much-needed comfort. As he made a final check of the door, giving it a firm push to confirm it was securely bolted, Polly couldn't help but admire his dedication.

With the house now secure, Tim brushed the rainwater from his jacket and hung it on the hall tree. "All set. I'll check the rest of the windows and doors when I'm warmed up."

As they stepped into the main reception room, the day's tension began to ease, replaced by a sense of security and comfort. Polly kicked off her shoes and settled onto the Chesterfield settee with a contented moan. She put her feet on a hassock, and Mr. Boots promptly claimed her lap as his comfy cushion. Polly claimed a flute of champagne from Tiara. "Heaven!" She sighed, taking a long sip. "And let's not discuss the horrors of this day," she said, drawing a line in the sand of appropriate cocktail conversation. "No details of threatening phone calls or the horrendous rehearsal—where only three of the twelve cast members bothered to show up, and Mildred had a meltdown because Sissy Kushner had been practicing the wrong song. And the costumes probably won't be ready for the show—and the lighting guy has trichinosis!"

As Polly sipped her drink and began to de-stress, she sighed again, trying to find a silver lining in having her phone taken away. "At least I don't have to live in fear of receiving a call from that tedious Audrey person! She hasn't called the landline, has she?"

Tim and Tiara exchanged glances and shook their heads.

"Nope, no calls from Audrey, and nothing else out of the ordinary around here," Tim replied, his tone reassuring.

Feeling more at ease, Polly chuckled softly. "Good. The last thing we need is another crisis." After hesitating, she added, "I did see something odd. Other than Mildred."

Tim raised an eyebrow.

Polly leaned back, her expression thoughtful. "Remember Jerry Corley's umbrella? You know, the one with the logo from his mother's record label?"

"It's pretty distinctive," Tim said. "Very retro."

"While I waited oh-so-patiently for my beloved and always thoughtful and considerate son this evening—you know my favorite thing in the world is twiddling my frozen thumbs in the pouring rain, waiting for a ride like a common hooker—I was shivering and miserable and saw someone with the same umbrella."

Tim ignored his mother's sarcasm. "It obviously couldn't have been Jerry's own umbrella. Someone else must have one just like it. RCA probably gave out hundreds over the years."

"Hmm," Polly said. "I'd never seen another. But Sarah said she saw one."

"Mystery solved," Tiara replied. "Someone in the village has a similar antique umbrella."

"Maybe. Sarah thought it might have belonged to one of those nosy tourists. She said they came into Bound to Read, talking or arguing with a man across the street who had the same umbrella. She was very specific: 'A cute dog sitting next to an antique gramophone, his head tilted to the side' is how she described it."

"Nipper," Tiara said, grinning. "Not Sarah. You know, the dog on the RCA Records logo. That's his name. Don't ask me how I know that—it was probably a *Jeopardy!* answer. Maybe the umbrella came from the Dusty Attic."

The trio agreed that a charity or antique shop was the most logical explanation for someone else having an umbrella that looked exactly like the one owned by Jerry Corley. But before they could consider any other possibilities about the umbrella, Mr. Boots suddenly raised his head, his ears swiveling sharply, as they did when he heard a mouse scurrying across the floorboards. The atmosphere in the room shifted instantly, and a chill ran down their spines. They followed Mr. Boots' lead and froze, straining to listen.

A subtle sound echoed through the room—like a table barely nudged. Their eyes darted around the dimly lit room, shadows dancing ominously along the walls.

In the oppressive silence that followed, the sound seemed almost like a figment of their imaginations. Hearts pounding, they exchanged nervous glances, each one silently questioning the reality of what they had heard. They decided it was probably nothing.

But Mr. Boots wasn't buying that. With a sudden, eerie grace, he leaped from Polly's lap. Everyone's eyes followed him as he prowled, muscles taut, towards the closed double pocket door separating the reception room from the dining room. He let out a low, plaintive meow and began pacing in front of the door, his body tense and his tail flicking back and forth.

Polly's heart pounded as she exchanged a worried glance with Tim and Tiara. The room seemed to grow colder, the shadows deepening around them. The once comforting glow of the fireplace now cast ominous silhouettes on the walls.

Mr. Boots stopped pacing and stared intently at the narrow center gap between the two sides of the door, his ears pinned back and his fur bristling. The tension was palpable, each second stretching out into an eternity. Polly could hear her own heartbeat in the silence.

Then a faint, almost imperceptible sound emanated from

the other side of the door—a soft creak, like the floorboards groaning under the weight of an unseen presence. Polly's breath caught in her throat, her eyes wide with fear. Tim reached for the nearest heavy object: his knuckles white as he tightly gripped an iron fireplace poker. Tiara moved closer to Polly, her hand trembling as she grasped her friend's arm.

Mr. Boots' low growl sent shivers down their spines. The cat stared through the space between the doors as if he could see what lay hidden in the darkness. At that moment, the walls of the reception room felt like a fragile barrier, barely holding back whatever terror lurked on the other side.

Another dull thud issued from the other side of the door. "Who's there?" Tim called out, his voice steady but his face pale.

"This is exactly why I hate being in this big old house at night," Tiara said, her voice quivering with fear and frustration. "We need armed security or ghost hunters to smudge the place clean of spirits. It's probably nothing more than the wind blowing down a chimney or that blasted door in the larder opening again, but it sets me on edge."

"Seriously, if a ghost pops out, I'm going to need a defibrillator and a stiff drink," Polly agreed.

Another ominous creak echoed through the room, causing Polly's eyes to dart nervously as she tried to find a logical explanation. Again, a dull thud came from behind the door, snapping everyone's attention back to the immediate threat. Tiara groaned, "Well, if it's not the wind... and it's not a ghost..."

"You saw me lock all the doors," Tim said, dividing his attention between Polly and the pocket doors.

"All the doors?" Polly said.

Tim's heart was pounding as he realized he hadn't checked the larder door—which opened to the outside—nor had he checked the windows upstairs.

Mr. Boots had not relaxed. His ears were flattened against his head, and his eyes were fixed on the closed pocket door. Polly, Tim, and Tiara exchanged uneasy glances, an unshakable sense of vulnerability gnawing at them.

Suddenly, a faint creak resonated from the hallway just beyond the reception room door behind them. Polly's breath hitched. Tim tightened his grip on the fireplace poker.

"It sounded like it came from the direction of the library," Tiara said, her eyes drawn to the reception room door.

Polly took a deep breath, trying to steady her racing heart. "It's probably the wind, like Tiara said." But deep down, she didn't believe that. The wind couldn't explain the persistent feeling of being watched, the unsettling sensation that someone —or something—was inside the house with them.

Mr. Boots meowed again as he focused on the pocket door.

Polly couldn't shake the feeling that she sensed a presence they couldn't see.

"I'm calling Gray," Tim whispered, his voice taut with urgency as he picked up his phone. But before he could tap his Contacts, the sliding pocket doors to the dining room flew open at breakneck speed, slamming into their compartments inside the walls with a deafening crash. Polly and her clan stood frozen in shock, face-to-face with...

28

Judging by the dark jacket and balaclava obscuring their face, as described by Elara, this was the same intruder who'd broken into Thistlethorne the other day. "Don't move, or you're dead!" The voice was male, thuggish, and with an unmistakably American accent—maybe New York? His words sliced through the air. Polly's heart leaped, and she could feel Tiara stiffen beside her.

His gloved hand gripped a sleek, black handgun, its barrel gleaming ominously in the chandelier's light. "Your phones. Over there," the voice demanded, pointing to a wing chair near the piano.

Tim hesitated. His finger poised over Grayson Jenkins' cell phone number. Polly, her mind racing, gently nudged his arm, urging him to comply with the intruder's demands. Reluctantly, he tossed his lifeline. Polly and Tiara followed suit, their devices landing together with soft thuds.

The intruder stepped forward, his eyes cold and calculating behind the mask. "Everyone take it nice and easy," he ordered, his voice dripping with menace. "No sudden moves."

"What do you want?" Polly asked, her voice trembling but

steady. She forced herself to meet the intruder's gaze, trying not to show fear.

"Don't play dumb," the man snarled. "You know what I want."

"Lester Lynch's notebooks."

"Aren't you clever."

The next moment, the door from the hallway into the reception room burst open, and another figure, clad in a wet, black puffer coat and black balaclava, stormed in. The intensity of the air doubled. "Stan, they're not there!" said an unmistakably female voice. Polly's blood ran cold. It was the voice she had heard several times before on the telephone: Audrey.

Audrey's eyes seemed to burn with anger as she looked at Polly. "Where are they?" she demanded, her voice sharp.

"Hand 'em over, and we'll leave. Nobody gets hurt," Stan, the male intruder, said.

Polly Pepper was a long-time survivor of Hollywood and its often-cutthroat underbelly. With a strength and tenacity that earned her respect and admiration from her peers, Polly had faced network executives who were notorious for their bullying tactics and capricious demands. Several times they'd wanted to change her vision for the show. But Polly, ever the diplomat, would listen politely, smile sweetly, and then find a way to get exactly what she wanted. She'd learned to stand up for herself, her show, and her team.

Now, as she stood facing a gun-wielding, hooded thief, Polly's Hollywood-honed instincts kicked in. She wasn't about to let anyone take advantage of her. Not this intruder. Not anyone.

"You've got the wrong castle, buddy," she said in an even, icy tone. "You're not getting so much as a crumb of our last scone, so I want you to leave now. I mean it."

Stan snorted with a derisive chuckle, his eyes glinting with malevolence. "We'll leave when we get what we came for," he hissed, taking a menacing step forward. "We can play rough if you want," he growled, brandishing the gun with a flick of his wrist. "Tell us where they are, or..."

His voice trailed off, the implication hanging heavily in the air. The tension in the room thickened like a dark, oppressive fog, and Polly imagined Stan smiling evilly behind his mask.

"No worries if you want to make this ugly," he continued, his voice a low, menacing rumble. "That's sort of the fun part for me."

Polly's heart pounded, but she stood her ground, drawing on every ounce of her Hollywood-honed courage. She wasn't about to let this thug intimidate her, not in her own home. "You'll get nothing from us," she said firmly, her voice steady despite the fear gnawing at her insides. "Not a word. Not a paragraph. Not a page."

"We're not leaving without the notebooks," Stan said, his voice a deadly growl. "And if you make us search for them, you won't like what happens next."

"Oh, please!" Polly spat, her eyes flashing with defiance. "I dealt with that infamous ogre Jerry Lewis, navigated the diva demands of JLo, and squared off against that Disney Studios exec Stephanie What's-her-face. After handling their tantrums, manipulations, and power plays, I could probably take on that fatso in North Korea and a couple of US senators. Compared to them, you're small potatoes... *Stan*." She now knew his name and spat it out like a bad taste in her mouth.

Stan's body language expressed his frustration as Polly took a step forward, closing the gap between them, her fearless demeanor challenging his dominance. "You think you're tough because you've got a gun? Everyone's got a gun in the US," she continued, her voice dripping with sarcasm. "I said get out of our house. Otherwise, you'll discover how phony baloney my Polly Pepper Pollyanna act is."

"Mom," Tim said hesitantly, "they're just notebooks. Lester wouldn't want anything to happen to us because we were protecting his stupid work."

"That's not the point, sweetums," Polly said, her gaze never wavering from the masked man. "It's the principle. I taught you never to take something that wasn't yours. Right? Well, these people need to learn that same lesson. Lester's notebooks don't belong to them. They don't belong to us, either. They belong to Lester's publisher. By golly, I will make sure they get all the showbiz dish that Lester promised. He might have written some mean or slanderous things. His book might upset some people. But that's not our problem. Our responsibility is to follow through with Lester's wishes. I won't let a few thugs scare me into breaking that commitment."

Polly stood silent for a long moment, trying to determine where she and Stan were in this negotiation. "You think you can waltz in here, threaten us, and take whatever you want? I've stared down Hollywood's fiercest. I've held my ground against moguls who could buy and sell you with a snap of their fingers. And I've done it all with a smile and a steely resolve that you can't even begin to comprehend."

"I've got this," Audrey said, interrupting Polly's soliloquy. Her voice was cold and commanding as she brandished a gleaming chef's knife. The blade caught the light, casting a sinister glint. She turned to Tiara. "You! Maid! Over here," she barked, calling Tiara to her side, her voice startling in its vicious intensity.

Tiara froze, her eyes wide with trepidation.

Polly felt a surge of protectiveness rise within her, a fierce determination not to let these intruders harm anyone she cared about. "Don't you dare lay a finger on her!" Polly shouted, stepping in front of Tiara, her fear masked by a façade of unwavering resolve.

Audrey's lips curled into a cruel smile beneath her mask, the knife held tightly in her grip. "Brave, are we? Or stupid," she sneered, taking a step closer, the knife hovering menacingly between them. "But bravery won't save you. You! Maid—" she called again.

"Her name is Tiara! Tiara is not a maid!" Polly interjected sharply, her eyes blazing with defiance. "She's my best friend. If you want to get to her, you have to go through me first."

With strength gleaned from Polly's loving pronouncement, Tiara squared her shoulders and glared at Audrey, her eyes blazing with defiance. "You'll have to come and get me," she said, her voice slicing through the tension. She crossed her arms and took a resolute stance, radiating an unyielding strength. "I'm not one of those obsequious Beverly Hills maids who take orders. I give them," she declared with a dramatic flourish. "Just ask Her Royal Highness." She jerked her head toward Polly. "She's still waiting for me to fluff her pillows and fetch her crown."

Audrey's eyes widened with a mix of surprise and frustration. She hadn't anticipated this level of defiance. Polly and Tiara's combined resolve seemed to electrify the air around them, leaving Audrey visibly unsettled.

"You heard Tiara," Polly said, her tone icy and commanding. "She isn't going anywhere with you."

In the next instant, Stan lunged at Tim with a ferocity that shocked everyone into silence. He twisted Tim's arm behind his back, eliciting a cry of excruciating pain that echoed through the room. "I swear to God," Stan snarled, his voice a low, menacing growl filled with deadly intent, "your darling son is about to have an accident falling off the castle tower if you don't hand over the notebooks!" His eyes burned with a dangerous intensity, making it clear that he wasn't bluffing.

Polly's heart lurched at the threat, her mind racing with the horrifying image of Tim, her steadfast and beloved son, plummeting from the ancient tower. A surge of fear, more intense than anything she'd ever felt, flooded through her, quickly giving way to a fierce protectiveness. "Let him go!" Polly's voice trembled, a mix of panic and desperate urgency coloring her words. "Okay, okay. We'll give you the notebooks. Just leave Tim and Tiara alone!" Her eyes pleaded with Stan, her hands clenched tightly as she braced herself to do whatever it took to save her family from the looming danger.

Stan's grip tightened, eliciting a sharp cry from Tim as pain shot through his twisted arm. "Now, that's more like it," Stan sneered, his eyes gleaming with a sense of triumph, a predator savoring his control over the situation. "Where are they? Get them. Now!" His voice dripped with menace, each word a dagger of intimidation. Polly's heart pounded in her chest, the room closing in around her as she frantically tried to think of a way to comply with Stan's demands while protecting her son. Every second felt like an eternity, the tension thick and suffocating, as the fate of her loved ones hung precariously in the balance.

"First, let Tim go," Polly demanded, her voice trembling yet filled with steely resolve. She stepped forward, her eyes locked onto Stan's. "You want the notebooks? Fine. But you release Tim. Now! I need to know he's safe before you get one damn thing."

The air was thick with tension as she awaited Stan's response. Her hands clenched into fists at her sides, nails digging into her palms as she braced herself for his reaction. Her son's safety hinged on this precarious moment, and she summoned every ounce of courage to stand firm against the malevolent force before her.

Stan shoved Tim onto another wing chair, where he groaned in pain. "I'll do it, Mom," Tim said through gritted teeth, still wincing from the pain. He glanced at Stan, his eyes filled with a mixture of defiance and fear. "This way," he said, rising and leading the way out from the reception room to the library.

As Tim led Stan down the hallway, the flickering light from the sconces on the walls cast long, ominous shadows. In the library, he moved directly to the partners desk. He reached for the secret compartment under the center drawer and withdrew the key. His hands trembled slightly as he unlocked the desk and pulled on the brass handle. The drawer scraping against the wood seemed loud in the otherwise tense silence.

But then Tim's blood ran cold. The drawer was empty. The notebooks were not there! Panic surged through him, his mind racing as he frantically rifled through the other drawers, each one yielding nothing but a growing sense of horror. "No, no, no," he muttered, his voice barely audible. The reality of the situation crashed down on him, the stakes higher than ever.

Stan's eyes bored into Tim, his sneer deepening. "Where are they?" he demanded, his voice a threatening growl.

Tim swallowed hard, trying to understand it all. "I don't know," he stammered, his voice shaking. "I swear to God, this is where I put them! I locked the desk myself!" Tim exclaimed, his voice a frantic mixture of confusion and desperation. His eyes darted wildly around the room as if willing the notebooks to materialize. "Honestly! I wouldn't lie. I don't care about Lester's stupid notebooks!"

"Don't play games with me," Stan snarled, his voice dripping with menace. He grabbed Tim by the collar, yanking him close with a vicious tug. Tim could feel Stan's hot breath on his face, the man's grip tightening like a vise.

"Where are they?" Stan's voice was a dangerous growl, each word punctuated by barely restrained violence. The room seemed to close around them, the air thick with tension and fear.

Tim's mind raced, desperately trying to recall any detail that could explain the missing notebooks. "I'm telling you the truth!" he insisted, his voice cracking under the pressure. "They were here. Someone moved them. They're around here somewhere. They have to be."

"You and your family are going to wish you were dead—long before you actually die.

"Audrey!" Stan hollered down the hallway.

29

P olly and Tiara were soon seated on the small settee in the library, their faces pale and tense. Tim sat in a wing chair, his eyes wide with fear and frustration. He looked at his mother, desperation etched across his features. "I locked the notebooks in the desk myself! I swear! Now they're not there."

Stan loomed over the trio, his presence a menacing shadow in the dimly lit room. "We'll go from room to room and shake this whole place upside down if we have to!" he spat, his voice filled with ruthless determination. His eyes glinted with a dangerous light, a predator zeroing in on its prey. "The secret hiding place. We'll start there!"

The room felt suffocating. Polly clutched the armrest of the settee, her knuckles white. Tiara's breath came in quick, shallow gasps, her eyes darting between Stan and Tim.

"Hurry up!" Stan barked, the edge of his voice slicing through the air.

Stan's expression darkened, his fury barely contained. "Then we keep searching," he hissed.

Polly's heart skipped a beat. "How did you know about that

secret space?" she asked, trying to keep the tremor out of her voice.

Stan chuckled again, a cold, sinister sound that sent shivers down Polly's spine. "Lester was persuaded to show us around the place," he said, his voice dripping with smug satisfaction. "He knew we were coming for his notebooks, so he hid them. He said nobody in the world knew about the space. Not even you. It didn't take much convincing for him to show us where the notebooks were. If you get what I mean," he added, brandishing his gun with a chilling smile.

"You were in our home the day Lester disappeared?" Tiara asked, her voice trembling. "While we were sleeping?"

Stan's grin widened. "That's right, maid. We slipped in quietly. Didn't want to disturb your beauty rest. Lester was very cooperative once he understood—the consequences." Stan waved the gun casually, the implied threat hanging heavy in the air.

Tim's hands clenched into fists, anger and fear battling for dominance. "You're a monster," he spat, his voice shaking.

Stan laughed, a dark, hollow sound. "I've been called worse, but I get results. Now, enough stalling." He took a step closer, the gun now trained on Tim.

Tim opened the panel, revealing the small, dusty hiding space. His heart sank as he peered inside. He turned to Stan, his face a mask of despair. "Empty," he whispered, his voice cracking.

Stan removed his wet balaclava. "It's too damn hot in here," he complained, tossing the polyester mask haphazardly onto the desktop. "Yeah. Lester Lynch was kind enough to give us a brief castle tour. Pretty amazing. Nothing like it where I live in Bedford-Stuy, that's for sure. Let's see what other fun places you can show me. Where to next, boy?" he ordered, his tone brooking no argument. "Remember, any funny business and your family pays the price."

Polly was furious that Lester had apparently brought strangers into the castle without her consent. "Why would Lester willingly invite you into our home without discussing it with us first?" she asked.

"Who said anything about being willing?" Audrey smiled evilly, removing her mask and shaking out the rain. She wiped her running nose with the palm of her hand, which made Polly almost cringe in revulsion.

Polly immediately recognized Audrey—and now Stan, too— from the sketches that David Durham had made. Sarah had done an excellent job describing them. He had a long rectangular face with high cheekbones. His eyes were set under prominent, expressive brows, and his nose was straight and somewhat elongated. His mouth was wide, with well-defined lips. He looked to be around forty-five years old.

Polly saw that Audrey was in her mid-forties, too. She was awkward and gangly and had an oval-shaped face, large brown eyes, a wide mouth full of too many teeth, and a pronounced overbite.

"Were you the caller who tormented him the night before he died?" Polly asked. "Why was he so upset?"

Stan looked at Polly for a long moment. Then he shrugged and made an ambiguous face that said maybe, maybe not. "Lester wasn't playing ball is all I can say. We were hired to knock some sense into him. We were told to grab some pages from a book he was writing."

Polly cleared her throat. "I'm not clear about a few things," she said, giving Stan a bewildered look. "Someone hired you? Who? You were supposed to remove some pages from Lester's notebooks? And how did this person even know Lester was writing a book?"

Stan shrugged again. "I don't ask questions. I'd never even heard of Lester the Dresser. That's what the boss called him. It's a stupid name. I just do the job. Get my cash. Then scram. Got it?"

"Who's the boss?" Polly asked, trying to fit the puzzle pieces together. "Why did he want pages from Lester's book?"

Stan took a deep breath. "None of your beeswax. Look, all I know is Lester the Dresser was being a prick. He was gonna publish something about someone who maybe didn't want some private stuff known. We all got secrets, ya know? We were with the boss when he picked Lester up early Wednesday morning, and as I said, Lester wasn't playing ball. So, we brought him back here. After he saw my gun, he handed over the pages. We were told to make sure he don't write no more. The boss was waiting in the car, so we had to do quick work. Lester put up a struggle and got himself a broken neck. Too bad. But we had this really convenient solution for getting rid of his body. His very own secret room—that nobody on the planet knew about."

"But why did you come back later for the other notebooks?" Tim asked. "You got what you wanted in the first place."

"Change of heart, I guess," Stan said. "Boss was wicked angry after he read Lester's pages. He guessed there was more private information about him in the book. He told us to swipe all the notebooks. Then your stupid house cleaner walked in."

It was all starting to fall into place now. Word had gotten out that Lester was writing a Hollywood potboiler, and someone didn't like what he might reveal. This person went so far as to hire goons—one brought from America, no less—to force Lester to hand over pages he'd written about one of his celebrity clients. But that wasn't enough. They'd decided they wanted Lester's whole kit and caboodle. And then they killed him.

Polly felt a wave of nausea as the full horror of Stan's deeds sank in. "You murdered poor Lester just so he wouldn't reveal something about a celebrity?" she whispered, her voice incredulous. "Whatever Lester had written, even if it was something explosive, would only have been news for a day. Two max. The news cycle moves fast. Who even remembers Lindsay Lohan being accused of stealing a necklace from a jewelry shop? Or Britney Spears' fifty-five-hour marriage? Or that *American Idol* scandal with Paula Abdul allegedly having sex with one of the contestants? They're all ancient history. Who cares? And no one remembers!"

Stan shrugged. "Not for me to say. And it's time for you to shut up. Where the hell are those notebooks?" he shouted, regaining his position as the upper hand. "The notebooks! Where are they!" he screamed again with all the intensity of a Marine drill sergeant roaring at a new recruit.

With excessive force, Stan hauled Tim up from his chair and forcefully shoved him against the library door. He grabbed him by the collar again and pointed the gun at his temple. "The notebooks! Even-Steven exchange!"

"All I can do is show you places where someone might hide valuables," Tim said, exhausted from being aggressively manhandled. "There's the secret passageway in the larder. We can try there."

"Go!" Stan growled as he opened the library door and pushed Tim into the corridor. "Try anything stupid, and you're dead meat!"

30

W hile Polly and Tiara were held captive in the library, praying fervently for Tim's survival, Audrey paced the floor, brandishing her knife and keeping a nervous close eye on her charges.

Polly, with her eyes glued to their captor, raced to piece together a theory about who "the boss" responsible for Audrey and Stan's presence here might be. Who would be so consumed with worry over the contents of a Hollywood tell-all that they'd commit murder? Sure, some of her friends had sued authors for defamation and invasion of privacy. Those types of lawsuits were common in her circle. Polly herself had sued L. R. Dawson over his unauthorized biography, *Pepper Spray: The Phony Face of Polly*, which was riddled with falsehoods and twisted truths. The book was mainly a "clip job," a word tapestry woven from hundreds of newspaper and magazine articles and old interviews spanning decades. Dawson's hastily constructed book had caused Polly immense emotional distress, leaving her no choice but to fight back.

But she hadn't won that court case. In fact, it was ultimately dismissed. The judge ruled that as a public figure, Polly had to prove intended malice by the author and that Dawson had knowingly published false information or acted with reckless disregard for the truth. Of course he was guilty. But Polly was unable to meet the high standard of proof. Many of her friends had similar outcomes with their failed attempts at retribution against a writer or website. And the legal costs for fighting were enormous.

The famous case of RayVen Black, the multi-Grammy Award-winning superstar, was darting through Polly's mind. One of the most popular young singers of her generation, RayVen had sued the author of *Blackout: RayVen Black Unmasked*, an unauthorized biography. The book purported to delve into RayVen's darkest secrets and painted her as a controlling and manipulative diva. RayVen claimed that the tell-all was full of malicious falsehoods that threatened to destroy her career and personal life. However, the court dismissed her claims, citing insufficient evidence of malice or falsity.

RayVen's world collapsed, and the author reaped enormous financial rewards.

As Polly sat thinking about her predicament, she wondered if that was precisely why someone decided to kill Lester Lynch. If a star as rich and powerful as RayVen Black couldn't succeed against a celebrity muckraker, what hope was there for anyone else? Maybe it was easier—and cheaper—to simply cut out the cancer before it spread to other vital tissues rather than try to treat it. She tried to recall what she'd read in Lester's notebooks that might provide a clue as to who would feel so defamed or misrepresented that they would take the ultimate step to silence him.

Lost in thought, Polly instinctively reached for Tiara's hand but was abruptly told to sit on the opposite side of the settee. Audrey seemed unusually agitated without her comrade, Stan, by her side. Without his presence, she didn't seem as tough.

As Polly and Tiara settled into their seats in the dimly lit room, the tension was palpable. Audrey, the menacing intruder who had turned their lives upside down, paced back and forth with a frantic energy that belied her cold exterior. Her eyes darted around the room, every creak of the floor heightening her paranoia.

Polly, trying to maintain a semblance of calm, glanced worriedly at Tiara. They both knew Audrey was dangerous, but her visible panic added a new layer of fear to their predicament. The threat was not just the trembling knife in Audrey's hand but the shadow of Stan lurking in their minds. "Don't try anything funny," Audrey warned.

Polly nodded slowly, her eyes never leaving Audrey's. She could see the opportunity, the brief moments when Audrey's guard faltered. But the thought of Tim, helpless in Stan's grip, held her back. "We're not going anywhere, Audrey. There's no need for this to get out of hand."

Audrey's laugh was brittle, almost hysterical. "Out of hand? It's already out of hand! This wasn't supposed to happen. None of this was supposed to happen!" She resumed her pacing, muttering to herself, her free hand running through her disheveled hair.

Tiara, muscles tense and ready despite her outward calm, tried to sound soothing. "Audrey, what are you so afraid of? Maybe we can help."

Audrey stopped in her tracks, turning to face them with wild eyes. "Help? You have no idea what's at stake here! I could go back to prison!" Her voice rose to a near scream, and she visibly struggled to regain control, taking deep, ragged breaths.

Polly and Tiara exchanged a fleeting look, an unspoken agreement that they could take Audrey down if needed. But the image of Stan with Tim in his clutches haunted them, keeping them rooted in place, their movements measured and slow, their eyes ever watchful.

Audrey's eyes flickered with desperation. "You don't get it," she snorted.

Polly shook her head. "As a matter of fact, I probably do get it. I've played a lot of different characters in my life. I had to know them all inside and out. That's why I know you're terrified. You've gotten involved in something bigger than you are. I don't think you're the kind of person who would devise a plan like this on your own."

"You mean I'm too stupid? Is that it?" Audrey barked, her voice shaking with a mix of anger and fear.

"No," Polly said softly. "You seem like an otherwise very nice person, and maybe you were talked into doing something you didn't want to do."

Audrey hesitated, her eyes flitting between Polly and Tiara. The knife wavered in her hand, and for a moment, it seemed like she might actually lower it. Polly could see the conflict in her eyes, the fear mingled with regret.

Polly pressed on gently. "Who got you into this, Audrey? If we know, we can maybe help you get out of it."

Audrey's grip on the knife tightened, but her resolve seemed to waver. "Stan," she whispered, her voice barely audible. "He's my cousin from America. He said it would be easy money. Just in and out, no one gets hurt. But now—" The sound of a door opening in the distance snapped her back into high alert. "Quiet!" she hissed. "Stan's coming."

Polly and Tiara exchanged one last, desperate glance and telepathic message. Polly nodded slightly, signaling they needed to act now. Tiara subtly shifted her position, ready to spring into action. They couldn't afford to wait any longer.

As Stan's footsteps grew louder, Polly took a deep breath and spoke in a firm, calming tone. "Audrey, listen to me. You can still get out of this. We can help you, but you need to help us."

Audrey's eyes darted towards the doorway, and in that fleeting nanosecond, Polly seized the opportunity. "Now!" she shouted to Tiara.

In a swift, coordinated move, Polly threw herself at Audrey, using her body weight to push her off balance. Tiara simultaneously lunged forward, grabbing Audrey's knife-wielding arm with both hands. Audrey gasped in surprise, the knife slipping from her grasp and clattering to the floor.

Polly and Tiara quickly pinned Audrey down, their combined strength overwhelming her resistance. "Stay still!" Polly commanded, her voice steady despite the adrenaline coursing through her veins.

Stan burst into the room, his eyes widening in shock at the scene before him. In his split second of shock and confusion, Tim turned and tackled him to the ground, wrenching the pistol from his hand and turning the tables. At nearly twenty years younger, Tim had an advantage.

"We've got them!" Tim shouted, reaching for the window curtain tiebacks and securing Stan's hands.

Polly and Tiara kept Audrey subdued until they were sure she was no longer a threat.

Then suddenly, the heavy iron doorknocker on the main entrance door sounded. "Thank God! It's Gray!" Polly shouted to Tim, relieved that rescue was at hand. "I knew you tapped his number before you relinquished your phone! Watch these three. I'll get the door. Don't make any moves!" she demanded of Stan and Audrey. "Tim's pretty handy with a gun. I used to date a cop who showed him the ropes!"

31

P olly raced for the entryway door, her heart pounding with adrenaline, fear, and hope. Breathless and desperate, she opened the door. But instead of Constable Grayson Jenkins, the familiar face of Jerry Corley appeared beneath his umbrella, droplets of rain cascading off its edges. For a split second, Polly was overwhelmed by a rush of surprise and gratitude for Jerry's unexpected arrival—and just in the nick of time.

"Oh, my God! Jerry!" Polly exclaimed, her voice quivering with desperation as she pulled him into the house with frantic urgency. "Call the police," she said, yanking him by the arm and practically dragging him down the hallway to the library. Her words tumbled out in a breathless rush. "We're in trouble! Burglars! Guns! Hostage! We need help!"

Jerry allowed himself to be dragged along. As they burst into the library, Tiara and Tim looked up, their faces a haunting blend of relief and exhaustion. "Jerry!" Tiara exclaimed, loosening her grip on Audrey.

"How did you know?" Tim asked, his curiosity piqued

despite his overwhelming gratitude for the unexpected backup. "You're supposed to be on your way back to America."

Polly's eyes suddenly took note of Jerry's relative composure at the sight of two people clad in black clothing, bound by curtain drawbacks, and held at gunpoint by Tim. Then, from between the folds of Jerry's dripping umbrella, the image of a dog's nose appeared. The RCA Records logo dog. A disconcerting wave of déjà vu washed over her. The world seemed to twist and warp around her as she realized the oddity of Jerry's unexpected arrival at the castle unannounced and at such a late hour. As she locked eyes with him, a million thoughts collided and coalesced into one.

Jerry knew exactly what Polly was thinking, and his face contorted into a fleeting, sinister smile that chilled Polly to her core. Her heart pounded in her chest, a cold realization slithering up her spine, leaving a trail of icy dread in its wake. The room seemed to close in on her as she made her sudden understanding known. "Jerry. You..." she began, her voice cracking with the terror of her dawning comprehension.

Before Polly could finish her sentence, Jerry moved with terrifying speed. In one swift motion, he seized her from behind, the crook of his arm engulfing her neck. "Sorry, Polly. Mom always liked you," he murmured, his voice dripping with cruel mockery. Jerry's chilling words sliced through the air as he barked commands, his tone sharp and angry. "Give me the gun," he yelled at Tim. "Kick it over here. Untie them." His eyes flickered to Tiara, making it brutally clear who was in control.

The room bristled with electrifying tension as Audrey moved to tie up Tim and Tiara. In mere seconds, the balance of power had shifted completely. Polly's heart hammered against her ribs as Jerry shoved her onto the Chesterfield. Her mind reeled, trying to grasp the magnitude of the peril that now engulfed them all.

"What is wrong with you people? What's taking so long? This was not a difficult job!" Jerry yelled at Stan and Audrey, his voice a furious roar. The oppressive silence that followed was broken only by the distant rumble of thunder, a sinister reminder of the storm both outside and within.

Amid the panic and fear, Polly's mind raced. She began to piece together all the signs that pointed to Jerry Corley as the man behind Lester's disappearance and death: his seemingly serendipitous appearance in Abbots Clover, his foreknowledge that Lester Lynch was writing a tell-all memoir, his distinctive umbrella that Sarah Rogers had spotted when the two mysterious tourists were seen arguing with someone, and his fervent interest in hidden places at Thistlethorne. Polly shook her head in disappointment with herself for missing so many clues.

When the grandfather clock in the hallway announced a new day, Polly wistfully said, "Silent shadows at midnight."

What did that mean? Everyone curiously looked at her, stupefied.

"Silent shadows at midnight," Polly repeated. "That's what Lester's spirit told me at the séance. Remember? And 'Silent Shadows at Midnight' was one of Dolores Hayes' most famous songs. I didn't make the connection at the time."

"Her theme song," Tim said.

"I remember her saying that she never particularly liked it," Polly continued. "She thought it was too old-fashioned and sentimental. But the world thought otherwise. I did, too. It became one of her signature hits."

Polly began to hum the memorable introduction to the melody. It had a timelessness and simplicity about it. Then she quietly sang:

In the quiet night, where the moon does glow,
Gentle winds hum soft and low.
'Neath the old willow tree,

Silent shadows at midnight dance and play,
Two hearts together, until the break of day.

For a fleeting moment, Jerry's hardened expression softened as memories of his mother singing him to sleep as a child with that song flooded his senses. "She sang it as a lullaby when I was little," he murmured, his voice tinged with vulnerability. "She called me her 'little shadow.' I *was* her shadow. I still am."

"That was probably my favorite of all your mother's songs," Polly said, her gaze locking with Jerry's, searching his soul and recognizing how lucky she was that her own son had been spared Jerry's emotional fate—the fate of so many children of celebrities. "It was hauntingly beautiful."

Polly suddenly saw Jerry with new eyes and thought she understood him. Despite the glamorous sheen of his childhood, filled with the trappings of fame and fortune, Jerry's life had unfolded in stark contrast to his mother's illustrious career. The constant comparisons to his mother's monumental successes probably left him feeling inadequate. Emotionally stunted, Jerry had never managed to carve out an identity of his own. He lived in the shadow of Dolores Hayes. He was haunted by her achievements. He'd retreated into a fantasy world with a mixture of bitterness and dependency, his charm only a thin veneer masking the deep-seated disappointment that defined his existence.

The room seemed still, the weight of unspoken emotions hanging in the air. Jerry's grip on his pistol tightened as he wrestled with the ghosts of his past, the echoes of his mother's voice whispering through the corridors of his memory. Jerry's eyes had softened, but scarcely a heartbeat later, the moment vanished. His hardened resolve snapped back into place—his gaze steely and determined as he regained his equilibrium.

"Now, if you hand over Lester Lynch's notebooks, we'll be on our way," he said, reminding everyone why they were in the position they'd found themselves.

"They've been stalling," Stan said. "Claim they don't know where they are."

Jerry shook his head and exhaled loudly, suggesting he was tired and impatient. "It's late. I have an early morning flight." He wandered around the room, appearing to admire all the celebrity-autographed photos hanging in tribute to the former castle owner's favorite stars.

As all eyes followed Jerry, an unsettling silence filled the room, broken only by the occasional creak of the old wooden floorboards under his footsteps. His gaze roamed over the rows of familiar framed faces until it landed on the black-and-white picture of Polly Pepper. Her eyes seemed to follow him, and her smile was frozen in time.

Without warning, Jerry raised his gun with both hands and fired!

The deafening bang shattered the stillness. The glass frame exploded, shards flying in every direction. The bullet tore through Polly's glossy publicity photo, leaving a gaping hole where her heart was.

Panic erupted through the room. The heavy, acrid odor of gunpowder mixed with the musty scent of aged wood and dust hung in the air. Eyes widened. Breaths caught in throats. The tension that had been simmering now boiled over, spilling into chaos.

Jerry turned slowly, his gaze sweeping over the shocked faces, and his gun pointing at potential victims. "Now," he said, his voice calm but laced with a dangerous edge, "does anyone else want to test my patience?"

The room remained in stunned silence, the gravity of the situation overwhelming Polly and her troupe. Jerry's display was a stark reminder that he wasn't bluffing. "Where are Lester Lynch's notebooks?" he quietly demanded, his eyes narrowing as they locked onto Polly.

Her face was pale, and her eyes were wide and full of fear. Polly shook her head. "I swear we locked them in the desk, and now they're gone!"

Jerry took a step closer, his gun still raised. "That's not the right answer, Polly. I'm not leaving until I get the notebooks."

Anger swelled in Tiara's eyes. "We swear, Jerry, we don't know where they are! Why would we lie?!"

"Everybody lies to me!" Jerry barked, his voice blazing with anger. "I've never been able to trust anybody. Do you know what it's like growing up with a famous movie-star mother? People either want something from you, or they're afraid of you. They lie to get close, thinking it'll open doors in Hollywood. They lie to keep their distance, afraid of saying the wrong thing and ending up on the wrong side of fame. Even my so-called friends lie, pretending to care about me when all they really care about is money. My teachers, my coaches—they all lied, telling me I was special, when all they saw was my mother's name. How am I supposed to trust anyone when all I've ever known is lies?"

Polly's hands trembled as she held them up defensively. "Please just listen to me, Jerry. We really don't know where the notebooks are. Why do you even want them so badly? They're basically just stream-of-consciousness notes. They don't make a lot of sense. Terrible penmanship and no regard for punctuation either."

Jerry's eyes flickered with a mix of anger and desperation. He hesitated, the gun still pointed at Polly. "I had to stop Lester from telling our secret. Mom and I promised never to ever talk about our secret."

The others in the room exchanged furtive glances, their faces masks of fear and uncertainty. Tim's mind raced, calculating his chances of overpowering Jerry—if he could. He knew they were slim. The cold steel of the gun pointing at him was a terrifying reminder of his powerlessness.

Across the room, Audrey's eyes darted between Jerry and Polly, trying to decipher his cryptic mention of a "secret." What could be so damning that Jerry would resort to hiring her and Stan to steal Lester's notebooks? And now this? She bit her lip, her mind a whirl of speculation and dread.

Each person was trapped in their own private hell of thoughts and fears. Jerry seemed to slip into a state of reverie, reliving fateful moments from his past. He saw snapshots of himself at Hillcrest Charter Academy, the elite private high school in Beverly Hills. He'd been an average student there—a young man more interested in fitting in and forging an identity distinct from his mother's than focusing on academia. "I knew a couple of guys," Jerry began. "You'll know the names: Brandon and Zachary—Prescott. Remember them?"

Polly, Tim, and Tiara instantly recalled the infamous Prescott brothers and the gruesome murders they committed. Their crimes had rocked Beverly Hills and the entertainment industry. The brothers became major news when they walked into their home with shotguns and blasted their wealthy parents to smithereens. Initially, the brothers claimed the murders were a result of a burglary gone wrong. But one of them later confessed to his shrink, thinking the revelation was protected under patient-therapist confidentiality laws.

"The thing is," Jerry continued, "I knew about their plans to murder their parents—and did nothing to stop it. Brandon and Zack were my friends. They confided their preparations to me. The staged break-in, and how they'd disable the security system. Their alibi and their escape plan. Even their post-murder behavior to avoid suspicion. They were good actors. I kept their secret because they were my only friends. They understood me."

Polly stared at Jerry, her mind racing to reconcile the man standing before her with the confession he had just made. She nodded, remembering the chilling investigation as it had played out in the press. The Beverly Hills police had done an outstanding job of peeling back the layers of a dysfunctional family and the brothers' cold-blooded ambition and greed.

"Eventually, it came out that I'd known about the plot," Jerry continued. "That threatened to not only mess with my life but also shatter Dolores Hayes' pristine image—if only by association. News of my complicity—even by omission—in such a brutal crime could have tainted her public image. The tabloids would have feasted on the scandal, casting shadows over all her achievements and questioning her fitness as a mother.

"So, Mom hired expensive lawyers. They leveraged every connection they could and exploited every legal loophole. They managed to keep my name—and hers—out of the press. The scandal was buried, and Mom's name preserved."

Polly's mind raced, her thoughts a jumble of confusion. Over the past few days, she'd viewed Jerry as a loyal, if overly intense, son and keeper of the Dolores Hayes flame. Now that all made sense. He was coming from a place of gratitude.

Tim was transfixed by Jerry's confession. His worship of Dolores Hayes wouldn't have changed if any of this had come to light. Surely, her other fans wouldn't have stopped loving her, either. None of it was her fault. But he completely understood Jerry's devotion to his famous mother and wanting to preserve her image. At the same time, he couldn't help believing that if Jerry and Dolores had just let their cards fall as they may, whatever scar the scandal left on her reputation would have been as forgotten by now as almost any other Hollywood scandal. Like the Fatty Arbuckle infamy from 1921. Or the William Desmond Taylor murder in 1922. Or even Natalie Wood's suspicious drowning in 1981 and her famous husband, Robert Wagner, being a person of interest in her death. These were all major headlines at the time. But today? Few remembered them.

Jerry shook his head as if trying to understand his life and actions. "From that moment on, my entire life was defined by a rigid devotion to my mother. I stopped doing all the typical things that teenagers do. I stopped having an independent life. I focused entirely on Mom and all she'd done to protect us.

"But the past has a way of resurfacing." Jerry chuckled uncomfortably. "Mom's friends Lawrence and Bob, who were hosting Lester at their place in Italy, called to tell me that Lester had given them a preview of his book. He was going to reveal our secret story. The manuscript threatened to unravel everything and maybe destroy my mother's legacy. I called Lester about it, and he just laughed and said I was being melodramatic. I knew I had to act. I had to silence him."

In the moments that followed, the room seemed to hold its breath. Each person grappled with their own tumultuous thoughts, the air thick with the realization that they knew the secret that Jerry had tried to protect. The walls seemed to close in as each of them—including Stan and Audrey—wondered what price they might have to pay for their knowledge of Jerry's secret.

Jerry took a deep breath and exhaled loudly. "You see, I had no choice," he said, his voice barely above a whisper. "And since no one will fess up about the notebooks…"

His voice trailed off, but the menace in his eyes spoke volumes. He raised the gun again, its cold barrel swinging ominously between Polly, Tim, and Tiara.

Polly's mind raced, her thoughts a whirlwind of terror and confusion. "Jerry, please," she implored, trying to keep her voice steady despite the panic in her chest. "We really don't know where the notebooks are. We had nothing to do with Lester's plans."

Tim felt a surge of anger. "This isn't the way to fix things, Jerry. You're only making it worse."

"Shut up!" Jerry snapped, his voice cracking like a whip. "You don't understand. None of you understand! I've sacrificed my entire life for my mother. I can't let it all be for nothing."

Polly, her voice trembling, dared to speak. "Jerry, think about what you're doing. This isn't you. I applaud your drive to protect your mother, but this—this is madness."

The room fell silent again. Polly could feel her heart pounding, and every beat reminded her of their precarious situation. She knew they needed a miracle.

32

Grayson gave up trying to phone Tim and went to bed. There were a million reasons why he was finding it impossible to sleep. The headline news reports that he'd consumed just before bed reminded him that a lot of people on the planet were having a lousy day. His too-late-in-the-evening cup of coffee now coursed through his veins, leaving him jittery and wide-eyed. The sharp strings and driving percussion music from the Liam Neeson movie he'd watched on Amazon Prime replayed in his ear, refusing to fade away. And then there was the disconcerting absence of a good-night call or text from Tim. However, he realized that most of his anxiety stemmed from the threats to Abbots Clover's famous resident, Polly Pepper. The village, with its quaint cottages and winding lanes, lacked a formal police force, leaving residents to depend on him alone or fend for themselves.

Trying every trick he knew to fall asleep Grayson attempted deep-breathing meditation, imagined himself floating on a raft on a placid misty lake, and even envisioned the many nearby fields of sheep, attempting to count the flocks. But nothing worked. He rolled over, punching his pillow in frustration, and questioned if he was truly doing all he could to protect Polly Pepper and her loved ones. What more could he do? He lay there, eyes wide open in the oppressive darkness, feeling the sting of inadequacy.

Finally, he flicked on his bedside lamp. His eyes landed on a heap of discarded clothes on the floor, begging for a wash—a metaphor, he suspected, for his chaotic life. The short stack of books on his nightstand held no interest, nor did the Sudoku game on his phone that he'd started earlier. Sighing in irritation, he swung his legs out of bed. He'd check one of his go-to blogs to fill the time and hopefully induce sleep.

With space at a premium in his small flat, his makeshift desk was a humble card table in the living room. The improvised workspace was a veritable collage of his daily life: old mail, crumpled receipts, takeaway coffee cups in various states of emptiness, and an assortment of keys. Even personal grooming items like lip balm and dental floss found their way into the mix.

Setting aside a pair of tangled earbuds and the remnants of a snack from the top of his police-department-issued laptop, he opened the cover and pressed the power button. The laptop was supposed to be for professional purposes only, but he ignored that rule. The screen flickered to life, and he quickly navigated to the lifestyle pages he'd started to haunt to keep up with Tim and his big-city sophistication: *UK Gent, Metro Man*, and the *London Ledger*. To his disappointment, the pages remained static. There were no new posts since the last time he'd checked.

Frankly, although the articles were sometimes informative, he was tired of reading about posh people facing the first-world challenges of putting together their wardrobes.

Whether you're attending a garden party, heading to the opera, or meeting friends for brunch, this guide will help you easily navigate a smart/casual dress code.

Gray had never been invited to a garden party (a picnic barbeque probably didn't count). He'd never been to the opera (or any theater other than the cinema) and had never met a friend for brunch. He felt it was unlikely he'd ever do any of those things.

Finally, he felt the gentle pull of sleep. He yawned and was about to log off when he noticed an official e-mail from Avon and Somerset Constabulary, the regional police office. He clicked on the message and quickly scanned the contents, his biggest fear becoming reality:

Subject: CASE #28492-37A Crucial Update. Forensic Findings

Dear Constable Jenkins,

I hope this message finds you well.

I am writing to provide a significant update from our forensic unit regarding investigating the threats against Polly Pepper. Our team has thoroughly analyzed the data extracted from Polly Pepper's and Lester Lynch's mobile phones and compiled a list of names and numbers found in their contacts and recent calls.

Upon cross-referencing these numbers with our criminal database, we have identified a noteworthy match: Audrey Watts, a person with a history of indictable offenses, including burglary, theft, fraud, and assault. Her contact number is +44 7700 900123.

During your preliminary investigation, it was noted that this number had previously contacted Polly Pepper's phone. This connection strongly suggests that Audrey Watts may be

directly involved in the threats against Ms. Pepper. Our forensics team has successfully traced a mobile phone signal belonging to Audrey Watts. As of 10:00 p.m. tonight, the signal was located within Abbots Clover, England.

Grayson's blood ran cold.

Please review the information and consider the appropriate next steps in light of this development. We recommend conducting further inquiries into Audrey Watts and taking necessary precautions when approaching her.

Please treat this information with the utmost confidentiality to preserve the integrity of our investigation. Thank you for your continued diligence and cooperation in this matter.

Our team will support your efforts if you need further assistance or analysis.

Best regards,
Inspector Amanda Wright
Bristol Police Department

Grayson Jenkins had never felt so alone in his entire life. As Abbots Clover's one-man-band police department, he was acutely aware of how in over his head he was—and there was no one in the immediate area to help. The weight of responsibility pressed down on him. The isolation of Abbots Clover, which he usually cherished for its peace and quiet, now felt suffocating. This was one of those moments where the silence screamed his vulnerability.

It was after midnight, but desperation drove him to dial the Wyre Piddle police department in the next village. His voice trembled as he begged for backup, but the cold reality set in that they were miles away. The seconds ticked by, each one a reminder that time was not on his side.

With no other options, Grayson bolted into his car, anxiety gnawing at him as he sped through the winding, narrow lanes of Abbots Clover. The darkness swallowed the village in his rearview mirror, intensifying his sense of urgency. The gravity of the situation was crystal clear: the person harassing Polly Pepper was right here in the village. More than likely at—Thistlethorne Lodge. His friends were probably in mortal danger and saving them was entirely up to him.

As he rolled into the gravel car park at the castle, his headlights caught sight of a vehicle he knew did not belong to Polly. His heart pounded harder as he noticed the license plate frame adorned with the name of a car rental agency: Crown Car Hire. Clearly, it belonged to a tourist.

Grayson killed the engine, plunging himself and the countryside into an impenetrable darkness. Stepping out of the car into the cold, misty rain, he tapped the torch icon on his phone, the faint beam cutting through the thick, inky blackness. Immediately, a soft, plaintive meow pierced the silence—Mr. Boots, whose black fur rendered him invisible in the night. Grayson spared the cat only a fleeting glance before moving swiftly towards the main curtain wall gate. The crunch of gravel beneath his sturdy shoes echoed ominously in the otherwise deadly silent night, each step a reminder of the potential danger ahead.

He registered with curiosity that the main gate in the curtain wall was ajar. He discovered the same anomaly at the front entryway door to the house. Holding his breath, Grayson eased the door open further, wincing as it creaked, a sound that echoed ominously through the otherwise silent vestibule. Dim light seeped from distant rooms, casting eerie, elongated shadows on the walls. His ears strained for any sound. The flickering light from wall sconces with tapered bulbs meant to simulate candles danced on the walls, created ghostly shapes that seemed to move and shift with every breath he took.

Suddenly, he could hear low, urgent conversation coming from the library. Grayson paused, his heart pounding and blood rushing in his ears. Doing whatever he could to steady himself, he edged closer, the weight of the situation pressing down on him almost like a physical force. With each step, the voices grew clearer, their words charged with tension and menace. "Time's up," a male voice that sounded American yelled. "It's over."

Grayson's pulse quickened. Polly and her troupe were definitely in grave danger. He had to act fast. Drawing another deep breath, he moved silently, using the shadows to his advantage. He couldn't barge into the room and risk harm to the captives or himself. He needed to draw the invaders away from their prey. Glancing around, he spotted a small decorative glass paperweight on a side table. Carefully, he picked it up and then let it drop. A dull thud echoed through the corridor.

"What was that?" the American voice said.

Grayson pressed himself against the wall in a shadow-filled alcove, his heart pounding so loudly he feared it would give him away. Every muscle in his body was coiled with tension. The library door creaked open, and a slight figure dressed in black stepped into the dimly lit hallway. Grayson held his breath, his senses on high alert.

The figure moved closer, their footsteps echoing softly off the wooden floor. As they passed by, Grayson sprang into action with a swift, silent motion. He reached out and seized the person from behind, locking the crook of his arm around their throat and clamping a gloved hand over their mouth. The figure struggled, but Grayson tightened his grip, using his strength and leverage to subdue them.

He dragged the figure down the hallway to the reception room and pulled off a glove. As he stuffed it into the person's mouth, he realized the captive was a woman. *Audrey Watts?* he wondered, but there was no time for further investigation.

Grayson cuffed her hands behind her back with practiced efficiency and then used a silk scarf draped over the Chesterfield settee to securely bind her feet. The woman's eyes widened with fear and anger, but she was effectively silenced and immobilized. Grayson stepped back, taking a brief moment to steady his breathing, his mind racing with the next steps in his plan to rescue Polly and her family.

"Stay quiet," Grayson hissed in her ear. "How many are you? One? Two? Three?"

Audrey nodded.

Grayson took another deep breath, every muscle in his body coiled with tension. He grabbed the iron fireplace poker on the floor where Tim had been forced to drop it and prepared to summon and subdue the next criminal.

"Where the hell is she?" Jerry's voice, edged with impatience, filtered into the hallway. "Check."

Grayson heard the sound of furtive footsteps approaching, the creak of the floorboards growing louder. He pressed himself against a wall again. As Stan got closer to the reception room, holding his gun in front of him like a shield, he could see Grayson's shadow stretching into the hallway. Suddenly, Mr. Boots wandered out from another shadow and into his path. In a skittish knee-jerk reaction, Stan pulled the trigger of his gun. He missed Mr. Boots by a mile but managed to pierce the canvas of an antique portrait. And in that very moment, he saw Audrey on the floor by the piano, bound and gagged.

With only that split second of distraction on his side,

Grayson raised the fireplace poker like a truncheon and brought
it down hard. It sliced through the air, striking Stan's wrist and
sending the gun flying from his grasp. Grayson grabbed the first
heavy object his eyes landed on—a marble bust of eighteenth-
century British naval hero Admiral Nelson—and smashed it, full
force, over Stan's head. He collapsed into an unconscious heap
as Grayson grabbed his gun.

Grayson took another deep breath, steeling himself for the
final confrontation. He moved silently down the corridor, the
gun's weight in his hand reassuring and daunting. As he
approached the library, he could hear an American's strained
and angry voice mixed with muffled recriminations from Polly
and her troupe.

"Nobody moves, or she gets it!" the American's threat was
clear, and Grayson could picture him holding Polly as a hostage.

Grayson positioned himself just outside the library door,
peeking in to assess the situation. Inside, Jerry was backing out
of the room, holding Polly tightly in front of him with a gun
pressed against her temple. Polly's eyes, wide with fear, caught
Grayson's reflection in the dark window across the room. He
gave her a small, reassuring nod.

In a movie, this would be the scene where Grayson yelled,
"Drop the gun!" and the villain would realize their cause was a
lost one. But here, in reality, Grayson couldn't risk the man
shooting his famous captive. He needed a distraction, something
unexpected to give him an advantage.

Just then, the flickering lights of the sconces dimmed
further, casting the room into deeper shadows. The air turned
unnaturally warm in this perpetually chilly house, and a stench
began to fill the air, thick and nauseating, like the reek of rotting
meat left out in the sun. The foul odor clawed at Jerry's throat
and made his eyes water. As his heart pounded, he heard a low,
guttural growl and remembered Polly's story about the legend of

Thistlethorne Lodge's canine ghost, Loki—a specter known to announce its presence with a smell that could turn even the strongest stomach.

"What the hell is that?" Jerry's voice wavered, the gun in his hand trembling.

Polly took a shallow breath, her eyes flicking to the dim corner of the room where the shadows seemed to coalesce into the faint, ghostly figure of a four-legged creature. "It's the spirit of the Loki dog!" she said. "The castle witch banished it into that painting in the hallway hundreds of years ago. He's supposed to guard this house."

Jerry's eyes darted around the room, his grip on the gun faltering as the ghostly figure moved closer, its form becoming more defined. The putrid odor grew stronger, wrapping around them like an invisible shroud, pressing down with an almost tangible weight.

Polly, sensing Jerry's attention shift, subtly shifted her own weight, ready to escape if the opportunity arose. Grayson, too, prepared himself, muscles tensed for the right moment.

Jerry's fear overtook him. "Stay back!" he shouted to the spectral dog, his voice cracking. "Go away! I don't like you!"

In the eerie glow, the ghost dog's eyes met Grayson's, a silent communication passing between them.

Grayson took a deep breath, drawing on the courage the ghost seemed to offer. "Now, Polly!" he shouted.

Polly ducked and rolled to the side just as Grayson lunged into the room, adrenaline sharpening his senses and his police training kicking in with precision. He grabbed Jerry's arm in a viselike grip, twisting it with force until the gun clattered to the floor. Grayson swept Jerry's legs out from under him with a fluid, powerful motion, sending the villain crashing to the ground. The impact reverberated through the floorboards. Grayson followed through, pinning Jerry's arm behind his back and pressing him down with his knee, his breath coming in controlled, steady bursts. The struggle ended as abruptly as it began, leaving Grayson towering over the subdued Jerry, the room heavy with the tension of the confrontation.

As the adrenaline faded, Grayson glanced back at the ghostly figure now retreating into the shadows.

Polly scrambled to her feet, her eyes wide with relief and overflowing with gratitude. "Grayson, you saved our lives!" she cried, her voice a powerful mix of amazement, joy, and raw emotion.

Tim nodded, his own expression, a mix of admiration and relief. "I knew you could handle it, Gray. But seeing it. Wow."

Grayson, still catching his breath, managed a modest smile. "It was a team effort. I couldn't have done it without a little help from your ghostly friend. But, God, he stinks!"

Polly and Tim exchanged glances, silently acknowledging the surreal yet undeniable presence that had aided them.

As the authorities from Wyre Piddle finally arrived to take Jerry and his accomplices into custody, the small community of Abbots Clover began to stir with the promise of a new day. Polly, Tim, Grayson, and Tiara stepped outside. The fresh morning air filled with the scent of the overnight rain. Rare patches of blue sky were visible, lighting up their faces with a sense of hope.

The nightmare was over, and the future felt bright for the first time in a long while.

33

The first light of dawn crept into Abbots Clover, casting a pale glow over Thistlethorne Lodge. The night of terror was over, but the air was still thick with the remnants of fear and adrenaline. The car park, which had been crowded with police vehicles only a short while ago, now lay empty except for Constable Grayson Jenkins' cruiser and Jerry's rental car. Inside, the house bore stark reminders of the night's chaos: furniture askew, fragments of a shattered antique porcelain figurine glinting on the carpet in the early morning light, bullet holes torn into the photo of Polly and the canvas portrait of the Duke of Droitwich.

Polly and Tiara huddled on the Chesterfield while Tim and Gray faced them in matching wing chairs. They were all in a state of exhaustion and relief, their faces etched with weariness. Polly, her usually impeccably coiffed hair now a mop and her eyes droopy with fatigue, leaned her head against Tiara, who had an arm wrapped securely around Polly's shoulders, offering silent comfort. Tim absently petted Mr. Boots, who basked in the attention, oblivious to all the chaos.

Grayson, the day's hero, was equally fatigued. His thoughts

were jumbled as the weight of his responsibility lifted. He glanced around the room, taking in the disarray and his friends' tired faces. "It's over now," he said softly, trying to inject some reassurance into the somber atmosphere. "You're safe."

Polly shivered, her mind replaying the terrifying moment when she realized that Jerry Corley was the one responsible for Lester Lynch's murder. "I should have suspected Jerry sooner," she said, ashamed of her failure to knit together the now glaringly obvious clues. "In retrospect, it wasn't coincidental that Dolores Hayes' son was in Abbots Clover at the very same time as Lester Lynch. This tiny village wouldn't be on any American tourist's list of must-see places to visit in England. It's like Brigadoon. It hardly exists. Lester was the only attraction here—other than yours truly, of course."

They all nodded in agreement, the puzzle pieces falling into place with an almost audible click. The isolation of Abbots Clover and its insignificance in the grand scheme of things only underscored the deliberate nature of Jerry's visit. The village was no tourist destination, but it was a perfect setting for a quiet murder.

"We're just as guilty for not being suspicious of Jerry," Tim countered. "He did a lousy job covering up his connection to Lester, even if it was tangential. Remember his comment about 'the prodigal son'? And he called Lester's death tragic despite not knowing the details of how he died. Remember, when we were having dinner at the Fox & Hare, he asked if we thought the burglars might come back for the rest of the notebooks? Only someone involved would know that the thieves hadn't taken everything. The village grapevine is short, but Jerry didn't know anyone here who could have told him that. Only Stan and Audrey knew the specifics."

Tiara nodded. "We didn't have any reason to mistrust him.

He was Hollywood royalty. Only Liza Minnelli and Lucie Arnaz have better showbiz pedigrees."

"And what about that damned umbrella?" Polly said, shaking her head. "The RCA Records logo? When I thought I saw an identical one, I shrugged it off."

"I dropped the ball, too," Grayson confessed. "First, I jumped to conclusions about Lester's cause of death. I shouldn't have said anything until the ME in Bristol filed their report. Then, when I didn't get a good-night call or text from Tim last night, I should have suspected that you might be in trouble."

Beating themselves up for missing all the indicators of trouble brewing was fruitless. But other questions about the ordeal they'd experienced gnawed at them as well; their thoughts were a tangled web of confusion and disbelief.

"If I didn't have eyewitnesses, I'd swear it was all just a very bad hallucination," Polly said. "That whole Loki the ghost dog thing is way too weird. Can you smell an illusion? Because, man, I nearly passed out from the stench of that dog! I prefer a whiff of rotting eggs, thank you. But I'm grateful for his appearance."

Polly's words hung in the air as she wrestled with doubts and fears. She'd seen the ghostly hound's glowing eyes, heard his ethereal growl, and smelled the sickening odor—these were details too vivid to be a mere dream or figments of her imagination. And yet, the rational part of her mind clung to the hope that there was a logical explanation, something less supernatural, something she could confront and understand.

"It was real," Tiara insisted. "Like Lester's spirit at the séance that I dismissed. And now we know the Old Granny Grumbles curse legend isn't just a shaggy-dog story—*pun* intended. Who's a good boy! You are! You are!" she said, looking around and praising the invisible hound. "I, for one, love that dog. Even if he's a ghost that farts."

"Another thing I can't get my head around is the disappearance of Lester's notebooks," Tim said, frustration evident in his voice. "I swear I locked them in the desk two days ago. Why did you move them? And why were you so stubborn about handing them over to Stan in the first place?" he asked his mother.

"I swear I never touched them," Polly insisted. "Trust me, if I'd known where they were, I would have given them up the moment Stan knocked my poor baby around. I wouldn't throw you under the bus to protect Lester's mean-spirited scribblings."

Polly's denial only deepened the mystery. Tim's and Polly's eyes then turned to Tiara, who immediately felt the pressure of their questioning stares.

"Don't look at me," Tiara said, deflecting their suspicion. "I don't touch what isn't mine. And Elara wouldn't have opened a locked drawer. Probably didn't know where the key was hidden."

"Speaking of Elara." Tim smiled as he looked up and saw the maid standing in the doorway, her face flushed with excitement and confusion.

"I think you should see something."

They all exchanged puzzled glances before following Elara down the hall to the kitchen, where she stopped in front of the old dumbwaiter, a relic from a bygone era. "Look," she said, pointing inside.

There, tied up with a red ribbon, were Lester Lynch's notebooks.

Polly gasped, her hand flying to her mouth. "But... how...? I swear I didn't put them there."

Tim's eyebrows shot up. "If you didn't, and Tiara didn't, and I didn't, and Elara didn't..."

Tiara's eyes widened. "Do you think...?"

And just as they were about to surrender to another paranormal theory, the bell at the main gate clanged impatiently.

"Who on earth...?" Polly said as she looked at her watch. She was desperate for sleep, her eyelids drooping from the long, stressful night. Suddenly, a look of panic crossed her face. "What day is it?" she blurted, her mind racing through the possible implications of their early-morning visitor.

The answer was Friday. And with that awareness, a fear nearly as horrible as being held hostage at gunpoint entered her head. It was the day of the opening night of *Cats on a Hot Tin Roof*.

34

The day at the village hall had been an unrelenting whirlwind, leaving Polly utterly exhausted. She had managed to snatch forty winks during the lunch break, but that was all the sleep she'd had in the past twenty-four hours. She was fueled by reserves of energy she hadn't had to access since her years in television.

The rehearsal for the show had been a chaotic mess and nowhere near ready for an audience. The cast's performances were rough and jagged. But it was far too late to turn back. Advertising posters had adorned the village for weeks, and tickets had nearly sold out. The theater gods were notoriously merciless, but Polly had to relinquish control to them. All she could do was hope for a miracle. The show must go on!

Backstage was a hive of frantic activity. Costumes hung half-finished on makeshift racks, and threads and fabric scraps littered the floor. Actors dashed about, scripts in hand, their faces pale and eyes wide with last-minute jitters. The makeup station was a topsy-turvy mess of lipsticks, blushes, powders, and brushes, with an ever-growing line of cast members awaiting their turn at the hands of Rebecca from the Clip & Curl, who'd volunteered her services.

The tech crew fumbled with ancient lighting equipment; bulbs flickered uncertainly as they tried to set the right mood for each scene. Props were scattered everywhere, some missing entirely, and a harried stagehand desperately tried to locate a crucial piece of set furniture.

Polly navigated through the clutter, giving encouragement to the amateur thespians. Like a bee flying from flower to flower, she offered her professional advice and encouragement:

"Nerves are natural, sweetheart, but don't let them control you...

"Forget about the audience and immerse yourself in your character...

"Remember, darling, you're not alone up there...

"Project your voice to the back of the hall, but don't shout...

"If something goes wrong, don't panic. Stay in character and improvise...

"Sweetums, I know you can do this!"

Easy for you to say, lady...

As she flitted from one terrified cast member to another, she sidled up to Mildred, who she noticed standing stock-still amidst the bedlam. Holding on to the back of a chair for support, Mildred looked nearly catatonic. Her wide eyes were staring at the illuminated screen of her phone.

Polly looked at the phone. Her own eyes widened with terror.

Down with fever after my nap. Can't talk. Can't walk.
No way I can perform tonight. Sorry. Frances.

Panic began to surge through Polly's veins as the reality began to set in. Frances was the linchpin of the production;

her role as Maggie was one of the leads and crucial to the show.

Of course, there was no understudy! Every cast member was essential in small village productions like this one, with limited resources and a small pool of available talent. Operating on a tight budget, the production relied completely on volunteers, and finding enough participants to fill all the roles was challenging enough, let alone having additional people available to understudy key parts. There were no professional-level contingencies.

Polly's mind raced in a frenzy as she and Mildred considered and discarded solutions. The clock ticked mercilessly, each second a reminder of the impending disaster.

"We don't have a choice," Mildred said.

Polly took a deep breath. A lead weight occupied her stomach.

"You have to step into Frances' role."

Polly had never sat down and read the entire script! Sure, she knew the basics of the classic Tennessee Williams play—she'd seen the Elizabeth Taylor, Paul Newman movie half a dozen times. And she certainly knew all of the famous Andrew Lloyd Webber songs. But she'd only coached other cast members during rehearsals. She hadn't even been at the dress rehearsal because of a little thing called *abduction at gunpoint*. The thought of performing in front of an audience with zero prep made her palms sweat and her heart pound. She wanted to throw up or die. *Please, dear God, let it be the latter.*

Mildred gathered the cast for the announcement. The reactions ranged from shock to supportive nods.

In a trancelike resolve, Polly donned Frances' ill-fitting costume. She stood backstage; the muffled sounds of the gathering audience reached her ears. *This can't be happening!* she cried to herself. *I'm a famous comedienne. I play to sold-out theaters.*

How could I have fallen this far? A dumb experimental musical in a tiny English village hall?

Polly had always had an inner strength. From her earliest memory, she held a deep trust not only in herself but in the theater gods. They'd proven their existence, taking her from obscurity to international acclaim. *Wait a minute. I'm an actress, right? A performer! Look at yourself! You've been bellyaching about not having any work. You prayed for another job to come along. And it has! So, it's not exactly the Netflix series you imagined. Next time, be more specific about what you want!* She chuckled at her own revelation. *Maybe this is the universe's way of reminding me what my life is all about: the thrill of being on a stage, connecting with an audience —no matter how small. This might not be the break you thought you wanted, but it's the one you got!*

The lights in the hall dimmed, and Mildred gave the signal. Polly took a deep breath. She stepped into the spotlight, feeling all eyes on her. She offered a warm, reassuring smile, hoping to convey confidence despite the turmoil inside.

"Good evening, everyone," she began, her voice steady. "You'll notice I'm *not* Frances Osmond."

She'd hoped for laughter, but the audience simply stared blankly at her. They'd come to see what dairy farmer Frances Osmond looked like on a stage wearing a costume instead of her coveralls, sturdy work boots, gloves, and cap. "Thank you all so much for coming out tonight. I know you've been looking forward to this performance, and we've been working hard to bring Mildred Banks' unique production to life for you." She paused, scanning the faces in the crowd. "I need to share some unexpected news. Unfortunately, our wonderful lead actress, Frances Osmond, has fallen ill and can't perform tonight."

A murmur of disappointment rippled through the audience. Whispers of "Where's Frances?" and "Well, this sucks" reached Polly's ears.

Polly took another breath, feeling the support from the cast and crew behind the curtain. "We had to make quick decisions to ensure the show could go on. So, tonight, I will be stepping into the role of Maggie. It's been a few years since I've trod the boards, but I promise to give it my all. We appreciate your understanding and support." The tepid applause that followed only served to heighten her nerves. Swallowing hard, she steeled herself, determined to prove that she could rise to the occasion despite the initial disenchantment from the crowd.

She let a small, genuine smile spread across her face. "The magic of theater is its unpredictability; we're all in this together. Thank you for your patience and kind indulgence. We hope you enjoy our show!"

With that, she gave a small nod and stepped back behind the curtain, grumbles from the audience telling her they weren't pleased.

The lights in the village hall went black, and then Mildred Banks, at the keyboard, began her musical introduction.

The opening number— "As If We Never Said Goodbye"— from the hit show *Sunset Blvd.* reflected Maggie and Brick's struggles with truth, lies, and relationships and provided a powerful and poignant start to *Cats on a Hot Tin Roof*. Polly found herself swept into the familiar rhythm of the music. The bright lights, costumes, and the cast's energy combined to create a whirlwind of activity around her. As she sang her first lines, she felt the initial wave of nerves subside, replaced by a deep focus.

In the audience, she saw Terrence giving her a thumbs-up, his face beaming with pride. It was a small gesture, but it fortified her resolve. Polly thought about all her years in show business and felt she was home again. Midway through the first act, during a particularly challenging scene, Polly thought, *This is where I belong.*

The audience seemed to be responding well. Their laughter and applause gave her a much-needed boost. She even performed an impromptu tap dance to "Masquerade" from *The Phantom of the Opera*. As she did a shuffle, hop, step, flap, she thought, *This is what my life is all about—a connection with an audience. They don't know the chaos backstage; they see the magic we create out here.*

In the second act, a particularly emotional scene tested her limits. *Stay in character, Polly! Feel the moment. Let them see the story through you,* she demanded of herself. She drew on her past experiences, the training and instincts honed from years in television, and poured everything into her performance.

As the final scene approached, Polly felt a mixture of exhaustion and exhilaration. *Almost there, kid. Just a little more. You've got this.* The cast rallied around her, their support palpable as they delivered their lines.

The closing number, "Love Changes Everything," from *Aspects of Love*, brought the entire cast together. As they took their bows, the audience erupted in applause. Polly's heart swelled with pride and relief. She raised her eyes toward Heaven and winked as if to say, *I knew you'd come through!*

Backstage, the cast and crew erupted in cheers, their faces glowing with the shared triumph. The energy was a mix of relief and exhilaration coursing through everyone.

Tim handed Polly a bottle of water, his eyes twinkling with admiration. "You were *amazing*, Mother! Absolutely *amazing*," he exclaimed, his voice barely audible over the excited chatter and laughter filling the room. Polly took a long sip, feeling the adrenaline begin to ebb. She looked around at her fellow performers, each an integral part of the night's success. *This is what I've missed most in life,* she thought. Tiara and Sarah were speechless, but she knew from their expressions they were supremely impressed.

Polly's heart swelled as she was swept into a cast group hug, the warmth of their embrace grounding her. She laughed along with their joyous banter, her cheeks flushed from both the performance and the overwhelming support. For the first time in a long while, she felt truly alive, her doubts dissolved in the shared triumph of the moment.

Despite not having a full rehearsal, she had been a captivating blend of warmth, wit, and comedic brilliance. Did she flub some lines? Many! But she was brilliant at covering her tracks. Polly's natural charm and relatable, down-to-earth presence instantly connected with the audience. Her ability to effortlessly switch between endearing vulnerability and a larger-than-life character showcased her remarkable versatility as a performer. And she'd inadvertently turned the dramatic play into a comedy.

"Congratulations—Peggy Sawyer!" Terrence said as he embraced Polly, referencing the iconic character from *42nd Street* who steps up to replace the lead at the last minute and becomes a star.

Then, out of the corner of her eye, she saw Mildred talking to a man wearing a serious disposition. Mildred pointed him toward Polly. The guy moved through the backstage crowd, and in a moment, he was face-to-face with her. "Ms. Pepper? I represent Sir Andrew Lloyd Webber..."

Suddenly, all the fun and excitement of the evening came to a crashing halt. Polly's eyes widened, and she put on her most contrite face. "This wasn't my idea! I swear! I was roped into it! I'll write you a check for whatever the Am-dram Society took in at the box office," she stammered, her words colliding. "Please, let's talk this out. There has to be a way to fix this without legal hassles," she pleaded, her voice trembling. "I swear I had no intention of violating any copyrights. Just give me a chance to make things right."

The man raised an eyebrow, a bemused smile playing on his lips. "Rather cheeky of someone to adapt Sir Andrew's songs for a different context... But that's for solicitors to deal with. I'm here on another matter," he said gently. "I loved you in the show!"

Polly blinked, confusion knitting her brows together.

"I wanted to let you know that I'll be reporting back to Sir Andrew about how wonderful this American Polly Pepper is. I'd never seen you perform before. I was only vaguely aware of your name. Sir Andrew's been looking for an old... um, old-*er*... actress for his next show, and I think you might be just right."

Polly's mouth fell open, her mind racing to catch up. "Really? Sir Andrew? You mean *the* Sir Andrew? As in *Sir Andrew Lloyd Webber*?"

The man nodded, his eyes twinkling. "The very same."

A slow, incredulous smile spread across Polly's face as the reality of the situation began to sink in. Her initial terror melted away, replaced by a glimmer of hope and excitement. "Thank you," she breathed, her voice barely above a whisper. "I don't know what else to say."

"Just say hello when Sir Andrew calls." The man smiled. As he turned to leave, Polly stood rooted to the spot, her heart pounding with a mixture of disbelief and exhilaration. The sounds of celebration and laughter from the cast and crew filled the room behind her, but everything seemed to fade into the background. She looked around at the amateur actors, still buzzing with post-performance adrenaline, and felt a profound sense of gratitude.

Despite the moment's joy, Polly's thoughts drifted back to the darker days of the past few weeks. The tragic loss of her friend Lester, who had met a cruel end at the hands of Jerry Corley and his henchmen, still weighed heavily on her heart. She, too, had narrowly escaped the same fate, surviving by sheer luck—and the appearance of a stinky ghost canine. The harrowing experience had left her scarred but also profoundly aware of her resilience.

Polly took a deep breath, savoring the bittersweetness of her journey. With its creaky floors and mismatched curtains, this tiny village hall had become the unlikely stage for her rebirth. She had found her spark again in a small English village, and her love for her art was rekindled.

As the night drew to a close, Polly Pepper knew one thing for certain: she was a survivor. She had weathered so many storms in her life and had found her footing once more. Now, she stood on the brink of a new and exciting chapter in her life. The best was yet to come. She was sure of it. She just hoped it was also the end of dead bodies littering her path!

But, as a corpse magnet, that was one thing she could never count on.

THE END[1]

---

1. It's never really "The End" where Polly Pepper is concerned. She's bound to stumble upon another murdered body very soon. Watch this space!

SNEAK PEAK: THE NEXT POLLY PEPPER MYSTERY

THE MYSTERY OF THE MISSING MANUSCRIPT

Abbots Clover's village library was a haven of tranquility in rural England. Housed in a quaint Victorian building along a narrow cobblestone lane, the library's ivy-covered stone walls and arched windows exuded old-world charm, inviting all to escape into the embrace of books.

It was nearly the end of the day, and Rose Wetherspoon, the librarian, quietly announced to the reading room: "Attention, please. The library will be closing in fifteen minutes. Bring any items you wish to check out to the lending desk. Thank you." How many times had she made the same declaration over the past twenty-five-plus years? She once calculated 6,522 workdays (including six leap years, and minus 200 bank holidays).

Rose Wetherspoon was the epitome of a stereotypical librarian. If you'd seen her at the weekly farmers market, you could have probably guessed her occupation simply by her appearance. Her silver-white hair was neatly pulled back and knotted into a tight bun. Fake-tortoiseshell-frame eyeglasses, which she frequently adjusted with a gentle unconscious touch, were perched on the bridge of her nose. She wore high-collared blouses fastened at the top by a cameo pin—a family heirloom. Her long, pleated, twill skirts fell just above her ankles. Her demeanor was almost always steady and composed (except when she found a wad of chewing gum stuck under a chair or reading table—that would make her go bat**** ballistic!). Rose exuded an air of intimidation and commanded, if not respect, at least guarded manners from those around her.

Rose hadn't planned on being a librarian. She had dreamed of becoming a famous writer like Emily Brontë (but without the tuberculosis). However, the Fickle Finger of Fate had led Rose down a less primrosy path. A flippant evaluation of her work from a creative writing professor had destroyed her already flimsy self-confidence. He'd dismissed her stories as "Merely collections of words with no cumulative value." Even now, a half-century later, she sometimes recalled those words—verbatim. They still held the power to pulverize her soul. The subsequent years had slipped by pretty much uneventfully until one day her only major goal in life was to rack up enough stamps on her Rodent-Ridderz loyalty card to earn a free vermin extermination visit to her cottage.

Occasionally, when alone in the library before or after hours, she faced the shelves lined with titles by Colleen Hoover, Stephen King, and Ben Tyler and ranted: "Oh, look at you! All smug with your fancy covers and million-dollar contracts. You think you're so special, don't you? Your words are immortalized and cherished by readers. Meanwhile, I'm over here, a literary ghost, haunting these aisles with unpublished dreams.

"You don't even know we exist—the almost authors, the manuscript misfits! I poured my heart and soul onto pages that will never be read. I imagined my work gracing these very shelves, but here I am, tending to *your* work! I dust your dust jackets, I straighten your spines, and what do I get? Paper cuts!

"Enjoy your fame and money. Not all stories are meant to

find an audience, and not all authors find their voice. Some of us are left to *shelve* books instead of *writing* them. But you know what? At least I can alphabetize faster than you can churn out sequels. So there's that!"

The Abbots Clover library became Rose's refuge. In this bibliophile's sanctuary, she was at least surrounded by stories, even if they weren't her own. "If you could have been, you would have been," she reasoned, parroting her wise mother and reluctantly reconciling to some unfair divine plan for her lack of success in life. The comforting fact that she wasn't a sewer inspector or slaughterhouse worker made it slightly easier to accept her fate.

As the last patron of the day left the library, Rose locked the door and glanced at the antique clock on the wall, its hands inching past six o'clock. She relished these last moments of solitude each evening. The day's bustle had faded, and she was alone in the literary domain she ruled. The familiar scent of aged paper and leather-bound volumes mingled with the faint fragrance of lavender sachets she had placed among the shelves, creating a soothing atmosphere that made the outside world feel distant and unimportant.

She didn't really want to go home to her cottage. It was a humdrum little place she shared with Danny—her Siamese cat —whom she named after her secret romantic movie-star crush, Dan Stevens. (She hung on every word of Dan's audiobook readings, imagining his seductive blue eyes locking with hers as he spoke directly to her. She'd never in a million years confess to a single soul—dead or alive—the lascivious fantasies that filled her thoughts whenever she heard his voice.)

Instead, Rose found herself grateful for the distraction of the library. As she moved about the silent library, tying up loose ends, she couldn't help but think about Abbots Clover's upcoming literary festival. It was always the highlight of her year

—and only a week away. The village population was already buzzing with anticipation. Colorful banners strung across the High Street fluttered in the springtime breeze. A vacant cow pasture would be transformed into a literary marketplace dotted with vendors' stalls and tents offering rare and secondhand books, literary-themed T-shirts and coffee mugs, and gourmet street food. Self-published authors, as well as renowned writers from all over England, would intermingle with readers.

Of course, the library—and the Bound to Read bookstore and coffee shop in the village—would be the festival's heart, hosting book readings, signings, intimate discussions with authors, and storytelling sessions for children.

Deeply involved in the festival's planning and execution, Rose loved the clout she held—organizing the schedules, coordinating with authors, and ensuring the library and bookshop were ready to welcome the influx of book lovers.

This year, the event would be especially momentous and unlike any other in Abbots Clover's history because Rose had the unique honor of unveiling the literary find of the century: *Virtue and Vanity*, the handwritten, unpublished book manuscript by Abigail Townsend, an obscure but admired nineteenth-century novelist and confidante of Jane Austen.

This extraordinary treasure had been discovered almost by accident, hidden beneath clothing in an antique steamer trunk in the attic at nearby Thistlethorne Lodge, the Abbots Clover castle inherited by iconic American comedienne and TV star Polly Pepper.

Polly had generously (if grudgingly) agreed to donate this priceless artifact to the village library, ensuring that Abigail Townsend's long-lost manuscript would finally be accessible to the world. The treasure, missing for more than two centuries, promised to shed new light on Townsend's enigmatic life and work, potentially revolutionizing the study of nineteenth-century literature. Its discovery was nothing short of a literary miracle—comparable to finding a lost diary written by Emily Dickinson—and would draw scholars of classic literature from around the world eager to immerse themselves in Townsend's previously unknown words.

By donating the manuscript instead of selling it for what would surely have secured a lottery-jackpot sum, Polly was making a profound contribution to the cultural and historical heritage of Abbots Clover, forever altering the landscape of literary history. It also ensured her respect and admiration from the other villagers. The festival's buzz about the manuscript's unveiling had cast Polly Pepper in the heroic role of a modern-day Sir Robert Cotton, the man who'd saved the last surviving copy of *Beowulf*.

However, not everyone shared the excitement. A shadow of controversy loomed over the event, fueled by the simmering rage of Arthur Townsend, Abigail's twenty-first-century descendant, who fervently believed the manuscript rightfully belonged to him and his family, not to Polly Hollywood-TV-star Pepper. Despite its discovery tucked away in Polly's castle attic, Arthur argued it was an heirloom of his lineage, a tangible piece of his family's heritage unjustly appropriated. A feud had been ignited, and the threats of a legal battle floated through the village. The dispute added a layer of tension to the otherwise celebratory atmosphere, casting Polly and the library in an unfairly contentious role. Some of the villagers, torn between admiration for Polly's generosity and sympathy for Abigail Townsend's descendant, couldn't help but feel the tension of the unfolding drama.

But Rose didn't want to think about that now as she gathered up stray books left on tables and chairs. She straightened misaligned rows on shelves and ran her fingers along the spines of particularly beloved volumes. Next, she moved to the reading nook, fluffing the cushions and throw pillows on the overstuffed armchairs and refolding handsewn quilts patrons draped around themselves for added warmth in the always cold library building. She switched off the reading lamps, leaving the nook in shadowy twilight. At her lending desk, she sorted and cataloged the day's harvest of returned books and placed them on a cart.

An hour later, as Rose finally slipped into her coat sleeves, collected her purse, turned off the lights in the main reading room, and headed toward the door, she was brought to a sudden standstill by an unexpected sound that broke through the otherwise silent library. She stopped for a moment to listen. It had sounded like a soft thud coming from the storage room behind the lending desk. "Don't tell me that damn badger's gotten in again," she groaned, remembering the mess the animal had made only a few weeks earlier. "Did someone leave the window open?"

There it was again, a muffled noise that piqued her curiosity. Setting her purse on the desk, she moved toward where she believed the source of the sound had come from. Her initial agitation gave way to annoyance as she imagined the furry, black-and-white-faced intruder turning the storeroom into a shambles again. She remembered the last time this happened; a mother badger had decided the library was a dandy place to burrow and raise her brood of rambunctious cubs.

Set on high alert, Rose stopped before the storage room door and listened.

Silence.

She didn't want to startle the creature—they could be vicious if frightened or cornered—but she had to investigate. Rose cautiously turned the doorknob and gingerly pushed open the door. She flipped the light switch on the wall and saw a discouraging view. *Oh, phooey!*

The room, which she always kept orderly despite the array of miscellaneous supplies, audio-visual equipment, and plastic bins filled with old magazines and newspapers, was untidy. "Darn you," she huffed and automatically glanced at the window. But the window was closed. Her eyes instantly darted to the back door. *That's how you got in!*

But as she started toward the door, her eyes were drawn to a shattering sight: The library's antique safe—a hulking, black behemoth of solid iron with a formidable combination lock—was open! Once a guardian of fortunes in the Trust & Savings bank in neighboring Wyre Piddle, its imposing presence dominated the room. Despite its age, it still exuded unyielding strength, daring anyone to challenge its security. Yet, to her disbelief, the seemingly impregnable strongbox stood wide open, revealing a dark, empty void within.

"The manuscript!" Rose cried, her hands covering her mouth in shock and confusion as she raced to the vacant repository.

Abigail Townsend's long-lost *Virtue and Vanity*—was gone!

A wave of anxiety crashed over her, nearly knocking her off balance. *Virtue and Vanity* was more than just an important piece of literary history; it was a priceless artifact. Rose's heart pounded as the catastrophe set in—*This isn't possible!*

What she saw next was another punch to the gut, leaving her paralyzed with terror. In a shadowy corner of the room, beside a box of used books to be sold at the festival, lay an even more ghastly sight: Dr. Jonathan Blackwood, the eminent historian and manuscript expert from the British Library in London. He had spent the past month in this very room, diligently studying and authenticating the purported work of Abigail Townsend. His familiar tweed jacket with elbow patches symbolizing tradition and intellectualism was unmistakable. Now he was lying on the floor, his eyes wide open, staring blankly at—nothing.

Rose's mind raced in a torrent of disbelief and horror. Desperation clawed at her as she looked from Dr. Blackwood's lifeless form to the safe and back again. She had to call for help! But at that moment, the enormity of the two losses weighed so heavily on her that she was immobilized.

The room seemed to close around her, every shape and shadow growing more menacing. Rose flashed on Dr. Blackwood's voice and pedantic, scholarly discussions, which were now replaced by a terrifying silence. His presence had brought a sense of gravitas to the library. Now, his inert body brought an overwhelming sense of doom. Rose felt the weight of the calamity pressing down on her. The sight of Dr. Blackwood, once so full of life and enthusiasm, now reduced to a cold, still figure, was a stark reminder of the fragility of life and the brutal reality of the moment.

Rose's pulse raced, and her body trembled as she reached for the doorframe for support. Her legs felt like lead as she staggered backward toward the main reading room, each step a battle against the paralyzing terror that gripped her.

Finally reaching the lending desk, she ransacked her purse to find her phone. Her fingers quivered as she tapped the emergency services numbers: 999.

"Help...!

"The library...!

"A body...! A dead body...!

"Maybe... murdered...!

"I could be next...!"

ABOUT THE AUTHOR

RICHARD TYLER JORDAN (self-proclaimed author) has stumbled through life with the kind of dumb luck that suggests he might have been Mr. Magoo in a past incarnation. Raised in Peabody, Massachusetts, he escaped in search of people who knew how to use more than one type of fork at dinner. In a stroke of kismet, or possibly confusion, the Walt Disney Studios saw potential in his enthusiasm and naivete. "They were initially charmed by what they believed to be a rare blend of gullibility and a tireless work ethic and decided I was the missing puzzle piece in Walt's empire of dreams."

Over the next three rollercoaster decades, Jordan was thrown into the meat grinder of over 500 feature-film publicity campaigns—though he swears he only remembers five of them. Amid crafting publicity materials for what he sarcastically calls "movies even popcorn with extra butter couldn't save," he began penning what he modestly calls "novels." His literary gems, with titles like *Overnight Sensation, Strangers in the Night, Gay Blades*, and *One Night Stand*, raised more than a few eyebrows—including his mother's. And Mickey Mouse wasn't thrilled about being the muse for Hollywood's latest scandalous potboilers either. "Who knew rodents were so sensitive?" Richard says.

When he tired of writing what friends called "Richard's naughty books," and to avoid any more awkward encounters on the Studio lot with judgmental anthropomorphic mice, Richard ventured into the realm of writing cozy murder mysteries. Thus, the Polly Pepper Mysteries series was created. With tantalizing titles like *A Corpse in the Castle* and *Final Curtain*, Jordan whipped up concoctions where the puns hit harder than Diana Ross's legendary temper tantrums, and the only thing sharper than his humor is has-been TV star Polly Pepper's knack for tripping over cadavers and unraveling the mysteries behind how they got that way.

Now, in what he cheekily dubs "the sequel to my already enviable life," Richard lives in England in a 500-year-old cottage and a ghost that's more "meh" than "boo." He loves nothing more than to visit ancient ruins and stay in castles-turned-boutique hotels. Richard Tyler Jordan is living proof that life can be just as much fun as a Hollywood rom-com.

To offer castle invitations, book club banters, or to inquire about his ghost's latest antics, visit **www.Richardtylerjordan.com**. Just don't expect him to remember the details of those 495 forgotten Disney films.